英語認知語法：結構、意義與功用

（中集）

湯　廷　池　著

臺灣　學生書局　印行

獻給朝夕相處的學生光明

還有嘉文、玲玉、玉霞、淑敏、縈、辰生、進歷、中慧、美玲、玉雪、芸如、靜慧、立中與志芬

湯 廷 池 教 授

著者簡介

　　湯廷池，臺灣省苗栗縣人。國立臺灣大學法學
士。美國德州大學（奧斯汀）語言學博士。歷任
德州大學在職英語教員訓練計劃語言學顧問、美國
各大學合辦中文研習所語言學顧問、國立師範大學
英語系與英語研究所、私立輔仁大學語言研究所教
授、《英語教學季刊》總編輯等。現任國立清華大
學外語系及語言研究所教授，並任《現代語言學論
叢》、《語文教學叢書》總編纂。著有《如何教英
語》、《英語教學新論：基本句型與變換》、《高
級英文文法》、《實用高級英語語法》、《最新實
用高級英語語法》、《英文翻譯與作文》、《日語
動詞變換語法》、《國語格變語法試論》、《國語

格變語法動詞分類的研究》、《國語變形語法研究第一集：移位變形》、《英語教學論集》、《國語語法研究論集》、《語言學與語文教學》、《英語語言分析入門：英語語法教學問答》、《英語語法修辭十二講》、《漢語詞法句法論集》、《英語認知語法：結構、意義與功用（上集）》、《漢語詞法句法續集》、《國中英語教學指引》、《漢語詞法句法三集》、《漢語詞法句法四集》、《英語認知語法：結構、意義與功用（中集）》等。

語文教學叢書緣起

　　現代語言學是行為科學的一環，當行為科學在我國逐漸受到重視的時候，現代語言學卻還停留在拓荒的階段。

　　為了在中國推展這門嶄新的學科，我們幾年前成立了「現代語言學論叢編輯委員會」，計畫有系統地介紹現代語言學的理論與方法，並利用這些理論與方法從事國語與其他語言有關語音、語法、語意、語用等各方面的分析與研究。經過這幾年來的努力耕耘，總算出版了幾本尚足稱道的書，逐漸受到中外學者與一般讀者的重視。

　　今天是羣策羣力 和衷共濟的時代 ， 少數幾個人究竟難成「氣候」。為了開展語言學的領域，我們決定在「現代語言學論叢」之外，編印「語文教學叢書」，專門出版討論中外語文教學理論與實際應用的著作。我們竭誠歡迎對現代語言學與語文教學懷有熱忱的朋友共同來開拓這塊「新生地」。

語文教學叢書編輯委員會　謹誌

「現代語言學論叢」緣起

　　語言與文字是人類歷史上最偉大的發明。有了語言，人類才能超越一切禽獸成爲萬物之靈。有了文字，祖先的文化遺產才能綿延不絕，相傳到現在。尤有進者，人的思維或推理都以語言爲媒介，因此如能揭開語言之謎，對於人心之探求至少就可以獲得一半的解答。

　　中國對於語文的研究有一段悠久而輝煌的歷史，成爲漢學中最受人重視的一環。爲了繼承這光榮的傳統並且繼續予以發揚光大起見，我們準備刊行「現代語言學論叢」。在這論叢裏，我們有系統地介紹並討論現代語言學的理論與方法，同時運用這些理論與方法，從事國語語音、語法、語意各方面的分析與研究。論叢將分爲兩大類：甲類用國文撰寫，乙類用英文撰寫。我們希望將來還能開闢第三類，以容納國內研究所學生的論文。

　　在人文科學普遍遭受歧視的今天，「現代語言學論叢」的出版可以說是一個相當勇敢的嘗試。我們除了感謝臺北學生書局提供這難得的機會以外，還虔誠地呼籲國內外從事漢語語言學研究的學者不斷給予支持與鼓勵。

湯　廷　池

民國六十五年九月二十九日於臺北

自　序

　　《英語認知語法：結構、意義與功用（中集）》收錄最近兩、三年來陸續發表的有關英語語法分析與應用教學的文章，包括「分析篇」四篇與「應用篇」五篇。

　　「分析篇」的第一篇文章〈語言教學、語言分析與語法理論〉以二十三個論題與兩百多個例句（其中還包含國立清華大學語言學研究所入學考試試題）來討論語言分析對語言教學的重要性，以及語法理論對語言分析的可能貢獻。第二篇文章〈英語情態助動詞的形態、意義與用法〉探討英語情態助動詞的形態特徵、句法功能、語意內涵與語用表現，特別是針對‘may, can, must, will’的「義務用法」與「認知用法」一一舉例說明。第三篇〈英語的副詞與狀語在「X標槓結構」上出現的位置：句法與語意功能〉從「X標槓理論」的觀點詳論各種英語副詞與狀語在動詞組、述詞組、小句子、大句子、名詞組、形容詞組等句法結構裏出現的位置與次序，並深入探討這些副詞與狀語的句法表現與語意功能。第四篇〈論旨網格與英漢對比分析〉則依照「原則參數語法」，利用述語動詞「論旨網格」的投射來衍生句子結構，並藉此詮釋英漢兩種語言在句子結構上的異同。讀者可以透過這些文章的內容逐步了解當代語法理論（特別是「原則參數語法」）的內容（如「X標槓理論」、「格位理論」、「論旨理

論」、「投射理論」等），同時也可以觀察如何整合語法、語意與語用來進行語言分析、貢獻語言教學。

「應用篇」的第一篇文章〈他山之石可以攻錯：評析日本大學英文科入學考試制度與試題〉與第二篇文章〈八十年度大學聯考英文試題的評析〉從英語測驗理論的觀點分別評析一九八七年度日本全國大學共同考試英文試題與一九九一年度我國大學聯考英文試題，指出其優點與缺失。第三篇〈英語疑難彙編〉回答國中與高中英文老師所提出有關英語詞彙與語法的疑難問題十一則。第四篇〈On Professor Fujii's 'Categories of Objects and the Verb BREAK: Conceptual Systems in Languages With and Without Classifiers'〉是講評別人論文的文章；討論的主題是英語動詞 'break' 的五種用法以及與此相對應的日語動詞的用法，並檢討以日語（漢語、韓語等）動詞類型與賓語名詞（以及名量詞）類型之間的搭配現象來詮釋不同的語言之間有關動詞對應關係的可能性。第五篇〈高中英語教學：回顧與展望〉則針對清末以來的我國英語教育，就時代背景、課程標準、師資培訓、教材教法等做歷史性的回顧與展望。讀者不難從這些文章的內容發現：所謂的「理論」與「應用」其實就是一體的兩面；二者的關係是相輔相成而密不可分的。

這本書，除了以上九篇文章以外，本來還想收錄兩篇已經寫好的論文，〈語法理論與對比分析：「格位理論」〉與〈語法理論與對比分析：「X標槓理論」〉。就是〈英語情態助動詞的形態、意義與用法〉這一篇文章也有意補充 'should, would, ought to, need, dare, have to, be to' 等助動詞，並且想討論英語

助動詞與「疑問句」、「否定句」、「被動句」、「主語身數」等的關係。但是學生書局的盧先生建議：以現有的文章都已經超出四百頁，實不宜再增加篇數；而且，本書的排版已經拖了快兩年了，應該早日出版。我只好欣然同意，而把這些文章也只得移到《英語認知語法：結構、意義與功用（下集）》去了。

　　或許是由於年齡的增加，對於文章的校對或索引的編製越來越覺得力不從心。想到這麼多年來，前前後後有那麼多的學生幫助我出書，心裏是說不出的感激。從最早年的嘉文、玲玉開始，經過玉霞、淑敏、縈、辰生、進匪、中慧、美玲、芸如到今天的玉雪、靜慧、立中、志芬，他們都不辭辛苦地幫我打字或校稿。尤其是來自澎湖的學生光明，從六年前在師大英語暑修班旁聽我的課開始就跟我結下了不解之緣，跟著我寫碩士論文、陪著我在十八尖山慢跑、聽著我天馬行空般的談論語言分析，去年終於在新竹市定居。我最近出版的七本書，幾乎每一頁原稿都有他汗水的痕跡。不但如此，他也即將達成我的心願把語言學帶進中文系裏去，因爲他的母系決定從下學期起聘任他講授語言學概論。感激與欣喜之餘，想把這一本書獻給光明以及所有曾經助我一臂之力的學生。謝謝你們，由於你們的愛心與奉獻，我今天又出了一本新書。

湯　廷　池

一九九二年八月八日父親節

英語認知語法：結構、意義與功用
（中 集）

目 錄

分 析 篇

應　用　篇

語言教學、語言分析與語法理論
(Language Teaching, Language Analysis and Linguistic Theory)

一、前　言

　　要成爲一位勝任愉快的語言教師，不但要注意本身聽、說、讀、寫四種「語言技能」(language skills) 的培養與充實，而且還要重視教學觀、教學法、教學技巧等「教學方法」(peda-gogical methodology) 的研究與改進。「教學觀」(approach)所闡釋的是有關語言教學的基本觀點與假設，「教學法」(meth-od) 所討論的是爲了達成語言教學的目標所使用的方法與步驟，而「教學技巧」(technique) 所研究的則是在語言教室裡爲了

實現教學觀與教學法所採取的具體而微的技巧。在教學方法的研究中，最重要的是教學技巧的改進。因為教學觀與教學法都僅提示基本的觀點、原則或大綱，而教學技巧則必須針對語音、詞彙、句法、語意與語用等各方面所遭遇到的實際問題提出簡明扼要的「解釋」（explication）與適切有效的「練習」（drill）。

教學技巧的研究與改進，不能全靠經驗與觀摩，有時候必須依賴自己的分析與創造。我們在實際教學中可能遭遇到的問題層出不窮，無法一一向人請教或在已出版的書本上找到答案。因此，我們必須設法自己發掘問題、自己分析問題、自己找出問題的答案。「語言分析」（linguistic analysis）基本上牽涉到三個步驟：(一)觀察有關的語言現象（observation）、(二)針對這個語言現象提出條理化的解釋（generalization）與(三)檢驗這個解釋的對錯（verification）。下面我們舉例討論如何進行語言分析，並且說明如何運用語言分析把「內化」（internalized）的「語言能力」（linguistic competence）、「語用能力」（prag-matic competence）與「溝通能力」（communicative compe-tence）「外現」（externalize）為清清楚楚、明明白白的語法規律。就這一點意義而言，我們支持「認知教學觀」（cognitive approach）的基本觀點：語法規律應該「有知有覺」的學習，然後經過不斷的練習與應用，最後纔能養成「不知不覺」的習慣。也就是說，我們不贊成讓學生暗中摸索、事倍功半的學習；而主張讓學生確實掌握語法規律，事半功倍的發揮學習的效果。我們也不贊成語言教學是"只可意會，不可言傳"的說法；而相信"既可意會，必可言傳"，任何語言教學上的問題都可以靠縝密的語

言分析來尋找簡要明確的答案。

二、'umpire' 與 'referee' 在意義與用法上的區別

英語裡各種競賽的裁判有 'umpire' 與 'referee' 兩種不同的說法。但是究竟什麼時候使用 'umpire' 而什麼時候使用 'referee'？這兩個同義詞在意義與用法上有怎麼樣的區別？我們首先把使用 'umpire' 的競賽項目與使用 'referee' 的競賽項目列舉於①與②。

① umpire: tennis（網球），table tennis（桌球），bad-minton（羽毛球），baseball（棒球），volley-ball（排球），softball（壘球），cricket（板球），swimming（游泳），...

② referee: basketball（籃球），（American）football（美式橄欖球），soccer（足球），rugby（foot-ball）（英式橄欖球），handball（手球），hockey（曲棍球），...

接著我們來觀察①與②裡的競賽內容或裁判方式具有什麼共同的特點來區別 'umpire' 與 'referee' 的意義與用法？ *Longman Dictionary of Contemporary English*（1978）對於 'umpire' 與 'referee' 的定義分別是 'a judge in charge of a game such as cricket or tennis or of a swimming' 與 'a judge in charge of a team such as football'，都採用例示的方式。如此，學生非得把①與②的競賽項目分類一一死記不可。但是①與②這兩類競賽項目的裁判方式有一個簡單明確的

區別：①類競賽項目的裁判都基本上在特定的位置坐著或站著執行裁判的工作；而②類競賽項目的裁判則必須隨著運動員在競賽場地上移動或奔跑來執行裁判的工作。如此，學生就不必把競賽項目的分類逐一死記，而只要從裁判的執行方式就可以推定應該用 'umpire' 或 'referee'。但是我們這個條理化是否周全，有無例外？因此，我們再列舉③的競賽項目來檢驗我們所擬定的小小「規律」。

③ boxing（拳擊），baseball（棒球），judo（柔道），sumo（相撲），wrestling（摔角），fencing（西洋劍術），kendo（東洋劍術），gymnastics（體操），...

拳擊賽有兩種裁判：一種是在拳擊場（the ring）隨著拳擊手（boxers）移動的一位裁判，叫做 'referee'；另一種是坐在拳擊場旁邊記分投票的三位裁判，叫做 'umpire'。棒球賽有四位裁判分別站在本壘、一壘、二壘、三壘執行裁判，統統都叫做 'umpire'。柔道賽有一位主審（referee）在賽場上隨著選手移動來執行裁判，而有兩位副審（umpire）坐或站在兩旁執行裁判。相撲也有一位主審（日語叫做'行司'）在賽場上（日語叫做'土俵'）執行裁判，而有五位副審（日語叫做'勝負審判'）坐在賽場四周執行裁判；前者的英語翻譯是 'referee'，而後者的英語翻譯則是 'umpire'（間亦有人稱 'judge'）。西洋劍術與東洋劍術（日語叫做'劍道'）的主審也都叫做 'referee'；如果有副審，就應該叫做'umpire'。體操、跳水、溜冰等好幾位裁判都坐在場地旁邊記分投票，所以統統叫做 'umpire'。如此，我們所擬定的小小規律就具有「詮釋」（explanation）與「預斷」（prediction）

的功能。❶

三、'glance'與'glimpse'以及'look'與'see'在意義與用法上的區別

'glance'與'glimpse'，無論是動詞或名詞用法，都是類義詞。*Longman Dictionary of Contemporary English* 對於'glance'的動詞與名詞用法分別註解爲'give a rapid look'與'rapid look'；而對於'glimpse'的動詞與名詞用法則分別註解爲'have a passive view of'與'a quick look at or incomplete view of'。這樣的英語註解並沒有把這對類義詞在意義與用法上的區別直截了當、清楚明白地告訴給學生。我們先談'glance'與'glimpse'的動詞用法。'glance'與'look'相似，一般都當不及物動詞使用；所以無法直接帶上賓語，必須在

---

❶ 'umpire'與'referee'在意義上與用法上的區別是否與這兩個詞的「詞源」（etymology）有關？'umpire'這個詞首先見於公元1400年左右，原係來自古法語的'nonper'（原義是'第三者；one who is not even, a third person'）在中古英語裏讀'n(o)umpere'，再變成'ompere'後經過'a *n*umpire'到'an umpire'的「重新分析」（reanalysis；同樣的現象見於從'a *n*apron'到'an apron'的變化）變成獨立的'umpire'；因爲指競賽的雙方當事人以外的第三者，而表示'裁判'的意思。另一方面，'referee'係由動詞'refer (to {someone/a dictionary/one's watch} for {information/the exact time})'加上表示'被V的人'的詞尾'-ee'而獲得（類似的造詞法還有'employee (cf. employer), nomin*ee*, pay*ee*'等）；諒係由競賽時有問題或糾紛時可以隨時請示或查詢而表示'裁判'之意。

介詞 'at, (a)round, down, through' 等引介之下纔能以名詞組為賓語。另一方面，'glimpse' 與 'see' 相似，都當及物動詞使用；所以可以直接帶上賓語。試比較：

④　a．{glance/look} {at/(a)round/down/through/...}
　　　　{someone/something}

　　b．{glimpse/see} {someone/something}

'glance' 也與 'look' 一樣，可以與 'up, down' 等介副詞連用；而 'glimpse' 與 'see' 則不能如此使用。試比較：

⑤　{glance/look/*glimpse/*see} {up/down/...}

但是 'glance' 與 'look' 不同，可以有⑥的及物用法。

⑥　{glance / *look / *glimpse / *see} one's eye {upon/
　　　down/over/through/...} {someone/something}

同時，'glance' 與 'look' 是「動態動詞」（actional verb），所以可以出現於祈使句或二元述語 'try' 與三元述語 'ask, force' 等的補語子句；而 'glimpse' 與 'see' 則是「靜態動詞」（stative verb），不能有如此用法。試比較：

⑦　a．{Glance at/Look at/*Glimpse/*See❷} the clock.

　　b．John tried to {glance at/look at/*glimpse/*see}
　　　the clock.

　　c．John forced Mary to {glance at/look at/
　　　*glimpse/*see} the clock.

---

❷　在英式英語中，祈使句 'See the clock' 可以做 'Look at the clock' 解。但是這裏的 'see' 做漢語的 '看' 解，而不做 '看見，看到' 解。

其次，我們談‘glance’與‘glimpse’的名詞用法。這兩個類義詞當名詞使用的時候，通常都在前面用動詞而在後面用介詞，但是‘glance, look’與‘glimpse’之間有關動詞與介詞的選擇呈現明顯有趣的對比。試比較：

⑧ {take/give/cast/shoot/dart/steal/exchange/...} a { glance/look } { at/over/through/... } {someone/something}

⑨ { get/have/catch/obtain/gain/... } a glimpse of {someone/something}

⑦，⑧與⑨裡有關例句與例詞的比較顯示：‘glance’與‘look’的動詞與名詞用法都以「主事者」(Agent)爲主語；而‘glimpse’與‘see’的動詞與名詞用法都以「感受者」(Experiencer) 爲主語。主事者好比是棒球的投手，所做的動作是自願、自發而積極參與的；而感受者卻好比是棒球的捕手，所做的動作是非自願、非自發或被動接受的。下面⑩的例句更顯示：與動詞‘see’有關的名詞‘sight’，在前面動詞與後面介詞的選擇上，與‘glimpse’頗爲相似。

⑩ {catch/lose} sight of {someone/something}

不過，名詞‘glance’與‘glimpse’的含義極爲相似，所以我們也發現下面⑪裡因爲「比照類推」（analogy）的結果，混用‘glance’與‘glimpse’的例詞；而⑫的例詞則顯示名詞‘look’也除了⑧的動詞以外，還可以用⑨裡的‘get, have’等本來應該與‘glimpse’連用的動詞。

⑪ *take a* glimpse *at, snatch* some glimpse *of,*

glimpses *into* plant life❸

⑫　{get/have} a look at {someone/something}

　　從以上的結論，我們可以知道：'glance'的名詞與動詞用法分別與 'look' 的名詞與動詞用法相似，都表示積極的參與'看'（事物)的動作；而 'glimpse' 的名詞與動詞用法則分別與 'see' 與 'sight' 相似，都含有消極的接受事物進入眼簾的意思。換句話說，動詞'glance'在語義上相當於 'look＋情狀（rapidly；匆匆)'；而動詞'glimpse'則在語義上相當於'see＋情狀（quickly and briefly；急速而短暫地)'。因此，'look', 'see','glance' 與 'glimpse' 的漢語解義分別如⑬。

⑬　'look'（看），'see'（看見，看到)；'glance'（看一眼，投以一瞥），'glimpse'（瞥見)

四、'receive', 'accept' 與 'acquire' 在意義與用法上的區別

Longman Dictionary of Contemporary English 對於 'receive', 'accept', 'acquire' 這三個英語動詞所下的定義分別是：'to get (something given or sent to one)', 'to take or receive (something offered or given), esp. willingly; receive with favor', 與 'to get for oneself by one's own work, skill, action, etc.'。只看這些定義，這三個動詞（特別是'receive'與'accept'）的含義似乎很相近，學生可能無法清楚的區別三者的用法。首先，'receive' 是「靜態動

---

❸　這些例詞採自 S. Katsumata（1958）*A New Dictionary of English Collocation*。

詞」，所以不能使用於祈使句(如(14a)句)、不能充當意圖動詞 'intend, mean, try, attempt, manage' 等補語子句的述語動詞(如(14b)句)、不能充當使役動詞 'tell, order, force, make' 等補語子句的述語動詞(如(14c句)、不能與表示「受益者」(Benefactive; Be) 的介詞組連用(如(14d)句)、很少使用於「進行貌」(progressive aspect；如(14e)句)。另一方面，'accept' 是「動態動詞」，所以可以使用於祈使句(如(14a)句)、可以充當意圖動詞補語子句的述語動詞(如(14b)句)、可以充當使役動詞補語子句的述語動詞(如(14c)句)、可以與表示受益者的介詞組連用(如(14d)句)、可以使用於進行貌(如(14e)句)。試比較：

⑭　a.　{*Accept/*Receive*} the money.

　　b.　John intended to {*accept/*receive*} the money.

　　c.　John told Mary to {*accept/*receive*} the money.

　　d.　John {*accepted/received*} the money for Mary.

　　e.　John is {*accepting the offer*/?? *receiving the money*❹ }。

這也就是說，動詞 'receive' 是以「客體」(Theme; Th) 為「內元」(internal argument) 或賓語，而以「終點」(Goal; Go) 為「外元」(external argument) 或主語的二元述語(可以用 '+[Th, Go]' 的「論旨網格」(theta-grid; θ-grid)

---

❹ 'receiving the money' 如果不做 '正在做…(be in the process of V-ing…)' 解，而做 '快要… (be about to V…)' 解，就可以通。

❺ 來標示）；而'accept'是以「客體」爲內元或賓語，而以「主事者」（Agent; Ag）爲外元或主語的二元述語（卽'+[Th, Ag]'）。凡是以「主事者」爲主語的述語動詞都屬於「動態動詞」；而以「終點」、「起點」（Source; So）、「感受者」（Experiencer; Ex）、「受惠者」、「時間」（Time; Ti）、「處所」（Location; Lo）等「論旨角色」（thematic role; θ-role）爲主語的述語動詞都屬於「靜態動詞」。

'acquire'與'accept'一樣，也都屬於以主事者爲主語，而以客體爲賓語的動態動詞。因此，在⑭的例句裡，'acquire'的句法表現與'accept'完全一樣。不過，'accept'的主事者主語只要說句'yes'，'OK'或點個頭就可以表示'accept'的意思；而'acquire'則要求主事者主語更積極的參與（more active participation），要靠些努力、下些功夫、憑些技巧纔能達成'acquire'的動作。試比較：

⑮　John {*acquired*/?*accepted} the job by offering a bribe. ❻

綜合上述討論，'receive', 'accept'與'acquire'這三個動詞的漢語解義分別如⑯。

⑯　'receive'（接到，收到），'accept'（接受），'acquire'

---

❺　參湯廷池（1990b）＜「論旨網格」與英漢對比分析＞、（1991c）＜原則參數語法、對比分析與機器翻譯＞與（1991d）＜從「論旨網格」談英漢對比分析＞。

❻　例句⑮裡'accept'在用法上的不適切，並不表示這個動詞不能與表示「手段」（Means）的'by V-ing…'連用。因此，'John accepted the offer *by nodding his head*'這樣的例句是通的。

（獲得，取得）

五、'eat', 'dine' 與 'devour' 在意義與用法上的區別

'eat', 'dine' 與 'devour' 都是與吃有關的動作，*Longman Dictoinary of Contemporary English* 對這三個動詞的定義分別是：'take in through the mouth and swallow (solid food or soup)', 'eat dinner' 與 'eat up quickly and hungrily'。但是了解有關動詞的語意內涵並不夠，還得進一步研究這些動詞的句法功能，包括「論元結構」(argument structure) 與「論旨屬性」(thematic property)。'eat' 可以有一元不及物動詞(可以用 '+[__ ♯]' 的(嚴密的)次類畫分框式 ((strict) subcategorization frame) 或 '+[Ag]' 的「論旨網格」來標示)與二元及物動詞(即 '+__[NP]' 或 '+[Th, Ag]') 兩種用法。這兩種用法可以統合為 '+[__ (NP)]' 的「次類畫分框式」或 '+[(Th) Ag]' 的「論旨網格」；其例句如下：

⑰ What time do we *eat* (dinner)?

'dine' 也有一元不及物與二元及物用法。一元不及物用法與 'eat' 的一元不及物用法相似(即 '+[Ag]')；以主事者為主語，但是不能以客體為賓語。試比較⑰與⑱的例句：

---

❼ 除此以外，'dine' 是比 'eat dinner' 更為「正式」(formal) 的說法。另外，'dine' 在 'wine and dine' 這個慣用說法(如 'When we go town, my brother *wines and dines* us splendly') 裏表示 '饗宴 (give a dinner party for)' 而具有 '+[Be, Ag]' 的論旨網格。

⑱ What time do we *dine* (*dinner)?❼

二元及物用法卻與 'eat' 的二元及物用法大不相同；以處所名詞組為主語，而以「數量」（Quantity; Qu）詞組為賓語（即 '+[Qu, Lo]'），例如：

⑲ a. This large table can *dine* twenty persons.

　b. How many people can this restaurant *dine*?

最後，'devour' 則只有二元及物用法，與 'eat' 的二元及物用法相似，以主事者為主語，而以客體為賓語（即 '+[Th, Ag]'）。但是賓語必須保留，不能加以省略。試比較⑰、⑱與⑳的例句：❽

⑳ The lion *devoured* * (the dinner).

以上 'eat', 'dine' 與 'devour' 這三個動詞在論元結構與論旨屬性上的區別，在「來自動詞的複合詞」（deverbal compound）的形成上顯現出來。下面㉑的例詞可以有兩種不同的解釋。動詞 'eat(ing)' 做及物動詞解釋時，'tree' 的論旨角色是客體；因而㉑做 '吃樹的動物' 解。但是如果動詞 'eat(ing)' 是做不及物動詞解的話，那麼 'tree' 的論旨角色就不能做為客體解，而只能做處所解；因而㉑就做 '在樹上吃東西的動物' 解。

㉑ a *tree-eating* creature

Selkirk（1982:29）也以下面（22a）與（22b）的例句來說明 'tree eater' 可能表達的兩種不同的解釋：(a) 'an eater of trees' 與 (b) 'a creature which habitually eats in trees'。試

---

❽　除此以外，'devour' 的含義可以分析為 'eat+情狀（quickly and hungrily；急速而飢餓地）。

比較：

㉒ a. He was a *tree eater* by choice and caused his parents great chagrin.

b. An avid *eater* in the *trees,* Cosimo refused the smallest bite with his feet on solid ground.

另一方面，在㉓與㉔的例詞裡，動詞 'dine（＞dining）' 與 'devour（＞devouring)' 則分別只能做不及物動詞或及物動詞解；因而（23a）與（23b）則分別只能做 '在樹上吃東西的動物' 與 '吃樹的動物' 解。

㉓ a. a *tree-dining* creature

b. a *tree-devouring* creature

六、'undoable' 的歧義以及其他問題

英語的「合成詞」(complex word；即由「語根」(root) 與「詞綴」(affix) 合成的詞) 'undoable' 可以有 (a) '無法做到的' (that cannot be done) 與 (b) '可以解開的，可以回復原狀的' (that can be unfastened, removed the effects of, etc.) 兩種含義。但是這兩種乍看全不相干的含義是怎麼來的？做 (a) 解釋時，詞根是動詞 'do'，而與「形容詞詞尾」(adjectival suffix) '-able' 合成形容詞 'doable' (可以做到的)，再以 'doable' 為「詞幹」(stem) 與「否定詞首」(negative prefix) 'un-' 合成含有否定意味的形容詞 'undoable' ((不可以＞) 無法做到的)。做 (a) 解釋時的 'undoable' 可以用下面㉔的「樹狀圖解」(tree diagram) 來表示內部結構與詞法範疇。'V'，'A'

與‘Ad’分別表示動詞、形容詞與副詞，而‘X-’與‘-X’則分別表示詞首與詞尾。

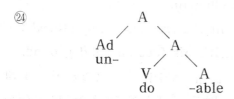

另一方面，做(b)解釋時，詞根也是動詞‘do’，與否定詞首‘un-’合成動詞‘undo’（解開，回復原狀）❾，再以‘undo’為詞幹與形容詞詞尾‘-able’合成表示可能性的形容詞‘undoable’（可以解開的、可以回復原狀的）。做(b)解釋時的‘undoable’可以用㉕的樹狀圖解來表示內部結構與詞法範疇。試比較：

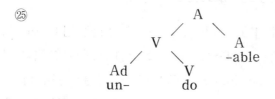

可見，做(a)解釋時的‘undoable’與做(b)解釋時的‘undoable’，雖然表面形態相同，內部結構卻顯然不同。而這種內部結構的差異則說明了(a)與(b)兩種不同解釋的由來。我們也發現：一般說來，英語合成詞的「主要語」(head) 都在右端。也就是說，合成詞右端「語素」(morpheme) 的詞類決定整個合成詞的

---

❾ ‘un-V’的相似用法，如‘unfasten, untie, unbutton, uncover, uncouple, unsaddle’等。

詞類❿。同樣的，'disproven'（＝'that has been proved
to be wrong'，已經證明爲錯誤的）與'unproven'（＝'that
has not yet been proved to be wrong or correct'，尚未
證明對或錯的）這兩個形容詞❶在語意解釋上的差異，也可以從
㉖與㉗的樹狀圖解裡內部結構上的差異來說明。試比較：

在㉖的'disproven'裡，動詞詞根'prove'與否定詞首'dis-'合
成動詞'disprove'（證明爲錯），再以'disprove'爲詞幹與形容
詞詞尾'-en'合成形容詞'disproven'（證明爲錯的）。另一方面
，在㉗的'unproven'裡，動詞詞根'prove'與形容詞詞尾'-en'
合成形容詞'proven'（已經證明的），再以'proven'爲詞根與否
定詞首'un-'合成形容詞'unproven'（尚未證明對錯的）。而決
定'disproven'與'unproven'這兩個合成形容詞的詞類都是居

---

❿　但是也有'*enlarge, enrich, encase, enthrone, dethrone, def-rost*'等例外以及'*enlighten, impoverish*'等不容易決定主要語
在左端或右端的例詞。

❶　動詞有'V-ed'與'V-en'兩種不同形式的過去分詞時，'V-en'形
多用於形容詞；例如'panic-stricken'與'panic-struck'以及
'awe-stricken'與'awe-struck'都可以用。複合形容詞'silver-wrought'與'iron-wrought'等的'wrought'本來也是'work'
的過去分詞。

於右端的形容詞詞尾語素‘-en’。又在十幾年前的大學聯考英文試題中，有一題考了‘…the telephone left unanswered’裡‘unanswered’的詞類；而聯招會所公佈的標準答案是動詞的過去分詞，而不是形容詞。但是如果我們比較下面㉘與㉙的樹狀圖解，那麼我們就立即明白英語裡並沒有‘unanswer’這樣的動詞（參㉘）；因此，正確的答案應該是形容詞（參㉙）。

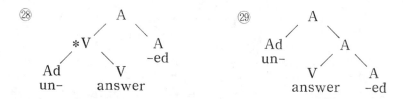

‘an *unanswered* letter’以及‘the letter {remained/seemed} {unopened/*unread*/*unanswered*}’等說法更顯示這種‘un-V-en’是形容詞用法❷；就如同‘unanswerable’只能分析爲形容詞用法，‘unanswered’也應該分析爲形容詞用法。*Longman Dictionary of Contemporary English* 雖然沒有列‘unanswered’爲獨立的詞，但是該詞典裡所列的‘un-[V-en]’，如‘unabated, unabridged, unaccompanied, unaccustomed, unadopted, unadulterated, unadvised, unaffected, unalloyed, unannounced, unarmed, unmasked, unattached, unattended’等都一律分析爲形容詞。我們手頭可以找到的英文

---

❷ 只有‘untie, uncover, unfasten, unmask’等具有‘un-V’形式的動詞的‘[un-V]-en’纔能有過去分詞用法，如‘He has *untied* his shoes’。

辭典(包括1987年纔出版的 *Collins Cobuild English Language Dictionary*)也統統都把'unanswered'分析爲形容詞。

七、'pay, sell, feed' 與 '(un)paid, (un)sold, (un)fed' 兩對詞在句法表現上的差異

'pay, sell, feed' 這三個動詞都可以充當「三元述語」(three-term predicate; three-place predicate) 而同時帶上間接與直接兩種賓語(因而又稱「雙賓動詞」(ditransitive verb; double-object verb)),例如:

㉚ a. John paid [the agent] [the money].

　　b. John sold [the customer] [the car].

　　c. John fed [the baby] [some oatmeal].

但是由動詞'pay, sell, feed'所衍生的形容詞'unpaid, unsold, unfed' 則在例句㉛的句法表現上有如下差異:(i)'unpaid'兼以㉚句的直接賓語(一般表示事物)與間接賓語(一般表示人)名詞組爲主語;(ii)'unsold' 只能以㉚句的直接賓語名詞組爲主語;而(iii)'unfed' 則只能以㉚句的間接賓語名詞組爲主語。試比較:

㉛ a. The [agent/money] seemed unpaid.

　　b. The [*customer/car] seemed unsold.

　　c. The [baby/*oatmeal] seemed unfed.

㉚的例句顯示'pay, sell, feed' 這三個動詞有相似的句法表現;而㉛的例句則顯示由這些動詞所衍生的形容詞 'unpaid, unsold, unfed'卻有不同的句法表現。但是其理由何在?

在未說明理由之前,我們要先了解動詞的過去分詞('V-en')

有動詞與形容詞兩種用法。以動詞'break'的過去分詞'broken'為例，㉜a被動句裡的'broken'是動詞用法（卽'vi., +[(by Ag) Th]'；而㉜b裡的'broken'是形容詞用法（卽'a.,+[Th]'）。試比較：

㉜　a. The glass was *broken* by John.（玻璃杯被約翰打破了）

　　b. The glass was *broken*.（玻璃杯是破的）

'broken'之具有形容詞用法可以從'broken'之(i)可以修飾名詞（如㉝a句），(ii)可以充當 Be 動詞等「連繫動詞」(linking verb) 的主語補語（如㉝b句），以及 (iii) 可以受'very much, badly'等加強詞或程度副詞的修飾（如㉝c句）等句法事實上看得出來。

㉝　a. Mary was hurt by a piece of *broken glass*.

　　b. The toy [*was/seemed/looked/remained*] *broken*.

　　c. The toy was [*very much/badly*] *broken*.

但是如果在過去分詞的前面加上表示否定的詞首'un-'，那麼就只具有形容詞用法，而不具有動詞用法。試比較：

㉞　a. * John's record was *unbroken* by *Bill*.

　　b.　John's record still remained *unbroken*.

其次，我們應該注意到'pay'的直接賓語與間接賓語都可以省略（但不能同時省略兩種賓語）；'sell'只能省略間接賓語；而'feed'則只能省略直接賓語。試比較：

㉟　a. John paid the agent.

　　b. John paid the money.

㊱　a. *John sold the customer.

　　b. John sold th car.

㊲　a. John fed the baby.

　　b. *John fed some oatmeal.

　　因此，'pay, sell, feed' 三個動詞的論旨網格分別如㊳a⓭；而與這些動詞相對應的形容詞'(un)paid, (un)sold, (un)fed'的論旨網格則分別如㊳b⓮。試比較：

㊳　a. pay (vt., +[(Go ⟨ Th) Ag]), sell (vt.,+[(Go)
　　　　Th, Ag]), feed (vt., +[Go (Th) Ag])

　　b. (un)paid (a., +[{Go/Th}]), (un)sold (a., +
　　　　[Th]), (un)fed (a., +[Go])

　　比較㊳a的動詞與㊳b的形容詞的論旨網格，我們發現：動詞'pay'的客體名詞組（'Th'）與終點名詞組（'Go'）都可以單獨充當賓語，因而這兩種名詞組也都可以充當形容詞'(un)paid'的主語；動詞'sell'只有客體名詞組（'Th'）可以單獨充當賓語，所以只有這個名詞組可以充當形容詞 '(un) sold' 的主語；而動詞'feed'則只有終點名詞組（'Go'）可以單獨充當賓語，因此只有這個名詞組可以充當形容詞 '(un) fed' 的主語。

八、動詞 'steal' 與 'rob' 等的論旨網格與句法功能

⓭　「交叉的內括弧」（linked　parentheses）連繫的論旨角色，如'(Xx ⟨ Yy)'，表示：'Xx'與'Yy'任何一方的論旨角色都可以省略，但是不可以同時把'Xx'與'Yy'都加以省略。

⓮　在「花括弧」（braces) 裏用斜扛畫開的論旨角色，如'{ Xx/Yy }'，表示：任選'Xx'或'Yy'一方的論旨角色。

在前一節的討論裡，我們用簡單明確的論旨網格來說明動詞與形容詞的句法表現。在這一節裡，我們再以動詞 'steal' 與 'rob' 爲例來說明述語動詞論旨網格的內容與句法功能之間的關係。這兩個表達「偷竊」與「搶劫」的動詞都牽涉到犯人（卽「主事者」，'Ag'）、贓物（卽「客體」；'Th'）與贓物的來源（卽「起點」，'So'）。但是 'steal' 與 'rob' 都各有不同內容的論旨網格，也就呈現不同的表面結構。試比較：

㊴ 'steal' vt., +[Th (So) Ag]

    a. [Ag He] stole [Th the money] [So from the bank].

    b. [Ag He] stole [Th the money].

㊵ 'rob' vt., +[〈(Th) So〉 Ag]⓯

    a. [Ag John] robbed [Th the money] [So from the bank].

    b. [Ag John] robbed [So the bank] [Th of the money].

    c. [Ag John] robbed [So the bank].

㊴裡動詞（steal）的論旨網格 '+[Th (So) Ag]' 表示：這個及物動詞（vt.）以客體（Th）爲內元（賓語），以主事者（Ag）爲外元（主語），並可以以起點（So）爲意元狀語（如㊴a句）⓰，但也可

⓯ 在「角括弧」（angle brackets）裏用逗號畫開的論旨角色，如 '〈Xx, Yy〉'，表示：'Xx' 與 'Yy' 的詞序可以調換，卽 '〈Xx, Yy〉'='Xx, Yy' 或 'Yy, Xx'。

⓰ 「內元」（internal argument）、「外元」（external argument）、（─→）

以不用這個狀語（如㊴b句）。客體賓語（'the money'）直接出現於及物動詞（'steal'）的後面，並由這個動詞獲得格位(Case)❼；而起點補語'the bank'則由表示起點的介詞'from'獲得格位。另一方面，㊵裡動詞'rob'的論旨網格'＋[〈(Th) So〉Ag]'則表示：這個及物動詞(vt.)以客體(Th)為賓語、以起點(So)為狀語、而以主事者(Ag)為主語時，形成㊵a的例句；以起點為賓語、以客體為狀語、而以主事者為主語時，形成㊵b的例句；以起點為賓語、以主事者為主語、而不用客體狀語時，則形成㊵c的例句。無論是以客體為賓語或以起點為賓語時，都直接出現於及物動詞'rob'的後面獲得格位；但是如果出現於賓語後面狀語的位置時，起點名詞組'the bank'必須由起點介詞'from'獲得格位，而客體名詞組'the money'則必須由客體介詞'of'獲得格位。因為根據「格位濾除」(Case Filter)，英語的名詞組必須由及物動詞、介詞或「呼應語素」(agreement morpheme)分別獲得「賓位」(accusative Case)、「斜位」(oblique Case)或「主位」(nominative Case)。

客體介詞'of'不僅出現於動詞'rob'的例句中，還出現於下面㊶與㊷有關動詞的例句中。

（→）「意元」(semantic argument)分別相當於賓語（或補語）、主語與狀語（adverbial）。關於這些術語以及有關動詞論旨網格與投射的詳細討論，參湯廷池（1991b）＜論旨網格與英漢對比分析＞，（1991c）＜原則參數語法、對比分析與機器翻譯＞，（1991d）＜從論旨網格談英漢對比分析＞。

❼ 關於「格位理論」(Case theory)的討論，參湯廷池（1989）＜原則參數語法與英漢對比分析＞與（1990）＜對照研究と文法理論(一)：格理論＞。

㊶　'deprive, relieve, ease, plunder, strip, ...'

　　vt., + [So, Th, Ag]

　　a. [Ag They] deprived [So the criminal] [Th *of* his rights].

　　b. [Ag You] had better relieve [So Mary] [Th *of* some of the housework].

　　c. [Ag I] eased [So him] [Th *of* his difficulty] by telling him what to do.

　　d. [Ag The crowds] plundered [So the shops] [Th *of* all their goods].

㊷　'inform, accuse, warn, convince, ...'

　　vt., + [Go, Th, Ag]

　　a. Did [Ag you] inform [Go the post office] [Th *of* the change of your address]?❸

　　b. [Ag The police] accused [Go the man] [Th *of* murder].

　　c. [Ag I] warned [Go him] [Th *of* the conse-quences of his action].

　　d. [Ag We] finally convinced [Go them] [Th *of* the futility of such a hope].

㊶的例詞與㊷的例詞在論旨網格的不同之點在於：前一類動詞以「起點」(So(urce)) 為內元賓語，而後一類動詞則以「終點」

---

❸　動詞 'inform' 的客體狀語，除了介詞 'of' 以外，也可以用介詞 'about' 來指派格位。

(Go(al)) 爲內元賓語。這個「論旨角色」(θ-role) 上的差別顯現於動詞 'plunder' 之可以與起點介詞 'from' 連用(如 'They plundered (*from*) the helpless villagers');以及由動詞 'warn' 所衍生的名詞 'warning' 之可以與終點介詞 'to' 連用(如 'as a warning *to* other youths; he is a warning *to* idle students')。

九、論旨角色「客體」與介詞 'of' 以及「格位指派」的關係

在前一節的討論裡,我們談到英語的名詞組必須獲得格位。以內元客體名詞組爲例,有兩種獲得格位的方法:一種是從及物動詞獲得賓位;而另一種是從客體介詞 'of' 獲得斜位。因此,在下面㊸與㊹的例句裡,動詞 'like' 與形容詞 'fond' 以及動詞 'fear' 與形容詞 'afraid' 都具有同樣的論旨網格(即以「客體」(Th(eme)) 爲內元賓語,而以「感受者」(Ex(periencer))爲外元主語);但是只有及物動詞 'like' 與 'fear' 可以指派「賓位」給客體名詞組,而形容詞 'fond' 與 'afraid' 則必須藉介詞 'of' 指派「斜位」給客體名詞組。試比較:

㊸ 'like' vt., +[Th, Ex]; 'fond' a., +[Th, Ex]

    a. [Ex John] likes [Th music].

    b. [Ex John] is fond *(of)* [Th music].

㊹ 'fear' vt., +[Th, Ex]; 'afraid' a., +[Th, Ex]

    a. [Ex We] fear [Th our teacher].

    b. [Ex We] are afraid *(of)* [Th our teacher].

又例句㊺的形容詞 'afraid' 與充當內元賓語的「that 子句」

⓳之間不能出現介詞'of'（如㊺a句）。這可能是由於「that 子句」與一般名詞組不同，不需要指派格位；也可能是由於「that 子句」已經由「補語連詞」（complementizer）'that'指派格位。但是如果因爲「準分裂句變形」（Pseudo-Clefting）而使'afraid'與「that 子句」隔開的時候，就需要插進介詞'of'（如㊺b句）⓴。試比較：

㊺　a. We are afraid (*of) [that our teacher will punish us].

　　b. What we are afraid *(of) is [that our teacher will punish us].

另外，㊻的動詞'destroy'與名詞'destruction'都具有以客體爲賓語而以主事者爲主語的論旨網格（卽'+[Th, Ag]'）。但是只有及物動詞'destroy'可以指派賓位給客體賓語，也只有'destroyed'裡所包含的「屈折語素」（inflection morpheme；如'-ed'）或「呼應語素」（agreement morpheme; Agr）可以指派主位給主事者主語（如㊻a句）。但是名詞'destruction'則不具有這種指派格位的能力；所以客體名詞組必須由介詞'of'來指派斜位或由「領位標誌」（genitive marker）'-'s'來指派

⓳　以「that 子句」爲內元的論旨角色，可以分析爲「命題」（Proposition）中的「陳述命題」（declarative proposition; Pd）。參考湯廷池（1991b, c, d）。

⓴　這可能是由於介詞'of'後面出現因爲「空號運符」（null operator; 'O$_i$'）移位所留下的「痕跡」（trace; t$_i$），所以必須受到主要語介詞的「管轄」（government）而滿足「空號原則」（the Empty Category Principle; ECP）。

「領位」(genitive case)，而主事者名詞組則必須由介詞‘by’來指派斜位或由領位標誌‘-’s’來指派領位(如⑯b、⑯c與⑯d句)。試比較：

⑯ a. [Ag The enemy] destroyed [Th the city].

b. [Ag the enemy's] destruction [Th of the city]

c. the destruction [Th of the city] [Ag by the enemy]

d. [Th the city's] destruction [Ag by the enemy]

十、「控制動詞」、「論旨角色」與「大代號」的關係

英語裡有不少二元述語(例如表示意圖、成敗或動貌的動詞，如‘intend, mean, try, attempt; manage, fail; begin, continue’等)與三元述語(例如表示使役的動詞，如‘order, ask, tell, force, compel’等)分別以由「空號代詞」(empty pronoun；卽不具語音形態的稱代詞)爲主語的「不定子句」(infinitival clause)爲主語補語或賓語補語。我們把這個空號代詞姑且稱爲「大代號」，並用‘PRO’的符號來表示。由於這個大代號必須受到母句主語或賓語的「控制」(control；卽大代號必須與母句主語或賓語的「指涉相同」(coreferential)或「同指標」(co-indexed)，而且必須受到母句主語或賓語的「成份統制」或「C統制」(c(onstituent)-command)㉑。我們把這類動詞統稱

㉑ 支配句法成份‘α’的「第一個分枝節點」(the first branching-node) 支配句法成份‘β’，而句法成份‘α’本身並不支配句法成份‘β’的時候，‘α’就「C統制」‘β’。這個時候，‘β’只能是與‘α’
(一→)

為「控制動詞」(control verb)。一般說來，二元控制動詞補語子句的大代號主語必須與母句主語同指標(如㊼句)；而三元控制動詞補語子句的大代號主語則必須與母句賓語同指標(如㊽句)❷。試比較：

㊼ a. John$_i$ { intended/meant/planned/tried/attempted/managed} [PRO$_i$ to help Mary].❷

b. Mary$_i$ {began/started/continued/ceased} [PRO$_i$ to go out with John].

c. Bill$_i$ {remembered/forgot} [PRO$_i$ to turn off the lights].

㊽ a. John$_i$ {ordered/told/commanded/forced/compelled} Mary$_j$ [PRO$_j$ to help him].

b. John$_i$ { asked/advised/requested/reminded/warned} Mary$_j$ [PRO$_j$ not to go out with Bill].

二元控制動詞包括靜態動詞與動態動詞；動態動詞(如 'try, begin, start, continue' 等)以主事者為外元主語，而靜態動詞(如 'intend, mean, forget' 等)則以感受者為外元主語。另一

(→)同輩的「姐妹成份」(sister constituent) 或比 'α' 晚輩的「姪女成份」(niece constituent)，但不可能是比 'α' 長輩的「姨母成份」(aunt constituent)。也就是說，'β' 在 'α' 的「句法領域」(syntactic domain) 裏面。

❷ 但是也有 'John$_i$ promised Mary$_j$ [PRO$_i$ to help her]' 等三元控制動詞補語子句的大代號主語與母句主語同指標的例外情形。

❷ 附於名詞組或大代號右下角的英文小寫字母 (如 'i') 表示「指涉指標」(referential index)。

方面，三元控制動詞則幾乎全屬於動態動詞，因而都以主事者爲外元主語。但是三元控制動詞的內元賓語應該分析爲什麼角色？㊾a的例句與這些例句的「名物化」（nominalization；即㊾b的例句）的比較顯示：三元述語動詞的內元賓語應該分析爲「終點」（Go(al)），因而與表示終點的介詞'to'連用。

㊾　a. John {ordered / requested / reminded / warned} Mary$_i$ [PRO$_i$ not to go].

　　b. John's { order/ request/ reminder/ warning } *to* Mary$_i$ [PRO$_i$ not to go]

另外，在與英語例句㊾相對應的日語例句㊿a與韓語例句㊿b裡，三元控制動詞的內元賓語也分別與表示終點的'に'與'ege'連用。

㊿　a. ［ジョンが］［メアリ$_i$に］［［PRO$_i$ 行くな］と］命令した。

　　b. [John] [Mary$_i$ *ege*] [[PRO$_i$ kat∫i malla] go] mjʌllʌŋ hæt'a.

至於充當二元控制動詞主語補語與三元控制動詞賓語補語的不定子句❷之所以以大代號爲主語，一方面是根據「投射原則」（Projection Principle）與「論旨準則」（theta-criterion; θ-criterion)❷補語子句的述語動詞（如'(not to) go'）必須有自己的

---

❷　湯廷池（1991b, 1991c, 1991d）把這種補語子句分析爲「以空號代詞爲主語的不定子句」（infinitival clause with an empty subject），並以'Pe'的符號來代表。

❷　「投射原則」要求述語動詞的「論元結構」（argument structure）與「論旨屬性」（thematic property）必須原原本本的投射到（→）

外元主語，而且根據「格位濾除」（Case Filter）與「約束條件」（Binding Condition）❷⑥，大代號只能出現於不定子句、動名子句與分詞子句等「非限定子句」（non-finite clause）裡主語的位置。例句⑭裡的大代號就出現於不定子句主語的位置，而例句⑤與⑫裡的大代號則分別出現於「wh不定子句」（wh-infinitival）、「動名子句」（gerundive clause）與「（現在）分詞關係子句」（(present) participial relative clause）或「不定關係子句」（infinitival relative clause）裡主語的位置。

⑤　a. I don't know [what$_i$ PRO to do t$_i$].❷⑦

（→）「深層結構」（D-structure）、「表層結構」（S-structure）與「邏輯形式」（logical form; LF）上面去。而「論旨準則」則要求論元與論旨角色之間必須形成「一對一的對應關係」（one-to-one correspondence）。

❷⑥　「格位濾除」要求具有語音形態的名詞組必須具有格位。「約束條件」的「條件A」要求反身詞、相互詞與名詞組痕跡等「照應詞」（anaphor）必須在其「管轄範疇」（governing category）內「受到約束」（be bound；即由同指標的「前行語」（antecedent）加以C統制）；而「條件B」則要求「稱代詞」（pronominal）必須在其管轄範疇內「不受約束」或「自由」（be free）。由於大代號兼具照應詞（＋〔anaphor〕）與稱代詞（＋〔pronominal〕）雙重性質，只得以「大代號原理」（the PRO Theorem）來假定大代號不具有管轄範疇或不受管轄。

❷⑦　符號‘t’代表句法成分移位後留下的「痕跡」（trace）。因此，‘what$_i$’與‘t$_i$’表示：‘what$_i$’在深層結構裡本來出現於‘t$_i$’的位置，然後由於「移動α」（Move α）或「影響α」（affected α）而移位到補語子句裡句首（即「大句子」（CP/S'）裡「補語連詞」（C））的位置。又出現於例句⑤裡的大代號（PRO）可以解釋為與主語名詞（→）

b. Can you tell me [how_i PRO to do it t_i]?

c. We are not sure [whether PRO to believe him or not].

d. Do you know [who (m)$_i$ PRO to ask t_i for help]?

e. * Do you know [who_i t_i to come]?

(52) a. I don't mind [{you(r)/PRO} wearing a red necktie].

b. [The man [PRO standing at the gate]] is my brother.

c. Do you know [the boys [PRO playing basket-ball]]?

d. [Those [PRO having finished the assignment]] may go home.

e. This is [the boy [PRO to send the message for you]].

f. I have [no book [O_i PRO to read t_i]].

例句(51)d的'who (m)'只能分析爲及物動詞'ask'的賓語(即在深

(一→)組同指標(叫做「由主語控制的大代號」(subject-control PRO)或與賓語名詞組同指標(叫做「由賓語控制的大代號」(object-control PRO));但是也可以解釋爲「泛指」(generic)或「任指」(arbitrary)的大代號。其他如'〔PRO to be〕or〔PRO not to be〕, that is, the question'或'〔PRO to see pro〕is〔PRO to believe pro〕'裏出現的'PRO'就是屬於「任指的大代號」。

層結構裡出現於痕跡't_i')的位置，不能分析爲出現於主語位置；因爲例句51e顯示：在深層結構裡出現於主語(即痕跡't_i')的位置，然後在表面結構裡移到「大句子」(CP；亦即S')「指示語」(specifier)位置的'who'不合語法。這是由於'who, who(m), what'等「wh 詞組」(wh-phrase)，與一般名詞組一樣，必須出現於賦有格位的位置；而不定子句主語的位置卻是不具有格位的位置。可見語法理論(我們在這裡所依據的是「原則參數語法」(Principles-and-Parameters Approach)的理論)不但能「描述」(describe)語法現象，而且還更進一步「詮釋」(explain)或「預斷」(predict)語法現象。

十一、動詞'persuade'、'prefer'與'believe'在句法表現上的差異

初看下面53a與53b的例句，我們很容易以爲'persuade'與'prefer'都屬於同一類動詞，而53a與53b的例句也屬於同一類句型。[28] 事實上，*Longman Dictionary of Contemporary English* 就是把這兩個動詞與例句53c的動詞'want'以及53d的動詞'believe'都統統分析爲以名詞組爲賓語('Bill')而以不定詞爲補語('to be honest')的'V3'類動詞。

53 a. John persuaded Bill to be honest.

b. John preferred Bill to be honest.

---

28 53到57有關動詞'persuade'與'prefer'的例句來自一九九一年度國立清華大學語言學研究所博士班句法學入學考試試題第Ⅲ題。

c. John wanted Bill to be honest.

d. John believed Bill to be honest.

但是例句⑭卻顯示：只有'prefer'與'want'這兩個動詞可以在'Bill'的前面插入程度副詞'very much'與介詞'for'；而'persuade'與'believe'這兩個動詞則不能。試比較：

⑭ a. *John persuaded (*very much*) *for* Bill to be honest.

b. John preferred (*very much*) *for* Bill to be honest.

c. John wanted (*very much*) *for* Bill to be honest.

d. *John believed (*very much*) *for* Bill to be honest.

例句⑮又顯示含有'persuade'與'believe'的主動句⑬a, d可以有與此相對應的被動句⑮a, b；而含有'prefer'與'want'的主動句⑬b, c則不可以。試比較：

⑮ a. *Bill was persuaded* to be honest by John.

b. **Bill was preferred* to be honest by John.

c. **Bill was wanted* to be honest by John.

d. *Bill was believed* to be honest by John.

另一方面，例句⑯卻顯示：含有'prefer'與'want'的主動句⑬b, c可以有與此相對應的被動句⑯b, c；而含有'persuade'與'believe'的主動句⑬a, d則不可以。試比較：

⑯ a. *(*For*) *Bill to be honest* was persuaded by John.

b. *For Bill to be honest* was preferred by John.

c. (?)*For Bill to be honest* was wanted by John.

d. **(For) Bill to be honest* was believed by John.

又例句⑰顯示：含有 'prefer' 與 'want' 的㊾b, c 句可以有與
此相對應的「準分裂句」（pseudo-cleft sentence）；而含有
'persuade' 與 'believe' 的㊾a, d句則不可以。試比較：

⑰ a. **What* John persuaded *was* (for) Bill to be
    honest.

b. *What* John preferred *was* for Bill to be honest.

c. *What* John wanted *was* for Bill to be honest.

d. **What* John believed *was* (for) Bill to be
   honest.

另外，動詞 'prefer', 'want', 'believe' 可以用稱代詞 'it' 或
指示詞 'that' 做為賓語(如㊿句)；'prefer', 'want' 可以用不
含主語的不定子句為賓語(如㊾句)；'prefer'可以用含主語的或
不含主語的「動名子句」（gerundive clause) 為賓語(如⑥句)
。試比較：

㊿ a. **John persuaded {it/that}.

b. John preferred {*it/that*}.

c. John wanted {*it/that*}.

d. John believed {*it/that*}. ㉙

㉙ 'believe' 是「非事實動詞」(nonfactive verb) ，所以也可以帶
上「肯定句替代詞」的 'so' 與「否定句替代詞」的 'not' ，如 'I believe {so/not}' 。

⑤ a. ＊John persuaded *to be honest.*

　 b. 　John preferred *to be honest.*

　 c. 　John wanted *to be honest.*

　 d. ＊John believed *to be honest.*

⑥ a. ＊John persuaded {φ/my/me} staying with her.

　 b. 　John preferred {φ/my/me} staying with her.

　 c. 　John wanted {＊φ/＊my/me} staying with her.❸

　 d. ＊John believed {φ/my/me}　staying with her.

綜合上述⑤句到⑥句所呈現的句法表現上的差異，可以從以 'want'、'prefer'、'persuade'、'believe' 爲述語動詞的例句 ⑤a,b,c,d 分別擬設下面⑥a,b,c,d 的深層結構。

⑥ a. John persuaded Bill [PRO to be honest].

　 b. John preferred [(for) Bill to be honest].

　 c. John wanted [(for) Bill to be honest].

　 d. John believed [Bill to be honest].

　首先，'persuade'是三元控制動詞，以名詞組（如'Bill'）爲 賓語，而以受賓語控制的大代號爲主語的不定子句（如 'PRO to be honest'）爲補語。因此，(i)不能在補語子句或 PRO 的前 面加上介詞'for'（如⑤a句）❸；(ii)可以以賓語名詞組（'Bill'）

---

❸ 'want' 還有 'John's uniform wants mending (＝needs to be mended)'這樣以不含主語的動名子句爲賓語的用法。

❸ 這裏的 'for' 是「介詞性的補語連詞」（prepositional comple- mentizer)，只能出現於「顯形名詞組」（overt NP；卽具有語音形 態的（實號）名詞組，與不具有語音形態的「隱性名詞組」（covert （→）

爲主語形成被動句（如⑤a句）；（iii）不能同時以賓語名詞組
（'(for) Bill'）與補語子句（'PRO to be honest'）充當被動
句的主語（如⑯a句）❷；（iv）不能同時以賓語名詞組與補語子句
（'Bill [PRO to be honest]'）爲信息焦點而形成「準分裂句」
如⑰a句）；（v）不能同時把賓語名詞組與補語子句以稱代詞'it'
或指示詞'that'來指涉（如⑱a句）；（vi）不能省略賓語名詞組而
僅帶上補語子句如（⑲a句）；（vii）不能由賓語名詞組與補語子句
共同形成「動名子句」或「(現在)分詞子句」（如⑳a）。

其次，'prefer'與'want'是二元及物動詞，可以以名詞組
爲賓語（如'They {preferred/wanted} Bill'），也可以以由介
詞'for'引介或不由介詞引介的不定子句（'(for) Bill to be
honest'）爲賓語。因此，（i）以不由介詞'for'引介的不定子句爲
賓語時，就分別產生⑬b與⑬c的例句；（ii）以由介詞'for'引介
的不定子句爲賓語時，就分別產生⑭b與⑭c的例句❸；（iii）以

NP）或「空號代詞」（empty pronoun, null pronoun；即「大
代號」（PRO）與「小代號」（pro））相對）的前面，以便指派格位
給這個名詞組。另一方面，大代號是不具語音形態的名詞組，不必也
不能指派格位，也不能受動詞、介詞或呼應語素等「格位指派語」
（Case-assigner）的管轄。

❷ 這裏的賓語名詞組與補語子句並沒有形成「詞組單元」（constituent
；即同受同一「節點」（node）的支配）。凡是沒有形成詞組單元的
句法成分都不能移位，不能由稱代詞來指涉或由替代詞來取代，也不
能充當「準分裂句」的信息焦點。

❸ 尤其是述語動詞與不定子句賓語之間出現'very much'等程度副詞
修飾語的時候。介詞'for'必須在表層結構裏存在，以便指派格位給
名詞組來滿足「格位濾除」的要求，但是在「語音形式」（phonetic
form; PF）部門則可以（或必須）省略。

名詞組爲賓語時固然可以有相對應的被動句(如'They {preferred/wanted} *Bill.* → *Bill* was {preferred/wanted} (by them)'),但是以不定子句爲賓語時卻不能把不定子句的主語('Bill')移出來充當被動句的主語(如⑤⑤b與⑤⑤c句);(iv)以由介詞'for'引介的不定子句爲賓語時,可以以整個不定子句爲主語來形成被動句(如⑤⑥b與⑤⑥c句❸)或成爲「準分裂句」的信息焦點(如⑤⑦b與⑤⑦c句);(v)賓語名詞組或不定子句可以用'it'或'that'來指涉(如⑤⑧b與⑤⑧c句);(vi)可以以不含主語(或以大代號爲主語)的不定子句爲賓語(如⑤⑨b與⑤⑨c句)❸ ;(vii)'prefer'可以以含有主語的「動名子句」('*my* staying with her')或不含有主語的動名子句('PRO staying with her',這時候的'PRO'必須受主語的控制而與主語名詞組同指標)爲賓語,動名子句的主語還可以用賓位('*me* staying with her',參⑥⑩b句)❸ ;(viii)'want'僅可以以含有賓位主語的「現(在)分詞子句」('*me* staying with her',參⑥⑩c句)❸ 。

---

❸ ⑤⑥c句的接受度「較受限制」或「較成問題」(marginal),所以在句首標上'(?)'的符號,但是顯然比⑤⑥a句或⑤⑥b句好。

❸ 這個句法事實似乎顯示:'prefer'與'want'兼具二元控制動詞的句法功能,如'I$_i$ {prefer/ want} 〔PRO$_i$ to go with you〕'。

❸ 這個句法事實似顯示:(i)這裏的'staying with her'是現在分詞,而不是動名詞(參❸);(ii)'me'的賓位是由(母句)述語動詞'prefer'來指派的。但是也有人主張'(me) staying with her'是動名子句,而賓位是由「動名語素」(gerundive morpheme)'-ing'來指派的。

❸ 試比較下列三個例句:
(i) I want you *to stay* with her.
　　(我要你跟她在一起(本來不在一起)。)
(──→)

　　最後，'believe' 也與 'prefer', 'want' 一樣屬於可以以名詞組或不定子句為賓語的二元及物動詞，但是與 'prefer', 'want' 不一樣的地方是不定子句賓語不能由介詞 'for' 來引介（如⑭d句），所以必須由（母句）述語動詞 'believe' 本身來指派格位給不定子句的主語名詞組（參⑬d句與 'John believed [*him to be honest*]' 的例句）。❸ 因此，(i) 可以以賓語名詞組為主語來形成被動句（如 'They believed {*Bill/his words*}.→{*Bill was/His words* were} believed (by them)'），或以不定子句的主語為主語來形成被動句（如⑮d句），但是不能以整個不定子句為被動句的主語（如⑯d句，因為這個時候不定子句的主語（Bill）無法由母句動詞（believed）或補語連詞（for）獲得格位的指派）；(ii) 不能成為準分裂句的信息焦點（如⑰d句，其理由與⑯d句不合語法的理由同）；(iii) 賓語名詞組或不定名詞子句

（──→）(ii) I want you *to be staying* with her.

　　　　（我要你跟她在一起並繼續在一起（本來不在一起）。）

(iii) I want you *staying* with her.

　　（我要你繼續跟她在一起（本來就在一起）。）

上面(ii)與(iii)的說法似乎顯示：這裏的 'you staying with her' 是現在分詞用法，而不是動名詞用法。

❸　一般語法學家都認為 'believe' 屬於「例外地指派格位的動詞」(exceptional Case-marking verb; ECM verb)，即例外地由母句述語動詞指派格位給不定子句的主語名詞組；而這是由於這裏的不定子句因「刪除大句子」(S'-Deletion) 或「透明大句子」(S'-transparenpy) 而成為「小句子」(S; IP)。但是也有一些語法學家認為這裏的不定子句主語升入母句而成為母句賓語。

可以用‘it’或‘that’或來指涉（如⑤⑧d句）**❸**；（iv）賓語不定子句不能以大代號爲主語（如⑤⑨d句）**❹**；（v）只能以不定詞爲賓語子句的述語，不能以動名詞或現在分詞爲賓語子句的述語（如⑥⑩d句）。

十二、冠詞‘a(n), some, φ, the’與指示詞‘that’的意義與用法

看下面例句⑥②的五個答案(a),(b),(c),(d),(e)中，那些答案妥當？那些答案不妥當？爲什麼妥當或爲什麼不妥當？又在幾個妥當的答案中，各個答案的意義與用法有什麼區別？

⑥②　Beware of {(a) *a* dog/(b) *some* dogs/(c) φ dogs/
　　(d) *the* dog/(e) *that* dog}.

英語的冠詞可以分爲「有定」與「無定」兩種。「有定冠詞」(definite article) 只有‘the’一個，可以與單數「不可數名詞」

---

❸ ‘believe’與‘prefer’相似，都可以以「that子句」(that-clause)爲賓語；但是‘believe’的賓語子句通常都是含有「時制」(tense；即「現在式」(present tense) 或「過去式」(past tense))的「限定子句」(finite clause)，而‘prefer’的賓語子句卻可能是以動詞原形爲述語的「原式限定子句」(subjunctive-present clause)。又‘believe’是「非事實動詞」，所以可以用‘so’與‘not’分別取代肯定式賓語子句與否定式賓語子句。另外，‘believe’的賓語子句述語限於「靜態動詞」（包括「動態動詞」的完成貌、進行貌與完成進行貌）。試比較：I believe John to {*have* a lot of money/*resemble* his mother/{**study*/*be* studying/*have* studied/*have been* studying} English}}。

❹ 這也就是說，‘believe’不屬於控制動詞，所以其補語不定子句或動名子句不能以大代號爲主語。

(noncount noun) 連用，也可以與單數或複數的「可數名詞」(count noun) 連用；而「無定冠詞」(non-definite article) 則可以包括'a(n)'（只能與單數「可數名詞」連用），'some'（只能與單數「不可數名詞」或複數「可數名詞」連用）與'ϕ'（只能與單數「不可數名詞」或複數「可數名詞」❹ 連用）三個。「有定冠詞」'the' 有兩種含義：「定指」(definite) 與「全稱」(inclusive 或 holistic)。而「無定冠詞」'a(n), some, ϕ' 也有兩種含義：「非定指」(indefinite) 與「偏稱」(exclusive 或 partitive)。所謂「定指」（或含有有定冠詞 'the' 的「定指名詞組」）表示「說話者」(the speaker) 與「聽話者」(the hearer 或 the addressee) 都知道這個定指名詞組的「指涉對象」(referent)是誰或是什麼。另一方面，所謂「非定指」（或不含有定冠詞'the' 的「非定指名詞組」）則指「定指」以外的一切情形，包括：

⑥ a. 「殊指」(specific)：只有說話者知道指涉對象是誰或什麼，聽話者却不知道，例如：

{*A* friend/*Some* friends} of mine came to see me yesterday.

b. 「任指」(arbitrary)：說話者與聽話者都不知道指涉

---

❹ 「零冠詞」(zero article) 'ϕ' 與「冠詞的省略」(omission of articles) 不同：前者是以不具語音形態的'ϕ'為冠詞；而後者是本來應該或可以用特定的冠詞卻加以省略，因而可能回復省略的冠詞（如'(*a*)father and (*a*) son, with (*a*) cigar in (*the*) hand' 等）。

對象是誰或什麼⑫，例如：

I {drink *a* glass of milk/eat *some* fruit} every morning.

c. 「虛指」(non-referring; non-referential)：沒有指涉對象，只是充當主語補語或賓語補語來表示屬性，例如：

{He is *a bachelor* (=single)/They are all ϕ *bachelors* (=single)}.⑬

其次，所謂的「全稱」是指把說話者與聽話者在「言談宇宙」(the universe of discourse) 裡所知道的指涉對象都要統統包括進去，一個都不能遺漏。而所謂的「偏稱」是指並沒有把說話者與聽話者在言談宇宙裡所知道的指涉對象統統包括進去，至

---

⑫ 有時候，同一個無定名詞組可以有「殊指」與「任指」兩種不同的解釋，例如：

(1) John wants to marry *a red-hair girl* (who lives next door). (殊指)

(2) John wants to marry *a red-hair girl* (but so far he has found none). (任指)

⑬ 也有人把含有「否定冠詞」('negative' article) 'no' 的名詞組 (如 'No student came yesterday', 'I found *no student* in the classroom' 的 'no student' 分析為「虛指」的名詞組)。又在「非定指」裏，除了「殊指」、「任指」與「虛指」外，還可能包括「泛指」(generic)，例如：'{*A dog* is/Dogs are/*The dog* is} a faithful animal'。其中，'a dog' 在形態與語意上都屬於單數，'dogs' 在形態與語意上都屬於複數，但 'the dog' 則形態上是單數，而語意上卻表示複數。

少有一個並未提到。「全稱」與「偏稱」的區別可以說明下面⑭句
的合法度判斷。

⑭　a. {the/* a} president of the university

　　b. {* the/a} student of the university

　　c. {the/some/ϕ} students of the university

就一般的情形而言，一所大學只有一位校長，所以⑭a句應該用
定指❹而全稱的‘the’，不能用非定指而偏稱的‘a’。另一方面，
一所大學的學生卻不可能只有一個，所以⑭b應該用非定指的‘a’
。最後，⑭c句的‘*the students* of this university’是指這
一所大學的全體學生，所以是「定指」而且是「全稱」；‘*some
students* of this university’是指這一所大學的某一些學生
（人數大概是三、四、五個），所以是「非定指」而且是「偏稱」；
‘ϕ *students* of this university’是指這一所大學不特定數目
的學生（人數是兩個人以上而少於全體），所以也是「非定指」而
且是「偏稱」。下面⑮與⑯的例句也可以用「定指、全稱」與「非
定指、偏稱」的區別來判斷冠詞的意義與用法。試把適當的冠詞
(the, a(n), some, ϕ)填入下面⑮與⑯的空白裡。

⑮　I've just been to inspect a house. I didn't buy it
　　because {(a) ＿＿ window was/(b) ＿＿ windows
　　were} broken and (c) ＿＿ roof was leaking.

⑯　That wedding was a disaster because Fred spilled
　　wine on {(a) ＿＿ bridesmaid/(b) ＿＿ bride}.

---

❹　「定指」並不要求說話者與聽話者都認識這一位校長，只要說話的當
　　事人知道指這一所大學的校長或有這麼一位大學校長就够了。

⑥a的空白應該填入‘a’，因爲依照常情來判斷，房屋的窗戶不太可能只有一個，所以應該填入「非定指」而「偏稱」的‘a’。⑥b的空白可以填入‘some’來表示有幾個窗戶是破的；也可以填入‘φ’來表示有不特定的數目的窗戶是破的；還可以填入‘the’來表示所有的窗戶統統都是破的。⑥c的空白應該填入‘the’，因爲這裡的‘roof’一定是指前面提到‘a house’（殊指）的屋頂，而且通常一棟房屋只有一個屋頂，所以應該填入「定指」而「全稱」的‘the’。同樣的，⑥a的空白可以填入‘the’來表示女儐相只有一個，也可以填入‘a’來表示不只一個女儐相中的一個；而⑥b則可以填入‘the’，因爲一般婚禮只有一個新娘。如果一定要在⑥b的空白裡填入‘a’，那就可能要解釋爲集團結婚裡的某一個新娘，甚或要解釋爲有一個新郎同時娶了兩個以上的新娘了。

綜合以上的分析與討論，我們可以針對前面⑥的例句做下面⑥的合法度判斷。

⑥ Beware of {(a) ?* *a* dog/(b) ?* *some* dogs/(c) (?) dogs/(d) *the* dog/(e) *that* dog}.

一般說來，‘Beware of’是用來警告人們要小心、當心或提防特定而實在的人、動物或事物。⑥a的‘a dog’係針對「非定指」而「偏稱」的‘某一隻狗’（殊指）或‘一隻狗’（任指）提出警告，所以不太妥當❹。同樣的，⑥b的‘some dogs’也是針對不特定的幾隻狗提出警告，所以並不妥當。⑥c的‘φ dogs’如果解釋爲不

---

❹ 如果把‘a dog’解釋爲泛指的狗則似乎可以通。但是這種以無定冠詞‘a(n)’與單數名詞表達的泛指，通常都出現於主語的位置，而不出現於賓語的位置。

特定的多隻狗而提出警告，也不妥當；但是如果把'∮ dogs'解釋爲「泛指」而當做'凡是狗都要{當心/提防}'解的話，就可以通❻。另一方面，⑥d的'the dog'與⑥e的'that dog'則針對特定而實在（「定指」而「全稱」）的狗提出警告，所以是妥當的說法。至於'the dog'與'that dog'的差異，則在於'the dog'所指涉的狗不必出現於說話者與聽話者的眼前（所以'（當心）家有惡狗'的警告牌都常寫做'Beware of the dog'），而'that dog'所指涉的狗則必須出現於說話者與聽話者的眼前（即看得見狗，或至少要聽得到狗叫聲）。如果把⑥（＝⑥）的例句跟與此相對應的漢語例句⑱加以比較的話，就不難發現這兩種語言之間有關例句的合法度與語意解釋都相當接近。試比較：

⑱　當心 {(a) *一隻狗／(b) *幾隻狗／(c) *多隻狗／(d)狗／(e)那隻狗}。

十三、「間接賓語提前」的「功能解釋」與「語用解釋」

英語的「雙賓動詞」（ditransitive verb; double-object verb）如'give, send, teach, write'等都可以用兩種不同的表面形態出現：一種是直接賓語（客體名詞組）出現於前，間接賓語（終點介詞組）出現於後；而另一種是間接賓語（終點名詞組）出現於前，直接賓語（客體名詞組）出現於後。例如：

---

❻　泛指的名詞組在信息結構上居於「有定」（determinate）；因此，無論在漢語或英語，泛指名詞組都可以出現於句首充當「論旨」（theme）或「焦點」（focus）、「主題」（topic），例如 '魚，我喜歡吃黃魚'與'Caramels I like; toffy I adore'。

⑥⑨　a．John taught [Th French] [Go to the students].

　　b．John taught [Go the students] [Th French].

⑥⑨a與⑥⑨b的例句在「認知意義上相同」(cognitively synony-mous)❹，但是這兩個例句的「信息結構」(information struc-ture) 與「功能背景」(functional perspective) 卻並不相同。根據「功能解釋」(functional explanation) 裡「從舊到新的原則」(From Old to New Principle)，代表舊信息或次要信息的句法成分盡量要靠近句首的位置出現，而代表新信息或重要信息的句法成分則要盡量靠近句尾的位置出現。因此，⑥⑨a與⑥⑨b 在語意與功能上的差別之一是：⑥⑨a 的信息焦點在於句尾的 'to the students'，而⑥⑨b 的信息焦點則在於句尾的 'French'。這個信息焦點上的差別，可以從⑦⑩與⑦① 含有「對比焦點」(con-trastive focus) 的例句中「可接受度」(acceptability) 的比較上看得出來。

⑦⑩　a．　John taught French *to the students, not to the neighbors.*

　　b．?* John taught *the students* French, *not (to) the neighbors.*

　　c．?? John taught *the students, not the neighbors, French.*

⑦①　a．　John taught the students *French, not German.*

---

❹　也就是說，如果⑥⑨a例句「命題」(proposition) 的「真假值」(truth-value) 是真的話，⑥⑨b例句的命題也是真；而且，反之亦然。

    b. ?? John taught *French* to the students, *not German.*

又根據「從輕到重的原則」（From Light to Heavy Principle），「份量」（weight）較輕(卽字數較短，句法結構較簡單)的句法成分要盡量靠近句首的位置出現，而份量較重(卽字數較長或句法結構較複雜)的句法成分則要盡量靠近句尾的位置出現。❹這個功能原則的適用，可以從⑫與⑬的例句中可接受度的比較上看得出來。

⑫ a. John taught French to *the students who came to his house every evening.*

    b. ?? John taught *the students who came to his house every evening* French.

⑬ a. John taught the students *French, with which language he was not very familiar.*

    b. ? John taught *French, with which language he was not very familiar,* to the students.

另外，Oehrle（1976）❹更指出：⑥a的例句只表示 John 敎一

---

❹ 有關「從舊到新的原則」、「從輕到重的原則」、「從低到高的原則」（From Low to High Principle）、「從親到疏的原則」（From Familiar to Strange Principle）等功能解釋對於英語語法或漢語語法的適用，請參湯廷池(1984)＜英語詞句的「言外之意」：「功用解釋」＞與(1985)＜國語語法與功用解釋＞，分別刊載於湯廷池（1988b）《英語認知語法：結構、意義與功用（上集）》247-319頁與(1988c)《漢語詞法句法論集》105-147頁。

❹ 參 R. Oehrle (1976) *The Grammatical Status of English Dative Alternation,* MIT Dissertation。

些學生的法文，而⑨b的例句則更進一步表達 John 把這些學生的法文敎會了。這是因爲在⑨b的例句裡終點名詞組緊跟著出現於及物動詞的後面而表示「受事者」(the affected; Patient)，所以多了'直接受影響'的含意，而表示'學生確實學會了法文'，(the students have actually learned the subject matter)。同樣的，在下面⑭的例句裡，⑭a的例句可能是正在懷孕的太太對丈夫說的話 (an utterance by a pregnant wife to her husband)，說話的時候孩子沒有出生；而⑭b的例句則說話的時候孩子已經出生，因爲只有已經存在的人或事物才能直接出現於動詞後面充當受事者❺⓪。試比較：

⑭　a. I'm knitting this sweater *for our baby.*

　　b. I'm knitting *our baby* this sweater.

十四、「介副詞移位」與「功能解釋」

英語的「介副詞」(adverbial particle; pre-ad) 與動詞形成「雙詞動詞」(two-word verb) 或「片語動詞」(phrasal verb) 的時候，賓語名詞組可以出現於動詞與介副詞之間，也可以出現於介副詞之後(如⑮a的例句)；但是賓語代詞則只能出現於動詞與介副詞之間，不能出現於介副詞之後(如⑮b的例句)。❺①

❺⓪　參 R. Kayne (1975) *French Syntax,* MIT Press, 並參 R.K. Larson (1988) 'On the Double Object Construction', *Linguistic Inquiry* (19, 335-391) 376頁至377頁脚㊽的說明。

❺①　早期的變形語法認爲動詞與介副詞在深層結構裏形成詞組單元，然後介副詞在表面結構裏移到賓語的後面，並稱這一種句式變化爲「介副詞移位」(Particle Movement)。

⑦⑤　a. I called {*John* up/up *John*} last night.

　　b. I called {*him* up/*up *him*} last night.

坊間的英文文法書只提出了「規範性」（normative）的「規定」
（stipulation）（卽"名詞賓語可以出現於兩種不同的位置，代詞
賓語只能出現於其中一個位置"），卻沒有提供「詮釋性」（ex-
planatory）的「說明」（explication）；也就是說，只回答了
'How?' 的問題，並沒有回答 'Why?' 的問題。爲什麼如果賓語
是名詞組的話，可以出現於「句中」（sentence-medial）與「句
尾」（sentence-final）這兩種位置；而如果是代詞的話，只能
出現句中的位置？就詞類所代表的「信息內涵」（informational
content）而言，名詞組可能代表新的信息，也可能代表舊的信
息；而代詞則只能代表舊的信息。因此，賓語名詞組出現於動詞
與介副詞的中間時，信息焦點在於雙詞動詞 'called up'（所以
「句重音」（sentence stress）或「音高峰」（pitch peak）落在
介副詞 'up' 上面，如 'called John UP' ❷）；賓語名詞組出現
於介副詞的後面時，信息焦點在於賓語名詞組 'John'（所以句
重音或音高峰落在賓語名詞組上面，如 'called up JOHN'）。
另一方面，代表舊信息的賓語代詞則只能出現於動詞與介副詞的
中間，句重音或音高峰也就落在介副詞的上面。這種句式變化上
的限制，也是上一節所提及的「從舊到新」這個功能原則的適用
。但這並不是說，賓語代詞決不能出現於介副詞的後面。至少，

---

❷　如果句重音或音高峰落在「動詞＋賓語＋介副詞」這個句式的賓語名
　　詞組上面（如 'called JOHN up'），那麼雙詞動詞 'called up' 與
　　賓語名詞組 'John' 都代表新信息而成爲信息焦點。

在兩種情形下，賓語代詞可以出現於介副詞的後面：(一)賓語代詞因爲獲得「對比重音」（contrastive stress）而成爲「對比焦點」（contrastive focus），如⑦的例句；(二)賓語代詞因爲連接而增加其份量，如⑦的例句。第一種情形是「從舊到新的原則」的適用，而第二種情形則是「從輕到重的原則」的適用。試比較：❸

⑦ a. I called up *him, not his wife.*

　　b. ?* I called *him, not his wife,* up.

⑦ a. I called up *him, her and their children*.

　　b. ?*I called *him, her and their children* up.

十五、「重量名詞組轉移」、「方向副詞提前」、「處所副詞提前」與「功能解釋」

「從舊到新」與「從輕到重」這兩個原則對於英文許多句式變化從「功能背景」（functional perspective）的觀點提出相當「合理」（plausible）的解釋。例如，⑦的例句顯示：表示客體的賓語名詞組（'a book'）應該出現於表示起點的狀語介詞組（'from John'）的前面。但是⑦的例句則顯示：如果賓語名詞組讀對比重音（如⑦a句）或份量較重（如⑦b句），那麼這個賓語名詞組就常出現於狀語介詞組的後面。❺

⑦ a.　　I bought *a book* from John.

---

❸ 賓語名詞組也不一定都可以出現於兩種不同的位置，有時候在特定的情形下只能出現於一種位置。關於這一點，參湯廷池(1981)＜介系詞與介副詞＞，收錄於湯廷池(1984)《英語語法修詞十二講》69-87頁。

❺ 這一種句式變化稱爲「重量名詞組轉移」（Heavy NP Shift）。

b. ?? I bought from John *a book*.

⑦⑨ a. I bought from John *a book, not a car*.

b. I bought from John *a book that deals with English prepositions*.

又⑧⓪到⑧①等含有終點「方位副詞」(directional particle)的句子都可以有兩種不同的詞序：(一)方位副詞出現於句尾的「狀語位置」(adjunct position)，如⑧⓪到⑧①的(a)句；(二)方位副詞出現於句首的「主題位置」(topic position) 而原來的主語名詞組則出現於句尾的位置而成為信息焦點，如⑧⓪到⑧①的(b)句❺❺。但是如果主語是代表舊信息的代詞，而不是代表新信息的名詞組；那麼主語代詞就必須出現於動詞的前面，不能出現於動詞的後面(即句尾的位置)，如⑧⓪與⑧①的(c)句。試比較：

⑧⓪ a. *John* comes here. *The bus* goes there.

b. Here comes *John*. There goes *the bus*.

c. Here *he* comes. There *it* goes.

⑧① a. *A policeman* came in. *A policewoman* went out.

b. In came *a policeman*. Out went *a policewoman*.

c. In *he* came and out *she* went.

⑧② a. *The sun* went in and *the rain* came down.

b. In went *the sun* and down came *the rain*.

同樣的，以表示處所的介詞組為補語的主語名詞組也可以有

---

❺❺ 在 (二) 的句式裏，句式 (一) 的主語名詞組出現於句尾而成為信息焦點。這種句式稱為「引介句」(presentative sentence; presentational sentence)。

⑧a與⑧b兩種不同的詞序；而主語代詞則只有⑧c的詞序，不能有⑧d的詞序。試比較：

⑧ a. *Trophies* were in the case.

b. In the case were *trophies.*

c. *They* were in the case.

d. *In the case {were *they/they* were}.

在⑧到⑧的例句裡，方位副詞或處所副詞的移首以及主語名詞組的移尾，都是爲了把代表舊信息的方位副詞與處所副詞移到句首主題的位置，而把代表新信息的主語名詞組移到句尾成爲信息焦點。因此，這種詞序的改變仍然遵守「從舊到新」的功能原則。這一點可以從例句⑧的「上下文語境」(contextual situation) 看得出來。在⑧a的例句裡，前一個句子 'The door opened' 的敍述暗示 'Someone came in'，所以在後一個句子裡 'came in → in came' 並不代表新的信息，而 'policeman' 則成爲最重要的新信息並出現於句尾的位置。同樣的，在⑧b的例句裡，出現於前一個句子裡的 'a glass case' 在後一個句子裡的 'in the case' 成爲舊信息，所以 'trophies' 就成爲最重要的新信息而出現於句尾代表信息焦點。因此，⑧a，b的後一個句子都是屬於介紹出場人或新事物的「引介句」。

⑧ a. The door opened. In came *a policeman.*

b. I found *a glass case* on the table. *In the case* were *trophies.* ㊼

㊼ 例句與說明參 H. Fukuchi (1983)<語順にみられる談話の原則>，《言語》12:2, 48-57。

十六、「移出變形」、「從名詞組的移出」與「從輕到重」的原則

英語裡由「補語連詞」（complementizer）'that' 引介的「that 子句」（如⑧⑤句或由介詞 'for' 引介的「不定子句」（如⑧⑥句)充當主語而出現於句首的時候，常常把這個「that 子句」與「不定子句」移到母句的句尾，並以沒有指涉對象的「填補詞」(expletive; pleonastic) 'it' 來充當句法上的主語❺⑦。這是由於英語的「節奏」(rhythm) 不喜歡「首重尾輕」(front-heavy) 的句子，而喜歡「首輕尾重」（end-weighty）的句子，以便符合「從輕到重」的原則。試比較：

⑧⑤ a. (?) *That she finished her job all by herself* seems impossible.

b. *It* seems impossible *that she finished her job all by herself.*

⑧⑥ a. (?) *For Mary to go to Europe this summer* will be difficult.

b. *It* will be difficult *for Mary to go to Europe this summer.*

同樣的，在⑧⑦的例句裡，充當賓語的不定子句出現於句中的位置時，也常把這個不定子句移到母句的句尾，以符合「從輕到重」的原則。❺⑧

---

❺⑦ 這種句式變化稱為「移出變形」(Extraposition)。

❺⑧ ⑧⑤a、⑧⑥a與⑧⑦a在可接受度的比較上顯示：「中重尾輕」的⑧⑦a句在可接受度上比「首重尾輕」的⑧⑤a與⑧⑥a句還要差。

⑧ a. ?* I think *for you to try to help your friends* right.

b. I think *it* right *for you to try to help your friends.*

同樣的，⑧a與⑧a也都是主語長而謂語短的「首重尾輕」的例句。因此，在⑧b與⑧b的例句裡分別把關係子句 'which I was cleaning' 與由介詞'of'引介(這個介詞也可以省略)的「wh 子句」'(of) what contribution the public should pay' 從主語名詞組中移出來，移到句尾的位置⑤，以符合「從輕到重」的原則。試比較：

⑧ a. (?) *A gun which I was cleaning* went off.

b. *A gun* went off *which I was cleaning.*

⑧ a. ? *The problem (of) what contribution the public should pay* arose.

b. *The problem* arose *(of) what contribution the public should pay.*

十七、‘動搖’與‘搖動’在意義與用法上的區別

語言分析與語言教學的密切關係不但成立於英語，而且對於所有「自然語言」(natural language) 都有效。在這一節與以下幾節裡，我們以漢語為例來更進一步說明語言分析與語言教學的關係。根據《國語日報辭典》的註解，‘動搖’是‘不穩定、不

---

⑤ 這種句式變化稱為「從名詞組移出」(Extraposition from NP)。

堅固'（103頁），而'搖動'是'（一）擺動（二）不穩'（353頁），但是讀者卻不容易從這些註解中去了解這一對字序相反的複合詞，在意義與用法上究竟有什麼樣的區別。尤其是'不穩定、不堅固'與'不穩'都是形容詞用法（如'很(不){穩定/堅固/穩}'）；以形容詞用法來註解'動搖'與'搖動'的動詞用法，顯然不妥。其實，'動搖'是由兩個字義相近而且詞類（動詞）與次類（如「及物」或「不及物」）相同的動詞'動'與'搖'並立合成的「並列式」（coordinative）複合動詞，含有'動之搖之'的意思。另一方面，'搖動'是由表示動作的'搖'與表示（動作）結果的'動'搭配合成的「述補式」（predicative-complement）複合動詞。因此，我們可以說'搖得動、搖不動'卻不能說'*動得搖、*動不搖'。

'動搖'與'搖動'不但「內部結構」（internal construction）不同，而且「外部功能」（external function）也有差別。'動搖'與'搖動'都可以兼充「使動及物」（causative-transitive）動詞與「起動不及物」（inchoative-intransitive）動詞。試比較：

⑩ a. 他的一番勸告{動搖/*搖動}了我的決心；我的決心{動搖/*搖動}了。

　　b. 他用力{搖動/*動搖}樹枝；樹枝{搖動/*動搖}了。

'動搖'常以抽象名詞組（如⑩a句的'他的一番勸告'）為「起因」主語，而且以「抽象」名詞組（如⑩a句的'我的決心'）為「客體」賓語。另一方面，'搖動'則常以「有生」（特別是「屬人」）名詞組（如⑩b句的'他'）為「主事者」主語，而且以具體名詞組（如⑩b句的'樹枝'）為「客體」賓語。

這裡附帶提一提語言變遷的問題。韓愈在〈祭十二郎〉一文中有'而視茫茫，而髮蒼蒼，而齒牙動搖'的詞句。依照現代漢語(北平話)的說法，'齒牙動搖'一般都說成'牙齒搖動'，由此可窺見從唐朝到現在約一千年之間漢語詞彙變化的一斑。

十八、'生產'與'產生'在意義與用法上的區別❻

'生產'與'產生'也是一對由兩個字義相近而字序卻相反的語素合成的複合動詞；在內部結構上都屬於「並列式」，而且在外部功能上都屬於及物動詞。那麼'生產'與'產生'在意義與用法上究竟有什麼樣的區別？《國語日報辭典》541頁對'生產'一詞所做的註解相當煩瑣，但是最重要的動詞用法可能是'(三)生息產業...憑勞作掙錢過生活(四)生孩子'。另外，542頁對'產生'所做的註解是'(一)生下來；耕作，製作(二)發生'。但是這個有關'產生'的註解中，(一)的註解實際上是'產'字字義的解釋，而不是'產生'這個複合詞詞義的註解。湯廷池(1983)❻認為做'製造'的意義解的時候，'生產'與'產生'二者之間重要的區別在於：前者以有形的具體名詞組為賓語，而後者則以無形的抽象名詞組為賓語。試比較：

⑨ a．我們的工廠一年可以{生產/*產生}一萬輛{汽車/自行車}。

---

❻ 這個問題是國立清華大學語言學研究所八十年度博士班入學考試現代漢語語法學試題之一。

❻ 參湯廷池(1983)〈如何研究華語詞彙的意義與用法〉，收錄於湯廷池(1988c)《漢語詞法句法論集》67-89頁。

　　b．工廠的廢液{產生/＊生產}了很大的{公害/金屬污染}。

但是更重要的區別可能在於：‘生產’是以「主事者」（包括‘公司

、工廠’等機構設施)或「工具」（如‘機器’)名詞組爲主語的動態

動詞，而‘產生’則是以「起因」名詞組爲主語的靜態動詞。試比

較：

⑨　a．({我們準備/他勸我們})生產{玩具/冰箱/電氣用品}。

　　b．(＊{我們準備/他勸我們不要})產生{弊端/影響/不良效

　　　　果}。

十九、‘幫助’與‘幫忙’在意義與用法上的區別⑥

　　《國語日報辭典》254 頁爲‘幫助’與‘幫忙’所做的註解，分

別是‘幫忙，援助’與‘助人辦事’。以‘幫忙’來註解‘幫助’，幾乎

暗示這兩個動詞是「可以互相代用」（mutually exchangeable）

的。其實，‘幫助’是由兩個字義相似的及物動詞‘幫’與‘助’合成

的「並列式」複合動詞，而‘幫忙’卻是動詞‘幫’與以由形容詞轉

爲名詞的‘忙’爲賓語合成的「述賓式」（predicative-object）複

合動詞。因此‘幫助’可以直接帶上名詞組賓語，但不能以領位名

詞組、數量詞、形容詞等修飾‘助’，也不能在‘幫’與‘助’之間挿

入動貌標誌‘了、過’等；而‘幫忙’則由於本身已含有賓語，所以

不能另外帶上賓語，但可以用領位名詞組、數量詞、形容詞等修

飾名詞的‘忙’，並在‘幫’與‘忙’之間挿入動貌標誌‘了、過’等動

---

⑥　這個問題也是國立淸華大學語言學硏究所八十年度博士班入學考試現
　　代漢語語法學試題之一。又這裏的討論仍然根據湯廷池（1983）的分
　　析。

貌標誌。試比較：

㉝　a. 幫 {助/*忙} 你

　　b. 幫你的 {*助/忙}；幫幾次 {*助/忙}；幫很大的 {*助/
　　忙}

　　c. 幫 {了/過} {*助/忙}

不過有許多人在詞義相近、用法相似的影響下，忽視了‘幫助’與
‘幫忙’在內部結構與外部功能上的差別，而比照‘幫助你’造句，
結果‘幫忙你’這樣的說法也就逐漸出現了❸。

廿、‘微笑、大笑、偷笑、狂笑、奸笑’等「偏正式」複合動詞與‘嘲笑、譏笑’等「並列式」複合動詞在句法功能上的差異

　　‘微笑、大笑、偷笑、狂笑、奸笑’與‘嘲笑、譏笑’這兩組複
合動詞都以動詞‘笑’為第二個語素。但是前一組複合動詞的第一
個語素‘微、大、偷、狂、奸’等在詞類上屬於形容詞（或由形容
詞轉為副詞），並與修飾第二個不及物動詞語素‘笑’合成「偏正
式」(modifier-head)複合動詞，因而分別表示：‘微微的笑、大
聲的笑、偷偷的笑、瘋狂似的笑、奸詐的笑’。另一方面，後一
組複合動詞則是由及物動詞語素‘嘲、譏’與及物動詞語素‘笑’並
列形成的「並列式」複合動詞。這種不及物動詞與及物動詞的區
別，可以從下面例句㉞的合法度判斷中看出來。試比較：

㉞　a. 他 {向/對著} 我 {微笑/大笑/偷笑/狂笑/奸笑/
　　?*嘲笑/?*譏笑}。

---

❸　例如褚文誼在《傳記文學》中刊載的自述中有‘幫忙我十年的朋友’這
　　樣一句話。

b. 不要 {嘲笑/譏笑/*微笑/*大笑/*偷笑/*奸笑} 別人。
另外，在「偏正式」複合動詞裡出現不及物動詞的'笑'既不表示
褒義，也不表示貶義，只能說是表示中立意義的'笑'。而在「並
列式」複合動詞裡出現的及物動詞的'笑'則與及物動詞'嘲、譏'
一樣表示貶義（即含有惡意的笑或不懷好意的笑）。這一點可以從
例⑨a句不及物動詞'笑'與⑨b句及物動詞'笑'不同用法的比較
中看得出來。

⑨ a. 他 {向/對著} 我笑。

b. 不要笑別人。

廿一、形容詞的「AABB型」重疊與「A裡AB型」重疊

漢語的形容詞可以藉「重疊」（reduplication）來表示形容
詞所表達的屬性或程度的加強並轉達說話者「主觀評價」（sub-
jective evaluation）的情緒意義❻。雙音節形容詞的重疊有
「AABB」與「A裡AB」兩種方式。有些形容詞（如⑨a的例詞）只
能有「AABB型」一種重疊，但是有些形容詞（如⑨b的例詞）卻
可以有「AABB型」與「A裡AB型」兩種不同的重疊。

⑨ a. 乾{乾淨/*裡乾}淨、漂{漂亮/*裡漂}亮、老{老實/*裏
老}實、大{大方/*裡大}方、端{端正/*裡端}正、快
{快樂/*裡快}樂、清{清楚/*裡清}楚...

❻ 試比較單音節形容詞的未重疊（A）與重疊（AA）這兩種說法之間在意
義與用法上的差異：如'大眼睛、高鼻子'（單純的屬性敘述）與'大大
的眼睛、高高的鼻子'（含有主觀或情緒色彩的主觀描寫）。同時，也
請注意閩語方言裏形容詞的單用（如'大、金'）、「雙疊」（如'大大
、金金'）與「三疊」（如'大大大、金金金'）之間程度加強上的差別。

　　b. 骯{骯髒／裡骯}髒、糊{糊塗／裡糊}塗、古{古怪／裡古}

　　　怪、荒{荒唐／裡荒}唐、迷 {迷糊／裡迷} 糊、囉{囉嗦／

　　　裡囉}嗦、嘮{嘮叨／裡嘮}叨...

究竟是什麼因素造成這兩類形容詞在重疊類型上的差別？是那一

類形容詞只有「AABB 型」一種重疊，而那一類形容詞纔有

「AABB型」與「A裡AB型」兩種重疊？一般說來，漢語的雙音

形容詞都可以有「AABB 型」的重疊❻，但是只有表示「貶義」

(pejorative) 的形容詞纔可以有「A裡AB型」的重疊。這種情

形不但見於⑯的「並列式」複合形容詞，而且還見於⑰的「偏正

式」形容詞。所不同的只是 ⑰b 的貶義形容詞只能有「A裡AB

型」的重疊，不能有「AABB型」的重疊。試比較：

⑰　a. 秀(秀)氣(氣)、客(客)氣(氣)、和(和)氣(氣)、福(福)

　　　氣(氣)

　　b. 小(裡小)氣、傻(裡傻)氣、傲(裡傲)氣、淘(裡淘)氣

　　　、寶(裡寶)氣、闊(裡闊)氣、神(裡神)氣、假裡假氣

貶義形容詞「A裡AB型」的重疊規律確實存在於我們的「語言能

力」(linguistic competence) 裡面，雖然我們在習得漢語的過

程中並沒有人教我們這樣的重疊規律，也沒有一本漢語詞典或漢

語語法書告訴我們那些形容詞可以這樣的重疊。因此，我們聽到

‘神裡神經’(這是演母親的楊惠珊女士在電影《小逃犯》裡罵兒

子時說的話)、‘女裡女氣’(這是常楓先生在電視連續劇《新孟麗

---

❻　關於漢語形容詞的重疊規律，請參湯廷池 (1982) ＜國語形容詞的重
　　疊規律＞ (收錄於湯廷池 (1988c)《漢語詞法句法論集》29-57 頁)
　　的分析與討論。

君》裡對演孟麗君的夏玲玲女士說的話)、'開開心心'(這是盛竹
如先生在臺視節目《強棒出擊》裡說的話)這樣的貶義或褒義重
疊，也都會"聽怪不怪"的了解這些話的意義，並自自然然的接受
這種用法。

廿二、'不、沒'、'二、兩'、'又、再'在意義與用法上的區別

漢語的'不'與'沒'都是表示否定的副詞，但是二者在意義與
用法上有什麼樣的區別？例如，我們如何說明例句⑱裡'不'與
'沒'的意義與用法？

⑱　a. 他明天不來開會。

　　b. 他昨天沒(有)來開會。

我們可以用下面⑲的「詞音規律」(morphophonemic rule) 來
直截了當的說明'不'與'沒'的區別。

⑲　a. 不 → 沒/＿＿有（必用規律）

　　b. 沒有 → 沒（可用規律）

⑲a的「必用規律」(obligatory rule) 表示：'不'與'沒'是屬
於同一個「語素」(morpheme) 的兩個「同位語」(allomorph)
。'沒'出現於完成貌動詞'有'的前面，而'不'則出現於"其他語
境"(elsewhere)；因而'不'與'沒'這兩個同位語形成不折不扣
的「互補分佈」(complementary distribution)。⑲b的「可
用規律」(optional rule) 則表示：由'不'(否定)與'有'(完成)
合成的'沒有'可以「簡縮」(contract) 成'沒'，但是仍然含有完
成貌'有'的意義。

　　其次，漢語的'二'與'兩'都是表示阿拉伯數字'２'的數詞，

但是二者在意義與用法上有什麼樣的區別？表示「基數」(cardinal number) 的時候，'二'與'兩'或者成「互補分佈」(如⑩ a,b,c 句)，或者形成「自由變異」(free variation；如⑩d句) ⑥；因而可以說是屬於同一個語素的兩個同位語。試比較：

⑩　a.{＊二/兩}{個/張/塊/支/...}（____量詞)⑥

　　b.十 {二/＊兩}({個/張/塊/支/...})（/____個位數)

　　c.{二/＊兩} 十 ({個/張/塊/支/...})（/____'十')

　　d.{二/兩}{百/千/萬/億/兆}(/____'{百/千/萬/億/兆}')

但是表示「序數」(ordinal number) 的時候，則只能用'二'，不能用'兩'。因此，⑩a的'二次革命'(序數，意即'第二次')與'兩次革命'(基數，意即'共兩次')分別表達不同的意思；⑩b與⑩c的例句也只能用表示序數的'二'，不能用基數的'兩'。試比較：

⑩　a.{二/兩} 次革命

　　b.第(十) {二/＊兩} 課

　　c.{二零二/＊二零兩/二百零二/(?)兩百零二/＊二百零兩/ ＊兩百零兩} 室

　　最後，漢語的副詞'又'與'再'翻成英語的時候都會變成'again'。那麼'又'與'再'究竟有什麼樣的區別？下面⑩的英文

---

⑥　'二'與'兩'可以互相代用的時候，'兩'似乎是比較口語體的用詞。

⑥　不帶量詞而單獨做個位數的時候，只能用'二'，不能用'兩'。連續數數目的時候，通常也用'二'而不用'兩'(如'一、{二/＊兩}、三')。不過，也有人在報電話號碼等一連串數目時，用音節結構較爲複雜的'兩'來代替音節結構較爲單純的'二'(同樣的以'拐'來代替'七'，以'洞'來代替'零')以求傳話的清晰。

例句可以有⑩與⑭兩種不同的解釋。做⑩解的時候，副詞'again'
修飾 '(I) forgot to call him'（「寬域解釋」（wide-scope
interpretation ））；而做⑭解的時候，副詞 'again' 則修飾 'to
call him'（「狹域解釋」（narrow-scope interpretation））。
試比較：

⑩ I forgot to call him *again*.

⑩ a. *Again*, I forgot to call him.

b. I forgot *again* to call him.

⑭ a. I forgot that I should call him *again*.

b. I called him once, but I forgot to call (him)
again.

在⑩的「解義」(paraphrase) 裡，副詞 'again' 出現於句首或
不定詞補語 'to call him' 的前面；因而獲得寬域解釋。而在⑭
的解義裡，或者副詞 'again' 出現於限定子句裡面（如⑭ a 句），
或者在前一句預先「肯定」(assert) '我已經打過一次電話'（如
⑭b 句）；因而獲得狹義解釋。另一方面，與⑩以及⑭的寬域與
狹域兩種不同的解釋相對應的漢語例句⑩與⑩則分別使用副詞
'又'與'再'，而且這些副詞在句子中出現的位置亦有差別。試比
較：

⑩ 我又忘記(了)打電話給他。

⑩ 我忘記再打(*了)電話給他。

在⑩的例句裡，副詞'又'出現於'忘記打電話給他'的前面（並且
，可以與完成貌標誌'了'連用）；因而獲得寬域解釋。而在⑩例
句裡，副詞'再'則出現於'忘記'的後面、'打電話給他'的中間

(同時，不常與完成貌標誌‘了’連用)；因而獲得狹義解釋。這些合法度判斷顯示：‘又’常與過去時間(或完成貌)連用(試比較：‘他昨天{又/*再}來了’)；而‘再’則常與未來時間(或單純貌)連用(試比較：‘他明天{再/*又}來’)。但是我們可以更進一步條理化而把‘再’與‘又’的用法訂為：‘再’與「未來時間」(future time；可以用‘＋[未來]’的符號表示)連用，而‘又’則與「非未來時間」(non-future time；包括「過去時間」(past time)、「現在時間」(present time)與「一切時間」(generic time)，可以用‘－[未來]’的符號表示)連用。如此，不但可以說明例句⑩與⑩的合法度判斷，而且還可以說明例句⑩的合法度判斷。

⑩ a. 他明天{*又/再}來。(未來時間)

　 b. 他昨天{又/*再}來了。(過去時間)

　 c. 他{又/*再}在吹牛了。(現在時間)⑱

　 d. 她{又/*再}漂亮{又/*再}賢慧。(一切時間)

　 e. 他{又/*再}會德語{又/*再}會法語。(一切時間)

廿三、‘死鬼’與‘死相’的語用解釋

假如一個初到中國的外國人聽到‘死鬼’或‘死相’這兩句話，而向我們打聽這兩句話的意義與用法時，我們應該如何說明？我們把這兩個詞翻成英語(不管是直譯的‘dead demon, deadly expression’或意譯的‘evil spirit, evil expression’)或分析

---

⑱　‘你又來了’(Here you go again’)可能解釋為過去時間、現在時間、甚至相當於英語的現在完成式用法，但都屬於「非未來時間」，所以應該用‘又’，不能用‘再’。

這兩個詞的內部結構(如‘死鬼’與‘死相’都由形容詞語素‘死’修飾名詞語素‘鬼’與‘相’合成的偏正式複合詞)都無法幫助他們了解這兩個詞的意義與用法，只能從「語用」（pragmatics）的觀點加以說明。

首先，我們要了解‘死鬼’是與‘（{你這/他那}個){傢伙/飯桶/白癡/兔崽子/老不羞/殺千刀的}’同類的「表示屬性的稱呼語」（pronominal epithet），在「稱呼者」（addresser；或「說話者」（speaker)）與「被稱呼者」（addressee；或「聽話者」（hearer)) 的性別、稱呼者的年齡、稱呼者與被稱呼者之間的關係、用這個稱呼語的社會背景或語言情景等各方面受下面⑩的限制。

⑩ a. 稱呼者限於女性，而被稱呼者則限於男性。

b. 稱呼者(與被稱呼者)多半是成年人，至少是年齡在思春期之後。

c. 稱呼者與被稱呼者之間具有相當親膩的關係，這種親膩關係從有肌膚之親到情侶之間等程度深淺上之不同，但可以說是一種男女雙方之間可以互相打情罵俏的關係。

d. 這個表示男女間親膩關係的稱呼語，一般說來是不登大雅之堂的用語，因而遭受“上流社會”的忌諱。使用的場合，多半限於私人家裡(如閨房之內)或私底下的範圍，很少在大庭廣眾之間或當著外人面前公開使用。

其次，‘死鬼’在詞類上是屬於名詞，而‘死相’卻屬於形容詞

⑥。⑩⑧的語用限制大致上也都適用於'死相'，不過⑩⑧a到⑩⑧d的限制可能稍微要放寬或補充，分別改爲⑩⑨a到⑩⑨d的語用限制。試比較：

⑩⑨ a. 稱呼者仍然限於女性，但被稱呼者除了男性以外，還可以包括同性膩友。

b. 稱呼者的年齡仍多半在思春期以後，但是使用者的年齡階層可能比'死鬼'較爲年輕。不過使用者仍然限於同輩之間，或長輩對於晚輩，絶少用於晚輩對長輩。

c. 稱呼者與被稱呼者之間的關係不限於男女之間，而可以擴大到女性之間，常含有'嬌瞋'的「情緒意義」(emotive meaning)。

d. 使用場合比'死鬼'較爲公開，尤其是在女性之間使用的時候。

從以上的分析與討論，可以知道'死鬼'與'死相'的意義與用法應該從「語用」(如稱呼者與被稱呼者之性別、年齡、關係、社會背景、使用場合等)加以解釋，而有關的語用解釋或語用限制也與詞法或句法規律一樣可以清清楚楚的加以條理化。

---

⑥ '死相'雖然很少說'{很／非常}死相'，卻似乎可以說'好死相！你怎麼這麼死相！'(這是清大中語系甘明惠同學的合法度判斷)。'死相'之比較不容易以程度副詞(如'很、大、常、特別、最、最'等)修飾，甚至不能重疊，可能是因爲'死'在這裏兼有程度副詞的作用(比較在'死緊的抓着不放、死硬派'等說法裏出現的'死')。其他如'雪白、血紅、鐵青、漆黑、冰冷'等複合形容詞的第一個修飾語語素，也兼具(最高級)程度副詞的作用，所以這些形容詞也都不容易用程度副詞來修飾。

廿四、「作格動詞」、「使動及物動詞」、「起動不及物動詞」：英、漢、日三種語言裡「開閉動詞」論旨網格的對比分析

英語裡表示開閉的動詞(如 'open, close, shut') 都有「使動及物」(causative-transitive；如⑩a句)與「起動不及物」(inchoative-intransitive；如⑩b句) 兩種用法。

⑩　a. John {opened/closed/shut} the door.

　　b. The door {opened/closed/shut} (of itself).

這些動詞的及物與不及物用法之間的關係與 'kick, hit, beat' 等動詞的及物與不及物的用法之間的關係不同：前者的及物句與不及物句分別以「主事者」與「客體」爲主語(如⑪句)，而後者的及物句與不及物句卻均以「主事者」爲主語(如⑫句)。另外，⑪a句「含蘊」(entail) ⑪b句；卽如果⑪a句裡命題的「眞假値」(truth-value) 是「眞」(true) 的話，⑪b裡的命題的眞假値必然也是眞。⑩這是由於 'open, close, shut' 的「使動及物」用法表示'cause to become {open/closed/shut}' 而其「起動不及物」用法則表示 'become {open/closed/shut}'；因此，使動及物用法的含義本身就含有起動不及物用法的含義的緣故。有些語法學家把這類動詞稱爲「作格動詞」(ergative verb)⑪。

---

⑩　但是⑩b句不一定含蘊⑩a句，因爲門可能自動的開，也可能由 John 以外的人來打開。

⑪　「作格動詞」、「作格」(ergative case) 與「作格語言」(ergative language) 等詞雖在語義上有關連，卻有區別。在 Eskimo 與 Basque 等「作格語言」裏不及物動詞的主語與及物動詞的賓語具有
（→）

試比較：

⑪ a. *John* {opened/closed/shut} the door.

　 b. *The door* {opened/closed/shut}.

　 c. *John {opened/closed/shut}.

⑫ a. *John* {kicked/hit/beat} the door.

　 b. *John* {kicked at/hit against/beat at} the door.

　 c. *The door {kicked/hit/beat}.

　漢語的‘開’與‘關’⓻也兼有使動及物(如⑬a句)與起動不及物(如⑬b句)兩種用法而屬於作格動詞。

⑬ a. 小明{開/關}了門。

　 b. 門{開/關}了。

至於日語，則有‘開(あ)ける；閉(し)める’、‘開(あ)く；閉(し)まる’、‘開(ひ)らく；閉(と)じる’這三對不同的開閉動詞。第一對開閉動詞只有(使動)及物用法，第二對開閉動詞只有(起動)不及物用法，而第三對開閉動詞則兼有使動及物與起動不及物的作格動詞用法。試比較：

(一)同樣的「形態格」(morphological case)，而與及物動詞的主語有別。這種語言的不及物句主語與及物句賓語的格就稱為「通格」(absolutive case)，而及物句主語的格就稱為「作格」。在英語裏，無論是及物句與不及物句的人稱代詞主語都用「主格」(nominative case)，而及物句的人稱代詞賓語都用「賓格」(accusative case)，所以不屬於「作格語言」，而屬於「賓格語言」(accusative language)。但是也有人把作格動詞及物句主語的格 (如⑪a句的‘John’) 稱爲作格的。

⓻ 另外，‘閉’在文言或書面語裏可做動詞使用(如‘閉門思過’)，但是現代口語裏卻變成「黏著語」(bound morph)，因而不能單獨使用。

⑭　a．太郎が戸を{開(あ)けた/*開(あ)いた/開(ひ)らいた/
　　閉(し)めた/*閉(し)まつた/閉(と)じた}。

　　b．戸が{*開(あ)けた/開(あ)いた/開(ひ)らいた/*閉(し)
　　めた/閉(し)まつた/閉(と)じた}。

因此，我們可以利用下面（⑮a,b,c）的「論指網格」(thetagrid;
θ-gird) 分別把英、漢、日三種語言裡開閉動詞的句法功能表示
出來，以便對照。

⑮　a．'open, close, shut': v(t)., +[Th (Ag)]

　　b．'開，關'： v(t)., +[Th (Ag)]

　　c．'開(あ)ける，閉(し)める'： vt., +[Th, Ag]
　　'開(あ)く，閉(し)まる'：vi., +[Th]
　　'開(ひ)らく，閉(と)じる'：v(t)., +[Th (Ag)]

廿五、英語「名前」、「名後」修飾語與漢語「名前」修飾語的對 比分析：「X標槓理論」與「主要語在首或在尾」的參數

　　請比較下面⑯英語與⑰漢語的例句與合法度判斷。❼❸爲什麼
英語的名詞組與漢語的名詞組在內部詞序上有其相似性，也有其
相異性？

⑯　a. the long-haired linguistics student

　　b. the student of linguistics with long hair

---

❼❸　這個題目也來自國立清華大學語言學研究所八十年度博士班入學考試
　　句法學試題。不過，我們把⑰的漢語例句稍微修改，以便與⑯的英語
　　例句加以對照。

  c. the long-haired student of linguistics

  d. the linguistics student with long hair

  e. *the linguistics long-haired student

  f. *the student with long hair of linguistics

⑪⑰ a. 長頭髮的語言學系學生

  b. *學生語言學系長頭髮的

  c. *長頭髮的學生語言學系

  d. *語言學系學生長頭髮的

  e. *語言學系長頭髮的學生

  f. *學生長頭髮的語言學系

名詞組（NP）的內部結構由「主要語」（head）名詞（N）與其「補述語」（complement; Comp）、「附加語」（adjunct; Adjt）、「指示語」（specifier; Spec）合成。根據「原則參數語法」（Principles-and-Parameters Approach）的「X標槓理論」（X-bar Theory），凡是自然語言各種「詞組」（以「變項」（variable）'XP'或'X"'（讀"X雙槓"或「詞組」）都必須遵守下面⑱的「X標槓公約」（X-bar Convention）。

 ⑱ a. X"（詞組）→ X'（詞節），X"（指示語）

  b. X'（詞節）→ X'（詞節），X"（附加語）

  c. X'（詞節）→ X（主要語），X"（補述語）

首先，⑱a規定：詞組（X"）由「詞節」（'X''；讀「X單槓」或「詞節」）與充當詞節指示語的詞組（X"）合成；在名詞組裡我們暫且把冠詞（如'the, a(n)'）、指示詞（如'this, that'）、領位名詞

組(如 'John's, the teachers'') 等視為指示語❼。其次，⑪b
規定：詞節(X')由詞節(X')與充當詞節附加語的詞組（X"）合
成；而在名詞組裡附加語係指修飾語或「定語」(adjectival)。
由於⑪b的「改寫箭號」(rewrite arrow；即'→'的改寫記號)
的左右兩邊都出現同樣的符號(即詞節'X'')，所以這條規律可
以連續適用的結果理論上可以衍生無限多個附加語❼。最後，⑪
c規定：詞節(X')也可以由主要語(X)與其補述語（X"）合成。
⑪a與⑪c的規律，與⑪b的規律不同，在箭號的左右兩邊並未出
現同樣的符號，所以原則上指示語與補述語僅限於一個。又⑪的
「X標槓公約」只規定詞組成分與成分之間「上下支配」(dominance) 的「階層組織」(hierarchical structure)，並不規定
這些成分之間「前後次序」(precedence) 的「線性序列」(linear order)。根據⑪的公約，補述語必須出現於主要語的左邊或
右邊成為主要語的「姊妹成分」(sister constituent)，而附加
語則出現於詞節的左邊或右邊成為主要語的「姨母成分」（aunt

---

❼　出現於「改寫箭號」(rewrite arrow；即'→')右邊而充當指示語
、附加語或補述語的詞組（X"）並不一定要與出現於改寫箭號左邊的
詞組(X")、詞節(X')屬於同一詞類。但是出現於改寫箭號左邊的詞
組、詞節以及出現於改寫箭號右邊的主要語(X)必則須屬於同一詞類
而形成「同心結構」(endocentric construction)。又名詞組的
「X標槓結構」(X-bar structure) 有主張應分析為「限定詞組」
(determiner phrase; DP) 的主要語(D)的補述語者，這裏不擬
詳論。

❼　因此，'A(djective) → very A(djective)' 這樣的規律連續適用
的結果可以衍生'very, very, very, very…happy' 這樣的例詞。

constituent)。至於指示語,則出現於「最高」(topmost)的
詞節的左邊或右邊,並「封閉」(close off)這個詞組,因而阻
止這一個名詞組更進一步的「擴展」(expansion)。另一方面
,詞組成分之間的前後次序,則可以依據「格位理論」(Case
Theory)中的「固有格位」(inherent Case)或「論旨理論」
(Theta Theory)中的「論旨角色」(θ-role))指派方向的
「參數」(parameter)⑯或「主要語在首」(head-first; head-
initial)與「主要語在尾」(head-last; head-final)的參數來
處理。

　　英語的'student, teacher, professor'是可以帶上「客體」
補述語的主要語名詞(比較:'a {student/teacher/professor/
*boy/*man/*woman} *of {English/linguistics/physics}*'),
並且可以帶上表示「情狀」的附加語(如'a {student/boy} *with*
{long hair/short legs/a round face}')。依照⑱的「X標槓
公約」、格位理論中「格位濾除」(Case Filter)與「固有格位
指派方向的參數」或「主要語在首或在尾的參數」,英語⑯a句與
⑯b句的詞組結構分析分別如⑱a與⑱b。

---

❼⑥　關於「X標槓理論」、「格位理論」、「論旨理論」以及有關參數在
　　漢語、英語、日語的分析與討論,請參照湯廷池(1989)＜原則參數語
　　法與英漢對比分析＞、(1990)＜對照研究と文法理論(一):格理論
　　＞、(1991a)＜對照研究と文法理論(二):Xバー理論＞、(1991b)
　　＜論旨網格與英漢對比分析＞、(1991c)＜原則參數語法、對比分析
　　與機器翻譯＞與(1991d)＜從「論旨網格」談英漢對比分析＞等。

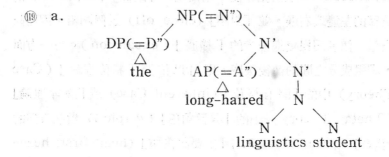

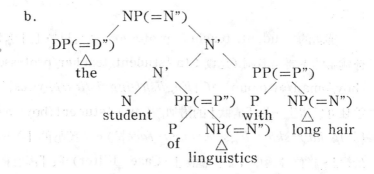

在⑲a的詞組結構裡，主要語名詞 'student' 在名詞組的組尾（卽右端），並與名詞 'linguistics' 合成複合名詞 'linguistics student'，再以複合形容詞 'long-haired' 爲附加語形成名詞節（N'），更以限定詞 'the' 爲指示語形成名詞組（NP＝N"）。在⑲b的詞組結構裡，主要語名詞 'student' 在名詞組的組首（卽左端），並以介詞組 'of linguistics' 爲補述語形成名詞節，再以介詞組 'with long hair' 爲附加語形成名詞節，最後以限定詞 'the' 爲指示語形成名詞組。在⑲a的詞組結構分析裡充當補述語

的名詞 'linguistics'、形容詞 'long-haired' 與限定詞 'the'
都不是名詞組，都不需要指派格位，所以都出現於主要語名詞
'student'的左邊。反之，在⑭b的詞組結構分析裡充當補述語的
'linguistics'與附加語的 'long hair' 卻是名詞組；因此，必須
出現於介詞的右邊，並由介詞獲得「斜位」（oblique Case）❼。
可見，英語的名詞組可能呈現「主要語在尾」（如⑭a）與「主要語
在首」（如⑭b）兩種不同的詞序。其次，⑯c句與⑯d句的詞組結
構分析，分別如⑭c與⑭d。

⑭　c.

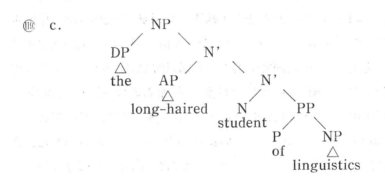

---

⑭　至於單詞修飾語，則必須出現於主要語名詞的左邊，而詞組（包括子
句）修飾語卻必須出現於主要語名詞右邊的理由，請參湯廷池（1988
a)〈英語的「名前」與「名後」修飾語：結構、意義與功用〉（收錄
於湯廷池(1988b)《英語認知語法：結構、意義與功用（上集）》453
頁至514頁）的分析與討論。

d.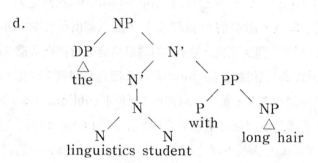

在⑩c的詞組結構裡，形容詞附加語‘long-haired’出現於主要語名詞‘student’的左邊；而補述語名詞組‘linguistics’則出現於主要語名詞‘student’的右邊，並由介詞‘of’來指派格位。另一方面，在⑩d的詞組結構裡，名詞組附加語‘long hair’出現於主要語名詞‘student’的右邊；而（補述語）名詞‘linguistics’則出現於（主要語）名詞‘student’的左邊，並與此形成複合名詞‘linguistics student’。因此，⑩a,b,c,d（＝⑩a,b,c,d）都是合語法的名詞組。最後，⑩e與⑩f的詞組結構分析，則分別如⑩ e與⑩f。

⑩ e.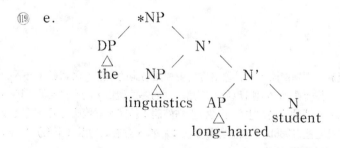

f.

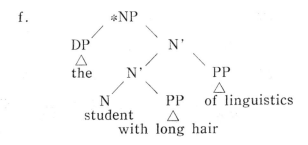

在⑲e的詞組結構裡，應該充當補述語的'linguistics'出現於附加語的位置⑱，而應該充當附加語的'long-haired'卻出現於補述語的位置，因而違反⑱的「X標槓公約」而不合語法。同樣的，在⑲f的詞組結構裡，應該充當補述語的'of linguistics'出現於附加語的位置，而應該充當附加語的'with long hair'卻出現於補述語的位置，所以也違反「X標槓公約」而不合語法。另一方面，漢語裡與英語⑯相對應的例句⑰a,b,c,d,e,f 則分別具有⑳a,b,c,d,e,f 的詞組結構分析。

⑳ a.　　　　　　　b.

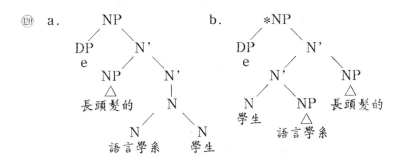

---

⑱　這裏的'linguistics'並未與主要語名詞'student'形成複合名詞；因此，應該分析為名詞組而必須指派格位。由於這個名詞組沒有獲得格位的指派，所以也違背「格位濾除」而不合語法。

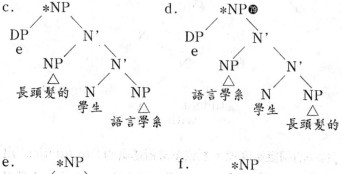

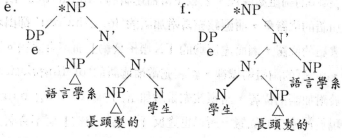

⑲ 例句⑪d的詞組結構也可以分析為如下（即名詞'語言學系'與名詞'學生'形成複合名詞'語言學系學生'）。

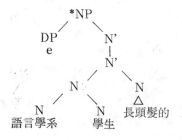

但是這個詞組結構分析也同時違背「主要語在尾」的參數與「X標槓公約」（應該充當附加語的'長頭髮的'卻出現於補述語的位置）而不合語法。

與英語不同，漢語的名詞組必須是「主要語在尾」❽；因此，除
了⑫a的主要語名詞'學生'出現於名詞組的右端而合語法以外，
其他⑫b,c,d,e,f的主要語名詞'學生'都未出現於名詞組的右端而
不合語法。同時，⑫b與⑫c的補述語名詞組'語言學系'既然未能
與主要語'學生'形成複合名詞，就必須指派格位；所以依照「格
位濾除」的規定而言，也要判定爲不合語法。又⑫d,e,f裡應該
充當補述語的'語言學系'卻出現於附加語的位置，而應該充當附
加語的'長頭髮的'卻出現於補述語的位置；因此，也都違背「X
標槓公約」而不合語法。另外，⑫d,e,f的名詞'語言學系'也都未
指派格位而不合語法。

廿六、結　語

　　以上就語言教學、語言分析與語法理論三者的關係，從英語
詞法、英語句法、漢語詞法、漢語語用以及英、漢、日三種語言
的詞法與英漢兩種語言句法之間的對比分析等各方面舉實際的例
詞與例句做了相當詳盡的分析與討論。語言教學並沒有所謂的
「唯一的最好的教學觀、教學方法或教學技巧」(the best approach, method or technique)，語言分析也不容易達成「最
後的已確定的分析」(the definite final analysis)。但是我們
可以在健全的語法理論的幫助與細心的語言分析的引導之下不斷
的改進我們的教學技巧；不但能清清楚楚、簡簡單單的說明我們
教學的重點，更能對症下藥、迅速有效的設計適當的練習。如此

---

❽　漢語的名詞修飾語，無論是單詞、詞組或子句，都出現於主要語名詞
　　的左邊。

，經過不斷的分析、研究實驗與改進，我們不斷的尋找以更少的時間為更多的學生帶來更大效果的教學技巧，一步一步的把我們的語言教學提昇到更高的境界。

　　＊　本文於1992年 5 月16日在臺中市國立中興大學舉行的「第九屆中華民國英語文教學研討會」上發表。

參 考 文 獻

Collins Cobuild (1987) *Collins Cobuild English Language Dictionary.*

Fukuchi, H. (1983) ＜語順にみられる談話の原則＞，《言語》12:2, 48-57.

Katumata, S. (1958) *A New Dictionary of English Collocation,* Kenkyusha, Tokyo, Japan.

Kayne, R. (1975) *French Syntax,* MIT Press, Cambridge, Massachusettes.

Longman (1978) *Longman Dictionary of Contemporary English,* Longman Group Ltd., Harlow and London.

Larson, R.K. (1988) 'On the Double Object Construction,' *Linguistic Inquiry* 19: 335-391.

Oehrle, R. (1976) *The Grammatical Status of the English Dative Alternation,* MIT Dissertation, Cambridge, Massachusettes.

Selkirk, E.O. (1982) *The Syntax of Words,* MIT Press, Cambridge, Massachusettes.

湯廷池（Tang, T.C.）(1982)＜國語形容詞的重疊規律＞。

……………(1983)＜如何研究華語詞彙的意義與用法＞。

……………(1984)＜英語詞句的「言外之意」：「功用解釋」＞。

……………(1985)＜國語語法與功用解釋＞。

……………(1988a)＜英語的「名前」與「名後」修飾語：結構、意義與功用＞。

……………(1988b)《英語認知語法：結構、意義與功用（上集）》，臺

灣學生書局。

……………………(1988c)《漢語詞法句法論集》，臺灣學生書局。

……………………(1989)＜原則參數語法與英漢對比分析＞。

……………………(1990)＜對照研究と文法理論（一）：格位理論＞，《東吳日本語教育》13：37-68。

……………………(1991a)＜對照研究と文法理論（二）：Ｘバー理論＞，《東吳日本語教育》14：5-25。

……………………(1991b)＜「論旨網路」與英漢對比分析＞。

……………………(1991c)＜原則參數語法、對比分析與機器翻譯＞。

(1991d)＜從「論旨網格」談英漢對比分析＞，「第三屆世界華語文教學研討會」發表論文。

英語情態助動詞的形態、意義與用法

一、前　言

　　就我國一般學生而言，英語的「情態助動詞」(modal aux-iliaries, 或簡稱 modals) 是僅次於冠詞在學習上最感到困難的「語法範疇」(grammatical category) 之一。我國學生，無論是說話或寫文章的時候，使用情態助動詞的頻率都遠比英美人士的使用頻率為低，常給對方說話語氣過分直率、冷漠甚至於倨傲的感覺。就是閱讀文章的時候，也常無法體會情態助動詞所明示或暗含的「情態意義」(modality)，特別是過去式情態助動詞所表達的含蓄而婉轉的語氣，或是連用完成貌或進行貌所表達

的虛擬的語氣。造成這些學習困難的原因，可能有下列幾點：

（一）國語的情態助動詞（如‘可以、可能、能夠、會、必須、要、應該’等）大都由「主要動詞」（main verb）演變而來，因而含有相當明確的「詞彙意義」（lexical meaning），在詞類畫分上屬於語意內涵比較具體的「實詞」（content word）。而英語的情態助動詞（如‘may, can, must, will, should’等）則與一般動詞不同而單獨成一類「虛詞」（function word），其語意內涵較爲抽象，較不容易掌握。

（二）英語每一種情態助動詞都可以表達幾種不同的情態意義，而同一種情態意義又可以用幾種不同的情態助動詞來表示。相形之下，國語卻一般說來都由不同的情態助動詞來表達不同的情態意義。雖然也有同義或近義的現象發生，但是其情形不若英語的晦澀，比較容易分辨。

（三）英語的情態助動詞與一般動詞不同，只有現在式（如‘may, can, must, will, shall’等）與過去式（如‘might, could, would, should’等）兩種形態，而「現在式」（present tense）不一定表示「現在時間」（present time），「過去式」（past tense）也不一定表示「過去時間」（past time），同一個情態助動詞的現在式與過去式所表示的情態意義可能有相當的差別。同時，英語情態助動詞的情態意義，除了「字面意義」（literal meaning）或「認知意義」（cognitive meaning）以外，常要考慮其「人際意義」（interpersonal meaning）、「情態意義」（emotive meaning）、「含蘊意義」（conveyed meaning）等「語用解釋」（pragmatic explanation）上的問題，情形更爲複

雜。

(四)英語的情態助動詞與一般動詞不同，在句法表現上不必依賴
'Do'動詞來形成疑問句、否定句、倒裝句、加強肯定句或省略
句等。在這一點，情態助動詞與表示完成貌（Have）與進行貌
（Be）的「動貌助動詞」（aspectual auxiliary）以及表示被動
態的'Be'動詞相似。但是表完成的'Have'動詞與表被動的
'Be'動詞要求後面的動詞用「過去分詞式」（past participle
form; V-en），表進行的'Be'動詞要求後面的動詞用「現在
分詞式」（present participle form; V-ing），而情態助動詞則
要求後面的動詞用「原式」（root form; V）。這種各類「助動
詞」（auxiliary verb）與其「主要動詞」（main verb）之間
在形態上幾種不同的「依賴關係」（dependency），也增加英語
助動詞的學習困難。

(五)英語的情態助動詞可以與「完成貌」動詞（have V-en）、
「進行貌」動詞（be V-ing）、「完成進行貌」動詞（have been
V-ing）、「被動態」動詞（be V-en, have been V-en）形成
相當複雜的句法結構，並且表達相當細緻的語意內涵。一般中學
生與大學生不容易掌握這些句法結構與語意內涵，因而既不能「
被動的了解」英語的助動詞結構、意義與用法，更不能「主動的
運用」英語的助動詞結構來適切有效的表達自己的情意。

　　已往的英語語法教學很少注意到英語情態助動詞與國語情態
助動詞在形態、意義與功用上的異同，更沒有從「形態」（mor-
phology）、「句法」（syntax）、「語意」（semantics）與「語用
」（pragmatics）各方面去研究英語情態助動詞並把這些情態助

動詞的意義與用法加以條理化。影響所及，英語情態助動詞的教學往往淪爲單純機械的詞彙學習，完全忽略了英語情態助動詞在形態、句法、語意與語用上的特殊性與條理性。本文有鑒於此，擬從認知的觀點研討英語情態助動詞的形態特徵、句法功能、語意內涵與語用解釋。爲了行文的流暢，從他人論著中引用的例句或觀點不在文中一一加註。但是這些論著都列在文尾的參考文獻中，以供讀者有意進修時的參考。

二、英語情態助動詞的形態特徵與句法功能

　　一般說來，英語的動詞在句法表現上可以有下面六種不同的形態❶：卽 (1) 第一、二身單複數與第三身複數現在式 (V, 如 'work, sing')；(2) 第三身單數現在式 (V-s, 如 'works, sings')；(3) 過去式 (V-ed, 如 'worked, sang')；(4) 過去分詞式 (V-en; 如 'worked, sung')；(5) 現在分詞式 (V-ing, 如 'working, singing')；(6) 不定式或原式 (to V; 如 'to work, to sing')。❷而英語的情態助動詞則只有「現在式」(V) 與「過去式」(V-ed) 兩種形態，而沒有「第三身單數現在式」(V-s)、「過去分詞式」(V-en)、「現在分詞式」或「動名詞式」(V-ing)、「不定式」(to V) 或「原式」(V)。其中，'must' 只有「現在式」，而 'ought (to)' 則只有「過去式」，其

---

❶　(1)的「第一、二身單複數，與第三身複數現在式」與(6)的「不定式或原式」在形態上並無區別，所以也可以視爲五種。

❷　英語的 'Be' 動詞可以有 'am, are, is, was, were, been, being, to be' 等八種不同的形態。

他 'may (might), can (could), will (would)' 與 'shall (should)' 則兼有「現在式」與「過去式」。

因為英語的情態助動詞只有現在式與過去式這兩種帶有「時制」(tense) 的「限定式」(finite form)，而沒有過去分詞式、現在分詞式（動名詞式）、不定式（原式）等不帶「時制」的「非限定式」(non-finite form)，我們可以推論出下面幾點英語情態助動詞的句法表現或功能。

(一)與動詞或其他助動詞（如表示「完成貌」的助動詞 'have' 以及表示「進行貌」或「被動態」的 'be'）連用時，情態助動詞必須出現於這些動詞或助動詞的前面，例如：

① a. I *should work* hard.

　　b. I *should have worked* hard.

　　c. I *should be working* hard.

　　d. I *should have been working* hard.

　　e. I *should be consulted*.

　　f. I *should have been consulted*.

因此，情態助動詞不能出現於過去分詞式、現在分詞式、動名詞、不定式或原式等一般動詞可以出現的位置。也就是說，情態助動詞不能出現於 'Have' 動詞、'Be' 動詞、'Do' 動詞或其他動詞的後面，例如：

② a. *He *has mayed* come.

　　b．*She *is musting* study.

　　c．*Does* he *may* come?

　　d．*She *does not must* study.

　　e．*I tried *to will* go.

　　f．*We made him *must* pay back.

　　g．*They enjoyed *canning* eat.

(二)不能同時連用兩個情態助動詞❸。試比較：

　③　a．*He *will can* tomorrow.

　　b．He *will be able to* come tomorrow.

　④　a．*You *may must* come along.

　　b．You *may have to* come along.

(三)情態助動詞與主語名詞之間沒有「身」（person）與「數」（number）的「呼應」（agreement）現象。試比較：

　⑤　a．John *comes* tomorrow.

　　b．*John *wills* come tomorrow.

　　c．John *will* come tomorrow.

───────────

❸　相形之下，有些國語的情態助動詞則可以連用，例如："他（不）可能（不）會（不）來"、"她（不）應該（不）會說英語"。國語有些情態助動詞也可以出現於及物動詞與賓語的補語子句裏，例如："我勸他一定要來"、"她叫我千萬要小心"。

(四)情態助動詞不能出現於「不定子句」(infinitival clause)
或「動名子句」(gerundive clause)。試比較：

⑥　a.　John will study English.

　　b.　It is important *for John to study English.*

　　c.　*It is important *for John to will study English.*

⑦　a.　It seems that *Dick can speak French.*

　　b.　Dick seems *to be able to speak French.*

　　c.　*Dick seems *to can speak French.*

⑧　a.　Mary must support her young sisters.

　　b.　We learned about *Mary's having to support her young sisters.*

　　c.　*We learned about *Mary's musting support her young sisters.*

同樣的，情態助動詞也不能出現於「派生名詞組」（derived
nominal)。試比較：

⑨　a.　John {*is able to / can*} deal with difficult
　　　　situations.

　　b.　*John's ability to deal with difficult situations*
　　　　is simply amazing.

　　c.　*John's can-ity to deal with difficult situa-*

　　　　tions is simply amazing.

(五)情態助動詞不需要依賴 'Do' 動詞來形成疑問句、否定句、
倒裝句、加強肯定句或省略句等。試比較：

⑩　a．You *speak* English.

　　b．*Do(n't)* you speak English?

　　c．You *don't* speak English, *do* you?

　　d．You *DO* speak English, *don't* you?

　　e．Neither *do* I speak English.

　　f．Yes, I *do.* /No, I *don't.*

⑪　a．You *can speak* English.

　　b．*Can('t)* you speak English?

　　c．You *can't* speak English, *can* you?

　　d．You *CAN* speak English, *can't* you?

　　e．Neither *can* I speak English.

　　f．Yes, I *can.*/No, I *can't.*

又含有情態助動詞、完成貌助動詞（have）、進行貌助動詞（be）
、被動態助動詞（be）與動詞（V）的句子可以有下列幾種不同
的省略方式。試比較：

⑫　John　*couldn't have been studying Japanese,* but
　　Dick

    a. *could have been studying Japanese.*

    b. *could have been φ.*

    c. *could have φ φ.*

    d. *could φ φ φ.*

⑬ Mary *should have been punished by the teacher* but Jane

    a. *shouldn't have been punished by the teacher.*

    b. *shouldn't have been φ.*

    c. *shouldn't have φ φ.*

    d. *shouldn't φ φ φ.*

但是在「動詞組提前」（VP-Preposing）中則只能把動詞與出現於動詞後面的賓語、補語、狀語等移到句首，其他出現於動詞前面的情態助動詞、完成貌助動詞、進行貌助動詞與被動態助動詞等都不能隨動詞移到句首來。試比較：

⑭ They say that John *will marry Alice,* and *marry her* he *will*!

⑮ They say that John *might have been taking dancing lessons,* and

    a. *taking dancing lessons* he *might have been*!

    b. **been taking lessons* he *might have*!

    c. **have been taking lessons* he *might*!

⑯ They say that Mary *must have been promoted*

>   *to a manager,* and
>
>   a.　*promoted to a manager* she *must have been*!
>   b.　**been promoted to a manager* she *must have*!*
>   c.　**have been promoted to a manager* she *must*!*

　　從以上的討論與分析，'may (might), can (could), must, will (would), shall (should), ought to' 等都具有（一）到（五）的句法表現。其他，如 'need, dare, had {better/sooner}, have to, used to, be to' 則並不具備所有的句法表現，但是在語意上仍然表達某種情態意義。我們把前一類情態助動詞稱爲「（狹義的）情態助動詞」，而把後一類情態助動詞稱爲「準情態助動詞」(quasi-modal auxiliaries)。

三、英語情態助動詞的語意與語用解釋

3.1　「義務意義」與「認知意義」

　　已往的英語語法教學視情態助動詞的學習爲單純的詞彙學習，因而常把每一個情態助動詞的意義與用法一一加以列舉，並且似乎認爲列舉得越多越詳盡越好。但是對於這些意義與用法卻很少加以條理化或規律化，也不說明這些意義與用法之間究竟有什麼句法上、語意上或語用上的關係存在。其實，英語情態助動詞的語意內涵主要可以分爲「義務意義」（deontic meaning）❹

---

❹　又稱「本義」(root meaning)。

與「認知意義」（epistemic meaning）❺兩種。這兩種不同意義的情態助動詞在「時制」（tense）、「動貌」（aspect）、「否定範域」（scope of negation）、「疑問」（interrogation）、「語態」（voice）等方面各有不同的句法表現、語意內涵與語用解釋。所謂義務意義或用法的情態助動詞，係指表示「許可」（permission）、「能力」（ability）、「需要」（necessity）、「義務」（obligation）、「命令」（command）等含義的情態助動詞。而所謂認知意義或用法的情態助動詞則指表示「可能性」（possibility）、「不可能性」（impossibility）、「或然性」（probability）、「必然性」（certainty）等含義的情態助動詞。前者表示「說話者」（the speaker）對於「聽話者」（the addressee; the hearer）或「第三者」（a third party）等所提出的有關積極的作為（肯定句）或消極的不作為（否定句）的要求；也就是說，許可或要求別人做某一件事或不做某一件事。而後者則表示「說話者」對於句子中「命題」（proposition）「真假值」（the truth-value）的看法；也就是說，推測某一件事可能、不可能或必然會發生。以下就英語的情態助動詞一一探討其「義務意義」與「認知意義」。

（一）may

（a）'may'的義務用法：情態助動詞'may'的義務用法，表示「（說話者的）許可」（permission（given by the speaker）），相當於國語的 '可以..'（be permitted to V），例如：

---

❺ 又譯「推測意義」。

⑰ You *may* smoke in this room. (＝You are permitted (by me) to smoke in this room.)

　"你可以在這個房間抽煙"

⑱ You *may* call further witnesses if you so desire. (＝I permit you, or court procedure permits you, to call further witnesses if you so desire.)

　"如果你需要，你可以〔本庭允許你〕傳喚其他證人"

在口語英語裏，'may' 一般都表示「說話者」對於「聽話者」的許可，如⑰與⑱句。但是在較爲正式的英語裏，'may' 也可以用來表示「一般性的許可」(general permission)，即不明示特定的許可來源或特定的許可對象，例如：

⑲ Visitors *may* park their cars in the field opposite. (＝The organizers, or the owners of the field, permit visitors to park their cars in the field opposite.)

　"（主辦單位或場地主人允許）參觀者可以在對面的場地停車"

⑳ Visitors *may* ascend the tower for one dollar.

　"參觀者付一元即可登塔"

如果 'may' 以第一人稱代詞 'I' 爲主語，那麼就可以解釋爲說話者對於本身的許可，或客觀的環境對於說話者的許可，例如：

㉑ I *may* say that I have never lied to her. (=I permit it of myself to say that I have never lied to her.) "我可以説我從未對她撒過謊"

㉒ I think we *may* assume it's murder. (=I think the evidence permits it of us to assume it's murder.)

"我想我們（有理由或證據）可以假定這是一件謀殺案"

(b)'may'的認知用法：情態助動詞'may'的認知用法，表示「（事實上的）可能性」((factual) possibility)，相當於國語的 "可能…" 或 "或許會…"(it is possible that…)，例如：

㉓ You *may* lose your way if you don't take a map. (= It is possible that you will lose your way if you don't take a map.)
"你不帶地圖去可能會迷路的"

㉔ Be careful; that gun *may* be loaded. (=It is possible that the gun is loaded.)
"小心，那把槍可能裝有子彈"

㉕ I *may* have misunderstood you. (=It is possible that I misunderstood you.) "我可能誤會了你"

表示「許可」的'may'不重讀，而表示「可能性」的'may'則

重讀。因此，下面㉖的例句可以有㉗與㉘兩種讀音與含義。試比較：

㉖ He may leave tomorrow.

㉗ He may *léave* tomorrow. "他可以明天走"

㉘ He *máy* leave tomorrow. "他可能明天走"

在科學 (scientific) 或 "準科學" (pseudo-scientific) 的文章裏，'may' 常以「非人稱」(impersonal) 名詞組爲主語。這種 'may' 可做「許可」解，亦可做「可能性」解，例如：

㉙ Transitive verbs *may* occur in the passive.

(=(a) The rules of English permit transitive verbs to occur in the passive;

=(b) It is possible that transitive verbs occur in the passive.)

"及物動詞 {可以／可能} 出現於被動句"

㉚ A camel *may* travel for many days without water.

(=(a) The physical constitution of a camel permits it to travel for many days without water;

(b) It is possible that a camel travels for many days without water.)

"駱駝{可以／可能}一連跋涉好多天而不喝水"

(c) 'may' 的其他用法

從 'may' 的「可能性」意義引申出下面的「讓步」用法 (concessive use)來，相當於國語的"或許、就算"，例如：

㉛ she *may* not be pretty, but at least she knows her job. (=Though she may not be pretty, yet she knows her job; =Whatever one thinks of her looks, she knows her job.)

"她或許長得不怎麼漂亮，却很能幹"

㉜ However hard he *may* try, he will never succeed. "不管他怎麼努力，他都不會成功"

另外在非常正式的英語裏，'may' 可以出現於主語名詞的前面來表示「願望」(desire)。這一種表示「祝禱」(benediction)或「詛咒」(malediction)的 'may'，只能出現於肯定直述句而動詞則必須用原式，不能出現於否定句、疑問句或條件句中。這一種 'may' 的用法，可以說是從 'may' 的「可能性」意義引申出來的，不過在現代英語中已經很少使用，例如：

㉝ *May* we never forget each other! (=I wish we never forgot each other.) "但願我倆永不相忘"

㉞ *May* God grant you happiness!

㉟ *May* his evil designs perish!

㊱ *May* grammar be hanged!

（二）can

（a）'can' 的「義務」用法：情態助動詞 'can' 的義務用法表示「能力」（ability），相當於國語的 "能（夠）…"(be able to V; be capable of V-ing) 或 "會"（know how to V），例如：

㊲ She *can* make (＝is capable of making) all her own dresses.

㊳ *Can* you (＝Do you know how to) swim well?

㊴ He *can* (＝is strong enough to) lift me up with one hand.

㊵ *Can* you (＝Are you free to) come to the meeting tomorrow?

'see, hear, feel, smell, taste' 等不能用於進行貌的「感受知覺動詞」（verbs of "inert perception"）常與表示「能力」的 'can' 連用來表示「知覺的狀態」（state of perception），即講話的時候正有這種知覺或感受，例如：

㊶ I *can see* John over there.❻

---

❻ 如果這類動詞不用 'can' 而直接以現在單純貌出現，就表示「瞬間的知覺」（momentary perception），例如 'I see(＝catch sight of) a bird!'。

㊷ I *can hear* a dog barking somewhere.

㊸ When I got off the train, I *could smell* the sea.

‘can’的另一種義務用法表示「許可」(permission)，相當於國語的 "可以…" (be allowed to V)，例如：

㊹ You *can* smoke in this room.(＝You are allowed to smoke in this room.) "你可以在這個房間抽煙"

㊺ Residents *can* use the car-park without a ticket. "房客可以免費停車"

在口語裏，表示許可的 ‘can’ 比表示許可的 ‘may’ 更為常用；而在正式的口語與書面語裏則常用 ‘may’ 來表示許可。另外 ‘may’ 表示「說話者的許可」(‘I give (you) permission to V…’)，而 ‘can’ 則不明示許可的來源 (‘(you) have permission to V…’)，所以在下面㊻的對話裏以用 ‘can’ 為妥當。試比較：

㊻ A: "{*Can/May*} I smoke in here?"

B: "So far as I know you {*can*/??*may*}—there's no notice to the contrary.

‘can’的「許可」意義還可以在語用上因為加強而表示 "帶有冒犯或無禮意味的" (offensive) 的「建議」(strong recommen-

dation）。 例如， 下面⑰的例句都表示帶有諷刺意味的建議，
聽話的人當然不會當眞而接受❼。

⑰ a. You *can* forget about your holiday.

　　　　"你不用想去度假了"

　　b. If he doesn't like it, he *can* lump it. ❽

　　　　"卽使他不喜歡也只得忍受"

　　c. You *can* jump in the lake.

　　　　"你去跳湖〔海〕好了"

　（b）'can'的「認知」用法：情態助動詞 'can' 的認知用法
表示「（理論上的）可能性」（(theoretical) possibility），相當
於國語的 "理論上可以，有…的可能"（it is possible for…to
V; sometimes V），例如：

⑱ Even expert drivers *can* make mistakes.

　　（=It is possible for even expert drivers to make

　　　　mistakes.

---

❼ 這種由情態助動詞的「義務」或「認知」用法引申出來的用法，可以
　稱爲「語用用法」（pragmatic use; pragmatic meaning）。又
　⑰例句裏的 'can' 都可以用 'may' 代替，所以表示「許可」的 '
　may' 也有類似的「語用用法」。

❽ 動詞 'lump' 在這裏做 "（勉強）忍受"（endure）解，常與動詞
　'like' 並用，如 'like it or lump it'。

=Even expert drivers sometimes make mistakes.)

"連最熟練的駕駛員也可能〔有時候〕會犯錯"

㊾ Lightning *can* be dangerous. (=Lightning is sometimes dangerous.)

㊿ He *can't* be working at this hour! (=It is impossible for him to be working at this hour!)

'may' 表示「事實上的可能性」，談的是在「現實世界」(the real world) 裏事情發生的可能性；而 'can' 則表示「理論上的可能性」，談的是在「假想世界」(the possible world) 裏事情發生的可能性。因此，在下面(51)的例句裏，(a) 句可能是我國工商界人士擔心美金更進一步貶值而發出的感嘆，而 (b) 句可能是美國財政官員在討論如何減少我國對美的出超時所表示的意見。試比較：

(51) a. The U. S. dollar *may* be further devalued.

b. The U. S. dollar *can* be further devalued.

同樣的，在下面(52)的例句裏：(a) 句可能是犯案的人企圖逃走而討論那一條逃亡的路線可能被警察封鎖時所說出的話，而 (b) 句則可能是追緝逃犯的警察在討論某一條路線能否架設路障封鎖時所說出的話。試比較：

⑫ a. The road *may* be blocked.

　　b. The road *can* be blocked.

由於‘may’表示「事實上的可能性」，所以㉝a句的‘a friend
’是暗指有那麼一位朋友可能會出賣你，是基於事實的警告。而
‘can’表示「理論上的可能性」，所以㉝b句的‘a friend’是
泛指一般朋友都有出賣朋友的可能，是基於假設的結論。試比
較：

㉝ a. A friend *may* betray you.

　　b. A friend *can* betray you.

又‘can’所表示的可能性比‘may’所表示的可能性更為肯定
。例如在下面㉞a句裏，說話者並不知道有沒有足球選手成為高
材生的實例，仍能可以用‘may’來表示他的推測。而在㉞b句
裏，說話者則知道至少有一位足球選手成為高材生的實例，因而
用‘can’做較為肯定的判斷。

㉞ a. Football players *may* be honor students.

　　b. Football players *can* be honor students.

　　表示「可能性」的‘can’與表示「能力」的‘can’有時
候並不容易分辨清楚，因為有「能力」就表示有「可能」。一般
說來，「能力」的義務用法限於「有生主語」(animate subject

)。因此，以「無生名詞」(inanimate noun) 'lightning' 為主說的例句⑭裏的'can'只能解釋為「可能性」，不能解釋為「能力」。下面⑮ a 的主動句以有生名詞 'children' 為主語，可以解釋為「能力」；⑮ b 的被動句以無生名詞 'this game' 為主語，只能解釋為「可能性」。試比較：

⑮　a.　Children *can* play this game.

　　b.　This game *can* be played by children.

(c) 'can' 的「語用」用法：從 'can' 的「可能性」意義引申出下面表示「未來建議」(a suggestion for future action) 的語用意義來，相當於國語的"可以、不妨…好了"，例如：

⑯　We *can* see about that tomorrow.

　　"我們明天再談這件事好了"

如果主語名詞是第二身人稱代詞、第三身人稱代詞或名詞，那麼 'can' 就可以傳達「圓通而親密的命令語氣」(a familiar though tactful imperative) 或「磋商性的命令語氣」(a "democratic" imperative) ❾。例如，下面⑰的例句可能是在學校戲劇公演的排練中學生導演對於擔任演員的同學以同輩的立

---

❾　這一點與後面所討論的情態助動詞 'will, shall' 等之傳達專橫而強制性的命令語氣 (an undemocratic coercive imperative) 者不同。

場徵求他們合作的指示。**❿**

⑤ Mike and Willy, you *can* be standing over there; and Janet *can* enter from behind the curtain.

(三)must

(a) 'must' 的「義務」用法：

情態助動詞 'must' 的義務用法表示「義務」(obligation) 或「(來自說話者的) 強制」(compulsion imposed by the speaker)，相當於國語的 "必須…，非…不可"(be obliged (by me) to V…)，例如：

⑤ You *must* be back by midnight.(＝You are obliged (by me) to be back by midnight.)

"你必須於午夜以前回來"

⑤ Soldiers *must* obey orders without questions. (＝Soldiers are required (by law) to obey orders without questions.) "士兵必須絕對服從命令"

⑥ Tell him he *must* stop this dishonest behavior.

"告訴他非停止這個不誠實的行為不可"

在含有「義務用法」'must' 的句子裏，義務或強制往往來自說

---

❿ 在⑤的例句裏進行貌動詞 'be standing' 出現於 'can' 的後面，因而可以認定這裏的 'can' 是表示「可能性」的認知用法。

話者（例如上面⑱與⑳的例句），但也可能來自其他比較不明確的來源（例如上面⑲的例句）。請注意在下面的例句裏義務或強制的來源❶。

⑥ You *must* apologize at once! (=I demand it of you, or politeness demands it of you, to apologize at once!)

⑥ When you pay your fare, you *must* receive a ticket.(=The rules of the bus-company demand it of you and the driver.)

⑥ This door *must* be kept closed. (=The authorities demand it of staff and visitors.)

⑥ All cars must have number-plates. (=The law demands it of car-drivers.)

⑥ All men *must* die. (=Nature or God demands that this should happen.)

⑥ The verb *must* agree with its subject. (=Grammar demands it of speakers and writers of English.)

如果‘must’以第一人稱代名詞‘I’或‘we’為主語，那麼就可以解釋為說話者對自己的要求或強制 (self-compulsion)，

---

❶ 下面部分例句與英語注解採自 Tregidgo (1982)。

或為客觀的環境所逼迫，例如：

⑥⑦ Well, I *must* go, or I'll be late. (=The exigen-
cies of the moment demand it of me, or I demand it of myself.)

⑥⑧ I *must* have a drink. (=My body demands it of
me, and of the potential.)

⑥⑨ I *must*n't tell lies. (=My teacher, or my conscience, demands it of me.)

另一方面，在含有 'must' 的疑問句與條件句裏義務或強制則常
來自第二人稱的「聽話者」(hearer; addressee)，例如：

⑦⓪ *Must* I answer all these letters myself? (=Are
these your orders?)

⑦① If I *must* go tomorrow, may I take my sister
with me?

(b) 'must' 的「認知」用法：

情態助動詞 'must' 的「認知」用法表示「邏輯上的必然
性」(logical necessity) 或「當前的猜測」(present conjec-
ture)，相當於國語的 "一定是…；準是…無疑"（V…very pro-
bably or certainly; it is necessarily the case that…V…
），例如：

⑦ John isn't home yet. He *must* be working late at the office. (=It is necessarily the case that John is working late at the office.)

"John 還沒有回家；他一定是留在辦公室裏工作"

⑦ Why isn't Jane here? She *must* have missed the train. (=That is necessarily the case—no other explanation is possible.)

"為什麼Jane還沒有來？她一定是沒有趕上火車"

⑦ There *must* be some mistake. (=Given the evidence, there can be no other conclusion.)

"一定有什麼差錯"

⑦ I *must* be dreaming! (=This cannot really be happening!) "我一定是在做夢；我簡直不敢相信"

認知用法的 'must' 表示說話者對於當前的事實根據邏輯的推理推論而得來的結論 (a conclusion arrived at by inference or reasoning)。因此，在上面⑦到⑦的每一例句後面都可以加上 "Given the evidence, there can be no other conclusion" 來強調這種邏輯上的必然性。有時候，情態助動詞 'must' 的「認知」語氣較為減弱，僅表示「邏輯上的假設」(logical assumption) 或「猜測」而相當於國語的 "我想…；我猜…" (I assume that…; I take it that…; I guess…)，例如：

⑦ You *must* be Mr. Taylor. (=I assume that you

・103・

　　are Mr. Taylor.) "我想您是 Taylor 先生吧"

⑦　You *must* be tired. "你 (一定) 累了吧"

⑧　He *must* be well over forty. "他總有四十多歲吧"

(c) 'must' 的「語用」用法：

從 'must' 的「義務」與「強制」意義引申出下面表示「厭煩與諷刺意味」(petulant irony) 的語用用法來，相當於國語的 "真愛…；偏要…；非…不可 (嗎)"，例如：❷

⑲　You *múst* go poking your nose into everything?
 (=It's unwise or unwanted for you to go poking your nose into everything.) "你真愛管閒事"

⑳　*Múst* you make that dreadful noise? (=For heaven's sake stop it!) "你非發出這樣可怕的聲音不可嗎？請你不要吵得這麼厲害"

㉑　*Múst* you shout so loudly!

㉒　If you *múst* smoke, use an ashtray. "(我真討厭你抽煙，但是) 如果你一定 (堅持) 要抽煙，那麼 (至少也得給我) 用烟灰缸吧"

㉓　If you *múst* behave like a savage, at least make sure the neighbors aren't watching.

㉔　Of course, after I gave her my advice, she *múst*

---

❷ 這種用法的 "must" 必須重讀。

go and do the opposite.

"當然囉，我雖然勸了她，她却偏不照我的話去做"

‘must’ 的義務意義也可以引申而解爲"應該"(should…; ought to V…)，例如

㊂ We *must* think about this very seriously. (＝ We should think about this very seriously.)

"我們應該認真考慮這個問題"

(四)will

(a) ‘will’的「義務」用法

情態助動詞 ‘will’ 的義務用法表示「意願」（willingness）、「意圖」（intention）與「堅持」（insistence）等。表示「意願」的 ‘will’ 相當於國語的 "願意…"(be willing to V…)，通常都不重讀，因而可以與主語名詞連續而簡縮成 ‘’ll’，例如：

㊆ "Who *will* lend me ten dollars?" "I *will*." ＝("Who is willing to lend me ten dollars?" "I'm willing." "誰願意借我十塊錢？" "我願意"

㊇ He'*ll* do anything for money.

"只要是爲了錢，他什麼事情都願意做"

㊈ *Will* you open the door for me?

"你願意替我開門嗎？"

以第二人稱代名詞 'you' 爲主語的疑問句⑧，在語用上表示「請求」（request），比直接表示「命令」（order）的 "Open the door for me" 客氣。爲了更進一步表示「客氣」（politeness），可以用 "Will you please V…"、"Will you kindly V…" 或 "Will you be {so kind as/so good as/kind enough/good enough} to V…" 的說法，還可以把情態助動詞 "will" 改爲 "would" 而表示更客氣的說法。試比較：

⑨ a.　*Will* you *please* open the door for me?

    b.　*Would* you *kindly* open the door for me?

    c.　*Would* you be *so kind as* to open the door for me?

與第一人稱代名詞 'I' 或 'we' 連用的情態助動詞 'will'，常表示「意圖」，相當於國語的 "打算…；有意…；準備…"（intend to V…; plan to V…; be going to V…），通常都不重讀，可以簡縮成 ''ll'，例如：

⑨ I *will* write tomorrow. (＝I'm going to write tomorrow.) "我打算明天寫"

⑨ We'*ll* celebrate this very night. (＝Let's celebrate this very night.) "我們今天晚上就來慶祝"

⑨ We'*ll* stop your pocket money if you don't behave. "如果你再不檢點，我們就不給你零用錢"

表示「堅持」的‘will’並不常用，而且通常都重讀，因而不能簡縮成‘'ll’。與第二人稱或第三人稱主語連用時，表示說話者對於這些人的執着頑固感到不快；與第一人稱主語連用時，表示說話者堅定不妥協的語氣。試比較：

⑭ He *will* go swimming in dangerous waters. (= He insists on going swimming in dangerous waters.) "他偏要在危險的地方游泳"

⑮ Jim, why *will* you keep making jokes about your brother? "Jim 你為什麼老愛開弟弟的玩笑？"

⑯ I *will* marry her, and no one shall stop me! (=I'm determined to marry her, and no one shall stop me!)

"我一定要跟她結婚，誰也阻擋不了我"

(b)‘will’的「認知」用法

情態助動詞‘will’的認知用法表示「對未來的預料」(future prediction)，相當於國語的 "會…" (be going to…)，通常都不重讀，因而可以簡縮成‘'ll’，例如

⑰ One day {I/you/he/she} *will* die.

"有一天{我/你/他/她}會死"

⑱ Tomorrow's weather *will* be cold and cloudy.

"明天的天氣會寒冷而多雲"

⑼ You'll feel better after taking this medicine.
"吃了藥以後你就會覺得舒服得多"

⑽ Perhaps I'll change my mind after I've spoken to my wife. "等跟太太商量之後我可能會改變主意的"

這種表示「預斷」的 'will' ，經常出現於條件子句的結果子句（如⑽句）或「預言性的宣告」(prophetic statement) (如⑽句)。

⑾ If you push this button, the door will slide open.
"如果你按這個鈕，門就會滑開"

⑿ In twenty years' time, the average employee will work a twenty-five hour week. "再過二十年，一般雇工（或雇員）都會每週工作二十五小時"

有時候，這種表示「預斷未來」的 'will' 在意義及用法上與表示「邏輯上必然性」或「當前猜測」的 'must' 很接近。例如，下面⑩到⑩裏的 'will' 都可以與 'must' 互相代用。⓭ 試比較：

⑩ That will be the milkman.(=That must be the

⓭ 這裏的'will'與'must'也可以與表示「邏輯上必然性」的 'should' 或 'ought to'（相當於國語的 "(照理) 應該"）互相代用。

milkman.) "那一定是送牛奶的"

⑩⑭ By now he *will* be eating dinner. (=By now he should be eating dinner)

"這個時候他一定在吃晚飯了"

⑩⑤ They *will* have arrived by now. (=They ought to have arrived by now.)

"這個時候他們應該已經到達了"

在下面⑩⑥到⑩⑨的例句裏，認知用法的‘will’則更進一步表示人、動物或事物的「典型或獨特的行為」(typical or characteristic behavior)，例如：

⑩⑥ He'*ll* go all day without eating. (=It is typical or characteristic of him that he goes all day without eating.) "他常整天不吃東西"

⑩⑦ A lion *will* attack a man only when hungry. (=It is predictable or characteristic of lions that they attack men only when hungry.)

"獅子只有餓的時候才會攻擊人"

⑩⑧ Accidents *will* happen. (=It is a predictable or characteristic fact about accidents that they happen.) "意外事件總會發生"

⑩⑨ Truth *will* out. (=It is typical of truth that

it makes itself known.) "真相總會大白"⓮

這一種表示「一般性的預斷」(habitual predictability) 或「必然性」(certainty) 的 'will' 在一般科學的文章裏可以用表示「一切時」(generic tense) 或「過現未」("for all time") 的「現在單純貌」(simple present) 來取代，例如：

⑪ Oil *will* float on water.⓯ (=Oil floats on water.)

⓮ 有時候，在同一個句子裏，'will' 可以做認知或義務用法解。例如，在下面 (i) 的例句裏，'will' 可以輕讀而做 (ii) 的「預斷」解，也可以重讀而做 (iii) 的「堅持」解。試比較：

(i) Boys *will* be boys.

(ii) It is predictable or characteristic of boys that they behave like boys. "男孩子總是男孩子"

(iii) Boys insist on behaving like boys. "男孩子難免會這樣"

⓯ 但這並不表示凡是真理、事實或常習的動作都可以用表示「預斷」的 'will' 來敍述。例如，下面 (i) 與 (ii) 的例句就不能用 'will'。

(i) Deciduous trees lose their leaves in fall.
"落葉樹於秋天落葉"

(ii) The CAL plane departs for Los Angeles at 10:30 daily. "華航班機每天上午十點半飛往洛山磯"

這是由於在⑪的例句裏，情態助動詞 'will' 含蘊條件句（如 '*if oil is mixed with water*, oil will float on water'）的存在，而 (i) 與 (ii) 的例句則不可能有類似的含蘊。同樣的，在 (iii) 的例句裏賽程的安排是「鐵定的事實」(utterly certain or predetermined fact)，所以可以不用表示「預斷」的 'will'，而在 (iv) 的例句裏比賽的結果無法未卜先知，所以必須用表示「預斷」的 'will'。試比較：

(iii) The Giants {play/*will* play} the Tigers tomorrow.
"巨人隊明天與老虎隊比賽"

(iv) The Giants {*defeat/*will* defeat} the Tigers tomorrow. "巨人隊明天會擊敗老虎隊"

"油會浮在水上"

另外，在下面⑪到⑬以「無生名詞」(inanimate noun) 為主語的例句裏，'will' 表示「傾向」(disposition)，常可以改寫成以「屬人名詞」(human noun) 為主語而與表示「可能性」的 'can' 連用的句子。試比較：

⑪ This auditorium *will* seat 1,000. (=One can seat 1,000 people in this auditorium.)
"這個禮堂可以容納一千人"
⑫ This watch *won't* work. (=I can't make this watch work.) "這個錶走不動了"
⑬ *Will* the window open? (=Can one open the window?) "這個窗戶打得開嗎？"

(五)shall

(a) 'shall' 的「義務」用法

情態助動詞 'shall' 的義務用法，與情態助動詞 'will' 的義務用法相似，也表示「意願」、「意圖」、「堅持」等三種意思。但是 'will' 表示的多半是主語名詞的意願、意圖、堅持，而 'shall' 則多半表示說話者的意願、意圖、堅持。表示說話者意願的 'shall'，多半以第二人稱或第三人稱為主語，因為含有「由說話者施惠」(the speaker is conferring a favor; "I'm willing for …to V…") 的意思，所以在現代英語裏除了對小

孩或寵物講話以外很少使用表示「意願」的 'shall'，例如：

⑭ You *shall* stay with us as long as you like. (= I'm willing for you to stay with us as long as you like.) "你想住多久就可以住多久"

⑮ Good dog, you *shall* have a bone when we get home. (=Good dog, I'll give you a bone when we get home.) "乖狗狗，回家以後賞根骨頭給你吃"

⑯ He *shall* be rewarded if he is patient.
"如果他有耐心的話，他就可以得賞〔＝我就給賞〕"

表示「意圖」的 'shall' 多以第一人稱為主語，因而其意義及用法幾乎與表示「意圖」的 'will' 相同。一般說來，'{I/we} shall' 多出現於英式英語，特別是書面語裏，例如：

⑰ I {*shall/will*} write tomorrow.

⑱ We {*shall/will*} celebrate this very night!

⑲ We {*shall/will*} stop your money if you don't behave.

表示「堅持」的 'shall' 通常都要重讀，而且以第二人稱或第三人稱為主語，表示說話者對這些人的堅持，相當於國語的 "我一定要⋯；⋯非⋯不可"（I insist that⋯），例如：

⑳ You *sháll* obey my orders! (=I insist that you obey my orders.) "我一定要你照我的話去做"

㉑ He *sháll* be mine! "他一定是我的;我非要他不可"

㉒ No one *sháll* stop me. "誰也阻擋不了我"

由於表示「堅持」的 'shall' 含有「驕橫」(imperious) 或「不民主」(undemocratic) 的語氣,這種 'shall' 在實際的語言情況裏很少使用❻,而由「義務」用法的 'must' 或「帶有民主意味的命令用法」(the democratic imperative) 的 'can' 來代替,例如:

㉓ You *must* obey my orders!

㉔ No one *can* stop me.

(b) 'shall' 的「認知」用法

---

❻ 這種 'shall' 在聖經的「十誡」(the Ten Commandments) 或「神仙故事」(fairy tale) 中巫婆嘴裏卻常出現,例如:

(i) Thou *shalt* not {kill/steal/lie}.

(ii) You *shall* turn into a frog.

另外在「法律(或類似法律)文件」(legal and quasi-legal documents) 中也可能出現這種 'shalll' 的用法,例如:

(iii) A player who bids incorrectly *shall* forfeit fifty points.

(iv) The hood *shall* be of scarlet cloth, with a silk linining of the color of the faculty.

　　'shall' 可以說是英語裏唯一沒有「認知」用法的情態助動詞，因爲「對於未來的預斷」都用 'will' 來表示，而不用 'shall' 來表示。另一方面，'shall' 的過去式 'should' 則兼有義務與認知兩種用法。

　　*本文曾刊載於《英語教學》（1988）12卷 3 期24-30頁；4 期12-20頁；13卷 1 期71-75頁；2 期 19-26 頁；14 卷 1 期 22-33 頁。由於全文仍未完成，擬將後續的文章以〈續談英語情態助動詞的意義與用法〉的標題連同參考文獻刊登於《英語認知語法：結構、意義與功用（下集》中。

英語副詞與狀語在「X標槓結構」中出現的位置：句法與語意功能

(Syntax and Semantics of English Adverbs and Adverbials: An X-Bar Structure Analysis)

一、前　言

　　在我國傳統的英語教學中，副詞與狀語可能是在所有詞類中僅次於感嘆詞而最不受重視的一項詞類。巷間的英語語法教科書或參考書，除了對英語的副詞籠統的下定義(如"副詞修飾動詞、形容詞或其他副詞")，並把副詞根據語意內涵籠統的加以分類(如「情狀副詞/狀語」、「情態副詞/狀語」、「處所副詞/狀語」、「時間副詞/狀語」、「工具狀語」、「手段狀語」、「受惠者狀語」等)，或者把副詞在句子中出現的位置籠統的加以交代(如「句首」、「句

中」、「句尾」三種位置）以外，很少做啓發性的說明或討論。其實，英語裏修飾動詞的「情狀副詞」（manner adverb）❶與修飾形容詞或副詞的「程度副詞」（degree adverb）❷，無論在形態上（情狀副詞常由形容詞加上副詞詞尾'-ly'而成；而程度副詞則常無相對的形容詞）、句法表現上（情狀副詞常出現於所修飾的動詞或其賓語後面；而程度副詞則常出現於所修飾的形容詞或副詞前面）、或語意功能上（情狀副詞用來描述或限制動詞所表達的動作或行動；而程度副詞則用來加強或緩和形容詞或副詞所表達的屬性或情狀），都有相當明確的區別。而且，副詞除了修飾動詞、形容詞、副詞以外，還可以修飾名詞組（如'*only* my son, *even* our teacher, *especially* John and Mary'）、介詞組（如'*right* in the middle, *all* over the place, *soon* after his arrival, *long* before their marriage, *ever* since their childhood'）、子句（如'*soon* after he arrived, *long* before they got married, *ever* since they were children, (pronounce the word) *exactly* as I do'）與句子（如'*Honestly*, John doesn't like her; *Frankly*, Mr. Lee is quite intelligent; *Fortunately*, she returned home safely; *Wisely*, he sold his old house and bought a new one'）。英語裏副詞與狀語出現的三種位置（句首、句中、句尾）也可以進一步細分爲七種：卽（一）「

---

❶　也就是McConnel-Ginet（1982）所謂的"ad-verb"（「飾動副詞」）。

❷　也就是所謂的"intensifier"（「加強副詞」）。

句首」(initial)，卽主語的前面❸(如'*By then* the book must have been placed on the shelf'❹)；(二)「句中首」(initial-medial)，卽主語的後面，情態助動詞的前面(如'The book *by then* must have been placed on the shelf')；(三)「句中」(medial)，卽情態助動詞的後面，動貌助動詞❺的前面(如'The book must *by then* have been placed on the shelf')；(四)「句中中」(medial-medial)，卽動貌助動詞與動貌助動詞的中間(如'The book must have *by then* been placed on the shelf')；(五)「句中尾」(end-medial)，卽動貌助動詞的後面，主要動詞的前面(如'The book must have been *by then* placed on the shelf')；(六)「句尾首」(initial-end)，卽

---

❸ 如果主語前面出現助動詞(如'*Seriously, do* you believe in ghosts?')、wh疑問詞(如'*Honestly, when did* you find this out?')或其他句法成分(如'*Anyhow, since when has* she been ill?')，那麼修飾整句的副詞與狀語就常出現於這些句法成分的前面。又在從屬子句與對等子句中，修飾整個子句的副詞與狀語常出現於從屬連詞(如'(I had scarcely got into the taxi) *when suddenly* the driver started the engine')與對等連詞(如'(Are you afraid of the dark,) *and, to be blunt,* do you believe in ghosts?', '(I know you are very charitable,) *but, seriously,* how can he be innocent?')的後面。例句參照 Quirk et al.(1985:491)，有關副詞與狀語出現的位置英文名稱也採自 Quirk et al.(1985:490-500)。

❹ 這些例句採自 Quirk et al.(1985:490)。

❺ 包括「完成貌助動詞」'have-en'、「進行貌助動詞」'be-ing' 與「被動態助動詞」'be-en'。

主要語動詞（或其賓語或補語）的後面❻，其他副詞或狀語的前面（如 'The book must have been placed *by then* on the shelf'）；（七）「句尾」（end），即句子的末尾（如 'The book must have been placed on the shelf *by then*'）。但是並非所有的副詞與狀語都可以出現於這些位置，因為副詞與狀語的「語意類型」（semantic typology）、「句法類型」（syntactic typology）以及句子的「信息結構」（information structure）等都對這些副詞與狀語在句子中出現的位置以及彼此間前後出現的次序具有相當密切的關係。本文從「X標槓理論」（X-bar theory）的觀點討論英語副詞與狀語在各種詞組結構中出現的位置與次序，藉以探討這些副詞與狀語的句法與語意功能。本文雖然比較偏重語法理論的檢討與語法結構的分析，但是本文所獲得的結論仍然可以做為英語語法教學的借鏡或參考，因而有其實踐上的價值。

二、「X標槓理論」與英語的詞組結構

「音素」（phoneme）或「單音」（phone）互相組合成為「語素」（morpheme）或「語」（morph）；語素或語互相組合成為「詞」（word）；而詞與詞則互相組合成為「詞組」（phrase）。「原則參數語法」（the principles-and-parameters approach）的

---

❻ 例如 'John was digging *a hole in the garden*', 'He gives *his car a wash every week*', 'They became *teachers in the end*', 'She put *the letter carefully on the table*'。

「X標槓理論」爲自然語言的組織結構提出下面①的「X標槓公約」(X-bar Convention)。

①　a.　X″ → Spec, X′

　　b.　X′ → Adjt, X′

　　c.　X′ → Comp, X

根據①的「規律母式」(rule schemata)，自然語言任何詞類的「詞組」(即「最大投影」(maximal projection; X″=XP)都由「詞節」(即「中介投影」(intermediate projeciton; X′)與其「指示語」(specifier; Spec)組成(參照①a)；而「詞節」則或由「詞節」與其「附加語」(adjunct; Adjt)組成(參照①b)，或由「詞語」(亦即「最小投影」(minimal projection)或「主要語」(head; X=X°))與其「補述語」(complement; Comp)組成(參照①c)。①的規律母式只規定詞組、詞節、詞語以及指示語、附加語、補述語之間「上下支配」(dominance)的「階層組織」(hierarchical structure)，而不涉及這些結構成分之間「前後出現」(precedence)的「線性次序」(linear order)。例如，詞組必須支配詞節與指示語①a，詞節可以支配詞節與附加語①b，但必須有一個詞節(如果同一個詞組結構裏有好幾個詞節，那麼必須是結構樹中最底下的一個詞節)支配詞語與補述語①c；而且，同一個詞組結構裏的詞組、詞節與詞語必須形成「同心結構」(endocentric construction)。另一方面，詞節與指示語之間，以及詞語與補述語之間的前後次序則與X標槓理論無關，而委由其他原則系統(如「論旨理論」(theta theory; θ-theory)與「格位理論」(Case theory)等)來加以詮釋。又

由於在①b 的規律母式裏，詞節出現於「改寫箭號」（rewrite arrow; 即'→'）的左右兩邊，所以在同一個詞組結構裏可以含有一個以上的詞節，因而可以反複衍生無數個附加語。因此，①的規律母式可以衍生下面②的詞組結構❼：

② a.　詞組(XP)　　　　　b.　詞組(XP)

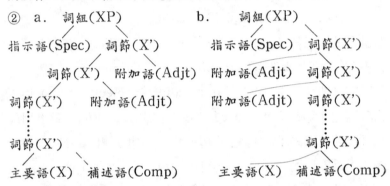

　　英語的詞組結構包括以「補語連詞」（complementizer; C）為主要語的「大句子」（S'; CP）、以「時制語素」（tense; T）為主要語的「小句子」（S; TP）❽、以「述詞」（predicate; Pr）為主要語的「述詞組」（predicate phrase; PrP）❾、以動詞為主

---

❼　根據「X標槓公約」，指示語不一定出現於主要語的左方，補述語不一定出現於主要語的右方，附加語也不一定一律出現於主要語的左方或右方。

❽　也有以「屈折語素」（inflection; I）或「動貌語素」（aspect; Asp）為小句子的主要語的。這裏參考 Bowers（1988）與 Pollock（1989）等人的分析，以「時制語素」為小句子的主要語。

❾　英語的「述詞」除了顯現為 'as'（如 'John regarded Bill *as* the biggest fool on earth'）以外，通常不具有語音形態；但在語意上連繫主語名詞與謂語詞組（相當於「述詞節」（Pr'）），並在二者之間建立「主謂關係」（predication）。參 Bowers（1988）。又有些語法學家（如 Pollock（1989））主張用以「呼應語素」（agreement; Agr）為主要語的「呼應詞組」（agreement phrase; AgrP）來代替「述詞組」。

要語的「動詞組」(VP)、以形容詞爲主要語的「形容詞組」(AP)
、以副詞爲主要語的「副詞組」(AdP)、以介詞或連詞爲主要語
的「介詞組」(PP)、以「量詞」(quantifier; Q) 爲主要語的「量
詞組」(quantifier phrase; QP)、以「限定詞」(determiner;
D) 爲主要語的「限定詞組」(determiner phrase; DP)、以
「名詞」爲主要語的「名詞組」(NP) 等。英語各種詞組結構的
內容舉例說明如下。

③ 大句子 (CP): 'Who will you see *tomorrow*?'

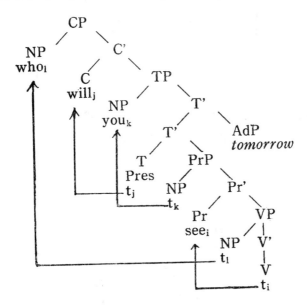

④ 大句子 (CP): '*Why* was he angry *yesterday*?'

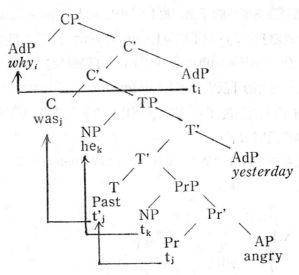

⑤ 形容詞組 (AP): '*so* angry with you'

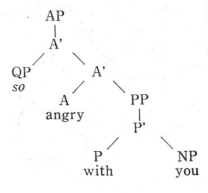

⑥副詞組 (AdP): '*ten times* faster *than a rabbit*'

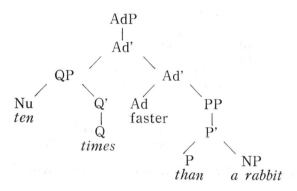

⑦ 介詞組 (PP): '*ever* since you left us'

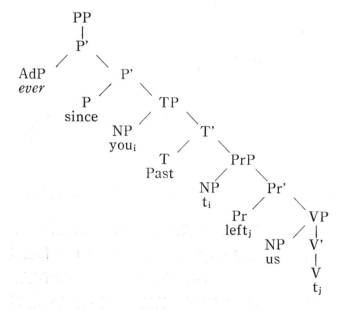

⑧ 量詞組 (QP): 'three copies of transcripts'

```
              QP
            /    \
         Nu        Q'
        three     /  \
                 Q      PP
              copies     |
                         P'
                        /  \
                       P     NP
                       of  transcripts
```

⑨ 限定詞組 (DP): '*even* John's three friends'

```
              DP
            /    \
         AdP       D'
        even      /  \
               NP      D'
              John    /  \
                    D      QP
                    's    /   \
                       Nu       Q'
                      three    /  \
                              Q     NP
                              e   friends
```

三、出現於動詞組補述語位置的副詞與狀語

　　英語的副詞與狀語一般都出現於Ｘ標槓結構裏附加語的位置來充當「可用論元」（optional argument）或「語意論元」（semantic argument）。但是有一些英語動詞的「次類畫分」（subcategorization）卻與表示情狀、處所、終點、受惠者副詞

或狀語有關。例如英語動詞 'behave, treat, word, phrase' ❿
等必須與情狀副詞或狀語連用,因此這些情狀副詞出現於動詞組
裏補述語的位置,例如:

⑩ a. He behaved {*badly* to his wife/*with great courage*}.

　 b. My car has been behaving *well* since it was repaired.

⑪ a. John treated Mary *politely*.

　 b. She always treated us {*well/like children/with the utmost courtesy*}.

⑫ a. He worded the explanation *well*.

　 b. *How* would one word such an announcement?

⑬ a. She phrased her refusal *politely*.

　 b. The moment I'd said it, I could see I'd phrased it *wrong*.

又如英語的存放動詞 'stay, live, lie; put, place, lay, keep'
等必須與表示處所的副詞、介副詞或介詞組連用,因此這些處

---

❿ 動詞'dress'也常與副詞或狀語連用,如'Mary dressed {*elegantly/in blue/in the cheapest clothes*}', 'She dresses *well* on very little money';但 'dress' 做'盛裝'解時可以不帶上副詞,如 'He said he would go to the party if he didn't have to *dress* (up)'。另外,動詞'pay'在 'The job on Tuesday paid us *handsomely*' 的「非人稱結構」(impersonal construction) 用法裏也必須與副詞連用。

所副詞、介副詞或介詞組也都出現於動詞組裏補述語的位置，例如：

⑭　John　stayed　{ *here/there/inside/outside/upstairs/ downstairs*}.

⑮　Mary put her coat {*up here/over there/down/away/ in the closet*}.

他如英語的雙賓動詞 'give, send, lend, rent, owe, pay, sell, tell, teach, bring, show, pass, leave, throw, hand' 等常與由介詞 'to' 所引導的「終點」（Goal）介詞組連用，例如：

⑯　John gave a Christmas present *to Mary*.

　　出現於動詞組裏補述語位置的副詞與狀語❶是動詞的「必要論元」（obligatory argument）或「域內論元」（internal argument），與主要語動詞形成「姊妹成分」（sister constituents），並由主要語動詞來指派「論旨角色」（thematic role; θ-role）給這些論元。我們參照 Larson (1988) 與 Bowers (1989b) 等人的分析，爲這些動詞組擬設下面的詞組結構分析❷。

---

❶　Takami（1987）把這類副詞與狀語稱爲「補述狀語」（adverbial complement）。

❷　根據⑰的詞組結構分析，賓語名詞組本來出現於動詞節左方指示語的位置，然後由於動詞提升而移入述詞組裏主要語的位置，所以賓語名詞組就出現於動詞的右方，並由動詞獲得格位。參湯(1990f)。

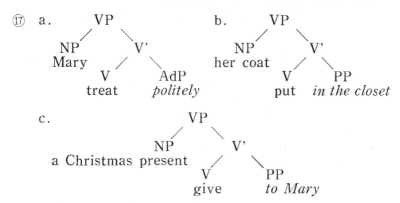

⑰ a. VP / NP V' Mary / V AdP treat *politely*

b. VP / NP V' her coat / V PP put *in the closet*

c. VP / NP V' a Christmas present / V PP give *to Mary*

出現於動詞組裏補述語位置的副詞或狀語，與非補述語的副詞或狀語，在句法表現上有下列幾點不同。

(一)補述語必須包含在「動詞組與述詞節的替代式」(pro-VP and -Pr' form❸) 'do so' 裏面（如⑱a、⑲a、⑳a句），而非補述語則可以包含在 'do so' 裏面，也可以出現於 'do so' 外面（如⑱b、⑲b、⑳b句）。試比較：

⑱ a. John treated Mary *politely*,

{ and Bob *did so*, too.
{ *but Bob *did so impolitely*,

b. John visited Mary *frequently*,

{ and Bob *did so*, too.
{ but Bob *did so only occasionally*.

---

❸ Speas (1988) 認爲所有語法規律(包括移位、「稱代」(pronominalization)、「對等連接」(conjoining)) 都不能提到「中介投影」(如這裏的 (Pr'))。因此，她主張把有關 'do so' 的句法限制改爲：必須指派論旨角色的域內論元(即補述語)不能出現於 'do so' 的外面或移到動詞組的外面。

⑲　a．John put the books *in the basement*,

　　　{ and Bob *did so*, too.
　　　{ *but Bob *did so in the attic*.

　　b．John burned the books *in the basement*,

　　　{ and Bob *did so*, too.
　　　{ but Bob *did so in the attic*.

⑳　a．John gave a book *to Mary*,

　　　and Bob *did so* {, too.
　　　　　　　　　　 { *to Alice.

　　b．John bought a book *for Mary*,

　　　and Bob *did so* {, too.
　　　　　　　　　　 { for Alice. ❹

　　(二)補述語必須包含於「準分裂句」（pseudo-cleft sentence) 的「焦點」（focus) 部分；而非補述語則可能包含於準分裂句的焦點部分，也可能包含於準分裂句的「預設」（presupposition) 部分。試比較：

㉑　a．What John did was (to) treat Mary *politely*.

　　b．*What John did *politely* was (to) treat Mary.

---

❹　⑳a與⑳b的對比顯示：雙賓動詞 'give' 等的終點介詞組屬於動詞組補述語，而 'buy, order, make, cook, save, spare' 等的「受惠者」（Benefactive)介詞組則屬於動詞組附加語。另外，下面的例句顯示：雙賓動詞 'give' 等的直接與間接賓語都可以充當被動句的主語，而 'buy' 等動詞則只有直接賓語可以充當被動句的主語。試比較：

(i) a．*The book* was given to Mary (by John).

　　b．*Mary* was given a book (by John).

(ii) a．*The book* was bought for Mary (by John).

　　b．*Mary* was bought a book (by John).

㉒ a. What John did was visit Mary *frequently*.

b. What John did *frequently* was (to) visit Mary.

㉓ a. What John did was (to) put the books *in the basement*.

b. *What John did *in the basement* was (to) put the books.

㉔ a. What John did was (to) burn the books *in the basement*.

b. What John did *in the basement* was (to) burn the books.

㉕ a. What John did was (to) give a book *to Mary*.

b. *What John did *to Mary* was (to) give a book.

㉖ a. What John did was (to) buy a book *for Mary*.

b. What John did *for Mary* was (to) buy a book.

❺

---

❺ 下面例句的合法度判斷顯示：第一個處所介詞組（'on the cheek'）雖然與主要語動詞（'kiss'）的次類畫分無關，卻不能出現於準分裂句的預設部分；而只能出現於焦點部分（參湯（1989c:367））。試比較：

（i）John kissed Mary *on the cheek on the platform*.

（ii）What John did *on the platform* was (to) kiss Mary *on the cheek*.

（iii）*What John did *on the cheek* was (to) kiss Mary *on the platform*.

但是(iii)句的不合語法似乎是：(i)由於 'on the cheek' 的有定冠詞'the' 是以 'Mary' 為前行語的「照應用法」（anaphoric use），

(三)Williams (1977) 與 Culicover & Wilkins (1984:27)
指出：在「多重 wh 回響問句」(multiple-wh echo question)
的「簡易回應」(short response) 中，'do' 必須取代動詞與補
述語。試比較：

㉗ a. John treated Mary *politely*.

b. Who treated Mary *how*?

c. *John did *politely*.

㉘ a. John visited Mary *frequently*.

b. Who visited Mary *how often*?

c. John did *frequently*.

㉙ a. John put the books *in the basement*.

b. Who put the books *where*?

c. *John did *on the desk*.

㉚ a. John burned the books *in the basement*.

b. Who burned the books *where*?

c. John did *in the basement*.

應在同一「管轄範疇」(governing category) 受到前行語'Mary'
的「約束」(be bound)；或者是(ii)由於 'on the cheek' 出現於前
行語 'Mary' 的左邊。因此，在例句(i)裏出現的 'on the cheek'
仍不應分析為補述語，因而可以包含於 'do so'裏面，也可以出現於
'do so' 外面。

(v) John kissed Mary *on the cheek on the platform*, and
Bill did so *at the gate*.

(vi) John kissed Mary *on the cheek*, and Bill did so *on the
mouth*.

㉛ a. John gave a book *to Mary.*

　　b. Who gave a book *to whom*?

　　c. *John did *to Mary.*

㉜ a. John bought a book *for Mary.*

　　b. Who bought a book *for whom*?

　　c. John did *for Mary.*

(四)Culicover & Wilkins (1984:27-28) 指出：修飾主語名詞組的「加強反身詞」(intensive reflexive) 可以出現於補述語與附加語之間，卻不能出現於主要語動詞與補述語之間❿。試比較：

㉝ a. *John treated Mary *himself politely.*

　　b. John visited Mary *himself frequently.*

㉞ a. *John put the books *himself in the basement.*

　　b. John burned the books *himself in the basement.*

㉟ a. ??John gave a book *himself to Mary.*

　　b. (?)John bought a book *himself for Mary.*⓱

---

❿　這是因為「加強反身詞」與「照應反身詞」(anaphoric reflexive) 不同，是出現於「非論元位置」(A-bar position) 的狀語用法；只有充當論元的照應反身詞可能出現於補述語的位置，充當非論元的加強反身詞只能出現於附加語的位置。

⓱　有些英美人士表示㉟a 的例句勉強可以接受，而㉟b 的例句也有些不自然。這一種合法度判斷似乎是在 ㉟ a,b 的例句與完全合語法的 'John gave a book to Mary *himself*'、John bought a book for Mary *himself*' 的比較對照之下所做的。不過這些英美人士都表示㉟b 的例句似乎比㉟ a 的例句通順自然。

　　(五)補述語副詞與介詞組必須出現於動詞組裏主要語動詞的右方，而非補述語的副詞或介詞組則常可以出現於主要語動詞的左方，甚至可以移到句首充當「論旨主題」(theme topic) 或「焦點主題」(focus topic)。試比較：

⑯　a.　*John *politely* treated Mary; *Politely* John treated Mary.

　　b.　John *frequently* visited Mary; *Frequently* John visited Mary.

⑰　a.　*In the basement* John put old papers.**⑱**

　　b.　*In the attic* John burned old papers.

---

⑱　補述語副詞與介詞組常可以移到句首充當「主題」(topic)，例如：

(1) *On the table*, John put his books.

　但是 Hornstein & Weingberg（1981:82）指出：「主題移位」(Topicalization) 與一般副詞或介詞組的提前移到句首應該加以區別；因為英語的主題句是比較特殊或「有標」(marked) 的句法結構，在語意與句法上比一般介詞組的提前受到更多的限制。試比較：

(ii) a. *On the table* John put his {books/?cards/?*hands}.

　　b. *On the defensive* John put his opponent.

(iii) a. *I know [that she believes [that I said [that *on the desk* John put his books]]].

　　b. I know [that she believes [that I said [that *since last Thursday* John has been sick]]].

　　c. I know [that she believes [that I said [that *on the boat* the man decided (to form a partnership)]]].

例句與合法度判斷採自 Hornstein & Weingberg（1981:82）。

㊳　a.　*To Mary John gave a diamond ring.**❶**

　　　b.　For Mary John bought a diamond ring.

Williams（1975:259-260）區別可以提前而出現於直接賓語前面的受惠者介詞組（如 'John found a book *for Mary*; John found *Mary* a book'），與不能提前而出現於直接賓語後面的受惠者介詞組（如 'John watched Sally *for Mary*; *John watched *Mary* Sally'），並對這兩種受惠者介詞組的移首做了如下的合法度判斷**❷**：

㊴　a.　?*For Mary*, John found a book.

　　　b.　*For Mary*, John watched Sally.

如果 Williams（1975）的觀察與判斷正確，那麼與雙賓動詞（如 'find, buy, cook, make, save' 等）連用的受惠者介詞組，以及與一般動詞（如 'watch, sell, sacrifice, die' 等）連用的受惠

---

❶ 如果㊳a是表示「焦點對比」（focus contrast）的例句，而把終點介詞組加以重讀（如 '*To Mary*, John gave a diamond ring, and to Sally, he gave a pearl necklace'），那麼這個例句就可以接受。又 Culicover & Wilkins（1984:29）雖然不接受 '**On the table*, John put the book carefully' 的例句，卻接受 '*Carefully on the table*, John put the book' 的例句，並且認為 'carefully on the table' 應該形成詞組成分。後面一個例句是因情狀副詞 'carefully' 的移首而引起處所介詞組的「隨伴移位」（piedpiping），因而提高這一個例句的合法度。

❷ Williams（1975）還認為：在㊴a的例句裏，直接賓語 'a book' 是間接賓語 'for Mary' 的「語意主語」（"semantic" subject）或「內部主語」（"inner" subject）；而在㊴b的例句裏，間接賓語 'for Mary' 的語意上的主語卻是 'watch Sally'。

者介詞組，在X標槓結構中出現的位置似應加以區別。我們在這
裏暫且把與雙賓動詞連用的受惠者介詞組分析爲出現於動詞組裏
附加語的位置，而把與一般動詞連用的受惠者介詞組分析爲出現
於述詞組裏附加語的位置。㉑

㉑ 有關英語動詞組X標槓結構的詳細討論，參湯 (1990e)。又 Culicover
& Wilkins (1984:29-30) 還提到補述語與非補述語在「動詞空缺」
(V-Gapping) 中的句法表現差異，認爲在「並列合句」(coordinate
compound sentence) 中因前後兩個對等子句都含有相同的主要語
動詞而刪除第二個對等子句的主要語動詞時，動詞空缺後只能留下一
個補述語，並且提出下面三個例句與合法度判斷爲例。

(i) John sells trucks on Thursdays, and Mary, *cars* on
　　　Fridays.

(ii) John gave a dog to Mary, and Sam, *a cat* to Susan.

(iii) *John put Fido in the dog house, and Sam, *Spot in
　　　the yard.*

Culicover & Wilkins (1984:30)承認這些例句的合法度判斷相當
微妙 ("the judgments perhaps subtle")。而且，在他們的分析
裏，例句 (ii)的終點介詞組 'to Susan' 出現於動詞組裏附加語的位
置，因而「單方面的c統制」(asymmetrically c-command) 出現
於動詞組裏補述語位置的直接賓語'a cat'。但是Barss & Lasnik
(1986) 與 Larson (1988) 先後指出：在雙賓結構中無論是(i)「反
身照應詞」與前行語之間的約束關係（如'I showed {*Mary* to *her-
self*/*herself to *Mary*/*Mary her*self/*herself Mary}'）、(ii)
「量詞組」與其被約束語之間的關係（如'I gave {*every paycheck*$_i$ to
its$_i$ owner/*its$_i$ owner *every pay*check$_i$/*every worker*$_i$ *his*$_i$
paycheck/??*his*$_i$ paycheck to *every worker*$_i$}、(iii) wh 詞組
與稱代詞之間的「輕微越位效應」(weak crossover effect；如
'{*Which check*$_i$ did you send t_i to his owner?/ **Which
worker*$_i$ did you send *his*$_i$ check to t_i ?/*Which man*$_i$ did

以上的分析與討論顯示：充當主要語動詞補述語的副詞與介詞組，必須與非充當主要語動詞補述語的副詞與介詞組加以區別。充當主要語動詞補述語的副詞與介詞組，與動詞的次類畫分有關，出現於動詞組裏面，而且必須與主要語動詞形成姐妹成分而受其「管轄」(be governed)，並獲得論旨角色的指派。在句法表現上，這些副詞與介詞組必須包含於 'do so' 與準分裂句的焦點裏面；在「多重wh回響問句」(multiple-wh echo question) 的簡易回應中，必須包含於「替代動詞」的 'do' 裏面，不允許加強反身詞 'oneself' 出現於賓語名詞組的後面，不能移到主要語動詞的前面，也比較不容易移到句首充當「論旨主題」。

四、出現於動詞組裏附加語位置的副詞與介詞組

動詞組的附加語與補述語不同，與動詞的次類畫分無關；不

---

you send t_i *his*$_i$ *paycheck*?/*Whose*$_i$ paycheck did you send *his* mother t?}')、(iv)「優位效應」(superiority effect)，卽wh詞組不能越過「c統制」這個wh詞組的wh詞組而移位 (如'{*Which check*$_i$ did you send t_i to *whom*?/*Whom*$_i$ did you send *which check* to t_i?/*Who*$_i$ did you give t_i *which paycheck*/*Which paycheck*$_i$ did you give *who* t?}')、(v)「相互代詞」(reciprocal pronoun)'each' 與 'the other' 之間的前後次序 (如 'I showed {*each* boy to *the other's* parents/*the other's* check to *each* boy/*each* man *the other's* socks/*the other's* friend *each* man}')、或是(vi)「連用否定詞」(negative polarity item) 與其「"觸動"語」("affective" element) 之間的前後次序 (如 'I showed {*nothing* to *any*one/*anything* to *no* one/*no* one *any*thing/*any*one *nothing*}')都顯示正確的結構佈局是：直接賓語「單方面的c統制」終點介詞組，而不能由終點介詞組來「單方面的c統制」直接賓語。

是主要語動詞的必要成分或域內論元，而只能說是主要語動詞的可用成分或語意論元。有些副詞與介詞組雖然與動詞的次類畫分無關，其句法功能卻頗似論元。Baker（1985c）曾經指出：能「併入」（be incorporated into）動詞的介詞僅限於表示「終點」（或「接受者」（Recipient））、「受惠者」（或「受害者」（Malefactive））、「工具」（Instrument）與「處所」等的介詞。他還指出：由這些介詞引導的「受事」（applicative）介詞組不一定都是動詞組的必要成分，但是這並不表示這些介詞組並未獲得論旨角色的指派。Speas（1988:33-34）因而主張把「具有論旨角色的附加語」（θ-marked adjunct）與「不具有論旨角色的附加語」（$\overline{\theta}$-marked adjunct）加以區別。我們暫且用下面⑩的 X 標槓結構佈局裏論旨角色的指派方式來加以區別：（a）出現於動詞組裏補述語位置的副詞與介詞組（如'to Mary'），由主要語動詞(X)來指派論旨角色；（b）出現於動詞組裏附加語位置的副詞與介詞組（如'for Mary'），由動詞節（V'）來指派論旨角色；與(c)出現於述詞組裏附加語位置的副詞與介詞組（如'for fun'），由介詞（P，即'for'）來指派論旨角色。試比較：

⑩　a.

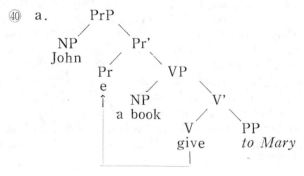

b.

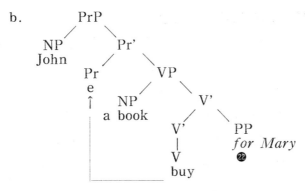

c.

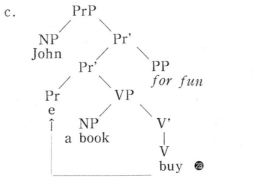

㉒　為了符合①的X標槓公約，並為了區別出現於補述語位置的介詞組(如
㊵a 的 'to Mary')是主要語動詞(V)的姐妹成分，並受主要語動詞
的「c統制」)，我們把這裏的'for Mary'分析為動詞節(V')的姐妹成
分，並受動詞(V)的「m 統制」(m-command)。但是 'to Mary'
與'for Mary' 主要的區別在於是否與動詞的次類畫分有關，而這個
訊息已經記載於「(嚴密的) 次類畫分框式」((strict) subcategorization frame) 或「論旨網格」(θ-grid) 中。因此，我們也可以用與
㊵ a 完全相同的結構樹來代表㊵ b。參 Larson (1989)與 Bowers
(1989b) 的有關詞組結構分析。

㉓　Speas (1988) 所提議的X標槓理論把「中介投影」(X')加以廢止，
就是「最大投影」(XP)也可以免除；因而連帶的也無需在X標槓結
構中做「補述語」、「附加語」、「指示語」等區別。她的 X 標槓理論允

出現於動詞組裏附加語位置的副詞與狀語(以下簡稱「動詞組狀語」(VP adverbial))，在論旨角色或「語意類型」(semantic type) 上包括「程度」(degree; 如'perfectly, completely, sufficiently'等)、「情狀」(如 'hard, early, late' 等)、「處所」(如'here, outside, upstairs, in the pool'等)、「受惠者」('for NP')、「工具」(Instrument; 如 'with NP')、「手段」(Means; 如'by VP, by means of NP'等)，例如：

④① a. John speaks English *perfectly.*

b. The tornado ruined his crops *completely.*

c. Mary had worked *sufficiently* that day.

④② a. John works very *hard* in the office every day.

b. I always get up *early* in the morning.

c. Mary went to bed *late*; let her sleep a little more while.

許所有主要語(X)都可以在不違背句法理論原則的條件下自由而連續的衍生。在她的理論裏，⑩b與⑩c 可能合成下面的 X 標槓結構樹。參 Speas (1988:35)。

㊸ a. We can't talk *here*; please come in.

b. I'll sleep *upstairs* tonight.

c. Mary is swimming *in the pool* now.

㊹ a. Mary bought this car *for John*.

㊺ b. John cut the salami *with a knife*.

㊻ a. *John*ᵢ forced the door open {*by means of a lever/by PRO*ᵢ *kicking it hard*}.

b. *John*ᵢ punished *Bill*ⱼ *for PRO*ⱼ *hitting Mary*.❷❹

動詞組狀語可以依據其「構詞形態」（morphological shape）分為三類。第一類是不含有副詞詞尾'-ly'的「單純副詞」(simple adverb; non-*ly* adverb)，包括(甲)在語音形態與句法功能上類似介詞或介詞組的副詞，如 'before, behind, afterward, inside, outside, upstairs, downstairs, around, alone, abroad, aboard, here, there' 等❷❺；(乙)與形容詞語音形態相同的副詞，如 'hard, early, late, (stay) long, (cut) short, fast, (drive) slow, (run) deep, (fly) high, (travel) light, (open) wide, well, (work) fine, (stay) close, (go) direct

---

❷❹ 在㊻a的例句裏出現的「大代號」(PRO) 以母句主語名詞組('John') 為「控制語」(controller)，而在㊻b的例句裏出現的「大代號」則以母句賓語名詞組 ('Bill') 為控制語。㊻b的例句顯示：這類表示手段的狀語子句必須出現於動詞組裏面才能受到賓語名詞組的「c統制」。

❷❺ 這類副詞是 Klima (1965) 所謂的「不及物介詞」(intransitive preposition)。這一類副詞不僅在語音形態上與介詞同形或含有介詞，而且在句法功能上相當於介詞組 (cf. '*after* that, *up* the stairs, *aboard* the ship, by himself, in here, over there' 等)。

(ly)'等。第二類是含有副詞詞尾'-ly'的單純副詞 (-*ly* adverb)，而第三類則是介詞組。第一、三類兩類副詞與狀語只能出現於動詞組右端的位置，而第二類副詞則可以出現於動詞組的右端，也可以出現於動詞組的左端。試比較：

㊼ a. The tornado ruined his crops *completely*.

　　 b. The tornado *completely* ruined his crops.

㊽ a. John works *very hard* in the office every day.

　　 b. *John *very hard* works in the office every day.

㊾ a. I'll sleep *upstairs* tonight.

　　 b. *I'll *upstairs* sleep tonight.

㊿ a. John cut the salami *with a knife*.

　　 b. *John *with a knife* cut the salami.

(51) a. John acquired the job *by offering a bribe*.

　　 b. *John *by offering a bribe* acquired the job.㉖

　在第二類副詞裏面，表示「程度」的副詞㉗ 常出現於動詞組

㉖　如果在(51)b的例句裏出現的'by offering a bribe'的前後加上逗號或停頓，那麼這個句子就可以通。但這是「整句副詞與狀語」(sentential adverb and adverbial) 的用法，與這裏所討論的動詞組狀語的用法不同。

㉗　表示程度的副詞，包括「增強」(amplification)與「縮減」(diminution)。英語裏常用的程度副詞包括：（一）「大小」，如 'greatly {admire/enjoy/exceed}, vastly, enormously, sufficiently, slightly, a little, not (very) much'；（二）「強度」，如 'strongly(deny), heartily(agree), vigorously,increasingly'；（三）「印象」，如 'imposingly, impressively'；（四）「情狀」，如 'wildly (reject), madly, furiously'；（五）「顯著」，如 'deeply {admire/provoke/insult/offend}, badly {need/want}, （→）

的左端。根據 Greenbaum (1970) 以七十名倫敦大學的學生爲
對象的調察結果顯示：在下面含有副詞 'badly' 的㉒a, b, c 三個
例句中，㉒ a 句的接受度爲 100%，㉒b 句的接受度爲 77%，而
㉒ c 句的接受度則爲34%。試比較：

㉒　a. He *badly* needed the money.

　　b. They *badly* wounded the elephant.

　　c. They *badly* treated the servant.

可是把㉒a, b, c 的三個例句分別改寫爲㉝ a, b, c 時，㉝三個例句
的接受度分別是：0%，21%，與66%。

㉝　a. He needed the money *badly*.

　　b. They wounded the elephant *badly*.

　　c. They treated the servant *badly*.❷

這些接受度上的差別是由於副詞 'badly' 可以做「增強程度副詞」

(→)terribly (sorry), dreadfully'；(六)「奇特」如'unusually, ex-
traordinarily'；(七)「全然」，如'completely {forget/ignore},
entirely (agree), genuinely (admire), perfectly {natural/
*unnatural}, entirely { mistaken/*correct }, totally, fully
(understand), thoroughly'等。

❷ Greenbaum (1970) 也提出下面(i)到 (iii) 的例句來要求學生判斷
合法度。結果，大多數學生都只接受增強程度副詞出現於動詞前面的
(iii)句而主張把(i)與(ii)句分別改爲(i')句與(ii')句。試比較：

(i) Did they *deeply* drill the hole?

(ii) Did he *deeply* sleep that night?

(iii) Did he *deeply* admire his speech?

(i') Did they drill the hole *deep(ly)*?

(ii') Did he sleep *deeply* (=soundly) that night?

'very much;非常'解，也可以做「情狀副詞」'in a bad manner；惡劣地'解；做程度副詞使用時較常出現於動詞的前面，而做情狀副詞解時則較常出現於動詞或補述語的後面。我們的X標槓結構分析允許動詞組狀語在這兩種不同的位置出現，例如：

(54)

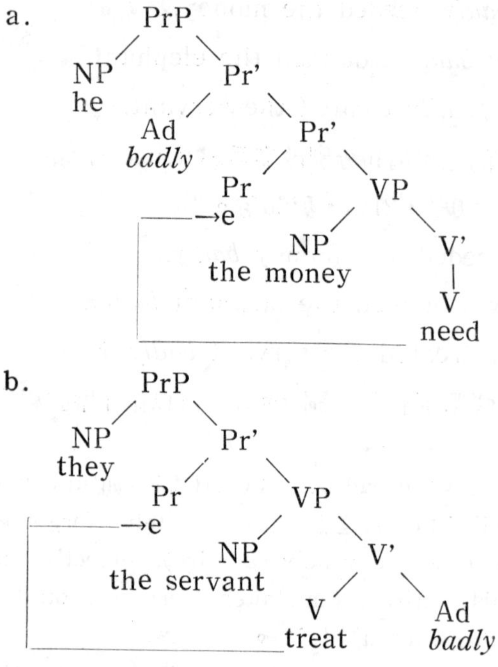

不過(54)a的詞組結構分析顯示：出現於動詞前面的程度副詞實際上出現於述詞組裏附加語位置。

無論在句法結構或語意關係上，動詞組狀語都比出現於述詞組或小句子裏附加語位置的副詞或狀語（以下簡稱「述詞組狀語」(PrP adverbial) 及「小句子狀語」(TP adverbial)）更接近主要語動詞而關係更爲緊密。因此，在句法表現上有下列幾點不

同。

(一)動詞組狀語與述詞組狀語或小句子狀語在同一個句子裏出現的時候，二者的前後次序通常是：動詞組狀語在前面，述詞組與小句子狀語在後面。試比較：

(55) a. John learned French *perfectly* (very) *quickly.*

b. *John learned French *quickly perfectly.*㉙

(56) a. John hasn't offended Bill *by telling jokes since returning home.*

b. *John hasn't offended Bill *since returning home by telling jokes.*㉚

(57) a. John bought this car *for Mary for fun.*

b. ?*John bought this car *for fun for Mary.*

(58) a. John donated 50 dollars *to charity to feel better.*

b. ?*John donated 50 dollars *to feel better to charity.*

(59) a. Mary swam *in the pool in her new swimsuit.*

b. ?*Mary swam *in her new swimsuit in the pool.*

㉙ 例句與合法度判斷採自 Bowers (1989b)。他還提供了下面的例句與合法度判斷。

(i) John *quickly* learned French *perfectly.*

(ii) *John *perfectly* learned French *quickly.*

(i) 句的合語法與 (ii) 句的不合語法似乎顯示：動詞組右端的情狀或程度副詞似乎包含於動詞組之內，而動詞組左端的情狀或程度副詞則出現於動詞組之外。

㉚ 例句與合法度判斷採自 Williams (1975:254)。

⑥ a. Mary cut the salami *with a knife with her eyes closed.*

　 b. ?*Mary cut the salami *with her eyes closed with a knife.*❸

　（二）因為「動詞組提前」(VP Preposing)而主要語動詞與補述語移到句首的時候，動詞組狀語通常都要隨同移位；而述詞組狀語與小句子狀語則可以隨同移位，也可以留在原位。試比較：

⑥ a. John said he would buy this car *for Mary,* and buy this car *for Mary* he did.

　 a'. *John said he would buy this car *for Mary,* and buy this car he did *for Mary.*

　 b. John said he would buy this car *for fun,* and buy this car *for fun* he did.

　 b'. John said he would buy this car *for fun,* and buy this car he did *for fun.*

⑥ a. John said he would donate 50 dollars *to charity,* and donate 50 dollars *to charity* he did.

　 a'. *John said he would donate 50 dollars *to charity,* and donate 50 dollars he did *to charity.*

　 b. John said he would donate 50 dollars *to feel better,* and donate 50 dollars *to feel better* he did.

---

❸　例句㊄到⑥曾參照 Speas (1988:33-34) 的例句。

b'. John said he would donate 50 dollars *to feel better*, and donate 50 dollars he did *to feel better*.

⑥²' a. Mary said she would swim *in the pool*, and swim *in the pool* she did.

a'. *Mary said she would swim *in the pool*, and swim she did *in the pool*.

b. Mary said she would swim *in her new swimsuit*, and swim *in her new swimsuit* she did.

b'. Mary said she would swim *in her new swimsuit*, and swim she did *in her new swimsuit*.

⑥³ a. Mary said she would cut the salami *with a knife*, and cut the salami *with a knife* she did.

a'. *Mary said she would cut the salami *with a knife*, and cut the salami she did *with a knife*.

b. Mary said she would cut the salami *with her eyes closed*, and cut the salami *with her eyes closed* she did.

b'. Mary said she would cut the salami *with her eyes closed*, and cut the salami she did *with her eyes closed*.㉜

㉜ ⑥¹到⑥³的例句與合法度判斷參照 Speas (1988:33-34) 的例句。

　　（三）在由從屬連詞 'though' 或 'as' 所引導的「讓步子句」(concessive clause) 裏，動詞組常因「Though 移位」(Though Movement: 又稱「Though 吸引」(Though Attraction)) 而移到句首。這個時候，動詞組狀語也常隨同主要語動詞與補述語移到句首；而述詞組狀語則可以隨同移位，也可以留在原位。試比較：❸

　⑭　a.　Buy a car *for Mary* though John did, she didn't appreciate it.

　　　b.　?Buy a car though John did *for Mary*, she didn't appreciate it.

　⑮　a.　Buy a car *for fun* though John did, he never actually drove it.

　　　b.　Buy a car though John did *for fun*, he never actually drove it.

　⑯　a.　Swim *in the pool* though Mary did, she still felt the heat unbearable.

　　　b.　?Swim though Mary did *in the pool*, she still felt the heat unbearable.

　⑰　a.　Swim *in her new swimsuit* though Mary did, no one paid attention to her.

　　　b.　Swim though Mary did *in her new swimsuit*, no one paid attention to her.

---

❸　以下⑭到⑮的例句有關 a 句與 b 句兩相比較之下所做的合法度判斷是「相對」(relative) 的而不是「絕對」(absolute) 的。

另一方面，小句子狀語則似乎比較不容易隨同移位，而留在原位。試比較：

⑱ a. Donate 50 dollars *to charity* though John did, they still thought he was a penny pincher.

b. ?Donate 50 dollars though John did *to charity*, they still thought he was a penny pincher.

⑲ a. ?Donate 50 dollars *to feel better* though John did, he was all the more depressed.

b. Donate 50 dollars though John did *to feel better,* he was all the more depressed.

⑳ a. Cut the salami *with a knife* though Mary did, she made a pretty bad mess of it.

b. ?Cut the salami though Mary did *with a knife,* she made a pretty bad mess of it.

㉑ a. ?Cut the salami *with her eyes closed* though Mary did, she made a pretty good job.

b. Cut the salami though Mary did *with her eyes closed,* she made a pretty good job.

(四)動詞組狀語與述詞組狀語或小句子狀語在同一個句子裏出現的時候，述詞組狀語與小句子狀語比動詞組狀語更容易移到句首。試比較：

㉒ a. John bought this car *for* Mary *for fun.*

b. ??*For Mary,* John bought this car *for fun.*

c. *For fun,* John bought this car *for Mary.*

⑺ a. John donated 50 dollars *to charity to feel better.*

　　b. ?**To charity,* John donated 50 dollars *to feel better.*

　　c. *To feel better,* John donated 50 dollars *to charity.*

⑺ a. Mary swam *in the pool in her new swimsuit.*

　　b. ??*In the pool,* Mary swam *in her new swimsuit.*

　　c. *In her new swimsuit,* Mary swam *in the pool.*

⑺ a. Mary cut the salami *with a knife with her eyes closed.*

　　b. ?**With a knife,* Mary cut the salami *with her eyes closed.*

　　c. *With her eyes closed,* Mary cut the salami *with a knife.*

⑺ a. John offended Mary *by telling jokes before leaving.*

　　b. ?**By telling jokes,* John offended Mary *before leaving.*

　　c. *Before leaving,* John offended Mary *by telling jokes.*❸

以上的分析與討論顯示：動詞組狀語雖然與動詞的次類畫分

---

❸　例句與合法度判斷採自 Williams (1975:256)。

無關，但是與動詞的語意關係相當密切；因而出現於動詞組裏附加語的位置，並受主要語動詞的管轄。動詞組狀語中，以副詞詞尾 '-ly' 收尾的單純副詞可以出現於動詞節的右邊，也可以出現於動詞節的左邊；不以副詞詞尾 '-ly' 收尾的單純副詞、不及物介詞㉟、以及介詞組狀語只能出現於動詞節的右邊㊱；而以副詞詞尾 'ly' 收尾的單純副詞中，表示程度的副詞則常出現於動詞的左方㊲。動詞組狀語與動詞的補述語一樣，在「信息結構」(information structure) 中常代表新的或重要的信息。因此，動詞組狀語(i)可以充當疑問句、否定句、「分裂句」(cleft-sentence) 或準分裂句的「焦點」(focus)；(ii)可以包含於 'do so' 裏面，也可以出現於 'do so' 外面；(iii)在「動詞組提前」與

㉟ Klima (1965) 以 "PP → P (NP)" 這樣的詞組結構規律來衍生及物介詞組 ('P NP'，如 'before dinner, behind the car') 與不及物介詞 ('P'，如 'before, behind' 等)。

㊱ 只有單純副詞可以出現於動詞的左邊，而狀語介詞組則無法出現於動詞的左邊。這個限制與句法結構有關而與語意無關。試比較：
(i) Bill dropped the bananas {*quickly/with a crash*}.
(ii) Bill {*quickly/*with a crash*} dropped the bananas.
參 Jackendoff (1977:73)。

㊲ 這些程度副詞在語意內涵與句法功能上與修飾形容詞或副詞的「增強詞」(amplifier; 'so, too, awfully, extremely' 等) 或「減弱詞」(down-toner; 'a bit, a little, barely, fairly, pretty, quite, rather, somewhat, slightly' 等) 相似，用來加強或緩和動詞、副詞、形容詞等所表達的情狀或屬性，因而可能概化爲量詞。另一方面，情狀、處所、工具、手段等副詞與狀語則有「陳述」(be predicated of) 動詞與其補述語的功能。

「Though 移位」中常隨動詞與補述語移到句首；（iv）可以單獨出現於句首充當「焦點主題」（focus topic），並且必須重讀；（v）在「句子照應」（sentential anaphora）中常包含於「代句詞」（pro-S）'it'、'that' 或 'so' 裏面，例如：

⑦ a. Did John buy the diamond ring *for Mary*?

b. John didn't buy the diamond ring *for Mary*.

c. It was *for Mary* that John bought the diamond ring.

d. What John did today was buy a diamond ring *for Mary*.

e. John bought a diamond ring *for Mary*, and Bill *did so* {, too/for Alice}.

f. John said he would buy a diamond ring *for Mary*, and buy a diamond ring *for Mary* he did today.

g. Buy a diamond ring *for Mary* though John did, he still could not win her heart.

h. *For Mary*, John bought a diamond ring (, and for Alice, a gold bracelet).

i. They said that 〔John bought a diamond ring *for Mary*〕ᵢ, but I don't believe *it*ᵢ.

j. ("Generously John bought a diamond ring *for Mary*".) "*That*'s surprising."

k. ("It was generous of John to buy a diamond

ring *for Mary*.") "I don't think *so*."

動詞組是由主要語動詞m統制的「最貼近」(minimal)的最大投影。在傳統的變形語法裏,「介副詞移位」(Particle Movement)、「終點賓語移位」(*To*-Dative Movement)與「受惠者賓語移位」(*For*-Dative Movement)等都在這個「句法領域」(syntactic domain)裏適用。❸由於這些變形或結構佈局的存在,再加上動詞組狀語本身的移位,所以動詞組狀語在動詞組裏出現的位置可能有所改變。試比較:

⑱ a.　John put the book on the desk *carefully*.

　　b.　John put the book *carefully* on the desk.

⑲ a.　John gave the book to Mary *carefully*.

　　b.　John gave the book *carefully* to Mary.

　　c.　John gave Mary the book *carefully*.

　　d.　??John gave Mary *carefully* the book.

⑱a,b的例句分別具有⑳a,b的結構佈局。試比較:

⑳ a.

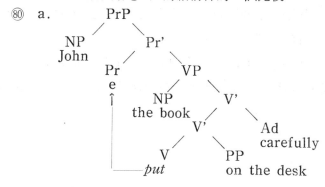

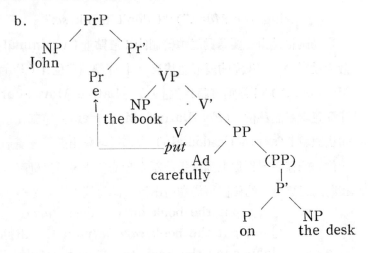

情狀副詞‘carefully’在⑧a的結構樹裏出現於動詞組附加語的位置，而在⑧b 的結構樹裏則「加接」(adjoin) 到處所介詞組的左端（或出現於介詞組裏附加語的位置）。由於‘carefully on the desk’在⑱b裏形成介詞組，所以整個「詞組單元」(constituent) 可以移到句首而衍生㉛句。**❸**

㉛ *Carefully on the desk*, John put the book.**❹**

另一方面，⑲a, b的例句則分別具有㉒a, b的結構佈局。試比較：

---

❸ 參 Culicover & Williams (1984:29)。

❹ 但是我們卻不可能從⑧a的深層結構來衍生不合語法‘*On the desk, John put the book carefully’。

⑧ a.

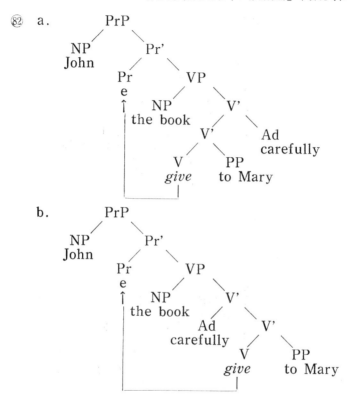

b.

在⑧b 的結構樹裏，'carefully to Mary' 並沒有形成詞組，所以不能移到句首而衍生⑧句。

⑧ *Carefully to Mary*, John gave the book.

至於⑲c,d 的例句，則應該分別從⑧a,b 的深層結構，(i)先經過由動詞節(V')到動詞 (V) 的「重新分析」(reanalysis)，(ii)把整個「合成述語」(complex predicate; 即 'give to Mary')移入主要語述詞的位置，(iii)再在「語音形式」(phonetic form; PF) 部門把介詞 'to' 加以刪除。❹ 結果，無論是⑧a與⑧b的深

---

❹ 參 Larson (1988)。

⑧ a.

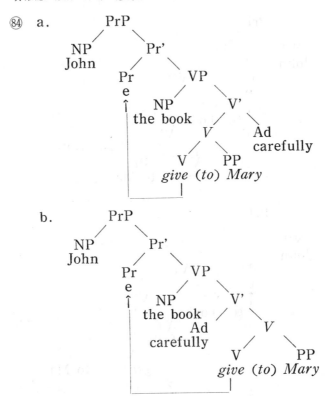

b.

層結構都只能衍生⑲c的表層結構，而無法衍生⑲b的表層結構。

雙賓動詞含有介副詞的時候，情況更爲複雜。例如，Keyser（1968: 369-371）提出下面含有「片語動詞」（phrasal verb）'send back' 與情狀副詞 'roughly' 的例句與合法度判斷。㊷

㊷ ⑧f到⑧h的例句是經過「介詞副詞移位」的句子。根據 Keyser（1968），⑧c的 'send back' 只能做 '回送'（"directional" reading）解，不能做 '退回'（"reiterative" reading）解。這就表示 'send something back to someone' 有兩種不同的詞組結構分析與含義：（──→）

⑧⑤　a.　John will *roughly* send back the money to the girl.

　b.　*John will send *roughly* back the money to the girl.

　c.　(?)John will send back *roughly* the money to the girl.

　d.　John will send back the money *roughly* to the girl.

　e.　John will send back the money to the girl *roughly*.

　f.　*John will send *roughly* the money back to the girl.

　g.　*John will send the money *roughly* back to

(一)　(i)'退回'：

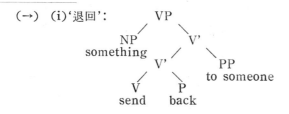

(i)'回送'：

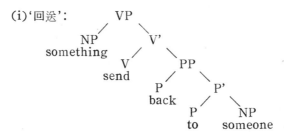

the girl.

h.　　John will send the money back *roughly* to the girl.

根據 Keyser (1968) 的分析，情狀副詞 'roughly' 具有「可以轉位」（〔+transportable〕）的句法屬性，並與動詞 'send'、名詞組 'the money'、介詞組 'to the girl' 形成姐妹成分；因此可以在⑧⑥的動詞組裏三種不同的位置出現。

⑧⑥

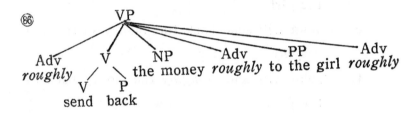

Keyser (1968) 的詞組結構分析只承認「一個槓次」(one bar-level) 的投影，因此必須假定：(i) 由最大投影所支配的詞組成分都形成姐妹成分；(ii) 情狀副詞在深層結構的某一個位置衍生以後，再靠「轉位」(transportation) 來移到其他位置；(iii) 情狀副詞的「修飾範域」(scope of modification) 不因情狀副詞的轉位而有所改變。而依照我們的分析，有關的情狀副詞都在深層結構裏直接衍生於動詞組附加語的位置，不必虛擬這些副詞的轉位❹❸；而且，也可以依據這些副詞所 c 統制或 m 統制的句法領域來決定其修飾範域，不必虛擬狹義的姐妹成分關係。在下面⑧⑦

---

❹❸　Chomsky (1986a, 1989) 認為「移位」是事非得已的「最後手段」(the "last resort")，在普遍語法的分析裏最好是備而不用。

到⑩的詞組結構分析裏，我們可以衍生⑧a, d, e, g, j等例句，而不會衍生⑧b, c, f等不合語法或有問題的例句，而且還比Keyser (1968) 的例句多衍生了⑧b與⑧b這兩個例句。

⑧ a. John will *send back* the money *roughly* to the girl. (=⑧d)

b. *John will *send* the money *roughly back* to the girl. (=⑧g)❹

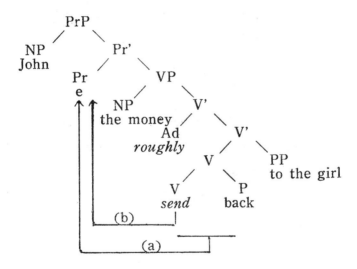

⑧ a. John will *send back* the money to the girl *roughly.* (=⑧e)

---

❹ 這個例句的不合語法是由於情狀副詞（'roughly'）出現於動詞（'send'）與介副詞（'back'）的中間所致。試比較：

（ⅰ）John looked up the information *quickly.*

（ⅱ）*John looked *quickly* up the information.

b. John will *send* the money *back* to the girl
   roughly.

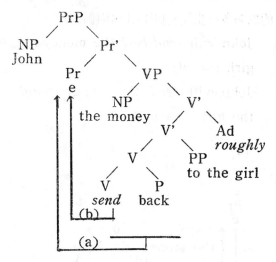

⑧⑨ a. John will *roughly send back* the money to the
   girl. (=⑧⑤a)

   b. John will *roughly send* the money *back* to the
   girl.

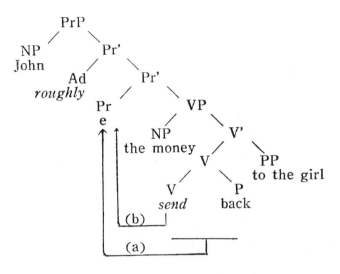

⑨ a. John will *send back* the money *roughly* to the girl. (=⑧d)

　b. John will *send* the money *back roughly* to the girl. (=⑧h)

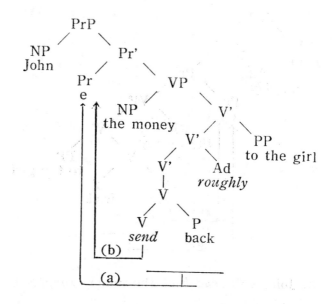

五、出現於述詞組附加語位置的副詞與狀語

　　述詞組以述詞爲主要語，以動詞組爲補述語合成述詞節，再以主語名詞組爲指示語合成述詞組。述詞節也可以由述詞節與附加語合成，並且可以反複衍生附加語。述詞組的附加語，與動詞組的附加語一樣，是與動詞的次類畫分無關的可用成分；因爲出現於動詞組的外面，所以不受主要語動詞的管轄或ｍ統制❹，也就不由主要語動詞來指派論旨角色。出現於述詞組裏的副詞或狀

────────

❹　這是就深層結構的結構佈局而言。由於主要語動詞的提升移入主要語
　　述詞的位置，所以在表層結構中主要語動詞也ｍ統制述詞組副詞與狀
　　語。

語 (以下簡稱「述詞組狀語」(PrP adverbial)) 包括「主事(者)」
(Agentive) 如⑨、「情狀」如⑨、「範圍」(Scope) 如⑨、「隨件」
(Comitative) 如⑨、「手段」如⑨、「程度」如⑨等,例如:

⑨ a. The instrument has been tested *by a techni-cian;* cf. *A technician* has tested the instru-ment.

b. Mary was proposed to *by a handsome million-aire;* cf. *A handsome millionaire* proposed to Mary.

⑨ a. John { *guickly/clumsily* } dropped his cup of coffee; cf. John dropped his cup of coffee { *quickly/clumsily* }.

b. Mary {*easily/readily*} ate her bananas; cf. Mary ate her bananas {*easily/readily*}.

c. The guest of honor arrived *in a blue gown.*

d. Pronounce the word (*exactly*) *as I do.*

e. John frequently talks *as if he knew everything about the GB-theory.*

⑨ a. I can run *three miles in ten minutes.*

b. They discussed the problem *for an hour.*

c. They have *all* prepared their lessons.

d. The men were *individually* asked to leave.

⑨ a. John went to New York (*together*) *with Mary.*

b. The stranger disappeared *with the purse.*

> c. Mary left the room *without even saying good-bye.*

⑨⑤ a. They plan to go to New York *by boat.*

> b. People used to travel *on horseback.*

> c. *John*ᵢ forced the door open *by PRO*ᵢ *kicking it hard.*

> d. *Bill*ᵢ offended Mary *by PRO*ᵢ *telling jokes.*

⑨⑥ a. The tornado *completey* ruined the crops.

> b. John *absolutely* refused to give up.

> c. Mary *merely* mentioned his name.

有些述詞組狀語（如「情狀」、「手段」、「程度」等）在語意類型上與動詞組狀語重複。其中，主事介詞組（'by NP'）與出現於述詞組裏指示語位置的主語名詞組相對（如⑨①的例句），所以似乎應該分析為出現於述詞組。手段介詞組（'by VP'）裏以主語名詞組為控制語的（如⑨⑤ c, d 的例句），似乎也應該分析為述詞組狀語。其他凡是出現於動詞前面的副詞（'A-ly'），也都應該分析為出現於述詞組附加語的位置。因為如果把這些副詞分析為出現於動詞組附加語的位置，那麼在主要語動詞提升而移入主要語述詞的位置以後，這些副詞就不可能出現於動詞的前面。試比較：

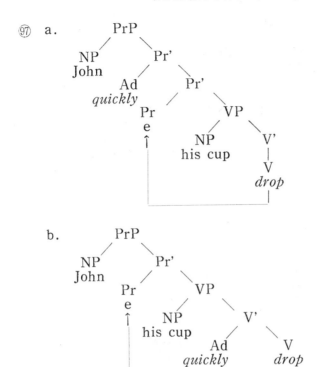

至於出現於動詞或賓語名詞組後面的副詞與狀語，則可以分析為出現於動詞組附加語的位置，也可以分析為出現於述詞組附加語的位置。試比較：⑱a,b

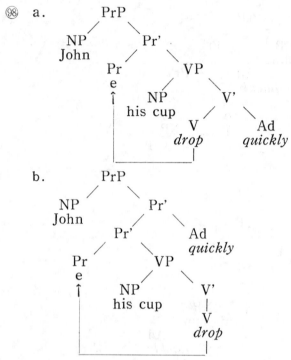

⑱ a.

b.

在前面有關動詞組狀語的分析裏，我們權宜的把無法出現於動詞前面的(i)不以詞尾'-ly'收尾的情狀副詞（如 'hard, fast, early, slow'）、(ii) 不及物介詞（如 'before, behind, along, inside, upstairs'）與 (iii) 具有準論元功能的介詞組（如處所介詞組、受惠者介詞組、工具介詞組、手段介詞組）歸入動詞組狀語。另外，程度副詞與情狀副詞同時出現的時候，程度副詞通常都出現於情狀副詞的前面⑯，因而也把出現於動詞或賓語後面的

---

⑯　參 Bowers (1989b) 下面的例句與合法度判斷：
　　（ⅰ）John learned French *perfectly* (very) *quickly*.
　　　　*John learned French *quickly perfectly*.
　　（ⅱ）John *quickly* learned French *perfectly*.
　　　　*John *perfectly* learned French *quickly*.
　　參註㉙。

程度副詞也歸入動詞組狀語。以母句賓語爲控制語的理由介詞組
（如 'John punished *Bill*ᵢ 〔*for PRO*ᵢ *hitting Mary*〕'），必
須受到母句賓語的 c 統制，所以也應該分析爲動詞組狀語。但是
以母句主語爲控制語的理由介詞組（如 '*John*ᵢ got sick 〔*from
PRO*ᵢ *eating too much*〕'）與手段介詞組（如 '*John*ᵢ acquired
the job 〔by *PRO*ᵢ *offering a bribe*〕'）則只要受到母句主
語的 c 統制，所以不一定要分析爲動詞組狀語，也可以分析爲述
詞組狀語。就語意上而言，動詞組狀語是以動詞組所表達的動作
或行動「爲陳述的對象」（be predicated of），而述詞組狀語則
以述詞組所表達的命題爲陳述的對象。但是二者的界限有時候並
不很明確，也就影響了動詞組狀語與述詞組狀語之間在分析上的
曖昧性。

　　動詞組狀語與述詞組狀語之間的曖昧性還牽涉到了英語「動
貌助動詞」（aspectual auxiliaries; 廣義的動貌助動詞包括
「完成貌」（perfective aspect; 'have-en'）、「進行貌」（pro-
gressive aspect; 'be-ing'）與「被動態」（passive voice;
'be-en'））與有關狀語在Ｘ標槓結構中出現的位置。關於英語動
貌助動詞在Ｘ標槓結構中應該如何分析，學者間仍有異論。❹
我們在這裏暫且採用⑨的分析來做爲 'John has been giving
money to Mary' 的Ｘ標槓結構。在這個分析裏，英語的「時制」
（tense; T）與「情態助動詞」（modal; M）出現於小句子（TP）

---

❹　參 Jackendoff (1977), Emonds (1970, 1976), Lapointe (1977,
　　1980), Akmajian et al. (1979) 等有關討論。

主要語(T)的位置；而完成貌助動詞 'have-en' 與進行貌助動詞
'be-ing' 則出現於動詞組裏，並以動詞組爲補述語❹。試比較
⑨a的深層結構與⑨b的表層結構：

⑨　a.

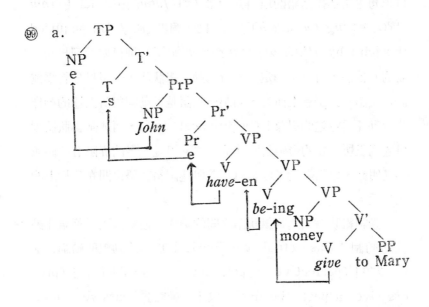

---

❹　動貌助動詞之以動詞組爲補述語，可以分析爲動貌助動詞的次類畫分
　　屬性。除了動貌助動詞以外，「動貌動詞」（aspectual verb；如
　　'begin, start, continue, cease' 等）也可以分析爲以動詞組爲補
　　述語。

b.

```
              TP
            /    \
          NP      T'
        Johnᵢ    /  \
               T      PrP
              hasⱼ   /   \
                   NP     Pr'
                   tᵢ    /   \
                       Pr      VP
                       tⱼ     /  \
                            V     VP
                          been   /  \
                               V      VP
                            givingₖ  /   \
                                   NP      V'
                                  money   /  \
                                         V    PP
                                         tₖ  to Mary
```

'John might have been giving money to Mary', 'John could have given money to Mary', 'John will be giving money to Mary' 與 'John did give money to Mary' 的詞組結構分析則分別如⑩a、⑩b、⑩c與⑩d。

⑩⑩ a.

```
              TP
          ／      ＼
        NP          T'
       John_i    ／    ＼
                T        PrP
              might   ／    ＼
                    NP         Pr'
                    t_i    ／      ＼
                          Pr          VP
                         have    ／      ＼
                                V          VP
                              been    ／      ＼
                                     V          VP
                                  giving_j  ／    ＼
                                          NP         V'
                                        money   ／    ＼
                                               V        PP
                                              t_j     to Mary
```

b.

```
              TP
          ／      ＼
        NP          T'
       John_i    ／    ＼
                T        PrP
              could   ／    ＼
                    NP         Pr'
                    t_i    ／      ＼
                          Pr          VP
                         have    ／      ＼
                                V          VP
                              given_j  ／    ＼
                                      NP         V'
                                    money   ／    ＼
                                           V        PP
                                          t_j     to Mary
```

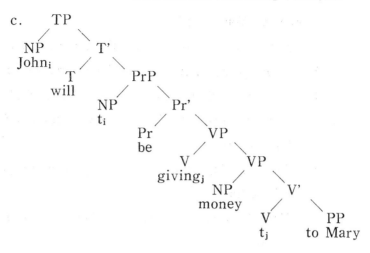

不過在⑩a 的詞組結構分析中，只有最底層的動詞組（'give money to Mary'）可以在「動詞組提前」與「Though 移位」中移位，也只有這個最底層的動詞組可以充當「準分裂句」的焦點。試比較：

⑩ They swore that John might have been giving

money to Mary, and

a. *giving money to her* he might have been!

b. **been giving money to her* he might have!

c. **have been giving money to her* he might!

⑩ a. *Giving money to Mary* though John might have been,

b. ***Been giving money to Mary* though John might have,

c. ***Have been giving money to Mary* though John might,

……he never took advantage of her.

⑩ a. What John might have been doing is *giving money to Mary.*

b. *What John might have done is *been giving money to Mary.*

c. *What John might do is *have been giving money to Mary.*

因此，我們不但要區別以動貌助動詞為主要語的動詞組與一般動詞為主要語的動詞組，而且還要考慮副詞與狀語在這幾種不同的動詞組結構中可能出現的位置。如果我們為述詞組擬設⑩的X標槓結構，那麼根據②的「X標槓結構公約」，述詞組底下可以包含四個附加語的位置；即「附加語 α」（adjt α）、「附加語 β」（Adjt β）、「附加語 γ」（Adjt γ）與「附加語 δ」（Adjt δ）。試比較：

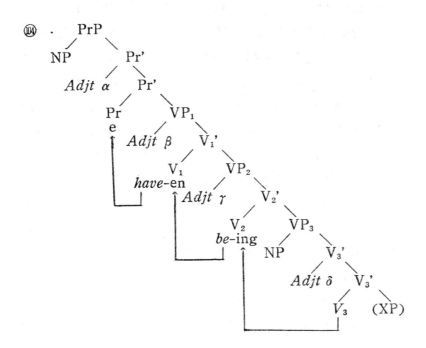

「附加語 δ」出現於最底層的（狹義的）動詞組裏面，也就是我們先前所討論的「動詞組狀語」的位置。「附加語 γ」出現於進行貌助動詞 'be (-ing)' 與主要動詞 'V' 之間；「附加語 β」出現於完成貌助動詞 'have (-en)' 與進行貌助動詞之間，而「附加語 α」則出現於時制或情態助動詞與完成貌助動詞之間。現在我們要討論的問題是：這三種不同的附加語位置是否都需要？如果這三種位置都需要，那麼各種不同類型的副詞與狀語在這三種不同的位置出現與分佈的情況究竟如何？

「附加語 α」的位置是各種「否定副詞」（negative adverb;

如‘not, never, hardly, scarcely’⑲）出現的位置。如果小句子
（TP）的時制語素（T）含有情態助動詞，那麼否定副詞就出現於
這個情態助動詞的後面（如‘could *not* have been studying
English’）；如果小句子不含有情態助動詞而述詞組裏面含有完
成貌助動詞（‘have’），那麼這個完成貌助動詞就移入時制語素的
位置以便獲得時制（如‘*had* not been studying English’）；
如果述詞組裏面不含有完成貌助動詞而含有進行貌助動詞（‘be’）
，那麼這個進行貌助動詞就 移入時制語素 的位置以便 獲得時制
（如‘*was* not studying English’）；如果不含有任何助動詞，
那麼「時制助動詞」（tense auxiliary）⑳‘do’就出現於時制語
素的位置（如‘*did* not study English’）。除了否定副詞以外，
「頻率副詞」（frequency adverb; 如 ‘always, usually, normally, generally, regularly, often, frequently, sometimes,
occasionally, rarely,（n）ever’）、「量詞」（quantifier; 如

---

⑲ 根據 Pollock（1989），否定詞本身也形成最大投影「否定詞組」
　　（negative phrase; NegP）。

⑳ 這是我們所杜撰的名稱，因為在英語疑問句、否定句、加強肯定句以
　　及「替代詞」（pro-form）所出現的助動詞‘do’（也就是所謂的「Do
　　支」援（Do Support）），其主要功能似乎在於顯示時制。又根據Pol-
　　lock（1989），英語的助動詞與「Be 動詞」（還有英式英語的「Have
　　動詞」）「提升」（raise）移入時制語素的位置來獲得時制，而其他一
　　般動詞則由時制語素（包括表示非限定式的 ‘to’）「降下」（lower）
　　移入主要語述詞的位置來授與時制。這樣的分析可以正確的詮釋「附
　　加語 α」在表層結構中可以出現於助動詞的前面或後面，但是只能出
　　現於一般動詞的前面。

'all, both, each')❺、「認知副詞」（epistemic adverb; 如 'probably, certainly, possibly, evidently, surely, undoubtedly, clearly, obviously, indeed')、「體裁副詞」（style adverb❷；如 'frankly, honestly, truthfully, confidentially, seriously, briefly, broadly, crudely')、「屬性副詞」（epithet adverb❸；如 'wisely, cleverly, artfully, prudently, foolishly, graciously, rightly, correctly, wrongly'）等也可以出現於「附加語α」的位置，例如：

⑩⑤ a. They'll {*always/all*} be faithful to their master.

　　b. They have {*always/all*} been nice to me.❺

⑩⑥ a. George will {*evidently/frankly*} have amused

---

❺ 關於這些量詞的來源，有主張由於主語名詞組裏量詞組本身的移位而來(即所謂的「量詞漂移」(Quantifier Floating))，亦有主張由於主語名詞組的移位而留下量詞的(即所謂的「量詞遺留」(Quantifier Stranding))。參 Sportiche (1988)。

❷ Quirk et al. (1985:615-618)把這類附加語稱爲 "style disjunct"。

❸ 這是 Schreiber (1970) 的名稱。

❺ 如果助動詞後面(包括 Be 動詞)有省略，那麼有關的副詞就出現於助動詞的前面，而且助動詞還要重讀，例如：'John has never been concerned about pollution, but Mary {*always HAS/*has always*}'。這個時候有關的副詞出現於小句子附加語的位置（即時制語素的左方)。雖然助動詞後面沒有省略，但是如果把助動詞重讀，有關副詞也出現於助動詞的前面，例如：

(ⅰ) My friends {*rarely/often/seldom*} are unhappy for long periods.

(ⅱ) My friends {*rarely/often/seldom*} have helped me.

(ⅲ) You *never* can get anything to eat in that restaurant!

(ⅴ) Well, I *never* did hear anything like that before!

例句與合法度判斷採自 Pollock (1989:fn.8)。

the children when we get there.

b. George will {*evidently/frankly*} be amusing the
children when we get there.

⑩⑦ a. John will {*artfully/prudently*} remind Mary of
their date.

b. John has {*artfully/prudently*} reminded Mary
of their date.

但是在這些副詞中否定副詞（如'not, never, hardly, scarcely'
❺❺）與少數表示範圍的副詞（如 'merely, simply, virtually,
utterly'）只能出現於「附加語 α」的位置，而其他副詞卻還可以
出現於其他附加語的位置。試比較：

⑩⑧ a. Albert is {*merely/truly/simply*} being a fool.

b. *{*Merely/truly/simply*} Albert is being a fool.

c. *Albert is being a fool {*merely/truly/simply*}.❺❻

⑩⑨ a. Albert is {*sometimes/evidently/frankly*} a fool.

b. {*Sometimes/evidently/frankly*} Albert is a

---

❺❺ 但是這些否定詞在「否定倒序」（Negative Inversion）中卻可以出
現於句首的位置，例如：

（ⅰ）*Never* have I seen him before.

（ⅱ）*Scarcely* had he begun his speech {when/before} the
door opened.

（ⅲ）*Not* that I know of.

❺❻ 例句與合法度判斷採自 Jackendoff（1972:51）。又如果例句⑩⑧ b 的
'truly' 後面附有停頓或逗號就可以通，但是這個句子與⑩⑧ a 的例句
含義不同。

fool.

    c.   Albert   is   a   fool   { *sometimes/, evidently/,* *frankly*}.

⑩   a.   Albert {*artfully/prudently*} dropped the subject.

    b.   {*Artfully/Prudently*} (,) Albert   dropped   the subject.

在後面有關小句子狀語與大句子狀語的討論裏，我們會更進一步詳細的討論這些副詞的句法功能與語意特徵。

其次，「附加語 β」的位置是介於完成貌助動詞與進行貌助動詞或主要動詞中間的位置。在我們所蒐集的語料中，有情態助動詞出現的時候，副詞出現於完成貌助動詞後面的例句並不多，例如：

⑪   a. They will have *seriously* considered him for the post.

    b. My answer may have *to some extent* displeased him.

    c. You would have {*probably/certainly*} missed the plane.

    d. The room must have been *quite carefully* searched by the police.

    e. They must have *often* been listening at the door.

    f. The car may have {*sometimes/indeed*} been

being used without permission.**❺**

在⑪的例句裏出現的副詞與狀語，包括「情狀」（⑪a,d句）、「程度」（⑪b句）、「頻率」（⑪e,f句）與「認知」（⑪c,f句）等。其中，表示頻率與認知的狀語還可以出現於小句子或大句子裏附加語的位置，但是表示情狀與程度的狀語則只能出現於述詞組或動詞組裏附加語的位置。試比較：

⑫　a.　John lost his mind *completely*.

　　b.　John *completely* lost his mind.

　　c.　*John *completely* {will lose/has lost} his mind.

　　d.　*John {*very much/to some extent*} will object to that.

　　e.　*Completely* John {will lose/has lost} his mind.

⑬　a.　Mary studied her lessons {*carefully/with diligence*}.

　　b.　Mary *carefully* studied her lessons.

　　c.　*Mary *carefully* {will study/has studied} her lessons.

　　d.　*Mary {*very diligently/with diligence*} will

---

❺　⑪的例句採自 Quirk et al. (1985:495;628)。他們也承認副詞出現於「句中中」（medial-medial）位置的例句（即⑪d,e,f句）不多（"to be found only rarely"）。又 Quirk et al. (1985:628)認為⑪c的例句合語法，而 Jackendoff (1977:48) 卻認為與此句相似的'?*George will have {*probably/evidently/frankly*} amused the children when we get there' 不合語法。可見英美人士對於這類例句的合法度判斷可能互有出入。

study her lessons.

e. *Carefully* Mary {will study/has studied} her lessons.❺❽

⑭ a. The car may have been used without permission *sometimes*.

b. The car may have been used *sometimes* without permission.

c. The car may *sometimes* have been used without permission.

d. The car *sometimes* may have been used without permission.

e. *Sometimes* the car may have been used without permission.

⑮ a. You would have missed the plane {*probably/certainly*}

b. You would {*probably/certainly*} have missed the plane.

c. You {*probably/certainly*} would have missed the plane.

d. {*Probably/Certainly*} you would have missed the plane.

---

❺❽ 參 Jackendoff (1972:50) 的例句與合法度判斷：

（ i ） Stanley ate his wheaties {*completely/easily*}.

（ii） Stanley {*completely/easily*} ate his wheaties.

(iii) *{*Completely/easily*} Stanley ate his wheaties.

這個區別似乎顯示：情狀副詞與程度副詞的修飾範域限於述詞組與動詞組，而頻率副詞與認知副詞的修飾範域則及於小句子或大句子。與情狀副詞、程度副詞一起屬於述詞組狀語或動詞組狀語的還有「主事」、「範圍」、「隨伴」、「手段」、「處所」等狀語；而與頻率副詞、認知副詞一起屬於小句子狀語或大句子狀語的則有量詞以及「體裁」、「觀點」、「領域」、「屬性」、「評價」等狀語。前一類狀語與情態助動詞、完成貌助動詞、進行貌助動詞或被動態助動詞連用的時候，常出現於「附加語 γ」的位置；而後一類狀語則與這些助動詞連用的時候，常出現於「附加語 α」的位置。

試比較：⑲

⑯ a. George will { *probably/completely* } finish his carrots.

b. George will have {*probably/*completely*} read the book.

c. George will be {*probably/*completely* } finishing his carrots.

d. George will be {*probably/*completely* } ruined by the tornado.

e. George has been {*probably/*completely* } finishing his carrots.

f. George has been {*probably/*completely*} ruined by the tornado.

---

⑲ ⑯的例句與合法度判斷，除 (a) 句以外均採自 Jackendoff (1972: 76)。

g. George is being {*probably/completely} ruined by the tornado.

⑪ a. George will {probably/?*completely} have read the book.**⑥⓪**

b. George will {probably/?*completely} be finishing his carrots by now.

c. George will {probably/?*completely} be ruined by the tornado.

d. George has {probably/?*completely} been finishing his carrots.

e. George has {probably/?*completely} been ruined by the tornado.

f. George is {probably/?*completely} being ruined by the tornado.

至於「附加語β」(即「句中中」(medial-medial))的位置，則兩類狀語都很少出現，特別是在進行貌的被動態中尤少出現。試比較：**⑥①**

⑱ a. John will have {?probably/*rapidly} been beaten by Bill.

b. John will have {?probably/*rapidly} been finishing the job.

---

⑥⓪ ⑪的例句與合法度判斷採自 Jackendoff (1972:74)。

⑥① ⑱的例句與合法度判斷採自 Jackendoff (1972:81)。

c. John will be {*probably/*rapidly} being beaten by Bill.

d. John has been {*probably/*rapidly} being beaten by Bill.

只有少數副詞（如 'merely, utterly, virtually, simply'）似乎可以出現於「附加語 α」（句中）、「附加語 β」（句中中）、「附加語 γ」（句中尾）的位置。但是「附加語 β」（句中中）的位置還是有點不自然，例如：❷

⑲ a. John will *merely* have been beaten by Bill.

b. ?John will have *merely* been beaten by Bill.

c. John will have been *merely* beaten by Bill.

d. John has *merely* been being beaten by Bill.

e. ?John has been *merely* being beaten by Bill.

f. John has been being *merely* beaten by Bill.

這類副詞與小句子狀語一樣，可以出現於主語與情態助動詞的中間（即「句中首」（initial-medial）的位置），但不能出現於主語的前面（即「句首」（initial）的位置）或（大）句子的末尾（即「句尾」（end）的位置）。試比較：

⑳ a. John {*probably/evidently/clumsily/merely*} will have been beaten by Bill.

b. {*Frankly/Probably/Evidently/Clumsily/*Merely*}(,) John will have been beaten by Bill.

---

❷ ⑲的例句與合法度判斷採自 Jackendoff (1972:82)。

c. John will have been beaten by Bill {(,) *clumsily/, evidently/, probably/, *merely*}.

另一方面，這類副詞與述詞組狀語一樣，可以出現於主要語動詞與助動詞的中間(即「句中尾」的位置)，卻不能出現於述詞組或小句子的末尾(即「句尾首」(initial-end) 的位置)。試比較：

⑿ a. John will have been { *completely/savagely/merely*} beaten by Bill.

b. John will have been beaten by Bill {*completely/savagely/ *merely*}.

根據以上的觀察與討論，我們把只能出現於助動詞（包括情態、完成貌、進行貌、被動態與時制助動詞）與主要語動詞中間的狀語分析為述詞組狀語；而把可以出現於助動詞與助動詞的中間或出現於助動詞與主語中間的狀語分析為小句子狀語或大句子狀語。副詞 'merely, utterly, virtually, simply' 等一方面可以出現於助動詞與主要語動詞的中間，另一方面又可以出現於助動詞與助動詞的中間或助動詞與主語的中間，因而可以說是介於二者之間的「"騎牆"狀語」("fence-sitting" adverb)。㊿

㊿ 英語的否定詞 'not' 在「限定子句」(finite clause) 裏面出現於助動詞(包括情態助動詞、完成貌助動詞('have')、進行貌助動詞('be')、被動態助動詞 ('be')、一般 'be' 動詞 (在英式英語裏還包括表示 '所有' 的 'have' 動詞) 與時制助動詞 'do')) 的後面，但是在「非限定子句」(non-finite clause;包括「不定子句」(infinitival clause)、「動名子句」(gerundive clause)、「分詞子句」(participial clause)) 與「假設子句」(subjunctive clause) 裏則分別出現於「不定式動詞」(infinitve;'to V')、「動名詞」(gerund;'V-ing')、「現在分詞」(present participles;'V-ing') 以及「動詞原式」(→)

（——）(root form; 'V') 的前面。這些句法現象可以由「動詞提升」（Verb Raising) 的移位規律來處理(Pollock (1988) 擬設以否定詞'not'為主要語的最大投影(稱爲「否定詞組」(negative phrase))，並受「小句子」主要語時制語素的支配，而主要語否定詞本身則支配述詞組)：(i) 情態助動詞出現於小句子主要語時制語素(T)下面，並與屈折語素(「過去式」(past tense; '-ed') 與「非過去式」(non-past tense; '-(s)')) 合成過去式與非過去式情態助動詞，因而出現於 'not' 的前面；(ii)助動詞'have' 與 'be' 必須從動詞組主要語的位置提升移入時制語素的位置，以便獲得時制（這就是所謂的「Have/Be 提升」(Have/Be Raising))，因而亦出現於'not'的前面；(iii) 其他一般限定動詞不能提升移入時制語素的位置，其肯定式由「限定時制標誌」(finite tense marker;即'-(s)'與'-ed') 降下移入主要語動詞的位置，以便指派時制（這就是所謂的「詞綴移位」(Affix Movement))；而其否定式則由助動詞 'do' 出現於時制語素的位置，以便獲得時制，因而助動詞'do'亦出現於'not' 的前面；(iv) 非限定動詞(包括一般動詞、助動詞 'have' 與(助)動詞 'be')亦不移入時制語素的位置，而由「非限定時制標誌」(non-finite tense marker；包括「不定式標誌」(infinitive marker) 'to'、「動名詞標誌」(gerund marker) 與 「現在分詞標誌」(present participle marker) '-ing') 降下移入主要語動詞的位置，因而'not' 出現於這些非限定動詞的前面；(v)「假設法動詞」(subjunctive verb; 即出現於「假設子句」(如 'John insisted that Mary (not) {be/come} here with us'裏的動詞原式)在時制語素底下含有「空號助動詞」(empty auxiliary ;參 Pollock (1988:401))，所以亦不移入時制語素的位置，因而'not'亦出現於假設法動詞的前面；(vi)「祈使句動詞」(imperative verb; 即出現於「祈使句」(如 *Finish* your work before I come back!' 與 '*Be* a good sport!' 裏的動詞原式)在時制語素底下含有特殊的「祈使語素」(Imp)，並在這個位置允許助動詞 'do' 的出現。試比較：

(i) John {*will/can/may/must/should*} not go with Mary.

(ii) a. John {has*n't* been/is*n't* living/is*n't*} here.

　　 b. Mary has*n't* (got) any money.

(iii) a. John {work*ed*/works} here.

　　 b. John {did*n't*/doesn't} love here any more.

(iv) a. For John {*not* to have left/?*to have *not* left} disturbs me. (Jackendoff (1972:78))

　　 b. For John {*not* to be/?*to be *not*} the man I'm
　　（——）

⑫到⑬的例句顯示：我們的分析會衍生似合語法的 (a) 句，而不會衍生不合語法的(c)句，可是卻無法衍生 Pollock(1988) 認為可以接受的 (b) 句，即「被割裂的不定詞」(split infinitive) ❻。Pollock (1988:381) 指出：⑫c與⑭c的例句都分別比⑫c與

───────────

(一)　　　looking for disturbs me. (Jackendoff (1972:78))

   c. {*Not* to be/?To be *not*} happy is a prerequisite for writing novels. (Pollock (1988:376))

   d. {*Not* to have had/(?)To have *not* had} a happy childhood is a prerequisite for writing novels. (Pollock (1988:376))

   e. {*Not* to be/?To be *not*} arrested under such a circumstance is a miracle. (Pollock (1988:376))

   f. John {*not* being/?being *not*} fond of beer, he ordered white wine.

（v）a. We suggest that you {*not* see/*see *not*} our daughter any more.

   b. It is absolutely necessary that he {*not* be/?be *not*} here when she visits us.

（vi）a. {Do*n't* (you) have finished/*Have *not* finished} your work when I come back! Pollock (1988:401))

   b. {Do*n't* be/*Be *not*} silly! (Pollock (1988:401))

   c. {Do*n't* (you) be/*Be *not*} singing when I come back! (Pollock (1988:401))

   d. *Do* be a good sport! Lend me five dollars. (Pollock (1988:401))

   e. Do*n't* you *not* be working when I come home! (Pollock (1988:fn.34))

   f. Do*n't* you *not* know your lesson when I come home! (Pollock (1988: fn.34))

⑱ c 的例句好，而 ⑬ c 的例句幾乎與 ⑬ b 的例句一樣好；可見英語裏動詞的提升基本上限於‘be’動詞與‘have’動詞。❻

⑫ {a.(?)*Hardly* to speak/b. To *hardly* speak/c. *To speak *hardly*} Italian after years of hard work means you have no gift for languages.

⑬ {a. (?)*Often* to look/b. To *often* look/c. *To look *often*} sad during one's honeymoon is rare.

⑭ {a. (?) *Almost* to forget/b. To *almost* forget /c. *To forget *almost*} one's name doesn't happen frequently.

⑮ {a. (?)*Completely* to lose/b. To *completely* lose/c. *To lose *completely*} one's head over pretty students is dangerous!

⑯ I believe John {a. (?)*often* to sound/b. to *often* sound/c. *to sound *often*} sarcastic.

⑰ I believe John { a. (?)*often* to be/b. to *often* be/c. (?)to be *often*} sarcastic.

⑱ John is said {a. (?)*seldom* to arrive/b. to *seldom* arrive/c.*to arrive *seldom*} on time at his ap-

---

❻ ⑫到⑬的例句與合法度判斷，除(a)句是由我們增添以外，均來自 Pollock（1988：381-382）。

❻ Pollock（1988）把這些例句裏動詞的移位稱爲「短程動詞移位」 (Short Verb Movement)，與我們所討論的「動詞提升」並不完全相同。

pointments.

⑫⑨ John is said {a. (?)*seldom* to be/b. to *seldom* be/c. (?)to be *seldom*} on time at his appointments.

⑬⓪ The English were then said {a. (?)*never* to have/ b. to *never* have/c. to have *never*} had it so good.

述詞組含有域外論元（即出現於述詞組指示語位置的主語名詞組）、述語動詞（由動詞組的主要語動詞提升移入述詞組的主要語述詞的位置）與域內論元（即出現於動詞組指示語位置的賓語名詞組，以及出現於動詞組補述語位置的補語介詞組），因而形成句子的「命題」（proposition）。述詞組狀語則以這個命題為陳述的對象，因而具有下列幾點句法與語意功能。

（一）述詞組狀語與動詞組狀語或句子（包括小句子與大句子）狀語在同一個句子裏出現的時候，述詞組狀語與主要語動詞的語意關係雖不如動詞組狀語的緊密，卻比句子狀語來得密切。因此，述詞組狀語總是出現於動詞組狀語的外圍，而句子狀語則又出現於述詞組狀語的外圍。試比較：

⑬① a. John has *often* been seeing Mary *secretly in her apartment for the past two months, evidently*.

b. *Evidently*, John has *often* been *secretly* seeing Mary *in her apartment for the past two months*.

⑬② a. John kissed Mary *gently on the cheek on the platform when the train arrived*.

· 185 ·

b. *When the train arrived*, John *gently* kissed Mary *on the cheek on the platform*.

(二)在「動詞組提前」與「Though 移位」中，動詞組狀語常隨主要語動詞與補述語移位；述詞組狀語則可以隨同移位，也可以留在原位；而句子狀語則比較不容易隨同移位。請參照例句㊶到㋁。

(三)動詞組狀語與述詞組狀語或句子狀語在同一個句子裏出現的時候，述詞組狀語比動詞組狀語更容易移到句首；而句子狀語又比述詞組狀語更容易移到句首。請參照㋂到㋆的例句。試比較：

(133) a. The burglar *hastily* opened the safe *with a blowtorch after midnight, evidently*.

b. *Evidently*, the burglar *hastily* opened the safe *with a blowtorch after midnight*.

c. *Evidently, after midnight* (,) the burglar *hastily* opened the safe *with a blowtorch*.

d. ?*After midnight*(,) the burglar *hastily* opened the safe *with a blowtorch, evidently*.

e. ?**Evidently, after midnight, with a blowtorch*(,) the burglar *hastily* opened the safe.

f. **With a blowtorch*, the burglar *hastily* opened the safe *after midnight, evidently*.

g. ***Evidently, after midnight, with a blowtorch, hastily* the burglar opened the safe.

h. ***Hastily,* the burglar opened the safe *with a blowtorch after midnight, evidently.*

(四)句子狀語可以出現於否定句的句首或「否定範域」之外，而動詞組狀語與述詞組狀語則不能出現於否定句的句首或否定範域之外。試比較：

⑭ a. {*Evidently,/After midnight(,)*} the burglar did*n't* open the safe.

b. ?**With a blowtorch(,)* the burglar did*n't* open the safe.

c. ?**Hastily(,)* the burglar did*n't* open the safe.

同樣的，句子狀語可以出現於疑問句的句首或「疑問範域」之外，而動詞組狀語與述詞組狀語則不能出現於疑問句的句首或疑問範域之外。試比較：

⑮ a. {*Frankly,/After midnight(,)*} did the burglar open the safe?

b. ?**With a blowtorch(,)* did the burglar open the safe?

c. ?**Hastily(,)* did the burglar open the safe?

這些事實顯示：動詞組狀語與述詞組狀語在信息結構中常代表新的信息，並在句法結構中受到否定詞（Neg）與疑問詞（Q;＋WH）的「m統制」。

(五)動詞組狀語與述詞組狀語在「句子照應」中必須包含在「代句詞」'it, that, so' 裏面。試比較：

⑯ a *Evidently,* 〔the burglar opened the safe *with a*

blowtorch]ᵢ, but nobody had expected *it*ᵢ.

b. (*"Surprisingly,* [the burglar *easily* opened the safe *with a screwdriver*]ᵢ.") *"That*ᵢ's unbelievable!"

c. *Probably,* [the burglar opened the safe *with a blowtorch*]ᵢ, *after midnight,* but *it*ᵢ wouldn't have happened before midnight.

d. (*"Certainly*(,) [John will pass the exam *with flying colors*]ᵢ.") "I don't think *so*ᵢ."

（六）正如有時候動詞組狀語與述詞組狀語之間的界限不很明確，有時候述詞組狀語與（小）句子狀語之間的界限也不十分清楚。出現於主要語左方的狀語固然可以根據能否出現於「附加語 α」（「句中」）與「附加語 γ」（「句中尾」）的位置來區別（小）句子狀語與述詞組狀語，但是出現於主要語右方的狀語則可能兼屬述詞組狀語與（小）句子狀語而產生「歧義」。例如，⑬的例句可以有（i）與（ii）兩種不同的解釋，因而分別具有⑬a與⑬b的詞組結構分析；即 'on Sunday' 在⑬a 出現於述詞組，而在⑬b 則出現於小句子。❻

⑬ John had kissed Mary on Sunday.

(i) 'John 在星期天(那一天)吻了Mary。'

(ii) 'John 在星期天(的時候)已經吻了Mary。'

---

❻ 參 Andrews (1982)。

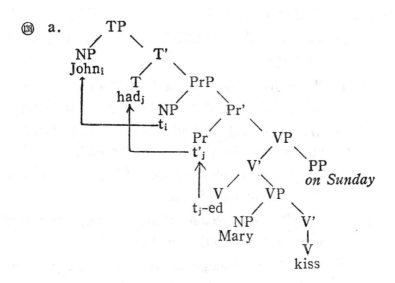

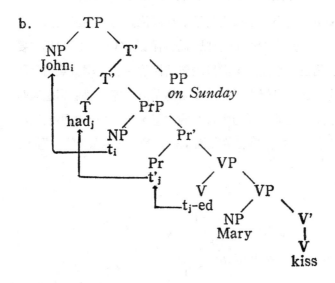

(138) a.

b.

⑬a與⑬b 這兩種不同的深層結構可以經過「準分裂句」、「動詞組提前」與「Though 移位」而分別變成⑲a,b、⑭a,b 與⑭a,b 的表層結構。試比較：

⑲ a. What John had done is kiss Mary *on Sunday*.

b. What John had done *on Sunday* is kiss Mary.

⑭ a. We thought John had kissed Mary *on Sunday*, and kissed Mary *on Sunday* he had.

b. We thought John had kissed Mary, and kissed Mary he had *on Sunday*.

⑭ a. Kiss Mary *on Sunday* though he had, John still went out with other girls.

b. Kiss Mary though he had *on Sunday*, John still went out with other girls.

六、出現於小句子與大句子附加語位置的副詞與狀語

「小句子」(S; TP) 以「時制語素」(tense; T)為主要語，並以述詞組為補述語，而以表層結構的主語名詞組為指示語。小句子的附加語可能出現於主要語的左方（卽主語名詞組與時制語素的中間；也就是「句中首」的位置，如⑭a），也可能出現於主要語的右方（卽述詞組的後面；也就是「句尾首」的位置，如⑭b）。試比較：

⑭ a.

```
              TP
            /    \
          NP      T'
         John    /  \
             Adjt     T'
           sometimes  /  \
                     T    PrP
                   takes  a walk in the park
```

b.

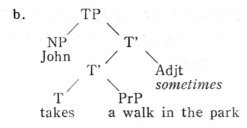

另一方面，「大句子」（S'; CP）則以「補語連詞」（complementizer; 'that, whether (...or not), if(...or not), for' ❻⑦，但也可能留為「空節」（empty node）❻⑧為主要語，並以小句子為補述語，而以「空節」為指示語❻⑨。大句子的附加語可能出現於

---

❻⑦ 因而會衍生下面的例句：

(i) I know *that Charles loves Suzanne.*

(ii) John wondered {*whether/if*} *Mary would answer his letter.*

(iii) Mary was not sure *whether PRO to tell her parents or not.*

(iv) John wanted very much *for Mary to have a date with him.*

❻⑧ 補語連詞如果是「空節」並且含有「疑問」（Q;〔＋wh〕）這個句法屬性，那麼就可以成為助動詞在「主語與助動詞調位」（Subject-Aux Inversion）中的「移入點」（landing site），例如：

(i) {*Will/Can/Did*} he *t* come?

(ii) Where *have* you *t* been?

在「否定倒序」中，補語連詞也可以成為助動詞的移入點，例如：

(iii) Never {*have/did*} I *t* put myself in his position before.

❻⑨ 這個空節可以成為「wh詞組」（wh-phrase）的移入點，例如：

(i) *Where*ᵢ do you come from *t*ᵢ?

(ii) *Why*ᵢ not bring your family with you *t*ᵢ?

這個空節還可能在深層結構衍生「主題」（topic）或成為主題的移入點，例如：

(i) *As for fish,* John likes to eat tunar.

(ii) *Mary*ᵢ, I've never met {*her*ᵢ/*t*ᵢ} before.

主要語的左方（即補語連詞的前面；也就是「句首」的位置，如⑭a），也可能出現於主要語的右方（即小句子的後面，也就是「句尾」的位置，如⑭b）。試比較：

⑭ a.

```
              CP
            /    \
          XP      C'
          e      /  \
              Adjt    C'
            Frankly, / \
                   C    TP
                    John is not very clever
```

b.

```
              CP
            /    \
          XP      C'
          e      /  \
              C'    Adjt
             / \    , frankly
            C   TP
            John is not very clever
```

　　由於小句子狀語與大句子狀語出現的位置很接近，我們必須設法區別這兩類狀語。一般說來，表示「頻率」（Frequency; 如 'twice (a day), every day, daily, occasionally, sometimes, from time to time, as often as I can, whenever I have time' 等）、「量詞」（如 'all, both, each'）、「處所」（Location; 如 'indoors, up here, over there, at the zoo, in the kitchen, three blocks away, where the post office used to be, wherever they could settle down' 等）、「時間」（Time; 如 'now, then, at 9 o'clock, on Sunday, in May, during {the vacation/the time (that) we were there, { before/after } { leaving for Japan/they left for Japan}, when {arriving at the airport/he arrived at the airport }, while { waiting for the interview/she was waiting for the interview}'等)、「起點」(Source; 如 'from Taipei, out of the kitchen; from seven'等)、「終點」(Goal; 如 'to Tainan, to the kitchen, into the room; till nine' 等)、「途徑」(Path; 如 'a long way, the whole distance; two hours, the whole morning, for three weeks, from Taipei to Tainan, from seven to nine, from Sunday till Monday' 等)、「目的」(Purpose; 如 'for a better job, to get a better job, so that he can get a better job, in order (for his wife) to get a better job' 等)、「原因」(Cause; 如 'because of the rain, out of charity, for fear of heart disease, on account of their high mortgage payments; because he was sick' 等) 常出現於小句子附加語的位置，但也可以出現於大句子附加語的位置 ⑩ ；而表示「理由」(Reason; 如 'because that's how people are, since you are so clever' 等) 的狀語多出現於大句子附加語的位置。例如，不能越過「句界」(sentence boundary) 而移位的「從名詞組

---

⑩　表示「時間關係」(Time-relationship) 的副詞（如 '(not) yet, already, just, just now, by now, at present, for the moment, still, any longer, any more'等）與完成貌或進行貌的語意關係甚為密切，二者之間常有「依存關係」(dependency)，因而宜分析爲出現於述詞組附加語的位置。

移出」(Extraposition from NP) 可以把修飾主要語名詞的關係子句、同位子句、介詞組等移到時間狀語的後面（即加接到小句子的右端），卻不能移到理由狀語的後面。試比較：**❼**

⑭　a. Many people *who were not very sick* had checkups *before coming to us*.

　　b. [CP[TP[TP Many people *t*i had checkups before coming to us] [cp who were not very sick]i]].

⑭⑤　a. Many people *who were very sick* lied to us *because that's how people are*.

　　b. *[CP[CP[TP Many people *t*i lied to us] [pp because that's how people are]❼ [cp who were very sick]i]].

同時，表示理由的 'why' 是唯一可以出現於否定句的句首或否定範域之外的疑問狀語。試比較：

⑭⑥　a. {*Why*/*When/*Where/*How} did*n't* John go?

　　b. {*Why*/*When/*Where/*How } *not* paint your house purple?

　　c. {*Why*/*When/*Where/*How} *not*?

因此，如果我們把表示理由的狀語詞組與其他狀語詞組加以區別而分析為出現於小句子之外，而否定詞的否定範域則只能及於小

---

❼　例句⑭a，⑭⑤a與合法度判斷採自 Williams (1975:258)。

❼　我們把「從屬連詞」(subordinate conjunction) 分析為介詞的次類，因而把從屬子句分析為介詞與小句子合成的介詞組。但是 Lasnik & Saito (1989) 則把從屬子句分析為由補語連詞與小句子合成。

句子，那麼上面⑭與⑮的例句裏理由狀語與其他狀語之間以及⑯的例句裏疑問詞'why'與其他疑問詞之間在句法表現上的差異就獲得了自然合理的詮釋。❼❸另外，下面⑰a,b裏出現的'because'子句似乎分別充當小句子狀語(「原因」)與大句子狀語(「理由」)。

---

❼❸ 英語疑問詞'why'還有下列幾點「特異性」(idiosyncracy)：(i) 其他疑問詞都有相對的「不定代詞」(indefinite pronoun) 或有關連的不定副詞 ('someone/somebody, something, somewhere/someplace, sometime, somehow, somewhat')，而唯獨 'why' 沒有 (*somewhy/*somereason)；(ii)其他的疑問詞都與'-ever' 合成「複合詞」(compound) (如'whoever, whatever, whichever, whenever, wherever, however')，而唯獨 'why' 沒有 ('*whyever')；(iii) 其他疑問詞常與 'ever' 連用以加強疑問語氣 (如'How *ever* did he escape?', 'What *ever* are you doing?')，而 'why' 的這種用法則似乎較為少見 ('??Why *ever* did he escape?', '??Why *ever* are you doing this to me?')；(iv)其他疑問詞都常出現於「wh不定子句」(wh-infinitival) (如'I don't know {*who(m)* PRO to ask for help/*which* (one) PRO to choose/*whose* book PRO to borrow/*whether* PRO to go or (to) stay/*when* PRO to start/*where* PRO to go/*how* PRO to do it}')，而'why'則很少出現於不定子句 (我們至今只能蒐集到兩個用例，'In this section, he tells the teacher not only *how to do certain things* but also *why to do them in certain ways*' (Yao Shen)與'The questions, *how* and *what to read* rise out of a far deeper one, namely, *why to read*'；但這裏的「why 不定子句」似乎是在與別的「wh 不定子句」對比之下所產生的特殊用法)。在這些有關 'why' 的特異性中，有大部分可能與'why'在X標槓結構中出現的特殊位置有關。

試比較：**⓻**

⑭⑦ a. We have no electricity (,) *because there's a power failure.*

　　b. I have no money in my bank account, *because I checked this morning.*

'because' 的小句子狀語用法與大句子狀語用法在句法功能上有下列幾點差別：(參 Quirk et al. (1985:1073-1074)。)

　　(一)充當小句子狀語的'because' 子句可以用來回答由主要子句得來的'why'問句，充當大句子狀語的'because'子句不能用來回答由主要子句得來的'why'問句。試比較：

⑭⑧ a. "*Why* do you have no electricity?"

　　　"*Because there's a power failure.*"

　　b. ##'*Why* do you have no money in your bank account?"**⓻**

　　　"*Because I checked this morning.*"

⑭⑦b句的'because'子句實際上是修飾⑭⑨a句的'I know that..'或說明 'I know that...' 的理由，因此⑭⑨ b的對話才是得體的對話。

⑭⑨ a. *I know that* I have no money in my bank

⓻ 例句⑭⑦與有關的語意解釋採自 Quirk et al.（1985:1072-1074）。Quirk et al. (1985) 把小句子狀語用法稱爲 "adjunct" 或 "subjunct"，而把大句子狀語用法稱爲 "style disjunct"。

⓻ 符號'##'表示這裏的對話「不得體」（infelicitous）或「不適當」（inappropriate)。

account, *because I checked this morning*.

b. *"How do you know that* you have no money in your bank account?"

"Because I checked this morning."

(二)充當小句子狀語的 'because' 子句可以 (加接小句子左端而) 移到句首，而充當大句子狀語的 'because' 子句則 (本已出現於大句子附加語的位置，所以) 不能 (加接小句子左端而) 移到句首。試比較：

⑤ a. *Because there's a power failure,* we have no electricity.

b. **Because I checked this morning,* I have no money in my bank account.

(三)充當小句子狀語的 'because' 子句可以互相「對等連接」 (coordinately conjoined)，而充當大句子狀語的 'because' 子句也可以互相對等連接；但是充當小句子狀語的 'because' 子句與充當大句子狀語的 'because' 子句卻不能對等連接。試比較：

⑤ a. He likes them *because they are always helpful*; he likes them *because they are really nice people*.

b. He likes them, *because his wife told me so*; he likes them, *because I have often seen him in their company*.

c. He likes them *because they are always helpful and because they are really nice people*.

    d. He likes them, *because his wife told me so and because I have often seen him in their company.*

    e. *He likes them *because they are always helpful and because his wife told me so.*

（四）小句子狀語與大句子狀語在同一個句子裏出現的時候，大句子狀語必須出現於小句子狀語的外圍。試比較：

⑮₂ a. ?He likes them *because they are always helpful, because his wife told me so.*

    b. *He likes them, *because his wife told me so, because they are always helpful.*

（五）大句子狀語必須以逗號與主要子句隔開，或自成獨立的「語調單元」（tone unit）；而小句子狀語則不必標逗號，也不必自成獨立的語調單元。在下面⑮₃到⑮₅的例句裏所出現的「理由」、「條件」與「讓步」狀語詞組都在（a）句裏充當小句子狀語，而在（b）句裏則充當大句子狀語。試比較：❼₆

⑮₃ a. *Since you know Latin,* you should be able to translate the inscription.

    b. I'm up to my ears in debt, *since you ask me.*❼₇

⑮₄ a. We'll take along Sharon(,) *if she's ready.*

    b. We can do with some more butter, *if you're*

---

❼₆ ⑮₃、⑮₄以及⑮₅的例句均採自 Quirk et al. (1985:1072-1074)。

❼₇ ⑮₃b的 'since' 子句可以出現於句首（即大句子左方附加語的位置），即 '*Since you ask me,* I'm up to my ears in debt'。參Quirk et al. (1985:1074, fn.c)。

in the kitchen.

⑮ a. She enjoys driving(,) *though she doesn't like to drive in heavy traffic.*

b. He deserved the promotion, *though it's not my place to say so.*❼❽

同樣的，在下面⑯的例句裏出現的狀語詞組都可以分析爲大句子狀語。試比較：❼❾

⑯ a. *While we're on the subject,* why didn't you send your children to a public school?

b. The latest unemployment figures are encouraging, *as it were.*

c. I'm in charge here, *in case you don't know.*

d. *Speaking of the devil,* here comes my nephew.

e. *Stated bluntly,* I have legal control over their estate.

f. *As far as its economy is concerned,* Germany shows signs of improvement.

g. *With John gone,* havoc will break loose.

h. *There being no taxi,* I had to walk home.

i. *Whether you believe or not,* our daughter is in love!

---

❼❽　⑮b 的 'though' 子句也可以出現於句首。

❼❾　例句⑯ a-f 與⑯ j 分別採自 Quirk et al.（1985:1073-1074）與 Jackendoff（1972:58）。

j. {*In all probability/In my opinion/According to Albert/In spite of his mother's admonitions/In order to kill his mother/By going to Cincinnati/(Being) sick at heart/Having lost the game/Now that he is married to Sally/To tell the truth/Taking all things into consideration*}, Bill has ruined his chances of an inheritance.

⑤⑦裏的「挿入句」(parenthetical expression) 似乎也可以分析爲大句子狀語。試比較：**⑳**

⑤⑦ a. John is, {*I think/I don't doubt*}, a fink.

b. We must continue to pay taxes, *I assume.*

c. The painters came, *I claim,* on Friday.

d. John usually has, {*I think/we suspect*}, been examined by the doctor.

e. John is a fink, {*Helen thinks/Margaret believes*}.

至於出現於⑤⑧裏句首的「時間」、「處所」與「情狀」狀語，固然可以分析爲大句子狀語，但也可以分析爲述詞組狀語或小句子狀語經過移位與加接而出現於小句子的左端來充當「論旨副詞」(thematic adverb)。試比較：

⑤⑧ a. John lost his wallet {*at 6:00/in the garden*}.

a'. {*At 6:00/In the garden*}, John lost his wallet *t.*

---

⑳ ⑤⑦與⑤⑧的例句分別採自 Jackendoff (1972:97-98,94)。

b. Mary visited the acquarium *yesterday.*

b'. *Yesterday,* Mary visited the acquarium *(t).*

c. It *suddenly* started to rain.

c'. *Suddenly,* it *(t)* started to rain.

d. John *usually* writes letters in red ink.

d'. *Usually* John *(t)* writes letters in red ink.

一般說來，出現於大句子附加語位置的狀語詞組都在「句子照應」中不包含於 'it, that, so' 等代句詞裏面，例如：**⑧**

⑮⑨ a. {*Frankly/To tell the truth/Probably/In all probability/If I may say so/By the way/With his mother-in-law living with them}*, 〔John hates Mary〕ᵢ, although you may not believe *it*ᵢ.

b. "{*In all likelihood/In my opinion/Frankly speaking/To my regret/Stated bluntly/Medically /Tragically}*, 〔Mary is an alchoholic〕ᵢ."

"*That*ᵢ's quite shocking!"

但是在例句⑮⑨裏出現於句首的狀語詞組則可以包含於代句詞裏面，也可以出現於代句詞外面（參 Takami (1984)）。試比較：

⑯⓪ a. 〔{*At 6:00/In the garden}*, John lost his wallet〕ᵢ but nobody realized *it*ᵢ.

a'. {*At 6:00/In the garden}*, 〔John lost his wallet〕ᵢ but nobody realized *it*ᵢ {then/there}.

---

⑧ 參 Takami (1984)。

　　　b. 〔*Yesterday* Mary visited the acquarium〕$_i$,
　　　　though her friends didn't know *it*$_i$.

　　　b'. *Yesterday* 〔Mary visited the acquarium〕$_i$, she
　　　　had long wanted *it*$_i$.

　　　c. 〔*Suddenly* it started to rain〕$_i$, but they say *it*$_i$
　　　　often happens here at this time of the year.

　　　c'. *Suddenly* 〔it started to rain〕$_i$, but nobody had
　　　　expected *it*$_i$ on such a fine day.

　　　d. 〔*Usually* John writes letters in red ink〕$_i$, and
　　　　everyone takes *it*$_i$ for granted.

　　　d'. *Usually* 〔John writes letters in red ink〕$_i$,
　　　　though his wife criticizes *it*$_i$.

在(a,b,c,d)句中這些狀語詞組都充當「焦點主題」(focus topic)
，因代表新信息而重讀；而在(a',b',c',d') 句中這些狀語詞組則
充當「論旨主題」(theme topic)，因代表舊信息而不重讀。同時
注意：這些狀語詞組出現於句尾的時候，前面不能標逗號或自成
一個獨立的語調單元。

⑩　a. ?*John lost his wallet, {*at* 6:00/*in the garden*}.

　　b. ?*Mary visited the acquarium, *yesterday*.

　　c. ?*It started to rain, *suddenly*.

　　d. ?*John writes letters in red ink, *usually*,

除了介詞組、從屬子句、不定詞組（如⑯j句）、分詞詞組（如⑯
d,e,j 句）、「獨立詞組」(absolute phrase; 如⑯d, f, g 句)
可以充當大句子狀語以外，還有一羣副詞可以修飾整個小句子而

出現於大句子附加語的位置。修飾大句子的「整句副詞」（sentence adverb; sentential adverb）可以根據語意與句法功能分爲下列幾類：

(A)「說話者取向」（speaker-oriented）的「體裁副詞」(style adverb)❷；如 'frankly, honestly, truthfully, confidentially, seriously, bluntly, crudely, briefly, broadly; to be frank, to speak frankly, frankly speaking, put frankly, if I may be frank, if I can speak frankly, in all frankness; by the way, to tell the truth' 等。

(B)「說話者取向」的「觀點副詞」(viewpoint adverb)❸；如 'geographically, ethnically, politically, economically, mathematically, linguistically, sociologically, medically, musically, technically, physically, visually, theatrically, ideologically, statistically; weatherwise, programwise; psychologically speaking, in one's opinion' 等。

(C)「說話者取向」的「認知副詞」(epistemic adverb)❹；如 'probably, possibly, maybe, perhaps, most likely, clearly, evidently, obviously, certainly, surely, assuredly,

---

❷ Bellert (1977) 把這類副詞稱爲「語用副詞」(pragmatic adverb)。

❸ Quirk et al. (1985:620-621) 把這類副詞稱爲表示「眞實度」(degree of truth) 的「內涵狀語」(content disjunct)，而 Ernst (1984b, 1985) 則稱此爲「領域副詞」(domain adverb)。

❹ Greenbaum (1969) 與 Schreiber (1971) 把這類副詞稱爲「情態副詞」(modal adverb)。

undoubtedly, doubtless; in all probability, in all likelihood, of course; sure enough, to be sure'等。

(D)「說話者取向」的「評價副詞」(evaluative adverb)[85]；如 'regrettably, surprisingly, amazingly, unexpectedly, (un)fortunately, luckily, happily, tragically, ideally, absurdly, ironically, annoyingly, hopefully, significantly, appropriately, oddly, strangely, curiously, naturally; to my regret, to our surprise, (what is) more important' 等。

(E)「主語取向」(subject-oriented)的「屬性副詞」(epithet adverb)[86]；如 'wisely, cleverly, intelligently, foolishly, stupidly, clumsily, carelessly, prudently, artfully, tactfully, creatively, graciously, bravely, rudely, rightly, correctly, wrongly' 等。

(F)「主語取向」的「觀感副詞」(mental attitude adverb)[87]；如 'delightedly, sadly, enthusiastically, anxiously, angrily, indignantly, boldly, desperately, frantically, nervously, eagerly, calmly, reluctantly, obstinately, absent-mindedly, resolutely, grudgingly, willingly, purposely' 等。

---

[85] 這是 Greenbaum (1969) 與 Schreiber (1971) 的用語。

[86] Quirk et al. (1985:621-623) 把(D)與(E)兩類狀語合稱為表示「價值判斷」(value judgment) 的「內涵狀語」。

[87] 這是 Ernst (1984b) 的用語。

這些整句副詞在句法與語意功能上有下列幾個共同的特點。

(一)這些整句副詞可以出現於「句首」(卽大句子裏附加語)的位置，並在後面常標以逗號或自成一個獨立的語調單元，例如：

⑯ a. {*Frankly/Honestly/Confidentially*}, John doesn't want to marry her.

   b. {*Politically/Morally/Linguistically*}, such an idea is pretty strange.

   c. {*Probably/Certainly/Evidently*}, John will pass the exam.

   d. {*Regrettably/Unfortunately/Tragically*}, hundreds of people were killed in the accident.

   e. {*Clumsily/Carelessly/Tactfully*}(,) Mary dropped her cup of coffee.❽❽

   f. {*Obstinately/Desperately/Reluctantly*}, Harry kept pushing his cause.

(二)這些副詞都可以出現於「句中首」(卽小句子裏左方附加語)的位置，前後不一定標逗號，但是通常自成獨立的語調單元，例如：

⑯ a. ?John, {*frankly/honestly/confidentially*}, doesn't want to marry her. ❽❾

   b. Such an idea, {*politically/morally/linguisti-*

---

❽❽ 整句副詞後面的逗號加上括弧是根據 Jackendoff (1972:49) 裏(3.2) 的例句。

　　　　　　 cally}, is pretty strange.⑧⑨

　c. John { *probably/certainly/evidently* } will pass
　　 the exam.

　d. Hundreds of people {*regrettably/unfortunately/*
　　 tragically} were killed in the accident.

　e. Mary { *clumsily/carelessly/tactfully* } dropped
　　 her cup of coffee.

　f. Harry {*obstinately/desperately/reluctantly*} kept
　　 pushing his cause.

　（三）這些副詞可以出現於「句中」（卽述詞組裏「附加語 α」）
的位置，「體裁副詞」與「觀點副詞」的前後比較常標逗號，也比
較容易自成獨立的語調單元，例如：

⑯⑷　a. ??John will, { *frankly/honestly/confidentially* },
　　　　 want to marry her.

　　　b. ??Such an idea will (,) { *politically/morally/*
　　　　 linguistically}, be pretty strange.

─────────────────────

⑧⑨　Ernst (1985:10) 認為觀點副詞不能出現於句中首的位置，並且自認
　　並無適當的方法來解釋這個問題。但是出現於句中首位置的體裁副詞
　　與觀點副詞，如果後面標以逗號或自成獨立的語調單元，那麼似乎可
　　以接受，例如：

　（ⅰ）John, { *frankly/frankly speaking* }, doesn't want to
　　　　 marry her.

　（ⅱ）Such an idea, { *politically/judging from a political*
　　　　 point of view}, is pretty strange.

　　　參註⑨⑩。

c. John will {*probably/certainly/evidently* } pass the exam.

d. Hundreds of people will {*regrettably/unfortunately/tragically*} be killed in case of an accident.

e. Mary will {*tactfully/artfully/dramatically* } dropped her cup of coffee, I'm sure.

f. Harry will {*obstinately/desperately/reluctantly*} kept pushing his cause.

(四)這些副詞除了「主語取向」的屬性副詞與觀感副詞以外，都可以出現於「句尾」（即大句子裏右方附加語）的位置，並在前面常標逗號或自成獨立的語調單元❾，例如：

⑯ a. John doesn't want to marry her, {*frankly/honestly/confidentially*}.

---

❾ 在「整句副詞」的各種句法表現中，體裁副詞與觀點副詞常自成一類（甲類），評價、屬性與觀感副詞則另成一類（丙類），而認知副詞則介於這兩類之間（乙類）。這是由於丙類副詞係針對小句子命題「有所陳述」（be predicated of）或「有所論斷」（make an assertion about）；因此，這些副詞可以說是以小句子為主語的「語意述語」（semantic predicate）。乙類副詞雖然也對小句子命題有所陳述，但並非針對命題內容本身提出評價或觀感，而只是就命題所描述的事態或事件之可能發生與否表示認知情態而已。至於甲類副詞則全無陳述或論斷的功能，而是與「說話者」言談題裁或觀點有關，或是修飾「行使動詞」（performative verb）的「語用副詞」（pragmatic adverb）而已。這三類副詞在語意功能上的微妙差異，似乎呈現於(二)、(三)、(四)、(五)、(六)幾點句法功能上的區別。

b. Such an idea is pretty strange, {*politically/ morally/linguistically*}.

c. John will pass the exam, {*probably/certainly/ evidently*}.

d. Hundreds of people were killed in the accident, {*regrettably/unfortunately/tragically*}.

e. ?Mary dropped her cup of coffee, {*clumsily/ carelessly/tactfully*}. ⑨

f. ?Harry kept pushing his cause, {*obstinately/ desperately/reluctantly*}.

（五）這些副詞都以小句子所表達的命題為陳述的對象。「說話者取向」的「體裁」、「觀點」、「評價」、「認知」副詞在語意內涵上分別表示說話者陳述命題內容時的體裁、觀點、命題內容發生與否的認知情態以及對於命題內容本身的價值判斷。因此，⑩的例句都可以「改寫」（paraphrase）成以說話者（'I, we'）為主語、以小句子命題為補語、而以整句副詞為「語用副詞」或「領域形容詞」（如⑯a,b）。或涵蓋整個補語子句的「陳述形容詞」（predicative adjective; 如⑯c,d句）的例句，例如：

⑯ a. *I tell you {frankly/honestly/confidentially}* that

John doesn't want to marry her.

b. *When we judge from a { political/moral/linguistic } point of view*, such an idea is pretty strange.

c. *I consider it { probable/certain/evident }* that John will pass the exam.

d. *I consider it {regrettable/unfortunate/tragical}* that hundreds of people are killed in the accident.

另一方面,「主語取向」的「屬性」與「觀感」副詞係表示說話者有關主語名詞組的評語或觀感;「屬性」副詞在述說的態度與語氣上似較「主觀」(subjective),而「觀感」副詞則似較「客觀」(objective)。試比較:

⑯⑦ a. *I consider it {clumsy/careless/tactful}* of Mary (for her) to drop her cup of coffee.

b. *{ Obstinacy / Desperation / Reluctance }* can be taken as a characteristic manifestation of Harry in his continuous pushing of his cause. ❷

(六)在「句子照應」中這些副詞都不包含於 'it, that, so' 等代句詞裏面,例如:

⑯⑧ a. *{ Frankly/Honestly / Confidentially }*, 〔 John doesn't want to marry her〕ᵢ, although you

---

❷ 參 Ernst (1985)。

may not believe *it*ᵢ.

b. {*Politically/Linguistically*}, 〔such an idea is pretty strange〕ᵢ, and you'd better admit *it*ᵢ.

c. { *Probably/Certainly/Evidently* }, 〔John will pass the exam〕ᵢ, and everyone expects *it*ᵢ.

d. { *Regrettably / Unfortunately / Tragically* }, 〔hundreds of people were killed in the accident〕ᵢ; *it*ᵢ is simply unbelievable.

e. { *Clumsily / Carelessly / Tactfully* }, 〔 Mary dropped her cup of coffee〕ᵢ; her boyfriend was not quite pleased about *it*ᵢ

f. (?){*Obstinately/Desperately/Reluctantly*}, 〔Harry kept pushing his cause〕ᵢ; *that*ᵢ is something I can never understand.

這些副詞通常都不代表新的或重要的信息。因此「句重音」(pitch peak) 或「對比重音」(contrastive stress)不可能落在這些副詞上面⑨⑬。這些副詞也不可能成為疑問句、否定句、分裂句或準

---

⑨⑬ 唯一的例外可能是觀感副詞，因為 'DEsperately, yet OBstinately, John kept pushing his cause'這樣的例句似乎可以接受。另外，有人認為⑯f例句裏的代句詞 'that' 亦可以包含 'obstinately, desperately, reluctantly' 等觀感副詞。 如果這些觀察正確的話，那麼觀感副詞可能是介於「整句副詞」(或「大句子狀語」；即體裁、觀點、評價、認知、屬性副詞)與「情狀副詞」(或「述詞組狀語」；如 'easily, deftly, softly, gently, roughly, safely, tightly, brightly, loudly'等)之間的「小句子狀語」。又在(A)到(F)的六類整句副詞中，越是位於前面的副詞，其修飾整句的功能越強。請參照註⑩與下面的有關討論。

分裂句的焦點。除了一些體裁與觀點副詞可能出現於疑問句與祈使句裏面以外，這些副詞也不能出現於疑問句、祈使句、間接疑問句或「控制結構」(control construction) 等。試比較：

⑯⑨ a. {*Frankly /Politically /*Probably /*Regrettably /*
   *Tactfully }, has he distanced himself from
   his former boss?❾❹

   b. {*Frankly /Politically /*Probably /*Regrettably /*
   *Tactfully}, what are the implications of that
   speech?❾❺

⑰⓪ a. {*Frankly/?*Politically/*Probably/*Regrettably/*
   *Tactfully}, contribute to the fund.

   b. {*Frankly/?*Politically/*Probably/*Regrettably/*
   *Tactfully}, don't tell him.

⑰① a. They want to know whether, {*frankly/*
   *politically/*probably /*regrettably /*tactfully},
   it is all right to contribute to the fund.

---

❾❹　參 Jackendoff (1972:84) 與 Ernst (1985)。

❾❺　Jackendoff (1972:84) 認爲認知副詞不能出現於疑問句裏面，並舉出 '*Did Frank *probably* beat all his opponents?', '*Who *certainly* finished eating dinner?', '?What has Charles *evidently* discovered?' 等例句。不過，Quirk et al. (1985:628) 卻認爲一些表示疑惑的認知副詞(如 'perhaps, possibly, conceivably') 可以出現於疑問句裏，但只能出現於「句中」的位置，例如：'Can I {*perhaps/possibly*} see her now?', 'What could he *possibly* do?'。

    b. He asked whether, {*frankly* /?**politically* / **probably*/**regrettably*/**tactfully*}, they knew anything about it.

⑫ a. John rushed into the street to pick up the little girl, {*frankly/politically/probably/regrettably/tactfully*}.

    b. *Mary told John 〔PRO to rush into the street to pick up the little girl, {*frankly/politically/probably/regrettably/tactfully*}〕.

有些整句副詞還可以在對話裏充當「回應」(response)，而不必另外加上 'yes' 或 'no'，例如：

⑬ a. "I'm going to resign." "*Seriously*?"❾❻

    b. "Are abortions very difficult?" "*Surgically*, no; but, morally, they may pose a problem."

    c. "Is he a detective?" "Well, *possibly*."

    d. "They won't be coming back." "*Unfortunately*, no."

    e. "They have returned to San Francisco." "Very *wisely*."

    f. "Is John ready to go?" "Yes, *reluctantly* so."

這些句法表現都與這些副詞之以小句子命題爲陳述的對象並且與說話者陳述命題內容時的體裁、觀點與認知情態或對命題內容本

---

❾❻ 例句⑬a, d, e 採自 Quirk et al. (1985:628)。

身的評價、評語、觀感有關。

(七)如果這些整句副詞與表示情狀的小句子狀語、述詞組或動詞組狀語連用，那麼前者的修飾範圍必須大於後者的修飾範圍；也就是說，前者必須出現於後者的外圍。**❾**

⑭ a. { *Frankly / Fortunately / Evidently* }, John has { *carefully / quickly / stealthily*} been studying the plan.

b. John {*frankly/fortunately/evidently*} has {*care-fully/quickly / stealthily* } been studying the plan.

c. John has { *carefully/quickly/stealthily* } been studying the plan, {*frankly/fortunately/evidently*}.

d. *{*Carefully/Quickly/Stealthily*}, John {*frankly/fortunately/evidently*} has been studying the plan.

---

❾ 參 Jackendoff (1972:89-91)。⑭a,b,c 句的合語法與下面(i)句的合語法相對，而⑭d,e,f句的不合語法則與下面 (ii) 句的不合語法相對。試比較：

（i）{I tell you *frankly*/It is *fortunate*/It is *evident*} that John has been { *careful/quick/stealthy* } in studying the plan.

（ii）*John has been {*careful/quick/stealthy*} in {*my telling you frankly/its being fortunate/its being evident*} that he has studied the plan.

e. *{ *Carefully / Quickly / Stealthily* }, John has {*frankly/fortunately/evidently*} been studying theplan.

f. *John {*carefully/quickly/stealthily*} has {*frankly/fortunately / evidently* } been studying the plan.

(八)這些整句副詞除了可以出現於大句子附加語的位置以外，有許多還可以出現於小句子、述詞組或動詞組附加語的位置做情狀副詞用。因此，情狀副詞常出現的位置是：「句中首」、「句中」與「句尾首」。試比較在例句⑰中出現的副詞 'clumsily, cleverly, tactfully'。這些副詞可以做「屬性副詞」使用，亦可做「情狀副詞」使用。

⑰ a. John { *clumsily/cleverly/tactfully* } *dropped his cup of coffee.*

b. John will {*clumsily/cleverly/tactfully* } dropped his cup of coffee.

c. John dropped his cup of coffee {*clumsily/cleverly/tactfully*}.

由於屬性副詞與情狀副詞都可以出現於「句中首」（如⑰a句）與「句中」（如⑰b句）的位置，所以⑰a,b兩句分別可以有⑯與⑰裏(a,b)兩種不同的解釋；而⑰c句裏出現於「句尾首」位置的副詞則只能當情狀副詞而做⑯b解。❾❽

---

❾❽ 如果這些副詞出現於句尾的位置，並標以逗號或自成獨立的語調單元（如'John dropped his coffee, {*clumsily/cleverly/tactfully*}'），那麼就只能當屬性副詞而做⑯a解。

⑯ a. I consider it {*clumsy/clever/tactful*} of John to drop his cup of coffee.

   b. John dropped his cup of coffee in a {*clumsy/ clever/tactful*} manner.

⑰ a. It will be {*clumsy/clever/tactful*} of ·John to drop his cup of coffee.

   b. The manner in which John dropps his cup of coffee will be {*clumsy/clever/tactful*}.

Ernst (1985:4) 認為觀點副詞出現於「句尾」的位置時不標逗號 ❾，因無法與出現於「句尾首」的情狀副詞分辨而產生歧義。例如⑱a的例句可做⑱b解(觀點副詞)，亦可做⑱c解(情狀副詞)。試比較：

⑱ a. We've solved many problems *financially*.

   b. *Financially*, we've solved many problems.

   c. We've solved many of our *financial* problems.

其他如體裁副詞(如 '*Frankly*, we always discuss our problems' 與 'We always discuss our problems *frankly*')、評價副詞 (如 '*Happily*, they returned home safely' 與 'They lived *happily* thereafter')、認知副詞 (如 '*Surely*, you're joking' 與 'The deer leaped *surely* from rock to rock')、觀感副詞 (如 '*Delightedly*, John abandoned his search while the robot looked for the keys' 與 'John and

---

❾ 出現於句尾的觀點副詞，似乎前面應該讀「降調」(falling tone)，因而自成獨立的語調單元。

the robot sang *delightedly*')等都可以有整句副詞與情狀副詞兩種用法。

（九）「主語取向」或「主事取向」(agent-oriented) 的屬性副詞與觀感副詞因出現於「主動句」抑或「被動句」以及出現的位置是「句中首」、「句中尾」或「句尾首」而可能有不同的解釋，例如：

⑰ a. The police {*easily/carelessly* } will arrest the thief.

　　 b. The police will {*easily/carelessly* } arrest the thief.

　　 c. The police will arrest the thief {*easily/care-lessly*}.

　　 d. The thief {*carelessly/easily*} will be arrested by the police.

　　 e. The thief will {*carelesly/easily*}be arrested by the police.

　　 f. The thief will be {*carelessly/easily* } arrested by the police.

　　 g. The thief will be arrested {*easily/carelessly*} by the police.

　　 h. The thief will be arrested by the police {*care-lessly/easily*}.

在⑰a, b, c的「主動句」裏，無論情狀副詞 'easily' 與 'carelessly' 出現於「句中首」(如(a)句)、「句中」(如(b)句)、或「句尾首」(如(c)句)都一律做 '警察會輕而易舉的抓到(或粗心大意的抓)小偷' 解。但是在⑰d, e, f, g, h 的「被動句」裏，情狀副詞在⑰d, e 兩句

裏分別出現於「句中首」(即小句子附加語)與「句中中」(即述詞組附加語)的位置時卻做‘小偷會因粗心大意(或很容易的)被警察抓到’解。同樣的,情狀副詞在⑰f,g分別出現於「句中尾」的左右方(即動詞組左方附加語與右方附加語)兩個位置時做‘小偷會被警察輕而易舉(或粗心大意)的抓到’解,因而與⑰a,b,c同義⑩。至於⑰h情狀副詞出現於「句尾首」的例句,則似乎‘做小偷會因粗心大意(或很容易的)被警察抓到’解,因而與⑰d,e同義。也就是說,在⑰的八個例句中,有五個例句(包括三個主動句(同時是「主語取向」)與兩個被動句)做「主事取向」解;而三個例句(都是被動句)則只能做「受事取向」(patient-oriented)解。我們現在把這八個例句的X標槓結構列舉在下面。

⑱　a. **主動句**:情狀副詞出現於「句中首」(小句子左方附加語)
　　(=⑰a)

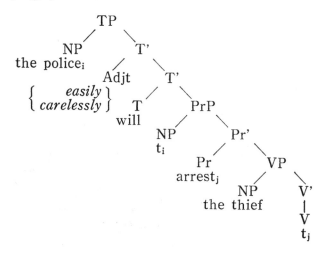

---

⑩　參 Jackendoff (1972:82-83) 與 Travis (1988:285)。

b. 主動句：情狀副詞出現於「句中尾」（述詞組左方附加語）
   (=⑰b)

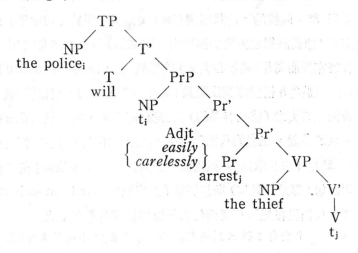

c. 主動句：情狀副詞出現於「句尾首」（述詞組右方附加語）
   (=⑰c)

d. 被動句：情狀副詞出現於「句中首」(小句子左方附加語)
(＝⑰d)

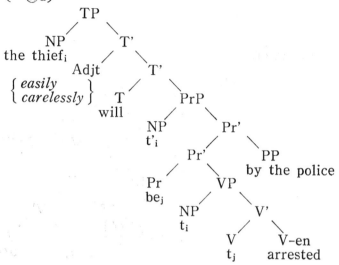

e. 被動句：情狀副詞出現於「句中(中)」(述詞組左方附加語)(＝⑰e)

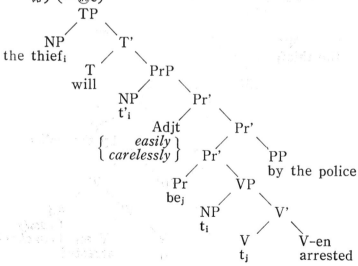

f. 被動句：情狀副詞出現於「句中尾」（動詞組左方附加語）
（＝⑰f）

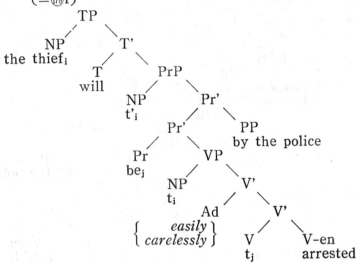

g. 被動句：情狀副詞出現於「句中尾」（動詞組右方附加語）
（＝⑰g）

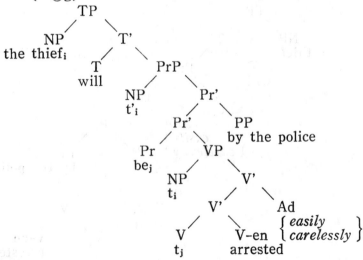

h. 被動句：情狀副詞出現於「句首尾」(小句子右方附加語)
(＝⑰h)

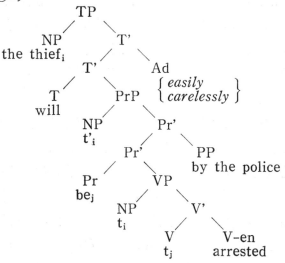

h' 被動句：情狀副詞出現於「句尾首」(述詞組右方附加語)
(＝⑰h)

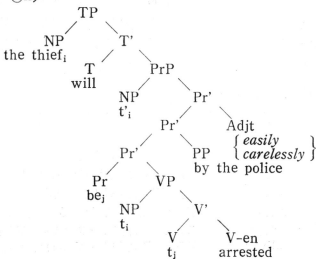

情狀副詞出現於「句尾首」的位置時，可能出現於小句子右方附加語的位置（如⑱h），也可能出現於述詞組右方附加語的位置（如⑱h'）；所以我們提供了⑱h與⑱h'這兩種可能的結構樹。「句尾」的位置是大句子（右方）附加語的位置，只有整句副詞或狀語才能出現這個位置（這個位置的前面常標以逗號，並自成一個獨立的語調單元）。

　　如果以上有關⑲a-h例句的語意解釋以及與這些例句相對的X標槓結構分析⑱a-h'是正確的話⑩，我們不難發現這些例句的語意解釋與X標槓結構之間存在著相當密切的關係。在⑱a-c的X標槓結構分析裏，主事名詞組（'the police'）都C統制有關的情狀副詞，因此都獲得「主事取向」的語意解釋。在⑱d,e的X標槓結構分析裏是受事名詞組（'the thief'）C統制有關的情狀副詞，因而獲得「受事取向」的語意解釋。在⑱f, g的X標槓結構分析裏，則是主事名詞組（'by the police'）C統制有關情狀副詞⑫，所以獲得「主事取向」的語意解釋。至於⑲h的例句，則可能分析爲⑱h或⑱h'的X標槓結構分析。但是無論是在⑱h或⑱h'都是受事名詞組c統制有關的情狀副詞，所以應該獲得「受事取向」的語意解釋。

　　⑱的X標槓結構不但可能就有關例句提供正確的語意解釋，

---

⑩　Jackendoff（1972:82-83）與Travis（1988:285）都只提到出現於主動句「句中首」與「句尾首」以及被動句「句中首」與「句中尾」的四個位置，並未討論出現於其他位置的情狀副詞。

⑫　雖然主語受事名詞組也c統制情狀副詞，但是受事名詞組與情狀副詞之間有最大投影述詞組（PrP）的介入，而且主事名詞是「就近」（locally）c統制情狀副詞的「最貼近」（minimal）的統制語。

而且也可能簡化語意解釋本身。關於如何解釋副詞與狀語的修飾範圍，學者間有不同的主張。Jackendoff (1972) 為各類副詞提出不同的「(語意)投射規律」((semantic) projection rule), McConnel-Ginet (1982) 建議在邏輯形式裏把副詞分析為「約束變項的運符」(variable-binding operator)，而Travis (1988) 則主張利用「屬性分析」(feature analysis；包括「屬性延伸」(feature extension)、「屬性傳遞」(feature transmission)、「屬性還原」(feature recoverability) 等概念) 為單純副詞與其他狀語分別提出不同的「認可條件」(licensing condition)。而我們則不但取消了專為副詞與狀語而設定的移位規律 ⑩，俾使所有的副詞與狀語都在深層結構直接衍生 ⑩；而且我們的語意解釋律也似可簡化為：副詞與狀語的修飾範圍以其姐妹成分 (或以其所能「C統制」的成分) 為限。因此，各種有關副詞與狀語的歧義問題 (如前面所出現的⑬⑦、⑦⑤a, b ⑩與⑦⑧a 的例句) 都可以利用不同的 X 標槓結構來說明；而且下面⑱⑩的例句裏(a) 與 (b) 兩句在語意解釋上的差異 ⑩也可以用⑱⑫的X標槓結構來說明。試

---

⑩ 我們雖然承認「論旨主題」的移位，但這個移位規律「有其獨立自主的存在理由」(independent motivation)，而且一律適用於所有的句法成分，不必專為副詞與狀語設定特定的條件或限制。

⑩ 因而也符合 Chomsky (1985a, 1989) 有關移位是事非得已的「最後手段」(last resort) 的主張。

⑩ ⑦⑤a 的觀點副詞出現於小句子右方附加語的位置，而情狀副詞則出現於述詞組右方附加語的位置。

⑩ 參 Andrews (1982)。他還提到 'John *intentionally* knocked on the door *twice*' 與 'John *twice* knocked on the door *intentionally*' 的歧義都可以用同樣的方式來處理。

比較：

⑱ a. John knocked the door *intentionally twice.*

　　‘John（前後）兩次故意的敲了門。’

　b. John knocked the door *twice intentionally.*

　　‘John 故意的敲門敲了兩下。’

⑱ a.

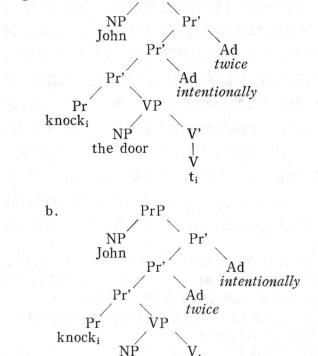

在 ⑱ a 的 X 標槓結構裏 ‘twice’ C 統制 ‘intentionally’，所以

'twice' 獲得了「寬域解釋」(wide-scope reading)；在⑱b的X標槓結構裏 'intentionally' C統制 'twice'，因此 'intentionally' 獲得寬域解釋。

　　有關各類副詞或狀語在各類X標槓結構上出現分佈的限制，則似乎可以用「次類畫分框式」(subcategorization frame) 的方式登錄於個別副詞的「詞項記載」(lexical entry) 裏面。如果某些副詞可以出現於X標槓結構上不同的位置，就悉數把這些位置登錄於次類畫分框式裏面。如果因為出現的位置不同而有不同的語意內涵，那麼就在詞項記載裏把次類畫分框式與語意解釋結合起來。如此，似可避免把同一個副詞做為「同音同形異義詞」(homonym) 的武斷處理。如果次類畫分框式之間，或次類畫分框式與語意解釋之間，發現「規律性」(regularity) 或「次規律性」(subregularity)，那麼就可以利用「詞彙冗贅規律」(lexical redundancy rule) 來處理。另外，介詞組（包括從屬子句）在X標槓結構上的出現分佈要比單純副詞的出現分佈更受限制，也應該在句法上統一解決或處理。❿

七、出現於其他詞組的副詞與狀語

　　副詞與狀語，除了可以出現於動詞組、述詞組、小句子與大句子以外，還可以出現於限定詞組、形容詞組、副詞組等。為了篇幅的關係，我們簡單的討論一下副詞與狀語在X標槓結構上出

---

❿ 「語用因素」(pragmatic factors) 對於英語副詞與狀語出現分佈的關係，參湯 (1984)〈英語詞句的「言外之意」：「功用解釋」〉，收錄於湯(1988e:247-319)。

現於這些詞組的位置。

(一)副詞與狀語在「限定詞組」裡出現的位置

「限定詞組」（determiner phrase; DP）以「限定詞」(determiner)為主要語，以名詞組為補述語合成「限定詞節」(D')，並以空節為指示語形成限定詞組。⓯限定詞節也可以由限定詞節與附加語合成，以便反復衍生附加語。限定詞組裏的副詞與狀語多半都出現於限定詞組裏附加語的位置，包括：(i)「加強詞」(如 'quite, rather')與「緩和詞」(如 '(a) sort of, a bit of, a heck of, a hell of')、(ii)「限制詞」(limiter；如 'even, just, only, especially; alone, else')、(iii)「倍數詞」(multiple；如 'half, twice, double, three times, four times…')、(iv)「精確程度的副詞」(adverb of degree of precision；如 'precisely, roughly, approximately, virtually, nearly, almost')、(v)「分集副詞」("set-dividing adverb"；如 'primarily, mostly')。例如 ⓰：

⑱ a. We had *quite* a party.

　　b. They'll be here for *quite* some time.

　　c. It's *rather* a big table.

⑱ a. This must be {*a sort of* joke/*sort of* a joke/*a sort of* a joke/a joke, *sort of*}.

⓯　有關英語限定詞組的詳細討論，參湯 (1990d)。

⓰　⑱、⑱與⑱的例句採自 Quirk et al. (1985:450-451)。

b. I had *a bit of* shock. ⑩

⑱ a. {*Only* the teacher/The teacher *alone*} knew the answer.

b. *Even* the teacher didn't know the answer.

⑱ a. I could do it at *double* the speed.

b. He earned *twice* the amount of money you did last year.

c. {No one/Who} *else* would come (?)

⑱ a. That is *precisely* the reason I suggested.

b. I paid him *roughly* the amount he asked for.

⑱ a. Are *primarily* horn players required for the job, or will bassoonists do?

b. *Mostly* my colleagues helped me tide over the period of difficulty.

表示「觀點」與「評價」的副詞也可能出現於限定詞組附加語的位置，但是實際上這些副詞並非修飾名詞組，而是修飾名詞組裏所包含的形容詞，例如：

⑱ a. {A *good* paper *editorially*/An *editorially good* paper} can also be {a *good* paper *commercially*/a *commercially good* paper}.

b. A cure had now been found for this *fortunately very rare* disease.

---

⑩ 湯 (1990d) 把'(a) sort of, a bit of'等分析爲「量詞」(quantifier)。

　　副詞與狀語也可以出現於名詞組裏附加語的位置來修飾名詞（或應該說是「名詞節」(N')），主要是 (i)「處所」副詞(如 'here, there. home; ahead, back, out, abroad, above, below; inside, outside, offside, upstairs, downstairs, backstage; three blocks away; in the room') 與 (ii)「時間」副詞 (如 'now, then, yesterday, tomorrow; last night, next month; before, afterward(s), overnight; at the time')，例如：

⑩　a. your friend *here,* that man *there,* the car *out-side,* the neighbor *upstairs,* the road *back,* the way {*out/ahead*}, the players *offside,* the noise *backstage,* his journey *home,* the garage *three blocks away*

　　b. the China {*now/then*}, the meeting *tomorrow,* the party *last night,* the day *before,* the meal *afterward(s),* their stay *overnight*

副詞與狀語不僅出現於「名後」(postnominal) 附加語的位置，還可以出現於「名前」(prenominal) 附加語的位置，例如：⑪

⑪　a. an *outside* door, *inside* information, the *above* quotation, the *backstage* noise, his *home* journey

　　b. the *now* generation, the *then* government, in *after* years

(二)副詞與狀語在形容詞組與副詞組裏出現的位置

---

⑪　例句多半採自 Quirk et al. (1985:453)。

形容詞組（AP）與副詞組（AdP）分別以形容詞（A）與副詞（Ad）爲主要語，與補述語合成形容詞節（A'）與副詞節（Ad'）。⑫但是形容詞節與副詞節也可以由形容詞節或副詞節與附加語合成，因而可以反複衍生附加語。出現於形容詞組或副詞組裏附加語的副詞或狀語多半是「程度」副詞（包括「加強詞」（或「增強詞」）與「緩和詞」（或「減弱詞」）⑬。由於這兩種詞類具有「互補分佈」（complementary distribution）或「互相排拒」（mutually exclusive）的關係，或許可以概化爲「（數）量詞組」（quantifier phrase; QP）。⑭

(三)副詞與狀語在介詞組裏出現的位置

介詞組（PP）以介詞（P；不但包括以名詞組與介詞組爲補述語的「介詞」，而且還包括以小句子爲補述語的「從屬連詞」）爲主要語，並與補述語合成介詞節（P'），再由介詞與附加語合成介詞節⑮。介詞組的附加語多半都是 'right, well, dead, straight, directly, soon, just' 等具有加強作用的單純副詞，而且通常都只出現於主要語左方的位置，例如：

⑲⑫ a. The nail went *right* through the wall.

---

⑫ 只有極少數的副詞（如 'independently, differently'）可以以介詞組（分別以 'of NP' 與 'from NP'）爲補述語；而且，形容詞組與副詞組都沒有指示語。

⑬ 關於修飾形容詞與副詞（包括「介副詞」）的附加語，參 Quirk et al. (1985:445-449)，這裏不再一一討論。

⑭ 參 湯 (1990d) 的有關討論。

⑮ 介詞組，與形容詞組和副詞組一樣，不含有指示語。

b. He made his application *well* within the time.

c. Her parents are *dead* against our marriage.

d. I married her *simply* because I loved her.

八、結　語

　　以上相當詳盡的討論了英語的副詞與狀語在Ｘ標槓結構上的位置，因而也討論了各種語意類型以及各種句法類型的副詞與狀語在各種Ｘ標槓 結構上的出現分佈 與前後次序 。 由於篇幅的限制，我們不準備在這裏總結本文的結論與要點，也不準備討論如何把這些結論與要點應用於課堂上實際的英語教學。不過做為英語老師有需要也有責任廣泛而深入的了解英語的語法事實、語法結構與語法表現 。 一般人對於英語的知識或能力往往是「內在」(internalized) 的、「隱形」(covert) 的、「抽象」(abstract) 的。英語老師的重要職責之一就是：如何把這個內在、隱形的知識或抽象的能力加以「條理化」(generalize) 與「外形化」(formalize)，設法明明白白、清清楚楚的傳授給學生，並且還要訓練他們如何利用這個知識或能力來造出一些他們從未聽過或讀過的句子。英語老師不能再以"只能意會，不可言傳"為藉口來規避英語教學上的責任或推諉英語教學上的失敗，而應該堅定" 既可意會，必可言傳 "的信念積極參與教材教法的改進。我們相信：英語教學必須以"有知有覺"的「認知」(cognition) 為基礎，然後經過不斷的練習與應用方能養成 "不知不覺" 而能 "運用自如" 的「習慣」(habit)。

　　＊ 本文於1990年「中華民國第七屆英語文教學研討會」上發表，並曾刊載於 (1990)《人文及社會學科教學通訊》一卷一期48-79頁、二期47-71頁。

參 考 文 獻

Abe, J., 1987, 'Generalized Binding Theory and the Behavior of Anaphors in Gerunds', English Linguistics 4, 165-185.

Abney, S., 1987, The English Noun Phrase in Its Sentential Aspect, Doctoral dissertation, MIT, Cambridge, Mass.

Akmajian, A., Steele, S. and Wasow, T., 1979, 'The Category AUX in Universal Grammar', Linguistic Inquiry 9, 261-268.

Allen, M., 1978, Morphological Investigations, Doctoral dissertation, University of Connecticut, Storrs, Conn.

Anderson, M., 1984, 'Prenominal Genitive NPs', The Linguistic Review 3, 1-24.

Anderson, S., 1982, 'Where's Morphology?', Linguistic Inquiry 13, 571-612.

Aoun, J., 1986, Generalized Binding: The Syntax and Logical Form of Wh-interrogatives, Foris, Dordrecht.

Aoun, J., and D. Sportiche, 1983, 'On the Formal Theory of Government', The Linguistic Review 3, 211-235.

Aoun, J., Hornstein, N., Lightfoot, D., and Weinberg, A., 1987, 'Two Types of Locality', Linguistic Inquiry 18, 537-577.

Aronoff, M., 1976, Word Formation in Generative Grammar, MIT Press, Cambridge, Mass.

Baker, M., 1985a, 'Syntactic Affixation and English Gerunds', WCCFL 4, 1-11.

Baker, M., 1985b, 'The Mirror Principle and Morpho-syntactic Explanation', Linguistic Inquiry 16, 373-415.

Baker, M., 1985c, Incorporation: A Theory of Grammatical Function Changing, Doctoral dissertation, MIT, Cambridge, Mass. (the University of Chicago Press, 1988)

Baltin, M., 1981, 'A Landing Site Theory of Movement Rules', Linguistic Inquiry 13, 1-38.

Barss, A. and H. Lasnik, 1986, 'A Note on Anaphora and Double Objects', Linguistic Inquiry 17, 347-354.

Bellert, I., 1977, 'On Semantic and Distributional Properties of Sentencial Adverbs', Linguistic Inquiry 8:2,337-351.

Booij, G. E., 1985, 'Review of Wordsyntax (Toman, J., 1983)', Lingua 65, 260-270.

Bouchard, D., 1984, On the Content of Empty Categories, Foris, Dordrecht.

Bowers, J., 1987, 'Extended X-Bar Theory, the ECP and the Left Branch Condition', Proceedings of WCCFL 6.

Bowers, J., 1988, 'A Structural Theory of Predication', ms.

Bowers, J., 1989a, 'Predication in Extended X-Bar Theory', ms.

Bowers, J., 1989b, 'The Syntax and Semantics of Nominals', ms.

Bresnan, J., 1972, Theory of Complementation in English Syntax, Doctoral dissertation, MIT, Cambridge, Mass.

Bresnan, J.W. and J. Grimshaw, 1978, 'The Syntax of Free Relatives in English', Linguistic Inquiry 9, 331-391.

Bresnan, J.W., 1976, 'On the Form and Functioning of Transformations', Linguistic Inquiry 7, 3-40.

Chao, Y.R. (趙元任), 1968, A Grammar of Spoken Chinese, University of California Berkeley, California.

Cheng, L. L.S., 1986, Clause Structures in Mandarin Chinese, MA thesis of the University of Toronto, Toronto, Ontario.

Chomsky, N., 1965, Aspects of the Theory of Syntax, MIT Press, Cambridge, Mass.

Chomsky, N., 1970, 'Remarks on Nominalization', in R. A. Jacobs and P. A. Rosenbaum (eds.) Reading in English Transformational Grammar, Ginn, Waltham, Mass.

Chomsky, N., 1981, Lectures on Government and Binding, Foris, Dordrecht.

Chomsky, N., 1986a, Knowledge of Language: Its Nature, Origin, and Use, Praeger, New York.

Chomsky, N., 1986b, Barriers, Linguistic Inquiry Monograph 13, MIT Press, Cambridge, Mass.

Chomsky, N., 1989, Some Notes on Economy of Derivation and Representation', MIT Working Papers in Linguistics 10.

Cole, P., G. Hermon, and L.-M. Sung, 1990, Principles and Parameters of Long-Distance Reflexives', Linguistic Inquiry 21, 1-22.

Culicover, P.W. and Wexler, K., 1977, 'Some Syntactic Implications of a Theory of Language Learnability', in P.W. Culicover, T. Wasow, and A. Akmajian (eds.) Formal Syntax, 7-30, Academic Press, New York.

Culicover, P.W. and Wilkins, W.K., 1984, Locality in Linguistic Theory, Academic Press, New York.

Di Sciullo, A.M., and E. Williams, 1987, On the Definition of Word, MIT Press, Cambridge, Mass.

Dougherty, R., 1968, A Transformational Grammar of Conjoined Coordinate Structures, Doctoral dissertation, MIT, Cambridge, Mass.

Emonds, J.E., 1970, Root and Structure Preserving Transformations, Doctoral dissertation, MIT, Cambridge, Mass.

Emonds, J.E., 1976, A Transformational Approach to English Syntax, Academic Press, New York.

Emonds, J.E., 1985, 'On the Odd Syntax of Domain Adverbs', ms.

Emonds, J.E., 1985, A Unified Theory of Syntactic Categories, Foris, Dordrecht.

Ernst, T., 1984, Towards an Integrated Theory of Adverb Position in English, IULC, Bloomington.

Fabb, N., 1984, Syntactic Affixation, Doctoral dissertation, MIT, Cambridge, Mass.

Farmer, A., 1980, On the Interaction of Morphology and Syntax, MIT Press, Cambridge, Mass.

Fillmore, C., 1968, Indirect Object Constructions in English and the Ordering of Transformations, Mouton, The Hague.

Franks, S., 1986, 'Theta-role Assignment in NPs and VPs', Paper read at LSA Winter Meeting.

Fukui, N., 1986, A Theory of Category Predication and Its Applications, Doctoral dissertation, MIT, Cambridge, Mass.

Fukui, N. and M. Speas, 1986, 'Specifiers and Projection', MIT Working Papers 8.

Fukuyasu, K., 1987, 'Government of PRO, by PRO, for PRO', English Linguistics 4, 186-200.

Greenbaum, S., 1969, Studies in English Adverbial Usage, Longman, London.

Greenbaum, S., 1970, Verb-Intensifier Collocations in English, Mouton, The Hague.

Grimshaw, J., 1979, 'Complement Selection and the Lexicon', Linguistic Inquiry 10, 279-326.

Gruber, J.R., 1965, Studies in Lexical Relations, Doctoral dissertation, MIT, Cambridge, Mass.

Gruber, J.R., 1976, Lexical Structures in Syntax and Semantics, North-Holland.

Haiman, J. (ed.) 1985, Iconicity in Syntax, John Benjamins, Amsterdam.

Haiman, J. 1986, Natural Syntax, Cambridge University Press, Cambridge.

Hsieh, H-I., (謝信一)1989, 'Time Imagery in Chinese', in J. H-Y. Tai & F. F. S. Hsueh (eds.), Functionalism and Chinese Grammar, 45-94, Chinese Language

Teachers Association, Monograph Series 1.

Hankamer, J., 1971, Constraints on Deletion in Syntax, Doctoral dissertation, Yale University.

Hantson, A., 1984, 'For, With and Without as Non-Finite Clause Introducers', English Studies 63, 54-67.

Hashimoto, A. Y., 1971, Mandarin Syntactic Structure, Unicorn 8, 1-149.

Hoekstra, T., H. van der Hulst, M. Moortgut, 1980, 'Introduction', in T. Hoekstra et al. (eds.), 1981, Lexical Grammar, 1-48, Foris, Dordrecht.

Hornstein, N. and Lightfoot, D., 1981, Explanation in Linguistics, Longman, London.

Hornstein, N. and Weinberg, A., 1981, 'Case Theory and Preposition Stranding', Linguistic Inquiry 12, 55-91.

Huang, C.T. (黃正德), 1982, Logical Relations in Chinese and Theory of Grammar, Doctoral dissertation, MIT, Cambridge, Mass.

Huang, C.T.(黃正德), 1987,, Remarks on Empty Categories in Chinese', Linguistic Inquiry 18, 321-336.

Huang, C.T.(黃正德), 1988, 'Wo Pao De Kuai in Chinese Phrase Structure', Language 64, 274-311.

Huang, C.T. (黃正德), 1989a, 'Pro-drop in Chinese: A Generalized Control Theory', O. Jaggeli and K. Safir (eds.), 1989, The Null Subject Parameter, 185-214.

Huang, C.T. （黃正德）, 1989b, 'Complex Predicates in Generalized Control', ms.

Hudson, R.A., 1976, 'Conjunction Reduction, Gapping, and Right-node Raising', Language 52, 535-562.

Jackendoff, R.S., 1968, 'Quantifiers in English', Foundations of Language 4, 422-442.

Jackendoff, R.S., 1971, 'Gapping and Related Rules', Linguistic Inquiry 2, 21-35.

Jackendoff, R.S., 1972, Semantic Interpretation in Generative Grammar, MIT Press, Cambridge, Mass.

Jackendoff, R.S., 1977, X-Syntax: A Study of Phrase Structure, Linguistic Inquiry Monograph 2, MIT Press, Cambridge. Mass.

Kageyama, T., 1980,《日英比較語彙の構造》，松柏社。

Kageyama, T., 1982, 'Word Formation in Japanese', Lingua 57, 215-288.

Kageyama, T., 1984, 'Three Types of Word Formation', Nebulae 10, 16-30.

Kageyama, T., and M. Shibatani, 1989,〈モジュール文法の語形成論──「の」名詞句からの複合語形成〉，in Kuno & Shibatani (eds.) 1989, 139-166.

Kayne, R., 1984, Connectedness and Binary Branching, Foris, Dordrecht.

Keyser, S.J., 1968, 'Review of S. Jacobsen, Adverbial Positions in English', Language, 357–373.

Kim, S–W., 1987, 'Remarks on Noun Phrase in English', Language Research 23, 217–232.

Kitagawa, Y., 1985, 'Small But Clausal', CLS 21/1, 210–220.

Kitagawa, Y., 1986, Subject in Japanese and English, Doctoral dissertation, University of Massachusetts at Amherst.

Klima, E.S., 1965, Studies in Diachronic Syntax, Doctoral dissertation, Harvard University, Cambridge, Mass.

Kobayashi, K., 1987, 'A Note on Bare-NP Adverbs', English Linguistics 4, 336–341.

Koopman, H., 1984, The Syntax of Verbs, Foris, Dordrecht.

Koster, J., 1987, Domains and Dynasties: the Radical Autonomy of Syntax, Foris, Dordrecht.

Koopman, H., and D. Sportiche, 1985, 'Theta Theory and Extraction', GLOW News letter.

Koopman, H., 1988, 'Subjects', ms.

Kuno, S. and M. Shibatani (eds.), 1989, 《日本語學の新展開》, くろしお出版。

Kuroda, S.-Y., 1981, 'Some Recent Trends in Syntactic Theory and the Japanese Language', Coyote Papers

2, 103-122.

Lapointe, S., 1977, 'A Lexical Reanalysis of the English Auxiliary System', ms.

Lapointe, S., 1980, 'A Note on Akmajian, Steele, and Wasow's Treatment of Verb Complement Types', Linguistic Inquiry 11, 770-787.

Larson, R.K., 1985, 'Bare-NP Adverbs', Linguistic Inquiry 16, 595-621.

Larson, R.K., 1988, 'On the Double Object Construction', Linguistic Inquiry 19, 335-391.

Lasnik, H. and M. Saito, 1984, 'On the Nature of Proper Government', Linguistic Inquiry 15, 235-289.

Lasnik, H. and M. Saito, 1989, Move α, ms.

Lees, R.B., 1960, The Grammar of English Nominalization, Mouton, The Hague.

Li, C. N. and A. Thompson, 1981, Mandarin Chinese: A Functional Reference Grammar, University of California Press, L. A., California.

Li, Jin-xi（黎錦熙）, 1969,《國語文法》，台灣商務印書館。

Li, M.-D.（李梅都）1988, Anaphoric Structures of Chinese, Student Book Co., Taipei, Taiwan.

Li, Y.H.（李艷惠）, 1985, Abstract Case in Chinese, Doctoral dissertation, University of Southern California, L.A., California.

Lieber, R., 1980, On the Organization of the Lexicon, MIT Press, Cambridge, Mass.

Longobardi, G., 1987, 'Extraction from NP and the Proper Notion of Head Government', ms.

Lu, Zhiwei (陸志韋) et al., 1975,《漢語的構詞法（修訂本）》，中華書局。

Lü, Shuxiang (呂叔湘), 1979,《漢語語法分析問題》，商務印書館。

Lü, Shuxiang(呂叔湘), 1984,《漢語語法論文集(增定本)》，商務印書館。

Lü, Shuxiang (呂叔湘), et al., 1980,《現代漢語八百詞》，商務印書館。

MacCawley, J.D., 1983, 'What's with With?', Language 59, 271-287.

MacCawley, J.D., 1988, 'Adverbial NPs: Bare or Clad in See-Through Garb?', Language 64, 583-590.

Manzini, R., 1983, Restructuring and Reanalysis, Doctoral dissertation, MIT, Cambridge, Mass.

Marantz, A.P., 1984, On the Nature of Grammatical Relations, MIT Press, Cambridge, Mass.

Mithun, M., 1984, 'The Evolution of Noun Incorporation', Language 60, 874-894.

Modini, P.E., 1977, 'Evidence from Chinese for an Extended Analysis of Exclamations', ms.

Mohanan, K.P., 1983, 'Functional and Anaphoric Control', Linguistic Inquiry 14, 641-674.

Muysken, P., 1982, 'Parametrizing the Notion 'Head', Journal of Linguistic Research 2:3, 57-75.

Nagasaki, M., 1988, 'θ-role Assignment Autonomous from Case Assignment', English Linguistics 5, 19-37.

Neijt, A.H., 1979, Gapping: A Contribution to Sentence Grammar, Foris, Dordrecht.

Ohta, Tasuo (太田辰夫), 1958,《中國語歷史文法》，江南書院。

Partee, B., 1973, 'Some Transformational Extensions of Montague Grammar', Journal of Philosophical Logic 2, 509-534.

Pollock, J.Y., 1989, 'Verb Movement, Universal Grammar, and the Structure of IP', Linguistic Inquiry 20, 265-424.

Postal, P.M., 1966, 'On So-Called 'Pronouns' in English', in D. Reibel and S. Schane (eds.) (1969) Modern Studies in English, 201-244, Englewood Cliff, New Jersey.

Postal, P.M., 1974, On Raising, MIT Press, Cambridge, Mass.

Pullum, G.K., 1985, 'Assuming Some Version of X-Bar Theory', CLS 21.

Quirk, R., Greenbaum, S., Leech, G. and Svartvick, J., 1985, A Comprehensive Grammar of the English

Language, Longman, London.

Radford, A., 1988, Transformational Grammar: A First Course, Cambridge University Press, Cambridge.

Reinhart, T., 1976, The Syntactic Domain of Anaphora, Doctoral dissertation, MIT, Cambridge, Mass.

Ren, Xueliang (任學良), 1981,《漢語造詞法》,中國社會科學出版社。

Reuland, E.J., 1983, 'Governing -ing', Linguistic Inquiry 14, 101–136.

Riemsdijk, H.C. van and Williams, E., 1986, Introduction to the Theory of Grammar, MIT Press, Cambridge, Mass.

Rizzi, L., (1990), Relativized Minimality, MIT Press, Cambridge, Mass.

Roeper, T. and M. Siegel, 1978, 'A Lexical Transformation for Verbal Compounds', Linguistic Inquiry 9, 199–260.

Ross, J.R., 1964, 'Auxiliaries as Main Verbs', in W. Todd (ed.) (1969) Studies in Philosophical Linguistics 1, 77–102, Evanston, Great Expectations Press, Illinois.

Ross, J.R., 1967, Constraints on Variables in Syntax, Doctoral dissertation, MIT, Cambridge, Mass.

Rothstein, S., 1983, The Syntactic Forms of Predication, Doctoral dissertation, MIT, Cambridge, Mass.

Rudanko, J., 1984, 'On Some Contrasts Between Infinitival and That Complement Clauses in English, English Studies 64, 141-161.

Rudanko, J., 1984, 'On the Grammar of For Clauses in English', English Studies 5, 433-452.

Sadock, J. 1980, 'Noun Incorporation in Greenlandic', Language 56, 300-319.

Sag, I.A., 1976, Deletion and Logical Form, Doctoral dissertation, MIT, Cambridge, Mass.

Selkirk, E.O., 1977, 'Some Remarks on Noun Phrase Structure', in A. Akmajian, P. Culicover and T. Wasow (eds.) (1977) Studies in Formal Syntax, Academic Press, New York.

Selkirk, E.O., 1982, The Syntax of Words, Linguistic Inquiry Monograph 7, MIT Press, Cambridge, Mass.

Selkirk, E. O., 1984, Phonology and Syntax: The Relation Between Sound and Structure, MIT Press, Cambridge, Mass.

Shibatani, M. and T. Kageyama, 'Word Formation in a Modular Theory of Grammar: Post-syntactic Compounds in Japanese', Language 64, 451-484.

Schreiber, P.A., 1970, 'Epithet Adverbs in English', Paper read at Summer Meeting, LSA, Columbus, Ohio.

Schreiber, P.A., 1971, 'Some Constraints on the Formation of English Sentence Adverb, Linguistic Inquiry 2, 83-101.

Siegel, D., 1974, Topics in English Morphology, Doctoral dissertation, MIT, Cambridge, Mass.

Speas, M., 1988, 'On Projection From the Lexicon', ms.

Sportiche, D., 1988, 'A Theory of Floating Quantifiers and Its Corollaries for Constituent Structure', Linguistic Inquiry 19, 425-449.

Stillings, J., 1975, 'The Formations of Gapping in English as Evidence for Variable Types in Syntactic Transformations', Linguistic Analysis 1, 247-274.

Stowell, T., 1981, Origins of Phrase Structure, Doctoral dissertation, MIT Press, Cambridge, Mass.

Stowell, T., 1983, 'Subjects Across Categories', The Linguistic Review 2, 258-312.

Sugioka, Y., 1984, Interaction of Derivational Morphology and Syntax in Japanese and English, Doctoral dissertation, the University of Chicago. (Garland Publishing, 1986)

Sugioka, Y., 1989, 〈派生語における動詞素性の受け繼ぎ〉in Kuno & Shibatani (eds.), 1989, 167-185.

Tai, J. H-Y. (戴浩一), 1973, 'A Derivational Constraint on Adverbial Placement in Mandarin', Journal of

Chinese Linguistics 1, 397–413.

Tai, J. H-Y. (戴浩一), 1985, 'Temporal Sequence and Chinese Word Order', in J. Haiman (ed.) 1985, Natural Syntax, 49–72, John Benjamins, Amsterdam.

Tai, J. H-Y. (戴浩一), 1989, 'Toward a Cognition-Based Functional Grammar of Chinese', in J. H-Y. Tai & F. F. S. Hsueh (eds.) Functionalism and Chinese Grammar, 187–226, Chinese Language Teachers Association, Monograph Series 1.

Takami, K., 1984,〈日本語の文照應と副詞・副詞句〉，《言語研究》 87, 68–94

Takami, K., 1987, 'Adjuncts and the Internal Structure of VP', English Linguistics 4, 55–71.

Tang, C. C. (湯志眞) 1988，漢語的移位、「承接條件」與「空號原則」，《第二屆世界華語文教學研討會論文集（理論分析篇)》83–118頁。

Tang, C.C. (湯志眞), 1989, 'Chinese Reflexives', Natural Language and Linguistic Theory 7, 93–121.

Tang, T.C. (湯廷池), 1972, A Case Grammar of Spoken Chinese, 海國書局。

Tang, T.C. (湯廷池), 1977a,《國語變形語法研究第一集：移位變形》，台灣學生書局。

Tang, T.C. (湯廷池), 1977b,《英語教學論集》，台灣學生書局。

Tang, T.C. （湯廷池）, 1979,《國語語法研究論集》,台灣學生書局。

Tang, T.C. （湯廷池）, 1981,《語言學與語言教學》,台灣學生書局。

Tang, T.C. （湯廷池）, 1984b,《英語語法修辭十二講：從傳統到現代》,台灣學生書局。

Tang, T.C. （湯廷池）, 1986,〈關於漢語的詞序類型〉,《中央研究院第二屆國際漢學會議論文集》519-569頁。

Tang, T.C. （湯廷池）, 1988a,《漢語詞法句法論集》,台灣學生書局。

Tang, T.C. （湯廷池）, 1988b,〈爲漢語動詞試定界說〉,《清華學報》第十八卷第一期,43-69 頁。

Tang, T.C. （湯廷池）, 1988c,〈漢語詞法與語言習得：漢語動詞〉,《中央研究院歷史語言研究所集刊》第五十九本第一分冊,211-247頁。

Tang, T.C. （湯廷池）, 1988d,〈新詞創造與漢語詞法〉,《大陸雜誌》第四期,5-19 頁;第五期,27-34 頁。

Tang, T.C. （湯廷池）, 1988e,《英語認知語法：結構、意義與功用（上冊）》,台灣學生書局。

Tang, T.C. （湯廷池）, 1988f,〈詞法與句法的相關性：漢、英、日三種語言複合動詞的對比分析〉,《清華學報》第十九卷第一期,51-94頁。

Tang, T.C. （湯廷池）, 1988g,〈普遍語法與漢英對比分析〉,《第二屆世界華語文教學研討會論文集（理論分析篇）》

119-146頁。

Tang, T.C. （湯廷池）, 1988h,〈英語的「名前」與「名後」修飾語：結構、意義與功用〉。《中華民國第五屆英語文教學研討會論文集》，1-38頁。

Tang, T.C. （湯廷池）, 1989a,〈普遍語法與英漢對比分析：「X標槓理論」與詞組結構〉，收錄於湯（1989c）。

Tang, T.C. （湯廷池）, 1989b,〈「X標槓理論」與英語名詞組的詞組結構〉，《中華民國第六屆英語文教學研討會論文集》，1-36 頁。

Tang, T.C. （湯廷池）, 1989c,《漢語詞法句法續集》，台灣學生書局

Tang, T. C. （湯廷池）, 1989d,〈漢語複合動詞的形態、結構與功能〉，ms.。

Tang, T. C. （湯廷池）, 1989e,〈「原則參數語法」與英漢對比分析〉，新加坡華文研究會世界華文教學研討會。

Tang, T. C. （湯廷池）, 1990a,〈漢語的「大代號」與「小代號」〉，ms.。

Tang, T.C. （湯廷池）, 1990b,〈漢語的「主題句」〉，ms.。

Tang, T.C. （湯廷池）, 1990c,〈漢語語法的「併入現象」〉《清華學報》新二十一卷第一期1-63頁；第二期337-376頁。

Tang, T.C. （湯廷池）, 1990d,〈「限定詞組」「量詞組」與「名詞組」的「X標槓結構」：英漢對比分析〉，ms.。

Tang, T.C. （湯廷池）, 1990e,〈英語副詞與狀語在「X標槓結構」中出現的位置：句法與語意功能〉，《人文及社會學科

教學通訊》一卷一期48-79頁；二期47-71頁。

Tang, T.C.（湯廷池), 1990f,〈「大句子」、「小句子」、「述詞組」與「動詞組」的「X標槓結構」：英漢對比分析〉，ms.。

Tang, T.C.（湯廷池), 撰寫中 a，當代語法理論與漢語句法分析。

Tang, T.C.（湯廷池), 撰寫中 b，漢語詞法初探。

Tang, T.C.（湯廷池), 撰寫中 c，普遍語法與漢英對比分析：（二）「論旨理論」、「格位理論」。

Teng, S.H.(鄧守信), 1977, A Semantic Study of Transitivity Relations in Chinese, Student Book Co., Taipei.

Thompson, S.A., 1970, 'Relative Clause Structures and Constraints on Types of Complex Sentence' Working Papers in Linguistics 6, the Ohio Uinversity.

Torrego, E., 1985, 'On Empty Categories in Nominals', ms.

Traugott, E.C., 1972, A History of English Syntax, Holt, Rinehart, Winston, New York.

Travis, L., 1984, Parameters and Effects of Word Order Variation, Doctoral dissertation, MIT Press, Cambridge, Mass.

Travis, L., 1988, 'The Syntax of Adverbs', McGill Working Papers in Linguistics, 280-310.

Tateishi, K., to appear, 'On the Universality of X-Bar Theory; The Case of Japanese' in WCCFL, 7.

Vergnaud, J.-R., 1974, French Relative Clauses, Doctoral dissertation, MIT Press, Cambridge, Mass.

Wang, Li（王力）, 1957,《漢語史稿(上)》，商務印書館。

Wells, R. S., 1947, 'Immediate Constituents', Language 23, 81-117.

Wible, D. S., 1989, 'A Barriers Account of the ECP in Chinese', ms.

Williams, E. S., 1975, 'Small Clauses in English', in J. Kimbal, ed. Syntax and Semantics 4, 249-273, Academic Press, New York.

Williams, E. S., 1977, 'Discourse and Logical Form', Linguistic Inquiry 8, 101-104.

Williams, E. S., 1980, 'Predication', Linguistic Inquiry 11, 203-238.

Williams, E. S., 1981, 'On the notions 'Lexically Related' and 'Head of a Word', Linguistic Inquiry 12, 245-274.

Williams, E.S., 1982, 'The NP Cycle', Linguistic Inquiry 13, 277-295.

Williams, E.S., 1983, 'Against Small clauses', Linguistic Inquiry 14, 287-343.

Xu, L.（徐烈炯）, 1986, 'Towards a Lexical-Thematic Theory of Control', The Linguistic Review 5, 345-376.

Xu, L., and Langendoen, D. T., 1985, 'Topic Structures

in Chinese', Language 61, 1-27.

Yamada, M., 1987, 'On NP-ing Constructions in English', English Linguistics 4, 144-164.

Yim, Y.-J., 1984, Case-tropism: The Nature of Phrasal and Clausal Case, Doctoral dissertation, University of Washington, Seattle, Washington.

Yoon, J. H.-S., 1989, 'Chinese Structure, Antipassives and the BA Construction', ms.

Zhu, Dexi(朱德熙), 1980,《現代漢語語法研究》,商務印書館。

Zhu, Dexi(朱德熙), 1982,《語法講義》,商務印書館。

論旨網格與英漢對比分析
(A "Theta-Grid" Approach to a Contrastive
Analysis of English and Chinese)

一、前　言

　　對比分析對於英語教學的重要性，早爲語言學家與語言教師所共認。但是國內至今尚無人針對英語與漢語這兩種語言提出有系統的對比分析來。考其原因，主要是由於缺少一套適當的語法理論把這兩種語言之間句法結構與句法現象上的異同簡單扼要的對照起來。本文有鑒於此，擬從「原則參數語法」(the Prin-ciplesand-Parameters Approach) 的觀點，利用述語動詞與形容詞的「論旨網格」(thematic grid; θ-grid)來演繹並詮釋英

漢兩種語言之間同義或近義動詞或形容詞在意義與用法上的異同。所謂論旨網格，乃是把有關述語動詞或形容詞的「論元結構」（argument structure; 如「域內論元」、「域外論元」、「語意論元」等）、「論旨關係」（thematic relation; 如「主事者」、「感受者」、「受事者」、「客體」、「起點」、「終點」、「工具」、「情狀」、「處所」、「時間」等）、「語法功能」（grammatical function; 如「主語」、「賓語」、「補語」、「定語」、「狀語」等）以及「前後次序」（linear order; 如主語出現於句首、賓語出現於動詞的後面、補語出現於賓語的後面、狀語出現於動詞的前面或賓語的後面等）四者的屬性結合起來，並且用簡要明確的符號與公式表達出來。

根據原則參數語法的理論，所謂「句法結構」（syntactic structure），包括各種「詞組」(phrase)、「子句」(clause)與「句子」（sentence），都是由述語動詞或形容詞在「詞彙」(lexicon)裏所登記的論旨網格「投射」（project）出來的。無論是多麼錯綜複雜的句法結構，都由有關述語動詞或形容詞的投射而來。不過論旨網格的投射必須經過有關「原則系統」(subsystems of principles; 如「投射理論」、「論旨理論」、「X標槓理論」、「格位理論」等) 的「認可」(licensing)，纔能成為「合格」(well-formed) 或「合語法」(grammatical) 的句子。

原則參數語法是有關自然語言「普遍語法」(universal grammar; UG) 與人類幼童「語言習得」(language acquisi-tion) 的理論，而原則系統裏所提出的各種「條件」(condition)與「限制」(constraint) 都是所有「個別語法」(particular grammar; PG) 共同遵守的。這就說明了為什麼英語與漢語之間可以發現這麼多相同或相似的句法現象。另一方面，這些條件與限制可能附有一些「參數」(parameter)，而這些參數的「值」(value) 是委由個別語言來選定的。這就說明了為什麼英語與漢語之間也可以出現不少相異的句法現象。

　　在未討論論旨網格的內容與功能以及論旨網格投射的條件與限制之前，我們先把有關的基本概念簡單扼要的介紹一下。

二、命題、述語與論元

　　「命題」(proposition)，簡單的說，就是句子的陳述內容❶

---

❶　「命題」是邏輯學最基本的概念之一。當我們在心中做思考('我想(＝I {believe/doubt})……') 或生疑問('不曉得 (＝I wonder) ……?')時，我們思考或疑問的對象（用虛擬'……'所表示的部分）叫做命題或「命題內容」(propositional content)，而不包括我們對這個命題內容所抱持的看法或態度（叫做「命題態度」(propositional attitude)；常用「情態副詞」如 'perhaps, surely, fortunately' 等)、「情態助動詞」(如'will, may, should'等)、「情態動詞」(如'I {believe/doubt/wonder}' 等) 來表示)；在自然語言裏常用'……是……的'或'……做……'等句式來表達。命題可以不改變其「認知意義」(cognitive meaning)翻譯成任何一種自然語言，可以有「真」(true) 或「假」(false) 的「真假值」(truth-value)，並且可以用「命題函數」(propositional function) 來表示。例如，'Caesar is a general' 可以用命題函數，'P(x)'（即 'x is a general'）來表示；'Brutus killed Caesar' 可以用命題函數 'Q(x,y)'（即 'x killed y') 來表示，而 'John gave a present to Mary'則可以用命題函數'R (x,y,z)' (即'x gave y to z') 來表示。命題函數裏的 'P, Q, R' 叫作「述語」(predicate)，而 'x, y, z' 則叫做「變項」(variable)。

，由「述語」（predicate）與「論元」（argument）構成。述語
是命題的核心，沒有述語就無法表達命題內容，也就不可能形成
句子。述語可能是動詞、形容詞、副詞、名詞組或介詞組。在英
語裏，除了動詞可以單獨充當述語以外，形容詞、副詞、名詞組
與介詞組通常都要藉 be 動詞或「連繫動詞」（如'seem, appear,
remain, look, sound, taste, feel'等）來引介。另一方面，在
漢語裏則動詞與形容詞都可以單獨充當述語，有時候連名詞組都
可以不經過動詞的引介而直接充當述語。但是漢語的副詞與介詞
組都不能直接充當述語，而必須藉動詞來引介。又無論是英語或
是漢語，述語動詞與形容詞都可以與表示「情態」（modality）、
「動貌」（aspect）與「動相」（phase）等助動詞或詞尾連用，還
可以帶上名詞組(NP)、形容詞組（AP）、動詞組（VP）、介詞組
(PP)、「副詞組」（AdP）、「子句」（S）❷、「小子句」（SC）❸ 等
論元充當賓語或補語。試比較：（英語的斜體部分與漢語的加黑
點部分，分別表示述語。）

---

❷ 「子句」包括「that 子句」（that-clause）、「不定子句」（infini-
tival clause）、「動名子句」（gerundive clause）、「分詞子句」
（participial clause）、「疑問子句」（wh-clause）、「疑問不定子
句」（wh-infinitival clause）等。

❸ 所謂「小子句」（small clause）係指不含有「時制」（tense；即「現
在式」與「過去式」）、「不定詞標誌」（infinitive marker；即'to'）
、「動名詞或現在分詞標誌」（gerundive or participial marker
；即'-ing'）、甚至根本不含有動詞的子句；如 'I consider〔him
a genius〕'、'We regard〔her as our best friend〕'、'I
believe〔John innocent〕'、'I found〔myself in trouble〕'、
'He made〔me do it〕'、'We saw〔him run away〕'。

① a. John 〔VP is *sleeping*〕.

　　小明〔VP 在睡覺〕。

b. Mary 〔VP will *study* 〔NP English〕〕.

　　小華〔VP 要讀〔NP 英語〕〕。

c. I 〔VP *felt* 〔AP very happy〕〕.

　　我〔VP 覺得〔AP 很快樂〕〕。

d. She 〔VP *remained* 〔VP sitting there〕〕.

　　她〔VP 繼續〔VP 坐在那裏〕〕。

e. John 〔VP did not *write* 〔NP a letter〕 〔PP to Mary
　　〕〕.

　　小明〔VP 沒有寫〔NP 信〕〔PP 給小華〕〕。

f. He〔VP has *told*〔NP me〕〔PP all about his troub-
　　le〕〕.

　　他〔VP 〔PP 把他所有的困難〕都告訴了〔NP 我〕〕。

g. John 〔VP *treated* 〔NP Mary〕〔AdP very kindly〕〕.

　　小明〔VP 待〔NP 小華〕〔AP 很親切〕〕。

h. We 〔VP all *know* 〔S' that you like him〕〕.

　　我們〔VP 都知道〔S' 你喜歡他〕〕。

i. I 〔VP *want* 〔S you to help him〕〕.

　　我〔VP 要〔S 你幫助他〕〕。

j. I 〔VP *saw* 〔S him walking across the street〕〕.

　　我〔VP 看到〔S 他在過馬路〕〕。

k. I 〔VP don't *mind* 〔S you(r) wearing my necktie
　　〕〕.

我〔VP 不在乎〔S 你戴我的領帶〕〕。

l. I〔VP *saw*〔SC him walk across the street〕〕.

我〔VP 看到〔S 他過馬路〕〕。

m. Mary〔VP *found*〔SC John very dependable〕〕.

小華〔VP 覺得〔S 小明很可靠〕〕。

n. He〔VP never *told*〔NP me〕〔S' that you are out of job〕〕.

他〔VP 從來沒有告訴〔NP 我〕〔S 你失了業〕〕。

o. I〔VP *know*〔S' who won first prize〕〕.

我〔VP 知道〔S 誰得了第一獎〕〕。

p. We〔VP should *ask*〔NP him〕〔S' when he will return our money〕〕.

我們〔VP應該問〔NP他〕〔S他什麼時候要還我們的錢〕〕。

q. She〔VP didn't *konw*〔S what to say〕〕.

她〔VP 不知道〔S（她）該說什麼〕〕。

② a. John〔VP is〔AP very *intelligent*〕〕.

小明〔AP 很聰明〕。

b. Mary〔VP seems〔AP *fond*〔PP of music〕〕〕.

小華好像〔AP 很喜歡〔NP 音樂〕〕〕。

c. They〔VP are〔AP *busy*〔VP talking about business〕〕〕.

他們〔AP 忙著〔VP 談生意〕〕。

d. She〔VP was *afraid*〔VP to go out alone in the dark〕〕.

她〔AP 怕〔S 一個人在黑夜裏出去〕〕。

e. I 〔VP am *glad* 〔S' that you can come〕〕.

我〔AP 很高興〔S 你能來〕〕。

③ a. Mr. Lee 〔VP is 〔NP a *teacher*〕〕.

李先生〔VP 是〔NP （位）老師〕〕。

b. He 〔VP is 〔NP a *teacher* 〔PP of English〕〕〕.

李先生〔VP 是〔NP （一位）〔NP 英語〕老師〕〕。

c. Today 〔VP is 〔NP *Sunday*〕〕.

今天（〔V 是〕）〔NP 星期天〕。

d. I 〔VP am 〔NP a *Cantonese*〕〕.

我（〔V 是〕）〔NP 廣東人〕。

e. We 〔VP consider 〔SC him 〔NP *our best friend*〕〕〕.

我們〔VP 認為〔S 他〔VP 是〔NP 我們最好的朋友〕〕〕〕。❹

④ a. The meeting 〔VP is 〔AdP *tomorrow afternoon*〕〕.

會議〔VP 在明天下午（舉行）〕。

b. The teacher 〔VP is 〔PP over *there*〕〕.

老師〔VP 在〔AdP 那裏〕〕。

c. John 〔VP has been 〔PP *up*〕 and 〔PP about〕〕.

小明〔VP 已經起來走動了〕。

d. Your mail 〔VP is 〔PP *on the desk*〕〕.

你的信〔VP 放〔PP 在桌子上面〕〕。

e. He 〔VP is 〔PP *out* 〔PP *of danger*〕〕 now〕.

---

❹ 亦可譯為'我們〔VP 把他當做〔NP 我們最好的朋友〕〕'。

他現在脫離〔NP 危險了〕）。

f. We 〔VP are 〔PP *in control* 〔PP *of everything*〕
now〕〕.

我們〔VP 現在控制〔NP 一切〕〕了。

三、論元、語法功能與語法範疇

在命題中與述語一起出現的各種詞組與子句（常用變數‘XP’
來表示）叫作「論元」（argument）。有些論元必須在句子裏與述
語共同出現（如‘*John* put *the book on the desk*’//‘小明把書
放在桌子上面’裏的‘John/小明’、‘the book/書’與‘on the
desk/在桌子上面’），否則句子就不成立或不合語法。這種論元
就叫做「必用論元」（obligatory argument）。必用論元又分爲
「域內論元」（internal argument; 簡稱「內元」）與「域外論元」
（external argument; 簡稱「外元」）。「內元」出現於動詞組裏
面充當述語動詞的「賓語」（object）或「補語」（complement）
，而「外元」則出現於動詞組的外面充當句子的「主語」（subject）
。另一方面，有些論元卻在句子裏不一定要與述語共同出現（如
‘John put the book *carefully* on the desk *in front of*
the teacher//小明在老師面前小心的把書放在桌子上面’❺裏的
‘carefully/小心的’與‘in front of the teacher/在老師面
前’），雖然可以使用，但也可以不使用。這種論元就叫做「可用
論元」（optional argument）或「語意論元」（semantic ar-

❺ 這一句英語也可以翻成‘小明小心的把書放在老師前面的桌子上面’。

gument; 簡稱「意元」)，常在句子裏充當「狀語」(adverbials; 包括副詞、現在分詞、過去分詞、不定詞、從屬子句等可以修飾動詞、形容詞、副詞、介詞組、從屬子句、句子的一切修飾語) 或「定語」(adjectivals; 包括形容詞、限定詞、數量詞、現在分詞、過去分詞、不定詞、名詞、副詞、介詞組、關係子句、同位子句等可以修飾名詞的一切修飾語) ❻。

　　述語可以依據其必用論元的數目分爲「一元述語」、「二元述語」、「三元述語」等。「一元述語」(one-place predicate) 只需要一個必用論元，而且只能有一個必用論元 (如‘laugh/笑、cry/哭、walk/走 (路)、jump/跳 (躍)、sleep/睡 (覺)’)。這個唯一的必用論元就充當一元述語的外元，也就是句子的主語。「二元述語」(two-place predicate) 必須與兩個必用論元連用 (如‘study/讀 (書)、drink/喝、kiss/吻、beat/打、kick/踢’) ；其中一個必要論元充當內元(賓語)，而另一個必要論元充當外元(主語)。「三元述語」(three-place predicate) 必須與三個必用論元連用：其中兩個必用論元屬於內元，分別充當述語動詞的賓語與補語；而第三個必用論元則充當外元，也就是句子的主語。英語的「氣象動詞」(meteorological verbs; 如‘rain、snow、frost’等) 本來是‘零元述語’(zero-place predicate) ，因爲這些動詞都不能以「指涉性的名詞組」(referential NP; R-expression) 爲外元或主語。但是英語的語法要求：每一個

---

❻ 「狀語」與「定語」可以合稱爲「附加語」(adjunct)。

句子都必須在表層結構有主語的存在❼；所以這些動詞就只好以「填補詞的'it'」(expletive 'it')❽做爲主語。其他在表示時刻、時令、天氣、天色等句子(如'*It* is {five o'clock/Monday/May/spring/a fine day/is getting dark}')裏充當主語的'it'，以及在以「that子句」或「不定子句」爲補語的句子 (如'*It* is {fortunate *that he has returned home safely*/impossible *for us to know the truth*}')裏充當主語的'it' 都屬於這種「填補詞的'it'」。

我們把表示「語法範疇」(grammatical category) 的「詞類」(part of speech)，如名詞、代詞、動詞、形容詞、副詞、介詞、連詞等，用「…詞」來表示；而把表示「語法功能」(grammatical function) 或「語法關係」(grammatical relation) 的概念，如主語、謂語、述語、賓語、補語、定語、狀語、附加語、修飾語、主要語、前行語等，用「…語」來表示。「…詞」基本上是「元素」(element)與「集合」(set)之間「歸屬關係」(class-membership; "…is a…") 的概念 ('John' is a noun; 'kiss' is a verb; 'Mary' is a noun)；而「…語」則是詞與詞形成「詞

---

❼ 這是所謂的「擴充的投射原則」(the Extended Projection Principle)。在漢語語法裏沒有這樣的要求，所以 '小明見到了小華沒有？' 這一句問話可以用 'pro見到了pro' 這一句不含顯形主語與賓語(「小代號」 'pro' 代表不具有語音形態的「空號代詞」(empty pronoun)) 的句子來回答。又英語祈使句裏第二身代詞 'you' 的消失可以分析爲在「語音形式」(phonetic form; PF) 部門裏刪除的結果。

❽ 又稱爲「冗贅詞的'it'」(pleonastic 'it')。

組結構」(phrase structure) 時「構成成分」(constituent) 與構成成分之間「結構關係」(structural relation; "…is the…of …") 的概念 ('John' is the subject of the sentence 'John kissed Mary'; 'Mary' is object of the verb 'kissed')。「…詞」是個別詞語的固有屬性,因而可以在詞典裏查到每一個詞的語法範疇或詞類。另一方面,「…語」卻是「…詞」在特定的句法結構出現時所擔任的語法功能或所發生的語法關係。同樣是名詞的 'John' 與 'Mary' 在 *'John* kissed *Mary'* 裏分別充當主語與賓語,在 *'Mary* kissed *John'* 裏分別充當賓語與主語,而在 *'John and Mary* kissed (each other)' 則共同充當主語。因此,「…詞」與「…語」兩個概念的釐清,在語法分析的觀念上相當重要。

四、論旨角色與論旨階層

在句子裏出現的論元,不但屬於一定的語法範疇(如名詞組、介詞組、形容詞組、副詞組、數量詞組、子句等)、擔任一定的語法功能(如主語、賓語、補語、狀語、定語等)、而且扮演一定的「論旨角色」(thematic-role; θ-role)。例如在下面⑤的例句裏,'John'、'the door'、'with this passkey' 都是述語動詞 'open' 的論元。其中,'John' 與 'the door' 都屬於名詞組,而 'with this passkey' 則是介詞組。又 'John' 是必要論元(外元),表示動作 'open' 的「主事者」(Agent),並在⑤a與⑤b的例句裏都充當主語。'the door' 也是必要論元(內元),表示動作 'open' 的對象或「客體」(Theme),在⑤a與⑤b的例句

裏都充當賓語，但是在⑤c的例句裏則由於主事者'John'的不存在而「升格」（promote）為主語。至於'with this passkey'則應該屬於可用論元（意元）；因為這個表示「工具」（Instrument）的論元雖然不存在，⑤b的例句也照樣可以成立。又這個論元在⑤a的例句裏與主事者'John'一起出現時，「降格」（demote）而成為狀語；但是在⑤d的例句裏主事者'John'不存在時，則「凌駕」（override）內元的'the door'而成為句子的主語。試比較：

⑤　a.　〔John〕opened〔the door〕〔with this passkey〕.

　　　　〔小明〕〔用這把總鑰匙〕開了〔門〕。

　　b.　〔John〕opened〔the door〕.

　　　　〔小明〕開了〔門〕。

　　c.　〔The door〕opened.

　　　　〔門〕開了。

　　d.　〔This passkey〕opened〔the door〕.

　　　　〔這把總鑰匙〕開了〔門〕。

又如在下面⑥a的例句裏，主語名詞組'John/小明'扮演「感受者」（Experiencer）的論旨角色，賓語名詞組'Mary/小華'扮演客體的論旨角色，而狀語介詞組'in the library/在圖書館裏'則扮演「處所」（Location）的論旨角色。但是如果把⑥a的主動句改為⑥b的被動句，那麼客體名詞組就充當句子的主語，而主事者名詞組'John/小明'就成為介詞'by/被'的賓語。試比

較：

⑥　a.　〔John〕 saw 〔Mary〕 〔in the library〕.

　　　　〔小明〕〔在圖書館裏〕看見了〔小華〕。

　　b.　〔Mary〕 was seen 〔by John〕 〔in the library〕.

　　　　〔小華〕〔在圖書館裏〕〔被小明〕看見了。

主事者與感受者通常都由「有生名詞」(animate noun)，特別是「屬人名詞」(human noun)，來充當，但是二者在論旨角色的功能上卻有差別：主事者表示自願或主動的積極參與行動，所以一般都與「動態動詞」(actional verb; 如 'look(at)/看、listen(to)/聽、look for/找、get/拿' 等) 連用，並且可以出現於 (i) 祈使句（如⑦a句）與 (ii) 使役句的補語子句（如⑦b句），也可以與 (iii)「進行貌」(progressive aspect)（如⑦c 句）及 (iv)「受惠者」(Beneficiary)（如⑦ d 句）連用；相反的，感受者表示非自願或被動的發生變化或接受行動，所以一般都與「靜態動詞」(stative verb; 如 'see/看見、understand/聽懂、find/找到、have/有' 等) 連用，並且不能出現於祈使句或使役句，也不能與進行貌或受惠者連用。試比較：

⑦　a.　{Look at/ Listen to/ *See/ *Understand} me!

　　　　{看/聽/*看見/*聽懂} 我。

　　b.　I asked him to {look at/ listen to/ *see❾/*un-

---

❾　這裏的動詞 'see' 如果解釋為動態動詞 '見（面）' 就可以通。

derstand} me.

我叫他 {看/聽/*看見/*聽懂} 我。

c. I am {looking for/ *finding} the money for him.

我在替他 {找/*找到} 錢。

d. Don't worry. I'll {get/ *have} the money for you.

別擔心。我為你去 {拿/*有} 錢。

　　再如在下面⑧a 的例句裏，主語名詞組 'John/小明' 扮演主事者，而賓語名詞組 'Mary/小華' 與補語子句 'PRO to go at once/PRO 馬上去' 則分別扮演「終點」(Goal) 與「命題」(Proposition) ⑩的論旨角色。我們在補語子句擬設不具語音形態的空號代詞 'PRO'（「大代號」）為主語，因為根據「投射原則」(the Projection Principle)⑪一元述語 'go/去' 應該以主事者名詞組為外元或主語。這個表示主事者的主語名詞組就以大代號 'PRO' 來表示；而且這個大代號必須與表示終點的賓語名詞組「同指標」(co-indexed)，所以例句裏的 'Mary/小華' 與 'PRO'

---

⑩　嚴格說來，這裏補語子句的命題內涵必須以主事者名詞組為主語而以動態動詞為述語，所以其所扮演的論旨角色似宜稱為「行動」(Action)。

⑪　原則參數語法的「投射原則」規定：在詞項記載裏所登記的述語動詞的「論元結構」（即述語必須有幾個論元）與「論旨屬性」（即這些論元必須扮演什麼論旨角色）必須原原本本的投射到「深層結構」、「表層結構」、「邏輯形式」等「句法表顯層次」上面去。

都加上同樣的「下標」(subscript)來表示這兩個名詞組的指涉對象是同一個人。又我們推測 'Mary/小華' 所扮演的論旨角色是終點，因為在與⑧a的英語例句相對應的「衍生名詞組」(derived nominal ⑫)，即例句⑧b的主語 'John's order *to Mary* to go' 裏，'Mary' 是由表示終點的介詞 'to' 來引介。⑬ 試比較：

⑧　a.　〔John〕ordered〔Mary〕i〔PROi to go at once〕.
　　　　〔小明〕命令〔小華〕i〔PROi 馬上去〕。

　　b.　〔〔John〕's order〔to Mary〕〔PRO to go at once〕surprised everyone.
　　　　〔小明要小華馬上去的命令〕使大家感到驚訝。

⑨的例句顯示：表示命令、請求、建議等動詞都以主事者名詞組為主語，終點名詞組為賓語，而以命題子句為補語。

⑨　a.　〔Bill〕{ requested/advised/reminded }〔Helen〕〔PRO to attend the party with him〕.

　　b.　〔〔Bill〕's { request/advice/reminder }〔to Helen〕〔PRO to attend the party with him〕proved

---

⑫　又稱「實質名詞組」(substantive nominal)。
⑬　漢語裏也有 '小明下命令給小華' 與 '司令下命令到隊部' 等說法，而 '給' 與 '到' 都是漢語裏表示終點的介詞。日語裏與⑧a的英語與漢語的例句同義的例句 '太郎は花子にすぐに行けと命令した' 裏 '花子' 也與表示終點的介詞 'に' 連用。

to be useless.

　　述語動詞的論元數目與論旨角色的認定，對於句法結構與句意內涵的了解有莫大的幫助。例如，如果我們知道英語與漢語動詞'steal/偷'都可以帶上三個論元：主事者（外元；主語）、客體（內元；賓語）與「起點」（Source）（意元；狀語），也就是'偷的人'、'偷的東西'與'（從那裏）偷來的地方'；那麼我們就可以依照在下文裏卽將討論的論旨網格的投射方式造出下面⑩的例句，也可以了解爲什麼在'the bank/銀行'前面出現表示起點的介詞'from/從'。

⑩　a.〔The thief〕（主事者）stole〔the money〕（客體）
　　　〔*from* the bank〕（起點）.
　　　〔小偷〕（主事者）〔從銀行〕（起點）偷了〔錢〕（客體）。
　　b.〔The thief〕（主事者）stole〔the bank〕's（起點）
　　　〔money〕（客體）.
　　　〔小偷〕（主事者）偷了〔銀行〕（起點）的〔錢〕（客體）。

但是與'steal/偷'近義的述語動詞'rob/搶'，英語與漢語的用法就有相同與相異之點。英語的'rob'與漢語的'搶'都可以有⑪a例句的用法，但是只有英語的'rob'可以有⑪b例句的用法。試比較：

⑪　a.〔The robber〕（主事者）robbed〔the money〕（客體）

〔*from* the bank〕(起點).

〔強盜〕(主事者)〔從銀行〕(起點)搶了〔錢〕(客體)。

b. 〔The robber〕(主事者) robbed〔the bank〕(起點)

〔*of* the money〕(客體).

在⑩a與⑪a裏客體名詞組'the money/錢'充當賓語並分別由及物動詞'steal/偷'與'rob/搶'獲得「格位」(Case)，所以不必也不可以帶上介詞；而起點名詞組'the bank/銀行'則必須從介詞獲得格位，所以必須帶上起點介詞'from/從'。另一方面，在⑪b裏起點名詞組'the bank/銀行'充當賓語而直接從及物動詞'rob'獲得格位，所以不帶介詞。但是出現於賓語後面的客體名詞組則再也無法從及物動詞獲得格位，因而必須從表示客體的介詞'of'獲得格位。至於⑩b的起點名詞組'the bank/銀行'，則從「領屬標誌」(genitive marker)'-'s/-的'獲得格位，所以也不必另外帶上介詞。英語介詞'of'之與客體名詞組連用，還可以從⑫與⑬的例句獲得證實。❶

⑫ a. 〔No one〕(主事者) can deprive〔me〕(起點)〔*of* my rights〕. (客體)。

b. 〔The doctor〕will relieve〔the patient〕〔*of* his pain〕.

---

❶ 在⑫裏"動詞＋起點＋'of'客體"的句式都可以改爲"動詞＋客體＋'from'起點"的句式；但是在⑬裏表示"動作＋終點＋'of'客體"的句式則不能有這種句式上的改變。

  c. What can 〔I〕 do is to ease 〔you〕〔*of* your grief〕?

  d. 〔The mob〕plundered〔the shops〕〔*of* their goods〕.

⑬ a. 〔John〕（主事者）informed〔Mary〕（終點）〔*of* the accident〕（客體）.

  b. 〔John〕reminded〔Mary〕〔*of* their appointment〕.

  c. 〔John〕convinced〔Mary〕〔*of* her victory〕.

  d. 〔John〕accused〔Mary〕〔*of* her carelessness〕.

  各種句法成分與其論旨角色的認定，不但有助於了解各種論元的語意功能以及論元裏名詞組與介詞之間的選擇關係，而且對於一些語法功能與表現的詮釋也有相當的貢獻。例如，Jackendoff（1972:43）爲英語提出下面⑭的「論旨階層」（The Thematic Hierarchy）與⑮的「論旨階層條件」（Thematic Hierarchy Condition）：

⑭ 「論旨階層」：主事者＞｛處所／起點／終點｝＞客體

⑮ 「論旨階層條件」：被動句裏由表示主事者的介詞‘by’所引介的名詞組必須在論旨階層上高於被動句主語名詞組。

  ⑭的「論旨階層」規定：在各種論旨角色的上下階層關係裏，主事者的位階高於處所、起點或終點的位階，而處所、起點與終點的位階又高於客體的位階。而⑮的「論旨階層條件」則規定：被

動句的主語名詞組所扮演的論旨角色在論旨階層上必須低於介詞 'by' 的賓語名詞組所扮演的論旨角色。這兩種條件可以說明下列例句的合法度判斷。試比較：

⑯ a. 〔John〕（主事者）was hitting 〔the car〕（客體）with force.

〔小明〕（主事者）正在用力的敲打〔汽車〕（客體）。

   b. 〔The car〕（客體）was being hit 〔by John〕（主事者）with force.

〔汽車〕（客體）正〔被小明〕（主事者）用力的敲打。

⑰ a. 〔John〕（客體）hit 〔the car〕（終點）with a crash.

〔小明〕（客體）砰然一聲撞(到)了〔汽車〕（終點）。

   b. ?〔The car〕（終點）was hit 〔by John〕（主事者）with a crash.

?〔汽車〕（終點）〔被小明〕（主事者）砰然一聲撞(到)了。

⑱ a. 〔The book〕（客體）costs 〔five dollars〕（數量(金額)）.

〔這一本書〕（客體）索價〔美金五元〕（金額）。

   b. *〔Five dollars〕（金額）are cost 〔by the book〕（客體）.

*〔美金五元〕（金額）〔被這一本書〕（客體）索價。❺

⑲ a. 〔John〕（客體）weighs 〔one hundred pounds〕（數

---

❺ ⑱漢語例句的不合語法，除了違反「論旨階層條件」以外，主語名詞組 '美金五元' 的「虛指」(non-referential) 也有關係。

　　　　量（重量）).

　　　　〔小明〕（客體）重〔一百磅〕（重量）.

　　b.　*〔One hundred pounds〕（重量）is weighed〔by
　　　　John〕（客體）.

　　　　*〔一百磅〕（重量）〔被小明〕（客體）重（了）。❻

⑳　a.　〔John〕（感受者）regards〔Bill〕（客體）〔as pom-
　　　　pous〕（屬性）❼.

　　　　〔小明〕（感受者）認爲〔小剛〕（客體）〔很自大〕（屬性）。

　　b.　〔Bill〕（客體）is regarded〔by John〕（感受者）〔as
　　　　pompous〕.

　　　　??〔小剛〕（客體）〔被小明〕（感受者）認爲（是）〔很自
　　　　大〕。❽

㉑　a.　〔Bill〕（客體）impresses〔John〕（終點）〔as pom-
　　　　pous〕（屬性）. ❾

---

　❻ ⑲b漢語例句的不合語法，除了違反「論旨階層條件」以外，主語名詞
　　組'一百磅'的虛指與述語'重'的屬於形容詞也有關係。

　❼ Jackendoff（1972:45）並未指明主語名詞組'John'的論旨角色，
　　卻認爲'as pompous'的論旨角色是「抽象的處所」（abstract
　　Location）。我們把這裏的'John'分析爲感受者（雖然在'Please
　　regard me as your best friend'的例句裏被省略的主語名詞組
　　'you'的論旨角色可能是主事者），並把'as pompous'的論旨角色
　　分析爲「屬性」（Attribute）。

　❽ ⑳b漢語例句的有瑕疵，可能與「論旨階層條件」無關，而與漢語動詞
　　'認爲'之以子句爲實語（英語動詞'regard'則似乎以小子句爲實語）
　　有關。

　❾ Jackendoff（1972:45）把這裏的'John'分析爲終點，因爲㉑a的例
　　句與'Bill（客體）is impressive〔to John〕（終點）'同義。同時
　　，請注意：在與㉑a的英語例句相對應的漢語例句'小剛給小明的印
　　（→）

〔小剛〕（客體）〔給小明〕（終點）的印象是（他）〔很自
大〕。

b. *〔John〕（終點）is impressed 〔by Bill〕（客體）〔as
pompous〕（屬性）.

*〔小明〕（終點）〔被小剛〕（客體）給的印象是（他）很自
大。

在以上⑯到㉑的例句裏，凡是合語法的被動句（⑯、⑰、⑳）都符
合「論旨階層條件」，而不合語法的被動句（⑱、⑲、㉑）都違背
這個條件。根據我們的初步觀察，同樣的「論旨階層條件」也大
致適用於漢語的被動句。不過⑮的「論旨階層條件」似乎並不周
全，因為⑮的「論旨階層條件」總共只列舉了五種論旨角色。如
果說在⑮裏並未列舉的論旨角色（如⑱與⑲句的「數量」）都在論旨
階層上低於「客體」，那麼在⑳與㉒裏合語法的被動句顯示「感
受者」在論旨階層上應高於「客體」。❹

──────────

（──）象是（他）很自大'或'小剛使小明覺得（他）很自大'裏出現的'給小明'
與'使小明'也都表示終點。

❹ 此外，Larson（1988:382）也是提出"「主事者」＞「客體」＞「終點」＞
其他介詞組論元（如「情狀」、「時間」、「處所」等）"的英語論旨階層，
並認為這些論旨角色依照從上到下的次序出現於動詞組的「X標槓結
構」（X-bar structure）裏。Bresnan & Kanerva（1989:23）也
提出 "「主事者」＞「受惠者」＞{「終點」/感受者}＞工具＞{客體/受事
者}＞處所" 的論旨階層來說明普遍語法裏「處所倒序」（Locative
Inversion）的現象。湯（1972）也提出 "「主事者」＞「工具」＞「受事
者」＞「客體」＞「終點」＞「處所」＞「時間」" 的漢語論旨階層來說明各
種論旨角色充當主語的優先次序。由於篇幅的限制，我們不擬在這裏
詳細評介這些論旨階層。

㉒　a.　〔John〕（感受者）saw〔Mary〕（客體）〔in　the
　　　　crowd〕（處所）.

　　　　〔小明〕（感受者）〔在羣衆裏〕（處所）看見了〔小華〕
　　　　（客體）。

　　　b.　〔Mary〕（客體）was seen〔in the crowd〕（處所）
　　　　〔by John〕（感受者）.

　　　　〔小華〕（客體）〔在羣衆裏〕（處所）〔被小明〕（感受者）
　　　　看見了。

　　又下面㉓的例句顯示，「使役動詞」（causative　verb; 如
'ask/請(求)、order/命令、force/強迫、make/逼'等)補語子
句的主語必須是「主事者」；㉔的例句顯示，不及物動詞'serve'
(做'用來(做……)'或'做……之用'解)的主語與補語子句主語都
必須是「工具」；㉕的例句顯示，及物動詞 'try'（做'試圖(做…
…)'解)的補語子句必須以「主事者」爲主語；而㉖的例句則顯示
，不及物動詞 'seem'（做'好像'解)的補語子句則不可以拿「主
事者」爲主語。試比較：

㉓　a.　John forced *Mary*〔*PRO*（主事者）to study En-
　　　　glish〕.

　　　　小明強迫小華〔*PRO*（主事者）學(習)英語〕。

　　　b.　*John forced *Mary*〔*PRO*（感受者）to understand
　　　　English〕.

　　　　*小明強迫小華〔*PRO*（感受者）懂(得)英語〕。

㉔　a.　*The ice*（工具）served〔*PRO*（工具）to chill the

beer〕.

那些冰塊（工具）用來〔PRO（工具）冰涼啤酒〕。

b. *The waiter（主事者）served〔PRO（主事者）to chill the beer〕.

*那位服務生（主事者）用來〔PRO（主事者）冰涼啤酒〕。

㉕ a. John tried〔PRO（主事者）to send the letter〕.

小明試圖〔PRO（主事者）送信〕。

b. *John tried〔PRO（終點）to receive the letter〕

*小明試圖〔PRO（終點）收到信〕。

㉖ a. John（感受者）seemed〔t㉑ to know the answer〕.

小明（感受者）好像知道答案。

b. *John（主事者）seemed〔t to copy the answer〕.㉒

㉑ 'seem'與'appear, prove, chance'等同屬於「提升動詞」（raising verb），主語'John'在深層結構裏本來出現於補語子句裏主語的位置，然後經過移位而提升移入主要子句主語的位置；結果，在原來的位置留下「痕跡」（trace），用符號't'來表示。

㉒ 但是如果把補語子句述語動詞改爲進行貌或完成貌（如'John seemed to {be copying/have copied} the answer'），就可以通。同樣的，如果把與此相對應的漢語例句的述語動詞改爲進行貌、完成貌或經驗貌（如'小明好像｛在抄（襲）/抄（襲）了/抄（襲）過｝答案'，就可以通。這個事實顯示；(i) ㉖a 的合語法與㉖b的不合語法，眞正的理由不是前者以「主事者」爲主語、後者不以「主事者」爲主語，而是前者的述語是「靜態動詞」、後者的動詞是「動態動詞」；(ii)「動貌助動詞」（aspect auxiliary；如'have (-en)'、'be (-ing)'、'在……'與「動貌標誌」（aspect marker；如'了、過'）在動詞屬性上屬於「靜態」，帶上了這些動貌助動詞或標誌的動態動詞都在句法功能上變成靜態動詞。

＊小明（主事者）好像抄（襲）答案。

　　論旨角色的分類與認定，不僅有助於解釋句法結構的形成與句法功能的表現，而且也有助於詞法結構的形成與語意內涵的表達。以與動詞詞根合成名詞的名詞詞尾 '-er' 為例，可以表示：(i)「主事者」，即做動詞詞根所表達的動作的人（如 'a(taxi-)driver' 表示 'a person who drives (a taxi)'）；(ii)「工具」，即用來做動詞詞根所表達的動作的工具（'a (can-)opener' 表示 'a tool which is used to open (cans)'）；與 (iii)「客體」，即適合於做動詞詞根所表達的動作的東西（如 'a broiler' 表示 'ayoung small chicken that is raised especially to be cooked by broiling'）。在派生名詞 'V-er' 的三種意義與用法中，句法結構最為「無標」(unmarkəd)、語意內涵最為「透明」(transparent)、在英語詞彙中用例最多❷、在幼兒的語言習得中最早學會，因而屬於最「典型」(prototypical) 的意義與用法是表示「主事者」的 'a taxidriver'，其次是表示「工具」的 'a can-opener'，而句法結構最為「有標」(marked)、語意內涵最為「含混」(opaque)、在英語詞彙中用例最少、在幼兒的語言習得中最晚學會的是表示「客體」的 'a broiler'。這是由於英語名詞詞尾 '-er' 的「核心意義」(core meaning) 是「主事者」，而「工具」與「客體」則屬於「引伸或周邊意義」(extended or peripheral meaning)；同時這個名詞詞尾充當派生名詞的「主

---

❷　也就是說，在形成 "動詞＋'er'" 這個派生詞的構詞規律中，衍生主事者名詞的「孳生能力」(productivity) 最強。

要語」(head)，與動詞詞根合成「主事者名詞」(agent noun)。又由於動詞‘drive’是二元述語，以「客體」(如‘taxi’)爲內元，而以「主事者」爲外元(但已爲名詞詞尾‘-er’所「吸收」(absorbed))，所以可以再帶上內元「客體」而形成複合名詞‘taxi-driver’。另一方面，動詞‘open’是兼充一元述語(如‘The door opened’的「起動」(inchoative)用法)與二元述語(如‘*John* opened *the door*’的「使動」(causative)用法)的「作格動詞」(ergative verb)，以「客體」爲內元、以「工具」爲意元、而以「主事者」爲外元。如‘*John* opened *the door* with a *passkey*)，所以可以再帶上內元「客體」而形成複合名詞‘can-opener’。至於動詞‘broil’，則是以「客體」爲內元而以「主事者」爲外元的二元述語，本來也可以與表示「主事者」的名詞詞尾‘-er’連用而帶上表示「客體」的‘chicken’合成「主事者」複合名詞‘a chicken-broiler’(‘烤雞的人’)、或名詞組‘a broiler of chickens’與‘one who broils chickens’，或與表示「工具」的名詞詞尾‘-er’連用而帶上表示「客體」的‘chicken’合成「工具」複合名詞‘a chicken-broiler’(‘烤雞的器具’)、或名詞組‘a broiler for chickens’與‘a tool which is used to broil chickens’。但是動詞‘broil’與表示「客體」的名詞詞尾‘-er’連用而表示‘適於烤來食的嫩雞’時，由於「客體」的論旨角色已爲詞尾‘-er’所吸收，所以不能再帶上內元的「客體」來形成複合名詞，但是仍然可以藉適當的動詞帶上外元的「主事者」或意元(如「處所」、「時間」等)而形成‘broilers raised *by the farmer*’、‘broilers sold *in the shop*’、‘broilers being sold *today*'等名詞組。❷

五、論旨角色的內涵、分類與分佈

　　上一節的討論顯示論旨角色在句法表現與語意功能上的重要性。我們所要提出的「論旨網格」既由論旨角色構成，我們就不能不詳細的討論各種論旨角色的語意內涵與語法功能。在討論英語與漢語裏需要擬設的論旨角色時，我們應該注意下列三點：

（i）　論旨角色的選定應該具有相當的「普遍性」（universality）。也就是說，我們不能任意武斷的專為英語或漢語擬設特定的論旨角色，而應該設法選定能夠適用於一切自然語言，而且能夠為一切自然語言詮釋語法現象的論旨角色。

（ii）　論旨角色的數目應該符合「最適宜性」（optimality）的要求；也就是說，所要擬設的論旨角色的數目應該不多也不少、而要恰到好處。因為如果論旨角色的數目太少，就無法區別各種論元的語意內涵，也就無法詮釋這些論元在句法表現上的差異。反之，如果論旨角色的數目太多，就難免失於浮濫，許多不該區別的論旨角色卻加以區別，結果論旨角色相互之間必然發生「重複」（overlapping）或「冗贅」（redundancy）的現象。

（iii）　論旨角色的界定與區分必須有相當的「客觀性」（objectivity）；也就是說，每一個論旨角色的認定都要有相當客

---

❷　'broiler'在美式英語的口語裏還可以做 "酷熱的日子" 解。

觀的依據或標準。在下面的討論裏，我們爲英語與漢語共
同提出一些論旨角色，並就其所代表的語意內涵、所歸屬
的句法範疇、所擔任的句法功能、以及與動詞、介詞等的
選擇關係等舉例說明。

（一）「Agent; Ag）：「自願」（voluntary）、「自發」（self-
controllable）或「積極」（active）參與行動的「主體」
(instigator)，原則上由「有生」（特別是「屬人」）名詞組
來充當，而且經常與「動態」動詞連用。由於主事者在論
旨階層中屬於最「顯要」(prominent) 的地位❷，所以常
出現於主動句主語的位置❷，不能出現於賓語的位置；而
在被動句裏則常由介詞 'by/被、讓、給'❷ 來引介。

㉗　a.　〔John〕rushed into the fire.
　　　〔小明〕衝進火窟裏。

---

❷　參 Grimshaw & Mester（1988）與 Y.F. Li（1990）。不過
Gruber (1976) 與 Jackendoff（1972）都認爲主事者名詞組在主
語的位置出現時常兼充「客體」（他們稱「客體」爲「論旨」(Theme)）
，所以客體才是論旨關係中居於最「核心」(central) 的地位。

❷　因而在句子的階層組織裏出現於「c 統制」(c-command) 其他論元
的位置。

㉗　漢語的主事者名詞組在主動句中也常由介詞 '由' 來引介，例如：'今
天由我來請客'、'這一批錢應該由他來付'。或許有人認爲介詞 '由'
不一定與主事者連用，因爲'今天由誰來當主席？'裏的述語 '當' 可
能不是動態動詞。不過，介詞'由'常與趨向助動詞'來、去'連用，而
這些趨向助動詞則可能是動態動詞。

b. 〔Mary〕fled out of the kitchen (?? in fright)㉘.

〔小華〕(??驚嚇的)從廚房裏逃出來。

c. 〔John〕intentionally sold the book to Mary (rather than to Jane).

〔小明〕故意把書賣給小華(而不賣給小惠)。

d. 〔The magician〕turned a handkerchief into a dove.

〔魔術家〕把手帕變成鴿子。

e. 〔John〕opened the door with a passkey.

〔小明〕用總鑰匙(給)打開了門。

f. The door was opened〔by John〕with a passkey.

門〔被小明〕用總鑰匙(給)打開了。

(二) 「感受者」(Experiencer; Ex)：「非自願」(nonvoluntary)、「非自主」(non-self-controllable)或「消極」(passive) 的參與者，跟知覺、感官、心態等有關的事件或受到影響的論元，與主事者一樣經常由「有生」(特別是「屬人」) 名詞組來充當，可能出現於主動句主語的位置或在被動句裏由介詞 'by/被、讓、給'來引介；但是與主事者不同，只能與「靜態」的知覺、感官、心態動詞或形容詞連用，並可以出現於主動句賓語的位置。

㉘ 'in fright'前面的「雙問號」(double question mark) 表示：主語'Mary'與這個狀語連用時可能要解釋爲「客體」。

㉘ a. 〔John〕(*intentionally) saw Mary. ㉙

　　〔小明〕(*故意的)看到了小華。

b. Mary was seen 〔by John〕 (*intentionally).

　　小華(*故意的)〔被小明〕看到了。

c. 〔Mary〕felt very sorry (*of her own free will).

　　〔小華〕(*自願的)覺得很難過。

d. John's presence pleased 〔Mary〕very much.

　　小明的在場使〔小華〕很高興；

　　〔小華〕因為小明的在場而覺得很高興。

e. Mary's remarks greatly surprised 〔everyone〕.

　　小華的話使〔大家〕大為驚訝。

f. John struck 〔Mary〕as pompous.

　　小明給〔小華〕的印象是為人自大。

(三) 「客體」（Theme；Th）㉚：存在、移動位置或發生變化

㉙　如果把這個例句的靜態動詞 'saw/看到、看見' 改為動態動詞 'looked at, took a look at/看了、看了一下'，句子就可以通。不過，這個時候主語 'John' 所扮演的論旨角色不是感受者，而是主事者。

㉚　'Theme' 本來可以翻成「論旨」，但是「論旨」這個術語的語意內涵較為含糊不清，所以我們參考 Fillmore（1968, 1971）的術語 'Objective' 與 'Object' 翻成語意內涵比較透明的「客體」。根據 Jackendoff (1972:29), 'Theme' 這個術語首由 Richard Stanley 提出，並且在 Gruber (1976) 有關英語詞彙結構的分析中居於核心的地位。Gruber 認為英語裏每一個句子都含有「論旨」，而其他的論元則環繞這個語意角色而存在；因而把述語與各種論元之間的語意關係統稱為「論旨關係」(thematic relation)。

的人或東西。與「存放動詞」(locational verb)連用時，
客體表示存在的人或東西(如㉙句)；與「移動動詞」(mo-
tional verb)連用時，客體表示移動的人或東西(如㉚句)
；而與「變化動詞」(transitional verb) 連用時，客體
則表示變化的人或東西(如㉛句)。客體原則上由名詞組來
充當，但是不限於有生名詞組或具體名詞組，也可能是無
生名詞組或抽象名詞組。由於英語的形容詞與名詞不能指
派格位，所以出現於英語形容詞或名詞後面的客體名詞組
常由介詞'of'來指派格位(如㉜句)。另一方面，漢語的客
體名詞組出現於及物動詞或及物形容詞的後面或右邊時，
由這些動詞或形容詞獲得格位；但是出現於這些動詞或形
容詞的前面或左邊時，則常分別由'把、將'與'對'❸來引
介並指派格位(如㉝句)。客體與不及物動詞連用時，常充
當句子的主語；而與及物動詞連用時，則可能充當主語或
賓語。試比較：

㉙　a.　〔John〕is in the room.

　　　　〔小明〕在教室裏。

　　b.　〔The book〕is lying on the floor.

　　　　〔書〕(擱)在地板上。

---

❸ 能否以及應否由介詞'把、將'或'對'引介客體名詞組，除了動詞與形
容詞的「及物性」(transitivity)以外，還與這些動詞與形容詞的語
意屬性(如動詞必須是「動態」動詞)以及動貌標誌與各種補語結構的
存在有關。

c. 〔The chest〕 is standing in the corner.

〔櫃子〕（放）在屋角。

d. 〔John〕 is staying under the bed.

〔小明〕留在床底下。

e. 〔The bed〕 will remain against the wall.

〔床〕會繼續放在靠牆壁的位置。

f. 〔The dot〕 is inside of the circle.

〔點〕在圓裏面。

g. The circle contains 〔the dot〕.

圓（裏面）包含〔點〕。

h. 〔The house〕 belongs to Mary.

〔房子〕（是）屬於小華（的）。

i. Mary owns 〔the house〕.

小華擁有〔（那棟）房子〕。

j. Mary knows 〔the answer〕.

小華知道〔答案〕。

k. John bought 〔the house〕 from Mary.

小明從小華買了〔那棟房子〕。

l. John inherited 〔a million dollars〕 from his father.

小明從他父親（那裏）繼承了〔一百萬元〕。

m. Mary kept 〔the book〕 on the bookshelf.

小華〔把書〕（繼續）放在書架上面。

n. The teacher explained 〔the proof〕 to his students.

老師〔把證明〕解釋給學生。

㉚ a. 〔The rock〕 rolled down the hill.

〔(那塊)岩石〕沿著山坡滾下來。

b. John rolled 〔the rock〕 down the hill.

小明〔把(那塊)岩石〕沿著山坡滾下來。

c. 〔The glass〕 dropped to the floor.

〔玻璃杯〕掉到地板上。

d. Mary dropped 〔the glass〕 to the floor.

小華〔把玻璃杯〕摔到地板上。

e. 〔John〕 went from Taipei to Tainan.

〔小明〕從臺北到臺南(去)。

f. Mother sent 〔 John 〕 from a public school to a private school.

母親〔把小明〕從公立學校送到私立學校(去)。

g. John gave 〔the book〕 to Mary.

小明〔把書〕送給小華。

㉛ a. 〔A pumpkin〕 turned into a coach.

〔南瓜〕變成了馬車。

b. The magic wand turned 〔a pumpkin〕 into a coach.

魔杖〔把南瓜〕變成了馬車。

c. 〔Mr. Lee〕 converted from a Republican into a Democrat.

〔李先生〕由共和黨轉為民主黨員。

d. The Watergate scandal converted 〔Mr. Lee〕 from a Republican into a Democrat.

水門案醜聞〔把李先生〕由共和黨員轉為民主黨員。

㉜ a. John {likes/is fond *of*} 〔music〕.

小明（很）喜歡〔音樂〕。

b. Mary { did not fear/was not afraid *of* } 〔the danger〕.

小華（並）沒有{恐懼/怕}〔危險〕。

c. We have not expected that the enemy should destroy 〔the city〕.

我們（並）沒有想到敵人竟然會摧毀〔（這座）城市〕。

d. The destruction 〔*of* the city〕 by the enemy is quite unexpected.

敵人的摧毀〔城市〕出了意料之外。

e. Mary is very much interested in studying 〔science〕.

小華對於研究〔科學〕很感興趣。

f. Mary is very much interested in the study 〔*of* science〕.

小華對於〔科學的〕研究很感興趣。㉜

㉜ 在㉜e的漢語例句裏出現於客體‘科學’前面的‘研究’是動詞用法，因而可以指派格位給賓語名詞組‘科學’；在㉜f的漢語例句裏出現於客體‘科學’後面的‘研究’是名詞用法，因為無法指派格位給‘科學’而必（→）

㉝ a. John has finished reading 〔the book〕.

　　小明看完了〔(那本)書〕了；小明〔把(那本)書〕看完了。

　b. Mary placed 〔the vase〕 on the table.

　　小華〔把花瓶〕擺在桌子上。

　c. John is very much concerned 〔*about* Mary〕.

　　小明非常關心〔小華〕；小明〔對小華〕非常關心。

　d. Mary is very sympathetic 〔to John〕.

　　小華很同情〔小明〕；小華〔對小明〕很同情。

(四)　「工具」(Instrument; In) 主事者所使用的手段或器具，常由無生名詞組來充當。英語與漢語的工具名詞組一般都由具體名詞組來充當，並分別由介詞 'with' 與 '用' 來引介。不過，英語裏表示「手段」(means) 的工具名詞組則常由抽象名詞組來充當，而由介詞 'by' 來引介。工具與主事者連用時，常做狀語使用（因而必須由介詞來指派格位）；但是在主事者主語不出現的情形下，工具也有可能升格成為主語❸。試比較：

㉞ a. John crushed the vase 〔with a hammer〕.

──────────

(一→)須由「領位標誌」(genitive marker) '的' 來指派格位。這種由領位標誌指派格位的情形也出現於英語，例如：'〔the enemy's〕 destruction of the city; 〔the city's〕 destruction by the enemy'（參㉜d的例句）。

❸ 相形之下，表示「手段」的名詞組則似乎比較不容易充當句子的主語。

　　　　　小明〔用鐵槌〕打碎了花瓶。

b.　〔The hammer〕crushed the vase.

　　　〔鐵槌〕打碎了花瓶。

c.　John got the money from Mary〔by a trick〕.

　　　小明〔用詭計〕從小華（那裏）得到了錢。

d.　Mary went to Boston〔by {plane/car/sea}〕.

　　　小華〔{搭飛機/坐汽車/經海路}〕到波斯頓。

我們把風雨、雷電、洪水、災荒、瘟疫等不可抗拒的自然力與現象（如㉟句）與引起心理反應的原因或刺激（如㊱句）也暫且分析為工具。我們的理由是：這些論旨角色都由無生名詞組來充當，可以充當句子的主語，而且不可能與表示工具的狀語連用（也就是說二者之間有「互相排斥」(mutually exclusive) 的關係）㉞。

㉞　但是這個分析的缺點是：無法區別下面(i)與(ii)裏的「原因」與「工具」用法。試比較：

　（i）a.〔The fire〕burned down the house.
　　　　　　〔那一場大譽〕把房子（給）燒毀了。
　　　　b. The house was burned down〔*by* the fire〕.
　　　　　　房子〔被那一場大譽〕（給）燒毀了。
　（ii）a. An arsonist burned down the house〔*with* fire〕.
　　　　　　放火犯〔用火〕把房子（給）燒毀了。
　　　　b. The house was burned down by an arsonist〔*with* fire〕.
　　　　　　房子被放火犯〔用火〕（給）燒毀了。

補救這個缺失的方法可能有兩個：（一）把自然力與自然現象等分析為「主事者」，並允許無生名詞組（甚至抽象名詞組）充當主事者；（二）另外擬設「起因」(Cause) 或類似的論旨角色來處理有關的問題。以上兩種方法中，似以後一種方法為宜，因為「起因」這個論旨角色在狀語的分類中確有其需要，而且也是由無生名詞組或子句來充當。

㉟ a. 〔The typhoon〕has blown down all trees.

〔颱風〕把所有的樹都吹倒了。

b. 〔The flood〕has caused great damages.

〔洪水〕造成了極大的損害。

㊱ a. 〔A blast of explosion〕frightened everyone.

〔一陣爆炸聲〕嚇壞了大家。

b. 〔The teacher's remarks〕moved us to tears.

〔老師的話〕使我們感動得流淚。

c. 〔His mother's sudden death〕left John an orphan.

〔他母親的忽然去世〕使小明變成孤兒。

(五) 「終點」(Goal; Go)：「客體」移動（包括具體或抽象的移動)的「目的地」(destination)、「時間(的)訖點」(end-point) 或「接受者」(recepient)，目的地與時間訖點通常都分別由處所與時間名詞組來充當，而接受者則一般都由有生（特別是屬人）名詞組來充當。出現於及物動詞後面並與及物動詞相鄰接的終點名詞組直接由及物動詞來指派格位；但是出現於不及物動詞或賓語名詞組後面的終點名詞組則必須由介詞來引介並指派格位。英語裏表示目的地、時間訖點或接受者的終點名詞組都常由介詞'to'來引介，但也可能「併入」(incorporate) 處所介詞而變成'into, onto'；而時間訖點介詞則除了'to'以外還可能用'till, until, through'等。漢語裏表示目的地與時間訖點

的終點名詞組經常由介詞'到'來引介，而表示接受者的終點名詞組則經常由介詞'給'來引介。在主事者未出現的情形下，終點有可能成爲句子的主語。但是如果句子裡含有主事者，那麼了被動句以外都由主事者充當主語。又英語的終點名詞組，除了與「雙賓動詞」(ditransitive verb; double object verb) 連用的接受者名詞組可以不經過介詞的引介出現於客體名詞組的前面充當賓語以外，一般都由介詞來引介出現於客體名詞組的後面充當補語或出現於動詞的後面充當狀語。漢語的終點名詞組也除了與雙賓動詞連用的接受者名詞組可以出現於客體名詞組的前面充當賓語㉟以外，表示終點的名詞組都一律以介詞組的結構形態出現於客體名詞組或動詞的後面充當補語或狀語，但是表示時間訖點的終點名詞組則可能出現於動詞的前面充當狀語。試比較：

㊲ a. The letter finally reached 〔John〕.

那一封信終於到達了〔小明(手裏)〕。

b. 〔John〕 finally received the letter.

〔小明〕 終於收到了那一封信。

c. John sent a Christmas present 〔*to* Mary〕.

小明送了一個聖誕禮物〔給小華〕。

d. John sent 〔Mary〕 a Christmas present.

㉟ 至於需要不需要經過介詞的引介，則視雙賓動詞的類型而定。參湯(1979:199-204, 364-369)。

小明送〔(給)小華〕一個聖誕禮物。

e. I sent a telegraph 〔*to* his old address〕.

我打了一封電報〔到他的舊地址〕。

f. They traveled from Boston 〔*to* New York〕.

他們從波斯頓旅行〔到紐約〕。

g. We will be staying here from May 〔{ *to/till/ until/ through*} December〕.

我們從五月〔到十二月〕會待在這裏。

但是漢語裏由介詞‘向’引介的屬人終點名詞則常出現於動詞的前面❸❻。試比較：

㊳ a. He made a proposal 〔*to* me〕.

他〔向我〕提出一個要求。

b. He has reminded 〔me〕 of tomorrow's meeting.❸❼

他 {提醒〔我〕/〔向我〕提醒} 明天的開會。

c. He {warned 〔John〕/gave a warning 〔to John〕} not to go out with his daughter again.

他 {警告〔小明〕/〔向小明〕提出警告} 不能再跟他女

---

❸❻ 但是也有‘走〔向光明〕’、‘奔〔向自由〕’等由介詞‘向’來引介抽象名詞組而出現於動詞後面的說法。這些比較偏向於書面語的說法，或許應該比照‘〔傾向〕贊成’、‘〔偏向〕勞方’等說法而分析爲由動詞‘走、奔、傾、偏’與動詞‘向’合成的複合動詞。

❸❼ 例句㊳a與㊳b的比較顯示：㊳b裏的‘me’除了「終點」以外，似乎還擔任「感受者」的論旨角色（試比較㊳b的例句與其被動句 ‘I have been reminded (by him) of tomorrow's meeting’）。

兒來往。

又與「變化動詞」連用時，終點名詞組常表示變化的「結果」(re-sult)。這個時候，英語的終點介詞常用 ‘into’，而漢語則常用 ‘成’或‘為’與述語動詞合成複合動詞。試比較：

㊲ a. The coach turned [*into* a pumpkin].

　　馬車變〔成(了)南瓜〕。

　　b. The little hut transformed [*into* a palace] over-night

　　一夜間小茅屋變〔為宮殿〕。

(六) 「起點」(Source; So)：「起點」與「終點」相對，而常與「終點」連用。「起點」常表示行動開始的時點或地點，或發生變化以前的狀態；而「終點」則表示行動終了的時點或地點，或表示發生變化以後的狀態。起點與終點一樣，常由表示時間或處所的名詞組來充當❸；但是如果與「交易動詞」(verb of trading) 連用時，也可能以屬人名詞組為起點。起點名詞組，除了在與「交易動詞」或「變

---

❸ 如果依 Jackendoff (1972) 的論旨關係分析，下面例句的主事者名詞組也兼充起點的論旨角色。

　(i) [John] sold the house to Mary.

　　〔小明〕把房子賣給小華。

　(ii) [Mary] mailed the check to John's address.

　　〔小華〕把支票寄到小明的地址。

化動詞」連用時可以充當主語或賓語❹以外，一般都在介
詞 'from, since' 與'從、由、自從、打從'等引介之下出
現於動詞的前面充當狀語。試比較：

⑩　a.　They moved 〔*from* a city〕into a countryside.

　　　　他們〔從都市〕搬到鄉間。❹

　　b.　The meeting lasted 〔*frcm* nine〕to eleven.

　　　　開會〔從九點〕繼續到十一點。

　　c.　They have been living in the countryside
　　　　〔*since* last year〕.

　　　　他們〔（{自/打}）從去年以來〕一直住在鄉下。

　　d.　John bought the house 〔*from* Mary〕.

　　　　小明〔從小華〕買了(那一棟)房子。

　　e.　〔Mary〕sold the house to John.

　　　　〔小華〕把(那一棟)房子賣給小明。

　　f.　〔A pumpkin〕turned into a coach.

　　　　〔南瓜〕變成了馬車。

　　g.　The magic wand turned 〔a pumpkin〕into a
　　　　coach.

----

❹　這個時候的起點主語或賓語常兼充「主事者」或「客體」的論旨角色
　　。例如在⑩e 的例句裏，主語名詞組 'Mary' 兼充主事者與起點；而
　　在⑩f 與⑩g 的例句裏，主語與賓語名詞組 'a pumpkin' 都兼充客
　　體與起點。

❹　'搬到鄉間'也可以插入完成貌標誌而說成'搬到了鄉間'；可見終點介
　　詞'到'已經「併入」述語動詞'搬'而合成複合動詞。

魔杖〔把南瓜〕變成了馬車。

h. I want to translate this article 〔*from* English〕 into Chinese.

我要把這一篇文章〔從英文〕翻成中文。

(七) 「受惠者」(Beneficiary; Be)：因主事者的行動而受益或受損❷的人，因而經常都是由有生(特別是屬人)名詞組來充當，通常都在介詞引介之下充當補語或狀語，但是在與雙賓動詞連用時可能出現於客體名詞組的前面充當賓語❸。在英語裏，無論是補語或狀語用法，受益者名詞組都多由介詞‘for’來引介，而受損者名詞組則多由介詞‘on’來引介。另一方面，在漢語裏，補語用法的受益者經常都由

---

❷ 因此，「受益者」這個論旨角色，除了狹義的「受益者」(beneficiary)以外，還包括「受損者」(maleficiary)。如果有需要，下面以方括弧標明的名詞組或介詞組都可以分析爲「受損者」或「受惠者」：

(i) The joke was 〔*on* me〕.
　　那個玩笑是〔對著我〕開的。

(ii) John walked out 〔*on* Mary〕.
　　小明遺棄〔小華〕出走。

(iii) The light went out 〔*on* us〕.
　　〔令/使我們困擾的是〕電燈熄滅了。

(iv) 〔John〕 {suffered a stroke/underwent an operation} last night.
　　〔小明〕昨天晚上{中了風/接受手術}。

(v) 〔Mary〕 {had/got} har arm broken.
　　〔小華〕把手臂給弄斷了；〔小華〕弄斷了手臂了。

❸ 並請注意❷ (iv) 與 (v) 裏受損者名詞組充當主語的情形。

介詞‘給’來引介，狀語用法的受益者多由介詞‘替’或‘給’來引介，而受損者則沒有什麼特別的介詞可以用來引介❹❹。試比較：

④ a. John bought a mink coat 〔*for* Mary〕.

　　小明買了一件貂皮大衣〔給小華〕。

　b. John bought 〔Mary〕a mink coat.

　　小明買了一件貂皮大衣〔給小華〕。

　c. John sent a mink coat 〔to Mary〕.❹❺

　　小明送了一件貂皮大衣〔給小華〕。

　d. John sent 〔Mary〕a mink coat.

　　小明送〔(給)小華〕一件貂皮大衣。

　e. John cleaned the room 〔*for* Mary〕.

　　小明〔{替/給}小華〕打掃了房間。

　f. John bought the book 〔*for* Mary〕〔*on behalf of* her mother〕.

　　小明〔{替/給}小華的母親〕買了這一本書〔給小華〕。

（八）「處所」（Location; Lo）：表示事情發生的地點或客體出

---

❹❹ 因此，常與❹❷的例句 (ii) 與 (iii) 那樣，常要用動詞（如(ii)的‘遺棄’）或其他「迂迴累贅的說法」（circumlocution；如(iii)的‘{令/使}……困擾的是’）來翻譯英語的受損者介詞‘on’。

❹❺ 請注意：‘to Mary’在英語裏表示「終點」，而‘給小華’在漢語裏則表示「受惠者」。同時，動詞‘send’在英語裏表示‘寄送’，而動詞‘送’在漢語裏則表示‘贈送’。

現或存在的地點，經常都由處所名詞組來擔任，並常由處
所介詞 'at, in, on, under, beside, across/在……(裏
(面)、上(面)、下面、旁邊、對面)' 等來引介出現於狀語
或補語的位置；但是也可能不由介詞引介而充當句子的主
語。試比較：

㊷ a. He is studying 〔*at* the library〕.

　　他〔在圖書館〕讀書。

b. She stayed 〔*in* the room〕.㊻

㊻ Jackendoff (1972:31) 在下面例句 (ia) 與 (ib) 的對照下，把(ib)
的形容詞'stay'比照(ia)的'in the room'分析爲「抽象處所」(abstract Location; the abstract domain (of 'quality space')
containing those things which are Adj)：

(i) a. John stayed 〔*in* the room〕.

　　　小明(繼續)留〔在房間〕。

b. John stayed 〔angry〕.

　　　小明{繼續/依然}〔生氣〕。

根據同樣的「比照類推」(analogy)，他也把 (iib) 的形容詞 'an-
gry'與(iiib)的形容詞'depressed' 分析爲「抽象終點」(abstract
Goal)，而把(iiib)的形容詞'elated'分析爲「抽象起點」(abstract
Source)。試比較：

(ii) a. George got 〔*to* Philadelphia〕.

　　　小強到達〔費城〕。

b. George got 〔angry〕.

　　　小強〔{變得生氣/生氣了}〕。

(iii) a. Harry went 〔*from* Bloomington〕〔*to* Boston〕.

　　　小剛〔從布城〕走〔到波城〕。

b. Harry went 〔from elated〕〔to depressed〕.

　　　小剛〔從興高采烈〕變得〔悒悒不樂〕。

　　　　　她留〔在屋裏〕。

c.　John put the book 〔on the desk〕.

　　　小明把書放〔在桌子上（面）〕。

d.　The dot is 〔*inside of* the circle〕.

　　　點在〔圓裏面〕。❹

e.　〔The circle〕 {contains/is around} the dot.

　　　{〔圓裏面〕包含/〔圓〕圍繞著} 點。

f.　It is very noisy 〔*in* the city〕;

　　　〔The city〕 is very noisy.

　　　〔城市裏〕很吵鬧。

（九）「時間」（Time; Ti）：表示事情發生的時刻、日期、年月等❹，經常都由時間名詞組來擔任，並常由時間介詞 'at, in, on, during, before, after/在……（的時候、當中、以前、以後）、於'等來引介出現於狀語或補語的位置；但是「由名詞充當的時間副詞」（'bare-NP' time adverb；如 'today, tomorrow, yesterday, last {night/ week/month/year}/今天、明天、昨天、昨天晚上、上星期、上個月、去年'等）則可以不由介詞引介而充當狀語或補語，甚至可以充當「連繫動詞」（copulative verb）的主語。試比較：

---

❹　⑫d 的漢語例句裏'（在）圓裏面'表示處所的介詞'在'可以分析爲由於與動詞'在'連續出現，所以經過「疊音刪除」（haplology）而刪除。

❹　我們把表示事情延續的「期間」（Duration）延入下面（十）的「數量」。

㊸ a. She came 〔*at* 10〕 and left 〔*at* 10:30〕.

　　她〔(在)十點鐘〕來，〔(在)十點半〕離開。

　b. Edison was born 〔*in* 1847〕 and died 〔*in* 1931〕.

　　愛迪生〔於1847年〕出生，〔於1931年〕逝世；

　　愛迪生生〔於1847年〕，卒〔於1931年〕。

　c. Mary set the date 〔*on* Monday〕㊾

　　小華把日期訂〔在星期一〕；

　　小華〔在星期一(那一天)〕訂了日期。

　d. I met John 〔yesterday〕.

　　我〔昨天〕遇到了小明。

　e. 〔Tomorrow〕 will be another day.

　　〔明天〕又是一個不同的日子。

(十) 「數量」(Quantity; Qu)：在我們的分析下，「數量」是一個「大角色」("archrole")，它的語意內涵是「概括的範域」(the generalized Range)，除了一般的「數量」(Qu) 以外，還包括下面許多「同位角色」("allorole")㊿：「期間」(duration; Qd)、「金額」(cost; Qc)、「長度」(length; Ql)、「重量」(weight; Qw)、「面積」(area;

㊾ 例句㊸c 裏的 'on Monday' 可以分析爲補語，也可以分析爲狀語，因此與這一個例句對應的漢語則有兩種不同的說法。

㊿ 這裏「大角色」與「同位角色」的關係，基本上相當於「大音素」(archphoneme) 與「音素」(phoneme) 的關係，或「音素」與「同位音」(allophone) 的關係。

Qa）、「容積」（volume; Qv）、「頻率」（frequency; Qf）等。「數量」多由「數量詞組」（quantifier phrase; QP），卽含有「數量詞」（quantifier）❺❶的名詞組來擔任，而且除了與特定的少數動詞連用時可以充當內元（卽賓語或補語）或外元（卽主語）以外，一般都充當意元（卽狀語）。英語裏充當意元的「期間」、「金額」、「長度（或距離）」等常在介詞'for'的引介下充當狀語。另一方面，漢語裏表示「數量」的狀語卻很少由介詞來引介，而直接出現於述語動詞的後面。試比較：

㊹　a.　We studied (English) 〔*for* two hours〕.

　　　我們（讀英語）讀了〔兩個小時〕。

　　b.　The meeting lasted 〔two hours〕.

　　　會議持續了〔兩個小時〕。

　　c.　〔Eight years〕 have elapsed since my son left.

　　　兒子走了以後已經過了〔八年〕了。

　　d.　I bought the book 〔*for* ten dollars〕.

　　　我〔以十塊錢（的代價）〕買了這一本書。

　　e.　I paid 〔ten dollars〕 for the book.

　　　我為了這一本書付了〔十塊錢〕。

　　f.　The book cost me 〔ten dollars〕.

---

❺❶　在概括的「數量詞組」下，除了表示度量衡的數量詞組以外，還可能包括「程度副詞」（degree adverb）。試比較：'He is {6 feet/very/rather/quite/extremely/more than 6 feet} tall'。

這一本書花了我〔十塊錢〕。

g. The forest streches 〔*for* miles〕.

那座樹林延伸〔好幾英里〕。

h. John stands 〔six feet〕.

小明身高〔六英尺〕；小明有〔六英尺〕高。

i. The boat measures 〔twenty feet〕.

這條船長〔二十英尺〕；這條船有〔二十英尺〕長。

j. Mary weighs 〔one hundred pounds〕.

小華體重〔一百磅〕；小華有〔一百磅〕重。

k. The cell measured 〔eight feet by five by eight high〕.

那個小房間有〔八英尺寬、五英尺長、八英尺高〕。

l. This hotel can accomodate 〔five hundred guests〕.

這家旅館可以容納〔五百位旅客〕。

m. This large dinner table can dine 〔twenty persons〕.

這一張大飯桌可以坐〔二十個人〕。

n. We met 〔twice a week〕.

我們〔每週〕{見面〔兩次〕/見〔兩次〕面}。

o. They dined together 〔every three days〕.

他們〔每三天〕一起 {吃飯〔一次〕/吃〔一次〕飯}。

(十一) 「命題」(Proposition)：具有「主述關係」(predication；亦卽含有外元與述語），以「狀態」(state)、「事件」(event) 或「行動」(action)等爲語意內涵的子句。與「數量」一樣，「命題」也是一個「大角色」，下面可以依據子句的「語意類型」(semantic type)分爲「陳述」(declaration 或 statement; Pd)、「疑問」(question; Pq) 與「感嘆」(exclamation; Px)。英語的陳述命題，因爲動詞具有「屈折變化」(inflection)，所以可以再依據子句的「句法類型」(syntactic type) 細分爲：(i)「限定子句」(finite clause; Pf)、(ii)「不定子句」(infinitival clause; Pi)、(iii)「動名子句」(gerundive clause; Pg)、(iv)「小子句」(small clause; Ps)、(v)「過去式限定子句」(finite clause with the past-tense verb; Pp)、(vi)「原式限定子句」(clause with theroot-form verb ❷: Pr)、(vii)「以空號代詞爲主語的不定子句」(infinitival clause with an empty subject; Pe) 等七種，而且述語動詞與陳述論元的句法類型之間有一定的選擇限制 ❸。另一方面，漢語的命題則雖然有陳述、疑問與感嘆

❷ 也就是所謂的「假設法現在式動詞」(subjunctive present verb)，參例句㊺q, r。

❸ 除了陳述命題以外，疑問命題也可以有「限定子句」(如 'what one should do')與「不定子句」(如 'what to do')之分。但是與陳述命題不同，述語動詞與疑問論元之間並沒有句法類型上的選擇限制；凡是以疑問子句爲賓語、補語或主語的述語動詞原則上都可以隨意選擇「限定疑問子句」(wh-clause) 或「不定疑問子句」(wh-infinitival)。唯一的例外是：由「疑問補語連詞」(interrogative complementizer) 'whether' 與 'if'引介的限定疑問子句不能改爲不定疑問子句。

等語意類型上的區分，但在陳述命題底下卻沒有英語裏那麼多句法類型上的差別，只要辨別一般陳述子句(Pd)與「以空號代詞爲主語的不定子句」(Pe) 兩種就夠了。也就是說，除了「控制動詞」(control verb；包括「主語控制」(subject-control) 的 'try, attempt, promise/設法，試圖，答應' 與「賓語控制」(object-control) 的'order, force, warn/命令、強迫、警告') 等需要以「以空號代詞爲主語的不定子句」(Pe) 爲賓語或補語以外，其他述語動詞都一概以「一般陳述子句」(Pd) 爲賓語或補語。試比較：

㊺ a. I know 〔Pf *that* John *is* a nice boy〕.

　　　我知道〔Pd 小明是個好男孩〕。

　　b. I asked Mary 〔Pq {*whether/if*} she *knew* the answer〕.

　　　我問小華〔Pq 她知不知道答案〕。

　　c. Do you know 〔Pq *what* {*we should/to*} do〕?

　　　你知道〔Pq（我們）該怎麼做〕嗎？

　　d. I didn't know 〔Px *what a* smart girl Mary *is*〕.

　　　我不知道〔Px 小華（竟然）是這麼聰明的女孩子〕。

　　e. I never imagined 〔Px *how very* smart she is〕.

　　　我沒有想到〔Px 她（竟然）這麼聰明〕。

　　f. We consider 〔Pf *that* Shakespeare *is* a great poet〕.

我們認為〔Pd 莎士比亞是偉大的詩人〕。

g. We consider 〔Pi Shakespeare *to be* a great poet〕.

我們認為〔Pd 莎士比亞是偉大的詩人〕。

h. We consider 〔Ps Shakespeare φ a great poet〕.

我們認為〔Pd 莎士比亞是偉大的詩人〕。

i. John wanted (it) very much 〔Pi *for* Mary *to* succeed〕.

小明渴望〔Pd 小華成功〕。

j. John expects 〔Pf *that* Mary *will* succeed〕.

小明期待〔Pd 小華會成功〕。

k. John expects 〔Pi Mary *to* succeed〕.

小明期待〔Pd 小華會成功〕。

l. Do you mind {Pg {me/my} wearing your necktie〕?

〔Pd 我戴你的領帶〕可以嗎？

m. I wish 〔Pp I *were* a bird〕.

但願〔Pd 我是隻鳥〕。

n. They found 〔Ps the place φ deserted〕.

他們發覺〔Pd 那個地方空無人影〕。

o. John saw 〔Ps Mary φ walk into the restaurant〕.

小明看見〔Pd 小華走進餐廳〕。

p. Mary made 〔Ps John φ admit that he was spying on her〕.

小華逼小明〔Pe PRO 承認他在暗中偵察她〕。

q. John insisted 〔Pr *that* Mary {*be*/stay} here with
   him〕.

   小明堅持〔Pd 小華要跟他在一起〕。

r. Mary suggested to John 〔Pr *that* he not *see*
   her any more〕.

   小華向小明提議〔Pd 他不要再來找她〕。

s. John tried 〔Pe PRO to reach Mary〕.

   小明試圖〔Pe PRO 連絡小華〕。

t. John promised Mary 〔Pe PRO to marry her〕.

   小明答應小華〔Pe PRO 跟她結婚〕。

u. John forced Mary 〔Pe PRO to marry him〕.

   小明強迫小華〔Pe PRO 跟他結婚〕。

以上我們根據「每句一例的原則」(the Principle of One-
Instance-per-Clause；即每一種論旨角色在同一個「單句」
(simple clause) 裏至多只能出現一個❸、「互補分佈的原則」

---

❸ 但是「每句一例的原則」應該允許「必用論元」與「可用論元」之間同
　時出現兩個同樣的論旨角色，因為在下面的例句裏「處所」與「受惠
　者」同時出現於「內元」(補語) 與「意元」(狀語)。
　（ i ）(While) 〔in the classroom〕 Mary placed the flowers 〔on
　　　the teacher's desk〕.
　　　〔在教室裏〕(的時候)小華把花擺〔在老師的桌子上〕。
　（ii）John bought a wristwatch 〔for Mary〕 〔on behalf of her
　　　mother〕.
　　　小明〔{替/給}小華的母親〕買了一隻手錶〔給小華〕。
　同時，英語裏由 "'out-' ＋不及物動詞" 所形成的及物動詞(如 'outrun,
　outtalk, outshoot/跑得過(跑得比……快)、說得過(說得比……好)
　、射得過(射得比……準)' 等)也似乎應該以兩個論旨角色相同的論元
　（→）

(the Principle of Complementary Distribution；即形成「互補分佈」(complementary distribution) 而絕不形成「對立」(opposition) 或「對比」(contrast) 的兩個或兩個以上的論旨角色屬於同一種論旨角色) 與「連接可能性的原則」(the Principle of Conjoinability；即只有論旨角色相同的論元才能互相連接❺）等來擬設英語與漢語所需要的論旨角色以及這些論旨角色所表達的語意內涵、所歸屬的句法範疇、所擔任的語法功能、論旨角色與介詞間的選擇關係等。如果我們要詳細討論充當副詞與狀語的論元，那麼我們可能還需要「情狀」(Manner; Ma)、「受事(者)」(Patient; Pa)、「起因」(Cause; Ca)、「結果」(Result; Re)、「條件」(Condition; Co) 等論旨角色。有了這些額外的論旨角色，我們不但能爲述語動詞與形容詞提出更

(→)爲主語與賓語(如 (iii) 句)；而必須「以語意上複數的名詞組爲主語」(semantically plural subject) 的「對稱述語」(如'kiss, meet, consult/接吻、見面、商量'等)以兩個(或兩個以上的名詞組)爲主語時，這些名詞組也似乎應該具有相同的論旨角色 (如 (iv) 句)。

 (iii)　〔John〕can {outrun/outtalk/outshoot} 〔Bill〕.
   〔小明〕能{跑得過/說得過/射得過}〔小剛〕。
 (iv)　〔John〕and 〔Mary〕{kissed/met/consulted}.
   〔小明〕跟〔小華〕{接了吻/見了面/商量了}。

❺ 這個原則也引導我們把英語與漢語的「比較結構」(comparative construction) 分析爲由兩個論旨結構相同的主句與從句合成，例如：

 (i)　John is 〔AP more intelligent 〔PP than 〔Bill pro〕〕〕.
   小明〔AP 〔PP 比 〔小剛 pro〕〕還要聰明。
 (ii)　John ran 〔AdP faster 〔PP than 〔Bill pro〕〕〕.
   小明〔VP 跑得 〔AP 〔PP 比 〔小剛 pro〕〕快〕〕。

例句裏的「小代號」(pro) 代表從句裏與主句裏相同的句法成分；如 (i)句裏的'pro'代表'is intelligent/聰明'，而(ii)句裏的'pro'則代表'ran fast/跑得快'。

細緻而明確的論旨網格,而且也可以爲介詞與連詞擬設適當的論旨網格。例如,㊻的例句裏,情狀副詞與狀語充當內元補語;在㊼與㊽的例句裏受事者與感受者的區別以及客體(或受事者)與結果的區別分別說明「準分裂句」(pseudo-cleft sentence)裏二者在句法表現上的差異;而在㊾的例句裏工具與起因的區別也說明了二者在被動句裏不同的句法表現。試比較:

㊻ a. He behaved {〔Ma *badly*〕 to his wife/〔Ma *uith great courage*〕}.

他 {對太太(表現得)〔Ma 很不好〕/表現得〔Ma 很勇敢〕}。

b. She always treated us {〔Ma *well*〕/〔Ma *with the utmost courtesy*〕}.

她經常待我們 {〔Ma 很好〕/〔Ma 非常有禮貌〕}。

c. I {phrased/worded} my execuse 〔Ma *politely*〕.

我(措辭)〔Ma 很禮貌地〕說出我的辯白。

㊼ a. 〔Pa *John*〕 suffered a stroke last night.

〔Pa 小明〕昨天晚上中了風。

b. What happened to 〔Pa *John*〕 last night was that 〔Pa *he*〕 suffered a stroke.

c. 〔Ex *John*〕 saw a friend last night.

〔Ex 小明〕昨天晚上見了一位朋友。

d. *What happened to 〔Pa *John*〕 last night was that 〔Ex *he*〕 saw a friend.

㊽ a. They finally destroyed 〔Th *the house*〕;
〔Th *The house*〕 was finally destroyed.

他們終於拆毀了〔Th 房子〕;

〔Th 房子〕終於被拆毀了。

b. What they finally did to 〔Th *house*〕 was destroy 〔Th *it*〕.

c. They finally built 〔Re the *house*〕;
〔Re *The house*〕 was finally built.

他們終於蓋了〔Re 房子〕；*〔Re 房子〕終於被蓋了。

d. *What they finally did to 〔Th *the house*〕 was build 〔Re *it*〕.

㊾ a. John burned down the house 〔In *with fire*〕.

小明〔In 放火〕燒毀了房子。

b. The house was burned down by John 〔In *with fire*〕.

房子被小明〔In 放火〕燒毀了。

c. 〔Ca *A fire*〕 burned down the house.

〔Ca 一場火警〕燒毀了房子。

d. The house was burned down 〔Ca *by a fire*〕.

房子〔Ca 被一場火警〕（給）燒毀了。

又如，表示處所（如'at, in, on/在'）、工具（如'with/用'）、客體（如'of /把，對'）、起點（如'from/從'）、終點（如'to/到，給'）、受益者（如'for/替，給'）、起因（如'for, because of/

為了，因為’）等介詞都可以分別用‘＋〔Lo〕，＋〔In〕，＋〔Th〕，＋〔So〕，＋〔Go〕，＋〔Be〕，＋〔Ca〕’的論旨網格來表示；而表示起因（如‘because, for/因為，由於’）、結果（如‘so that/所以’）、條件（如‘if, unless/如果，除非’）等連詞也都可以分別用‘＋〔Ca, Re〕，＋〔Re, Ca〕，＋〔Co, Re〕’的論旨網格來表示。

六、論旨網格與其投射條件

從以上的討論可以知道：如果把所有大大小小的句法結構視為述語動詞、形容詞、名詞以及主要語介詞、連詞、名詞、副詞、數量詞等的投射，那麼我們必須在這些詞語的詞項記載裏把有關的句法屬性登記下來，才可以設法投射出去。以述語動詞為例，動詞的詞項記載裏應該登記下列四種句法屬性。

(一) 有關動詞的論元屬性；卽這些動詞究竟是一元述語、二元述語、還是三元述語？

(二) 有關動詞的論旨屬性；卽與這些動詞連用的必用論元究竟扮演什麼樣的論旨角色？是客體、起點、終點、主事者、感受者、受惠者、工具、起因、時間、處所、數量、命題、還是其他論旨角色？

(三) 有關論元的範疇屬性；卽扮演各種論旨角色的論元應該屬於什麼樣的句法範疇？是名詞組、介詞組、數量詞組、還是命題？如果是命題，那麼究竟是陳述命題、疑問命題、還是感嘆命題？如果是陳述命題，那麼究竟是限定子句、不定子句、動名子句、小子句、過去式限定子句、原式動詞限定子句、還是以空號代詞為主語的不定子句？

(四) 有關論元的語法功能；即扮演各種論旨角色的論元應該擔任什麼樣的句法功能？是賓語、補語、主語、狀語、還是定語？

我們可以用「論旨網格」(theta-grid; θ-grid) 把以上四種句法屬性整合起來。以一元述語'cry/哭'為例，可以用'+〔Ag〕'這個論旨網格來表示有關的句法屬性：即這個動詞是只需要主事者這個必要論元的一元述語；而主事者這個論旨角色必須由有生名詞組來擔任，而且也由這一個主事者論元來充當外元或主語；因而能投射成為'John cried/小明哭了'這樣的例句。再以二元述語'see/看到'為例，可以用'+〔Th, Ex〕'這個論旨網格來表示有關的句法屬性：即這個動詞是需要以客體為內元，而以感受者為外元的二元述語；客體內元由名詞組來擔任並充當賓語，感受者外元由有生名詞組來擔任並充當主語；因而能投射成為'John saw Mary/小明看到小華'這樣的例句。更以三元述語'force/強迫'為例，則可以用'+〔Go, Pe, Ag〕'這個論旨網格來表示有關的句法屬性：即這個動詞是以終點與以空號代詞為主語的不定子句命題為內元，而以主事者為外元的三元述語；終點內元由名詞組來擔任並充當賓語❺，命題內元由以空號代詞為主語的不定子句來擔任並充當補語，而主事者外元則由有生名詞組來擔任並充當主語；因而能投射成為'John forced Mary to study English/小明強迫小華讀英語'這樣的例句。又以三元述

---

❺ 充當不及物動詞內元賓語或及物動詞內元補語的終點一概由介詞組來擔任，但是充當外元主語或及物動詞內元賓語的終點則由於必須獲得「格位」(Case) 的指派而一概由名詞組來擔任。

語‘rob/搶（走）’爲例，則可以用‘＋〔〈Th (So)〉Ag〕’/＋〔Th (So)Ag〕❺這個論旨網格來表示有關的句法屬性：卽這個動詞在英語裏是以客體名詞組爲賓語、起點介詞組爲補語、主事者名詞組爲主語，或以起點名詞組爲賓語、客體介詞組❺爲補語、主事者名詞組爲主語的三元述語；因而能投射成爲‘John robbed the money from the bank’或‘John robbed the bank of the money’這樣的例句。另一方面，在漢語裏‘搶（走）’是以客體名詞組爲賓語、起點介詞組爲狀語❺，而以主事者名詞組爲主語；因而能投射成爲‘小明從銀行搶（走）了錢’這樣的例句。最後以‘buy/買’爲例，則可以用‘＋〔〈Th (Be)〉Ag〕/＋〔Th (Be) Ag〕’這個論旨網格來表示：卽這個動詞是以客體名詞組爲賓語、受惠者介詞組爲補語、而以主事者名詞組爲主語的三元述語；因而可以投射成爲‘John bought a coat (for Mary)/小明買了一件大衣(給小華)’這樣的例句。另外，英語動詞‘buy’的論旨網格裏的角括弧（〈……〉）：表示除了客體出現於受惠者的前面

---

❺　「角括弧」（angle brackets）‘〈……〉’表示：括弧裏面的兩個符號可以調換位置；因此，‘〈Th, So〉’可以有‘Th, So’與So, Th’兩個不同的詞序。又「圓括弧」（parentheses)‘(……)’表示：括弧裏面的符號可有可無；因此，‘(So)’表示起點這個論旨角色可以不出現。

❺　客體名詞組充當及物動詞的賓語時，由及物動詞直接獲得格位；而客體名詞組充當及物動詞的補語時，則必須由客體介詞‘of’獲得格位。

❺　漢語的起點，與終點、處所不同，無法出現於賓語名詞組後面充當補語，只能出現於述語動詞前面充當狀語。同樣的，英語裏出現於賓語名詞組後面的起點（‘from the bank’)或客體(‘of the money’)也可以分析爲狀語。

以外，受惠者也可以出現於客體的前面；而論旨網格裏標在客體下面的「下線」（underline）（卽'Th'）表示出現於受惠者後面的客體具有「固有格位」（inherent Case），所以不必再由介詞來引介或指派格位；因而可以投射成爲'John bought Mary a coat'這樣的例句⑥。

　　從以上的舉例與說明，我們可以知道：論旨網格是以論旨角色爲單元來規畫的。在論旨網格裏所登記的論元，原則上都屬於必用論元，所以論旨網格裏所登記的論元數目決定這個動詞是幾元述語。又論旨角色的語意內涵與擔任這些論旨角色的語法範疇之間有極密切的關係，所以我們常可以從論旨角色來推定這個論旨角色的句法範疇⑥。另外，論旨角色是依內元（賓語先、補語後）到外元（卽主語）的前後次序排定的，所以我們也可以從論旨網格裏論旨角色的排列次序來推定由那些論旨角色來分別充當動詞的賓語、補語或句子的主語。關於論旨網格的設計，我們還應該注意下列幾點：

　　（一）　在論旨網格裏，我們原則上只登記必用論元，不登記可用論元。但是有些動詞可以兼用「及物」與「不及物」動詞，而有些及物動詞又可以帶上「單一」或「雙重」賓語。這個時候，把及物與不及物用法，或單賓與雙賓用法，合併登記的結果，論旨網格

---

⑥　與及物動詞 'buy' 相鄰接而出現於後面的受惠者名詞組 'Mary' 由動詞直接獲得格位，不必再由介詞 'for' 來引介或指派格位。與英語 'buy' 相應的漢語 '買'，在論旨網格裏找不到 '<Th, Be>' 的符號，所以不能投射成爲 '*小明買（給）小華一件大衣' 這樣的例句。

⑥　Chomsky（1986a）把這種論旨角色與句法範疇之間的連帶關係稱爲「典型的結構句式」（canonical structural realization; CSR）。

裏必然有些論旨角色出現於圓括弧裏面。例如，英語'eat, dine, devour'這三個動詞都與'吃'有關。但是這三個動詞的論旨網格分別是'+〔(Th) Ag〕'(如'What time do we *eat* (dinner)?')，'+〔Ag〕'(如'What time do we *dine?*') ❷ 與 '+〔Th, Ag〕'(如 'The lion *devoured* the deer')。再如英語與漢語的「作格動詞」(ergative verb)'open/開，close/關'等都可以有「使動」(causative) 及物用法(如'如John {opened/closed} the door/小明{開/關}了門')與「起動」(inchoative) 不及物用法(如'The door {opened/closed}/門{開/關}了')；因而可以用 '+〔Th (Ag)〕'的論旨網格來表示。也就是說，如果動詞是及物動詞，那麼以主事者名詞組為主語而以客體名詞組為賓語；如果動詞是不及物動詞，那麼以客體名詞組為主語 ❸ 。又如英語與漢語的「雙賓動詞」'teach/教，ask/問'等都可以有雙賓用法 (如 'Mr. Lee taught us English/李先生教我們英語'，'We asked Mr. Lee a question/我們問了李先生一個問題')與單賓用法 (如'Mr. Lee taught {us/English}/李先生教{我們/英語}'，'We asked {Mr. Lee/a question}/我們問了{李先生/一個問題}')。因此，英語與漢語的'teach/教'與'ask/問'可

❷ 英語動詞 'dine' 除了'+〔Ag〕'的論旨網格以外，還可以有'+〔Lo, Qu〕'這個論旨網格 (如'This table can dine twelve persons'，'How many people can this restaurant dine?')；而'+〔Ag〕'與'+〔Lo, Qu〕'這兩種論旨網格可以合併為'+〔{Ag/Lo, Qu}〕'。

❸ 這是由於不及物動詞無法指派格位，所以客體名詞組只得出現於主語的位置來獲得主位。

以分別用‘+〔〈(Th⊗Go)〉Ag〕/+〔(Go⊗Th) Ag〕’與‘+〔〈(Th⊗of So)〉Ag〕/+〔(So⊗Th)Ag〕’⑭ 的論旨角色來表示。

　　（二）　可用論元不必一一登記於論旨網格裏，而可以用「語彙冗贅規律」(lexical redundancy rule) 來處理。例如，以主事者為主語的動態動詞一般都可以與情狀、工具、受惠者、時間、處所等可用論元連用，而這種連用的情形則可以用‘+〔……Ag〕→+〔……(Ma) (In) (Be) (Lo) (Ti) Ag〕’這樣的詞彙冗贅規律來表示。如此，英語與漢語的二元述語‘cut/切’不但可以衍生‘John cut the cake/小明切了蛋糕’這樣只含有必用論元的例句，而且還可以衍生‘John cut the cake *carefully with a knife for Mary at the party last night*/小明昨天晚上在宴會裏替小華用刀子小心的切了蛋糕’這樣含有許多可用論元的例句。

　　（三）　對於必用論元，我們嚴格遵守「每句一例的原則」；即在同一個單句裏不能由兩個或兩個以上的同一種論旨角色來充當必用論元。但是這個原則並不排斥以下三種情形：（甲）同一個論旨角色可以同時充當必用論元與可用論元；（乙）「對稱述語」

---

⑭ 「交叉的圓括弧」(linked parentheses) ‘(…⊗…)’表示：包含在圓括弧裏的兩個成分中，任何一個成分都可以在表層結構中不出現，但是不能兩個成分都不出現。又英語動詞論旨網格裏的「角括弧」表示角括弧裏的兩個成分在表面結構中可以有兩個不同的詞序；而論旨角色底下的「下線」則表示這些論旨角色可以直接出現於賓語的後面充當補語，而不必由介詞來引介或指派格位。因此，除了前面所舉的例句以外，英語還可以有‘Mr. Lee taught English to us’，‘Mr. Lee taught to us’，‘We asked a question of Mr. Lee’，‘We asked of Mr. Lee’這樣的例句。

(symmetric predicate；如'kiss/接吻，meet/見面，consult/商量；mix/混合')在語意上要求複數主語或賓語，因此允許兩個或兩個以上的同一種論旨角色為內元或外元；（丙）有些述語（例如由'out-'與不及物動詞形成的及物動詞'outrun/跑得過（跑得比……快），outtalk/談得過(談得比……好)，outshoot/射得過(射得比……準)')在語意上要求以同一種論旨角色為賓語（內元）與主語（外元）❻⑤。因此，我們可以從'place/擺'的論旨網格'+〔Th, Lo, Ag〕'衍生'〔Lo In the classroom〕John placed the flowers〔Lo on the teacher's desk〕/小明〔Lo 在教室裏〕把花擺在〔Lo 老師的桌子上面〕'這樣的例句；也可以從'kiss/接吻'的論旨網格'+〔Ag Ag'〕'衍生'〔Ag John〕and〔Ag' Mary〕kissed/〔Ag小明〕跟〔Ag' 小華〕接吻了'這樣的例句❻⑥；還可以從'outrun/跑得過'的論旨網格'+〔Th, Th'〕衍生'〔Th John〕outran〔Th' Mary〕/〔Th 小明〕跑得過〔Th' 小華〕'這樣的例句。

（四） 關於論元與論旨角色之間，我們也嚴格遵守「論旨準則」(theta-criterion; θ-criterion)的規定：即論元與論旨角色之間的關係是一對一的對應關係；每一個論元都只能獲得一種論旨角色，而每一種論旨角色也只能指派給一個論元。但是一個句子有兩種以上的歧義的時候，我們例外允許以'{Xx, Yy}'的符

---

❻⑤ 這三種情形的例句與說明，請參照❻④。

❻⑥ 英語的'kiss'還具有'+〔Th, Ag〕'的論旨網格，因而還可以衍生'〔Ag John〕kissed〔Th Mary〕'這樣的例句。

號 ❻❼來表示這一個論元可以解釋爲 'Xx' 或 'Yy' 兩種不同的論旨角色。例如，英語與漢語的動詞 'roll/(翻) 滾' 都具有 '+〔{Ag, Th}（Ro）〕' ❻❽ 的論旨網格。因此，'John rolled down the hill/小明沿著山坡滾下來' 這樣的例句可以解釋爲 '小明（故意）沿著山坡滾下來'（'小明'是主事者），也可以解釋爲 '小明（不小心）沿著山坡滾下來'（'小明'是客體）。又如，'buy/買' 與 'sell/賣' 分別具有 '+〔Th (So) {Ag, Go}〕' 與 '+〔Th (Go) {Ag, So}〕' 的論旨角色。因此，'John bought a book from Mary/小明從小華（那裏）買了一本書' 的 'John/小明' 可以解釋爲主事者，也可以解釋爲終點。'Mary sold a book to John/小華賣了一本書給小明' 的 'Mary/小華' 可以解釋爲主事者，也可以解釋爲起點。

（五）　爲了不使論旨角色的數目無限制的膨脹，也爲了適當的處理論旨角色裏介詞與名詞組之間的選擇關係，我們在某種情況下把特定的介詞或名詞直接登記於論旨網格中。例如，英語

❻❼　請注意 '{Xx, Yy}' 與 '{Xx/Yy}' 兩種不同的符號代表兩種不同的情形；前者（如 '{Ag, Th}'）表示這一個論元可以解釋爲兩種不同的論旨角色（如主事者與客體），而後者（如 '{Ag/Th}'）則表示這兩種論旨角色中任選一種（如主事者或客體）。

❻❽　'Ro' 代表「途徑」（Route; Ro），常由 'along, up, down/沿著……（{上/下}{來/去}）' 來引介。又嚴格說來，'roll/(翻)滾' 的論旨網格應該寫成 '+〔{{Ag,Th}/Th(Ag)}(Ro)〕'；如此，不但可以衍生 '{ John/The rock} rolled down the slope/{小明/石塊}沿著山坡（翻）滾下來' 的例句，而且還可以衍生 'John rolled the rock down the slope/小明把石塊沿著斜坡滾下去' 的例句。

的不及物動詞'talk'具有'+〔〈Go, about Th〉Ag〕'的論旨網格（與此相對應的漢語動詞'談'則具有'+〔（有關）Th 的事情，跟 Go, Ag〕'的論旨網格）；因而可以衍生'John talked to Mary about the party/小明跟小華談了（有關）宴會的事情'與'John talked about the party to Mary'這樣的例句。又如，英語的及物動詞'load'具有'+〔{Th, on Lo/Lo, with Th} Ag〕'的論旨網格（與此相對應的漢語動詞'裝（載）'則具有'+〔Th, Lo 上面, Ag〕'的論旨網格；因而可以衍生'John loaded the furniture on the truck/小明把家具裝在卡車上面'與'John loaded truck with the furniture'這樣的例句。再如，英語的及物動詞'blame'具有'+〔{Be, for Ca/Ca, on Be} Ag〕'的論旨網格（與此相對應的漢語動詞'怪罪'則具有'+〔Be, Ca, Ag〕'的論旨網格）；因而可以衍生'John blamed Mary for the accident/小明為了車禍怪罪了小華'與'John blamed the accident on Mary'這樣的例句❻❾。

（六）以「成語」(idiom)或「片語」(phrase)的形式出現的述語動詞，把論旨網格賦給這個成語動詞或片語動詞。例如，英語的成語動詞'kick the bucket (=pass away=die)'具有'+〔Be〕'的論旨網格（與此相當的漢語成語動詞'翹辮子'、'兩腳伸直'、'穿木長衫等也具有'+〔Be〕'的論旨網格）；因而

---

❻❾ 'blame'是及物動詞，因此無論是受惠者或起因出現於動詞的後面充當賓語時，這些名詞組都不經過介詞的引介而直接由及物動詞獲得格位。但是受惠者或起因出現於賓語的後面充當補語時，這些名詞組都必須由介詞來引介並指派格位。

可以衍生 'John kicked the bucket last night/小明昨天晚上翹辮子了'這樣的例句。他如, 英語的片語動詞 'give {birth/rise} to'都具有'+〔Go, So〕'的論旨網格(與此相對應的漢語'生(產)'與'引起/導致'也都具有'+〔Go, So〕'的論旨網格)；因而可以衍生 'She gave a birth to a son last night/她昨天晚上生了一個男孩子'與'A privilege often gives rise to abuses/特權常導致濫用'這樣的例句。又如英語的片語動詞'look down (up)on(=despise)'與'take……into consideration'都具有'+〔Th, Ag〕'的論旨網格 (與此相對應的漢語動詞'輕視'與'考慮'也都具有'+〔Th, Ag〕'的論旨網格)；因而可以衍生 'Never look down on your neighbors/絕不要輕視你的鄰居'與'Please take my health into consideration/請考慮我的健康'這樣的例句。

至於論旨網格的投射，則必須遵守下面的原則或條件。

（一） 述語動詞的論旨網格，包括論元屬性與論旨屬性，都要從詞項記載裏原原本本的投射到深層結構、表層結構與邏輯形式上面❼⓿。

（二） 述語動詞與內元、意元、外元之間的「上下支配關係」(dominance) 或「階層組織」(hierarchical structure)，必須依照「X標槓理論」(X-Bar Theory) 的規定。根據湯 (1988a, 1990d, 1990e, 1990f) 所提出的X標槓理論，主要語動詞（V）以

----

❼⓿ 在「原則參數語法」裏，以「投射原則」(Projection Principle) 與「擴張的投射原則」(Extended Projection Principle) 或「主謂理論」(Predication Theory)來規範或詮釋這個現象。

補語內元為「補述語」(Complement) 形成「動詞節」(V'),動詞節以賓語內元為「指示語」(Specifier) 形成「動詞組」(V"; VP);主要語述詞 (Pr) 以動詞組為補述語形成「述詞節」(Pr'),述詞節以主語外元為指示語形成「述詞組」(Pr"; PrP);「屈折語素」(INFL; I) 以述詞組為補述語形成「謂語」(I'),謂語以「空號節點」(empty node)為指示語形成「小句子」(S; I"; IP);「補語連詞」(complementizer; C) 以小句子為補述語形成「子句」(C'),子句以空號節點為指示語形成「大句子」(S'; C"; CP)。而狀語與定語等可用意元,則以「附加語」(adjunct) 的身分與各種詞節 (X') 反複衍生詞節;因此,附加語的數目原則上沒有限制。又根據這種X標槓理論,所有的詞組結構都屬於「同心結構」(endocentric construction),而且是「兩叉分枝」(binary branching)。因此,只要把充當狀語與定語的句法成分依照句法與語意功能細加分類,那麼述語動詞與有關內元、意元、外元之間的階層組織不難從論旨網格裏直接推演出來。

(三) 述語動詞與內元、意元、外元之間的「前後出現位置」(precedence)或「線性次序」(linear order)則可以從「格位理論」(Case Theory) 中「固有格位」(inherent Case)與「結構格位」(structural Case) 的指派方向裏推演出來。我們假定英語的固有格位原則上由主要語動詞、形容詞、名詞從左方(前面)到右方(後面)的方向指派給充當內元、意元與外元的名詞組、介詞組、小句子與大句子;而英語的結構格位則原則上由及物動詞、介詞、連詞、補語連詞從左方到右方的方向指派「賓位」(accusative Case;包括「斜位」(obligue Case)) 給名詞組與子句,而「主

位」(nominative Case) 則由「呼應語素」(AGR)在「同指標」的
條件下指派給出現於小句子指示語位置的主語名詞組。另一方面
，漢語的固有格位則原則上由主要語動詞、形容詞、名詞從右方
(後面)到左方(前面)的方向指派給充當內元、意元與外元的名詞
組、介詞組、小句子與大句子；而結構格位則與英語一樣原則上
由及物動詞、及物形容詞、介詞、連詞從左方到右方的方向指派
賓位給名詞組與子句❼，並由呼應語素在同指標的條件下指派主
位給出現於小句子主語位置的主語名詞組。英語與漢語之間，固有
格位指派方向之相異，說明爲什麼這兩種語言之間有那麼多詞序
相反的「鏡像現象」(mirror image)❼；而結構格位指派方向之
相同，則說明爲什麼漢語的賓語出現於動詞或形容詞的右方時不
要由介詞來引介，而出現於動詞或形容詞的左方時則常由介詞'把
、對'等來引介。各種格位的指派也說明，爲什麼除了出現於及
物動詞(與形容詞)右方的賓語名詞組可以從這些動詞(與形容詞)
獲得格位以外，其他名詞組都必須由介詞來引介並指派格位❼。

❼　表示「終點」的內元介詞組與名詞組例外的出現於動詞或賓語的右方。
　　關於這一點，我們不在此詳論。

❼　有些英語的副詞 (如 'hardly, scarcely, simply, merely, just,
　　not, never' 等) 只能出現於主要語動詞的左方，而有些英語的副詞
　　與狀語(如表示情態與頻率的副詞以及修飾整句的副詞與狀語等)則可
　　以出現於句子裏幾種不同的位置，包括各種主要語左方的位置。這些
　　副詞與狀語的「獨特性」(idiosyncracy) 都在有關的論旨網格裏加
　　以登記(例如 'hardly, scarcely, simply, merely, not, never'
　　等都登記爲'＋〔__X'〕') 或依照其語意類型用詞彙冗贅規律加以處理
　　(例如表示時間(＋Ti) 與起因 (Ca) 的副詞與狀語可以出現於句首與
　　句尾的位置)；參 湯 (1990e)。

❼　漢語裏出現於大句子指示語位置的「主題名詞組」(topic NP) (如
　　'魚，我喜歡吃黃魚)與加接於小句子右端的名詞組(如'{我那一本書/
　　那一本書我} 昨天看完了')則例外的不必指派格位。

（四）　述語動詞與內元、意元、外元之間的線性次序，除了由論旨網格裏論旨角色從左到右的排列次序以及固有格位與結構格位的指派方向來規範以外，還可能因爲「移動 α」（Move α）的變形規律（如「從名詞組的移出」（Extraposition from NP）、「重量名詞組的轉移」（Heavy　NP　Shift）、「主題化變形」（Topicalization）等）而改變詞序；而這些移位變形都要受原則參數語法裏原則系統一定的限制❼ 。

七、論旨網格與英漢對比分析

從以上的介紹與討論，我們已經可以了解如何從英語與漢語述語動詞的論旨網格與其投射來推演或詮釋英語與漢語在句法結構上的異同。在這一節裏，我們再舉幾類較爲特殊的動詞來比較這些動詞在論旨網格上的異同如何導致英漢兩種語言在表層結構上的異同。

（一）　「交易動詞」（verbs of trading）：

⑩　a.　'spend' vt.,+〔Qc (on Th) Ag〕；

　　　　'花(費)' vt.,+〔Qc(Th上面) Ag〕

　　　　John spent ten dollars（on the book）.

　　　　小明（在這本書上）花了十塊錢；小明花了十塊錢買這本書。❼

　　b.　'pay' vt.,+〔＜Qc (Go)＞ (for Th) Ag〕；

---

❼　關於原則參數語法與英漢對比分析，參湯（1989e）。

❼　有兩個相對應的漢語例句時，一般說來前一例句比較偏向「直譯」，而後一例句則比較偏向「意譯」。

‘付’ vt.,+〔<Qc (Go)> (為了Th) Ag〕

John paid {ten dollars (to Mary)/(Mary) ten dollars} (for the book)}.

小明(為了這本書)付了{十塊錢 (給小華)/小華十塊錢}；

小明付了{十塊錢(給小華)/小華十塊錢}買這一本書。

    c. ‘buy’ vt., +〔Th (So) (Qc) Ag〕；

      ‘買’ vt.,+〔Th(So) (以Qc) Ag〕

John bought the book (from Mary) (for ten dollars).

小明(以十塊錢) (從小華)買了這本書。

    d. ‘sell’ vt.,+〔Th (Go) (Qc) Ag〕；

      ‘賣’ vt., +〔Th (Go)(以 Qc) Ag〕

Mary sold the book (to John) (for ten dollars).

小華(以十塊錢)賣了這本書(給小明)。

    e. ‘cost’ vt., +〔(So) Qc, Th〕；

      ‘花’ vt.,+〔(So) Qc, Th〕

The book cost (me) ten dollars.

這本書花了(我)十塊錢。

（二）「雙賓動詞」（ditransitive verbs; double-object verbs）

㉕ a. ‘spare’ vt.,+〔(Be) Th, Ag〕；

      ‘饒，不給’ vt.,+〔Be 的 Th, Ag〕

Please spare (me) my life;

Please spare me your opinions.

請饒我的命吧；請不要{給我/跟我談}你的意見吧❼❻。

b. 'forgive' vt.,+〔Be (Th) Ag〕；

'原諒,赦免' vt.,+〔Be Th, Ag〕

Please forgive us (our {sins/trespasses}).

請{原諒/赦免}我們(的罪)吧。❼❼

c. 'deny' vt.,+〔Go, Th,Ag〕；'拒絕' vt.,+〔Go的Th,Ag〕

He cannot deny us our privileges；

He never denied us anything.

他不能拒絕我們的權利；他從未拒絕我們任何事情。

d. 'envy' vt.,+〔Be, Ca, Ex〕；

'羨慕,嫉妒' vt.,+〔Be(的),Ca, Ex〕

John envied Bill (because of) his { good luck/
beautiful girl friend}.

小明(因為小剛{運氣好/女朋友漂亮}而)羨慕他；

小明羨慕小剛的{漂亮女朋友/好運氣}。❼❽

---

❼❻ 英語動詞 'spare' 還可以有'+〔<{Qd/Qc} (Be)>Ag〕'的論旨網
格,而與漢語動詞'撥出(Du),借(Am)'(+〔{Qd/Qc} (Be) Ag〕)
相對應,例如：'Can you spare a few {minutes/dollars} (for
me)；Can you spare me a few {minutes/dollars}？你能
{撥出幾分鐘/借幾塊錢}給我嗎？'。

❼❼ 英語動詞 'forgive'還有'+〔Be, Qc, Ag〕' 的論旨網格,而與漢語
動詞'意見,不要'(+〔Be, Qc, Ag〕) 相對應,例如：'I lent you
fifty-two dollars a month ago; I'll forgive you the two
dollars, but I want the fifty dollars back；我一個月以前借
你五十二塊錢；我不要你兩塊錢,但我要你還我五十塊錢'。

❼❽ 英語動詞 'envy'論旨網格裏的'Ca'底下圓括下弧線'(＿＿)'表示：
這個論旨角色可以不由介詞來引介(如⑤d 句的 'his {good luck/
beautiful girlfrienrd}'),也可以由有關的介詞來引介(如⑤d句的
'because of his {good luck/beautiful girlfriend}')。與此相
對應的漢語動詞的論旨網格裏,'Ca'底下沒有畫這種符號,所以沒
有類似的用法。

　　e.　'give' vt.,+〔＜Th, Go＞ Ag〕；

　　　　'給' vt.,+〔Go, Th, Ag〕

　　　　John gave a present to Mary;

　　　　John gave Mary a present.

　　　　小明給了小華一件禮物。

　　f.　'introduce' vt.,+〔Th, Go, Ag〕；

　　　　'介紹' vt.,+〔Th, Go, Ag〕

　　　　John introduced Mary to Bill.

　　　　小明介紹小華給小剛；小明把小華介紹給小剛。

　　g.　'telex' vt.,+〔＜Th, Go＞ Ag〕；

　　　　'打 telex（用 telex 通知）' vt.,+〔Th, Go, Ag〕

　　　　John telexed the news to Bill;

　　　　John telexed Bill the news.

　　　　小明把消息打 telex 給小剛；

　　　　小明用 telex 把消息通知(給)小剛。

　　h.　'send' vt.,+〔＜Th, Go＞ Ag〕；

　　　　'送' vt.,+〔＜Th,(給) Go＞ Ag〕

　　　　John will send some cookies to Mary;

　　　　John will send Mary some cookies.

　　　　小明會送一些餅乾給小華；

　　　　小明會送(給)小華一些餅乾。

（三）「以"可以調換詞序"的名詞組與介詞組爲補語的動詞」
(verbs with "alternating" NP-PP complements)

㉜　a.　'blame' vt.,+〔{Be, for Ca/Ca, on Be} Ag〕；

'怪罪,責難' vt.,+〔Be, Ca, Ag〕

John blamed Mary for the accident;

John blamed the accident on Mary.

小明為了車禍(而)怪罪小華。

b. 'load' vt.,+〔{Th, Lo/Lo, with Th} Ag〕;

'裝(載)' vt.,+〔Lo, Th, Ag〕

John loaded the furniture { on/onto/into } the truck; John loaded the truck with the furniture.

小明把家具放在卡車{上面/裏面}。

c. 'tap' vt.,+〔{ Lo, In/In, on Lo} Ag〕;

'敲' vt.,+〔Lo, In, Ag〕

John tapped the desk with a pencil;

John tapped a pencil on the desk.

小明用鉛筆敲桌子。

(四)「以"可以調換詞序"的兩個介詞組為補語的動詞」

(verbs with "alternating" double PP complements)

⑬ a. 'talk' vi.,+〔<Go, about Th> Ag〕;

'談論' vt.,+〔(有關)Th的事情,跟 Go, Ag〕

John talked to Mary about the party;

John talked about the party to Mary.

小明跟小華談(有關)宴會的事情。

b. 'hear' vi.,+〔<So, about Th> Ex〕⑲;

---

⑲ 英語動詞'hear'另外具有 'vt.,+〔{Th (So)/(So) Pf} Ex〕' 的論旨網格(與漢語動詞'聽到Th,聽So說(Pd)'vt.,+〔{Th/Pd} (So)(→)

'聽到' vt.,+〔(有關)Th的消息, So, Ex〕

I heard from him about the accident;

I heard about the accident from him.

我從他(那裏)聽到(有關)車禍的消息。

（五）「以處所爲"轉位"主語的動詞」(verbs with Locative as "transposed" subject)(80)

(54) a. 'swarm' vi.,+〔〈Lo, with Th〉〕;

'充滿' vt.,+〔Th, Lo〕

Bees are swarming in the garden;

The garden is swarming with bees.

院子裏充滿了許多蜜蜂。

b. 'dazzle' vi., +〔〈Lo, with Th〉〕;

'閃耀' vi., +〔Th, Lo〕

Diamonds dazzled in the setting;

The setting dazzled with diamonds.

鑲臺中閃耀著許多鑽石。(81)

c. 'reek' vi.,+〔〈Lo, with Th〉〕;

'有……的氣味' vt.,+〔Th, Lo〕

(──→)Ex〕' 相對應)而衍生 'I heard the news (from him); I heard (from him) that his wife was ill. 我從(他(那裏))聽到這個消息；我聽(他)說他的太太病了'這樣的例句。

(80) 關於這類動詞的詳細討論，參 Slakoff (1983)。

(81) (54)a句裏述語動詞的動貌詞尾用'了'，而(54)b句裏述語動詞的動貌詞尾卻用'著'；顯然與處所詞的出現於句首（因而處所介詞'在'常加以省略)以及'充滿'的及物用法與'閃耀'的不及物用法有關。

Garlic reeks in his breath;

His breath reeks witn garlic.

他的呼吸裏有大蒜的氣味。

(六) 「非賓位動詞」(unaccusative verbs)

⑤ a.　'arise' v.,+〔Th (there)〕;

'發生' v.,+〔(有)Th(φ)〕㉜

There arose a problem; A problem arose.

發生了一件問題;有一件問題發生了。

b.　'arrive' v.,+〔Th (there)〕;

'到,來' v.,+〔(有)Th (φ)〕

There arrrived a guest yesterday;

A guest arrived yesterday.

昨天{到/來}了一位客人;有一位客人昨天{到/來}了。

c.　'emerge' v.,+〔Th (there)〕;

'顯現(出來)' v.,+〔(有)Th (φ)〕

{There emerged some important facts/Some important facts emerged} as a result of the investigation.

(由於)調查的結果,{顯現了一些重要的事實/有些重要

㉜　我們暫用 'v.' 的符號來代表「非賓位動詞」(unaccusative verb)。這類動詞後面雖然可以出現名詞組,卻不宜分析爲賓語。根據「格位理論」,出現於這類動詞後面的名詞組所獲得的不是「賓位」(accusative Case),而是「份位」(partitive Case)。因此,這些名詞組通常都是「無定」(indefinite) 的,而且常可以出現於述語動詞的前面或後面。

的事實顯現（出來）了}。

（七）「作格動詞」（ergative verbs)⑧

⑤⑥　　a.　'open' v(t).,+〔Th (Ag)〕；

'（打）開' v(t).,+〔Th(Ag)〕

John opened the door;

The door opened (automatically).

小明（打）開了門；門（自動的）（打）開了。

b.　'thicken' v(t).,+〔Th ({Ca/Ag})〕；

'（使）變{厚/濁/濃/複雜}' v(t).,+〔Th ({Ca/Ag})〕

Smog has thickened the air;

The air has thickened (with smog).

煙霧使空氣變濁了；空氣（因煙霧）變濁了。

c.　'beautify' v(t).,+〔Th ({Ca/Ag})〕；

'美化' v(t).,+〔Th ({Ca/Ag})〕

Flowers have beautified the garden;

The garden has beautified.

花卉美化了庭園；庭園（因花卉）美化了。

（八）「非人稱動詞」（impersonal verbs)⑧

---

⑧　「作格動詞」兼有「使動及物」(causative transitive) 用法與「起
　　動不及物」(inchoative intransitive) 兩種用法，而且在起動不
　　及物用法時並不含蘊主事者的存在。我們暫用的 'v(t).' 的符號來代
　　表作格動詞。

⑧　「非人動詞」包括「氣象動詞」(meteorological verbs) 與「提升
　　動詞」(raising verbs) 等。

(57) a. ‘rain’ vi.,+〔it〕；‘下’v.,+〔雨（ϕ)〕

It is (still) raining.

下雨了；雨還在下。

b. ‘snow’vi.,+〔it〕；‘下’v.,+〔雪（ϕ)〕

It has stopped snowing.

沒有下雪了；雪{沒有下/停}了。

c. ‘seem’ vi.,+〔{Pd, it/Pe, Th}〕；

‘好像’ ad.,+〔Pd〕[85]

It seems that he is sick; He seems to be sick.

好像他不舒服；他好像不舒服。

d. ‘happen’ vi.,+〔{Pd, it/Pe, Th}；‘湊巧’ad.,+〔Pd〕

It happened that she was at home;

She happened to be at home.

湊巧她在家；她湊巧在家。

（九）「控制動詞」(control verbs)

(58) a. ‘remember’ vt.,+〔{Pe, Ag/Pg, Ex}〕[86]；

---

[85] 與英語動詞‘seem’相對應的是漢語副詞‘好像’（論旨網格‘+〔Pd〕’表示：‘好像’是修飾整句的(情態)副詞，因此可以出現於句首或主語與謂語之間)。請注意：‘seem’與‘好像’都分別要求補語子句與所要修飾的句子裏面的述語是靜態動詞（比較：‘He seems to {know/*study} English；他好像{懂/*學}英語’），但是與動貌助動詞或動貌詞尾連用的動態動詞則視爲靜態動詞（例如‘He seems to {have studied/be studying} English；他好像{在學/學過}英語’）。

[86] 英語動詞‘remember’還具有‘vt.,+〔{Pd/Pq} Ex〕’（與漢語‘記得 vt.,+〔{Pd/Pq} Ex〕’相對應，如‘I remembered {that he came too/who else came}；我記得{他也來了/還有誰來了}’與‘vt.,+〔Be, Go (Ag)〕’（與漢語的‘問候/致意’vi/t.,+〔(向) Go, Be (Ag)〕’相對應，如‘Please remember me to your wife；請替我{向您太太問候/問候您太太}’)等論旨網格。

'記得(要V/V過)'vt.,+〔{Pe, Ag/Pg, Ex}〕,

Remember to turn off the lights;

I remembered {having seen/seeing} him once;

I remembered him saying that.

記得要關燈；我記得見過他一次；我記得他說過那樣的

話。⑧

b.　'try' vt.,+〔{Pe/Pg} Ag〕；

'試著(去),(嘗)試過,試一試' vt.,+〔Pe, Ag〕

I tried to help him; I tried communicating with

him; Why don't you try taking this medicine?

我試著去幫助他；我試過跟他溝通；你不妨試一試(吃)

這個藥。

c.　'manage' vt.,+〔Pe, Ex〕⑧ ；

'設法（辦到)' vt.,+〔Pe, Ex〕

I managed to see him in his office.

我設法在他辦公室裏見了他。

d.　'warn' vt.,+〔Go, Pe, Ag〕；

'警告' vt.,+〔Go, Pe, Ag〕

He warned me not to see his daughter any

more.

---

⑧　英語動詞 'manage'除了 '+〔Pe, Ag〕' 的及物用法之外，還有'＋
〔Ag〕'的不及物用法而與漢語的'應付, vi/t.,+〔(Th) Ag〕'相對應
，例如 'I think I can manage by myself；我想我能自個兒應
付'。

他警告我不要再見他女兒。

e.　'promise' vt.,+〔Go, Pe, Ag〕；

　　'答應' vt.,+〔Go, Go, Pe, Ag〕

　　She promised me to buy me a new bicycle.

　　她答應我買一輛腳踏車給我。

（十）「"併入論元"的動詞」（"argument-incorporating" verbs)❽

⑤　a.　'butter' vt.,+〔Lo, Ag〕；'塗奶油' vi.,+〔Lo, Ag〕

　　He buttered the bread heavily.

　　他在麵包上厚厚的塗奶油。

　　b.　'bottle' vt.,+〔Th, Ag〕；

　　'裝進瓶子' vi.,+〔Th,Ag〕

　　They are bottling the wine.

　　他們在把葡萄酒裝進瓶子。

　　c.　'gut' vt.,+〔So, Ag〕；

　　'拿掉(So的)內臟' vi.,+〔So, Ag〕

　　I have already gutted the fish.

　　我已經拿掉了魚的內臟；我已經把魚的內臟拿掉了。

---

❽　所謂「"併入論元"的動詞」是這些動詞本來是名詞，但是轉爲動詞以後原來的名詞就變成動詞語義的一部分；也就是說，原來的論元名詞被動詞「併入」(incorporation) 進去。原來的名詞在動詞用法裏可能充當客體（如⑤a、⑤c句）、終點（如⑤b句）、工具（如⑤d句）等；這種名詞論元被動詞併入的情形，以及這些名詞論元所充當的論旨角色，可以從與英語動詞相對應的漢語動詞裏清楚的看出來。

d. 'knife' vt.,+〔Be, Ag〕；'用刀子捅' vt.,+〔Be, Ag〕
John knifed Mary's boy friend.

小明用刀子捅了小華的男朋友；小明捅了小華的男朋友
一刀。

八、結　論

以上應用原則參數語法的基本概念來設計述語動詞的論旨網
格，並利用論旨網格的投射來衍生句子。由於篇幅的限制，我們
主要討論了述語動詞與必用論元的投射，但是述語形容詞、述語
名詞以及各種體語、狀語、定語的句法結構都可以用同樣的方法
來衍生。對於不習慣當代語法理論的術語與分析方法的讀者而言
，論旨網格的內容與投射條件可能顯得太複雜、太麻煩。但是
如果把論旨網格的內容拿來與 Advanced Learners' English
Dictionary ⑧⑨ 或 Longman Dictionary of Contemporary
English ⑨⓪ 所採用的動詞與句型的分類比較的話，那麼論旨網格

---

⑧⑨　這一本辭典的動詞與句型的分類，主要依據 A. S. Hornby (1959)
　　的 A Guide to Patterns and Usage in English 一書中第一
　　頁到八十二頁的 'Verbs and Verb Patterns'。根據這裏的動詞
　　分類，英語的動詞類型分為二十五大類與六十九小類。

⑨⓪　有關用這一本辭典的動詞類型，參該辭典 xxviii 頁到 xxxix 頁（特
　　別是 xxxvi 頁到 xxxvii 頁）的說明以及封面底裏頁的 'Table of
　　Codes'。這一本辭典的動詞分類似比 A. S. Hornby 的動詞分類較
　　為簡單，但是除了「不及物動詞」（intransitive verb）、「連繫動
　　詞」（linking verb; intensive verb）、「單賓動詞」（transitive
　　verb）、「雙賓動詞」（ditransitive verb）、與「複賓動詞」（com-
　　plex-transitive verb；即兼帶賓語與補語的及物動詞）分別用 'I,
　　L, T, V, X' 的符號代表之外，還根據賓語與補語在句法結構上的不
　　同而加上 '1' 到 '18' 等不同的阿拉伯數字來區別；因此，無論是查詢
　　或記憶都相當複雜而不方便。

的內容就較爲簡單，用英文單詞的簡寫來代表的論旨角色也比較
方便於查詢或記憶，而且論旨網格裏所包含的資訊非常豐富。論
旨網格所提供的資訊包括(一)必用論元的數目、(二)重要的可用
論元、(三)這些論元所扮演的論旨角色、(四)這些論元所歸屬的
句法範疇、(五)這些論元所擔任的句法功能、(六)這些論元在表
面結構的前後次序❾與可能的詞序變化、(七)「塡補詞」(ex-
pletive) 或「冗贅詞」(pleonastic) 'it'與 'there'的出現等。
同時，利用共同的符號與統一的格式把英語與漢語之間相對應的
述語動詞的論旨網格加以並列對照的結果，不但可以利用論旨網
格的資訊從英語翻成漢語，也可以利用同樣的資訊從漢語翻成英
語❾ 。

在語言教學上，英漢兩種語言的論旨網格分析可能做出的貢
獻是：（一）爲英漢對比分析提供具體可行而簡便有效的方法；
(二)可以利用英漢兩種語言論旨網格的比較來預測英語系學生學
習漢語時可能遭遇的問題與困難，以及中國學生學習英語時可能
遭遇到的問題與困難；(三)英漢兩種語言論旨網格的分析、比較

---

❾ 如果有需要，也可以提供述語動詞與各種論元間之階層組織。

❾ 這一點在機器翻譯上有相當重要的意義，因爲論旨網格的設計不但簡
化詞項記載的內容，可以眞正做到「由詞彙來驅動」(lexicon-dri-
ven) 的機器翻譯，而且不必爲英翻中與中翻英設計兩套不同的詞組結
構規律與詞庫。理論上，無論是多少種語言，只要能設計適當的論旨
網格並明確的規畫其投射條件，機器翻譯就可以依「多方向」(multi-
directional) 進行。關於依據這種觀點並針對英、漢、日三種語言
所能做的論旨網格分析與機器翻譯的關係，參拙著＜原則參數語法、
對比分析與機器翻譯＞。

與對照以及從此所獲得的結論，可以促進對兩種語言共同性與相異性的了解，因而有助於這兩種語言教材教法的改進；(四)論旨網格的設計與改良，對於英語辭典、漢語辭典、英漢辭典、漢英辭典裏動詞句型分類以及例句的選擇方面提供寶貴的參考；(五)在文法、翻譯、作文、修辭教學上，對於如何用詞或選詞，提供簡單扼要的說明。不過，本文是從論旨網格討論英漢對比分析的初步嘗試，許多問題可能尚未發現或尚待解決。因此，虔誠的希望有更多的學者老師對這個問題感到興趣，大家共同來研究論旨網格在語文教學、辭典編纂、機器翻譯等各方面的應用價值。

　　＊ 本文原於1991年5月18日在新竹國立清華大學舉行的第八屆中華民國英語文教學研討會發表，並刊載於《人文社會學科教學通訊》(1991) 2卷3期129-145頁；4期76-97頁與《中華民國第八屆英語文教學研討會英語文教學論文集》235-289頁。

他山之石可以攻錯：
評析日本大學英文科入學考試制度與試題

一、前　言

　　日本大學入學考試從昭和五十四年（即一九七九年）起採取「共同第一次考試」（正式名稱爲「國立大學選拔共通第一次學力測驗」；簡稱「共同考試」）與「個別第二次考試」的兩段式考試制度。日本之所以要舉行共同第一次考試，主要是爲了防止各大學在自辦入學考試時盡出一些高難度、甚至冷僻怪異的題目，因而以共同考試的方式要求入學考試的命題內容必須符合高中授課的範圍。從平成二年（即一九九○年）起，共同第一次考試更由專

設的「大學入學考試中心」（大學入試センター）負責出題與評分，名稱也由「共同第一次考試」改為「大學入學考試中心考試」（大學入試センター試驗；簡稱「中心考試」）。另一方面，「個別第二次考試」（簡稱「個別考試」）則仍由全國各國立、公立、私立大學自行負責出題與閱卷；而其考試內容除了一般的筆試以外，還可以兼採小論文、面試、推薦（包括自我推薦）甄試、術科考試等方式，藉以補救已往入學考試偏重學科知識的缺失。

這些改進措施顯示了日本大學入學考試與甄選的「正常化」與「多元化」，但也無可避免地產生一些弊端。例如，共同考試不但提供了全國統一的評量考生成績的尺度，而且也提供了全國各國立與公立大學錄取標準的高低序列。結果，一般考生在報名個別考試時難免抱有安全第一的想法；即根據共同考試的自我評分（共同考試的成績並不對外公佈）選擇自己有把握考進去的學校，而不敢選擇自己真正想進去的學校。如此，各校系錄取標準高低的畫分越來越明顯，造成日人所謂的「輪切り」現象。另一方面，一般考生所嚮往而競爭劇烈的明星大學也常以共同考試的成績做為能否報名個別考試的主要依據。結果，有不少考生雖然報名卻不准應考，或雖能應考卻不能錄取。因此，一九九〇年開始，日本國立與公立大學便舉辦中心考試。除了規定大學入學考試的科目與主要範圍必須事先公佈以外，還規定中心考試與個別考試的成績必須依照比例合併計分。同時，大學入學考試中心，除了統籌主辦中心考試以外，還輔導考生的升學與就業，並建立 HEART 電腦諮詢系統 (Higher Education ARTiculation support system) 以便向外界提供有關國內大學的各種資訊。

昭和六十年(一九八五年)所舉行的臨時教育審議會更建議各大學
的入學考試應朝各校自主的方向發展，期能甄選眞正具有特色與
潛力的學生。在現行制度下，國立與公立大學的考生必須參加中
心考試才能報名個別考試；而私立大學的招生則不硬性規定必須
參加中心考試（以平成二年爲例，參加中心考試的私立大學共十
三所、十四個學院），而可以逕自舉行個別考試。

　　中心考試的考試科目總共有五科，包括：(一)國語（配分兩
百分考試時間八十分鐘）、(二)社會（配分一百分考試時間六十分
鐘）、(三)數學（分爲A與B兩組，每組配分一百分，考試時間六
十分鐘）、(四)理化（分爲A、B、C三組，每組配分一百分，考
試時間六十分鐘）、(五)外國語（從英語、德語與法語中任選一
科，總分兩百分，考試時間八十分鐘）。至於這些科目的配分是
否要加重計分，則委由各大學或各學系自行決定。

　　本文擬就日本昭和六十二年度（即一九八七年度）的共同考
試英文科試題內容加以評介，期能做爲改進我國大學入學考試英
文科試題的參考。

二、昭和六十二(一九八七)年度共同考試英文試題
　　評介

第一問：同答下列問題（A，B）。（配分21分）

A.　從下列問題（1—5）的單詞（1—4）中，選出第一重音節
　　的母音讀法與其他三個單詞不同的單詞來。

問1　　　　| 1 |

1 circumstance　　2 pursue　　　3 universal
4 permanent

問2　　　　| 2 |

1 definite　　　　2 delicate　　3 recently
4 estimate

問3　　　　| 3 |

1 patience　　　　2 magic　　　3 manager
4 balance

問4　　　　| 4 |

1 conference　　　2 confidence　　3 continent
4 concern

問5　　　　| 5 |

1 photograph　　　2 profit　　　3 notice
4 oppose

　　試題評析：這一個試題的目的在於要求考生分辨單詞的「第一重音」（primary accent）以及出現於這個重音節的母音讀法。有很多人認爲這是考「發音」（pronunciation) 的題目。但是事實上考生並沒有實際的「聽音」，更沒有實際的「發音」；能做對這些題目的考生，並不一定能正確的聽出或發出英語的音來

。同時，英語裏第一重音節在單詞裏出現的位置常有一定的規則（例如，雙音節單詞的第一重音大多數都出現於第一個音節，三音節與三音節以上單詞的第一重音節大多數都出現於倒數第三個音節），英文拼字與發音之間也常有一定的對應關係（參湯廷池(1989)《國中英語教學指引》，〈國中英語與音標教學〉100-132頁）。就第一問A問的第一重音節為例，'circumstance, permanent, definite, delicate, recently, estimate, patience, magic, manager, balance, conference, confidence, continent, photograph, profit, notice' 十六個單詞的第一重音節都可以用上面所提出來的非常簡單的規則找出來，只有'pursue, universal, concern, oppose' 四個單詞是屬於例外的情形（連這些例外的情形都可以利用「詞根」（root）與「詞綴」（affix）的區別來加以條理化）。同時，問1（第一重音節的 '{i, e} r' 都讀/ɝ/音與問4（第一重音的 'o' 都讀/ɑ/音，輕音節的 'o' 都讀/ə/音）裏拼字與母音都形成規則的對應，只有問2的 'recently'、問3的 'patience' 與問5的 'profit' 是屬於例外的情形，而這些例外的情形正是試題所要求的正確答案。因此，這一類試題不但不能真正測驗考生的英語發音，而且如果試題的答案完全可以利用對應規則找出來即更失去考發音的意義，如果盡出一些屬於例外的情形即容易出現冷僻罕用的單詞。近幾年來，我國的大學聯考英文試題很少出現這一類題目，或許是基於這一種考慮。

B.　下面一段文章（問1—2）裏1到3與4到6裏分別有一個單詞要讀得特別重。請選出這一個詞。

問1　　　　　　　6

Susan and Tim were waiting for their friend Akira at the airport. Tim shouted, "There he
　　　　　　　　　　　　　　　　　　　　　　　1　　2
is! He's just beside the man with the red shirt."
　　3

Both were excited to see their friend from Japan.

問2　　　　　　　7

It had been a long time since they were to-
　　　　　　　　　　　　　　　　　4
gether at the last ski tournament.

"It's good to see you again," said Akira. "You
　　　　　　　　　5

both look great."

"So do you! We could hardly wait for you to
　　　　6

get here."

　　試題評析：這一個試題的目的在於要求考生指出一個句子或一段文章裏的「信息焦點」(information focus)。由於句子的「信息焦點」經常都是這一個句子裏「音高峰」(pitch peak) 或「句重音」(sentence stress) 出現的地方，所以許多人誤以為這是考發音的題目。其實，這一類題目也沒有真正要求考生聽音

或發音，考生只要能了解這一般文章的大意，並且能夠指出那一個答案代表「最重要的信息」（most important information）就可以答對題目。因此，只能說是考「語意」或「閱讀」的題目，不能說是考「語音」或「發音」的題目。以第一問A問為例，代詞 'there, he, they, you' 通常都代表舊的不重要的信息。但是問1裏1的 'There (he is)' 是「引介句」（presentative sentence），整個句子都代表新的重要信息（'他在那裏！我看到他了！'），所以例外的要讀句重音（在英式英語裏句尾常讀「降升調」（falling-rising tone））。另一方面，6 的 '(So do) you' 是 'You look great (,too)' 的「簡縮倒裝句」：為了避免 'You look great' 的重複而用 'so do' 來代替；而且為了強調 '你看來也蠻好啊！' 而把 'you' 移到句尾來充當信息焦點，以便符合「從舊到新的原則」（"From Old to New" Principle）。可見，考生只要能判斷句子成份所代表的信息重要或不重要，就能答對這些題目。

第二問：同答下列問題（A，B）。（配分73分）

A. 從下列問題（1—19的答案1到4中，選出最適當的答案填入空白（ 8 — 26 ）中。

問1　It would be good for you to send your baggage

　　 8 　 to avoid any inconvenience

　　1 far advanced　　　　　　　2 in advance

　　3 with advantage　　　　　　4 at advantage

問2　You'll feel ┃ 9 ┃ in English if you have more practice.

　　　1 at home　　　　　　2 at liberty

　　　3 at rest　　　　　　4 at school

問3　Many accidents ┃ 10 ┃ the icy road conditions.

　　　1 resulted by　　　　2 resulted from

　　　3 took place　　　　4 were caused

問4　I can't ┃ 11 ┃ to eat in such an expensive restaurant.

　　　1 have　　　　　　　2 find

　　　3 spend　　　　　　4 afford

問5　When I bought the book ten years ago, it just cost ┃ 12 ┃ .

　　　1 one and a half dollar

　　　2 one and a half dollars

　　　3 one and half dollar

　　　4 one and half dollars

問6　Nothing more ┃ 13 ┃ because of the storm.

　　　1 could be doing　　　2 could do

　　　3 could be done　　　4 could have done

問7　My mother was happy to see her guest ┃ 14 ┃

her cakes eagerly.

1 eaten   2 eats

3 to eat   4 eating

問8   I want to   15   . It seems out of order.

1 have fixed this cassette recorder

2 have this cassette recorder fix

3 have this cassette recorder fixed

4 have this cassette recorder fixing

問9   A: I'm afraid I've spilt some milk on the tablecloth.

B; Oh, don't   16   about that.

1 care   2 matter

3 suffer   4 worry

問10 A: Can you tell me where the nearest bus stop is?

B: I'm sorry, I've no   17   .

1 idea   2 mind

3 plan   4 thought

問11 A: I've been studying English for seven years but I can speak only broken English.

B: But your English is very good. Don't be so   18   .

      1 careless   2 frank

      3 modest   4 kind

問12 A: I didn't know that she was so troubled about money matters.

     B: I wish you ⬚19⬚ her some a couple of weeks earlier.

      1 had sent   2 send

      3 sent   4 will send

問13 A: Does Jack live in the suburbs or in the center of the city?

     B: ⬚20⬚ I know, he lives near the center.

      1 As far as   2 As long as

      3 As much as   4 So long as

問14 A: Can you lend me two thousand yen?

     B: Sure. How long?

     A: Is it all right if I pay it back next week?

     B: ⬚21⬚

      1 Yes, thank you.   2 Yes, that's O.K.

      3 Not at all.   4 I'd be glad to.

問15 A: Do you have all your suitcases with you?

     B: No, I have some more.

     A: ⬚22⬚

B: I left the other two at the baggage room.

1 Where are the rest?

2 Why do you still have them with you?

3 Can I help you find the baggage room?

4 You should leave this one, too, shouldn't you?

問16　A: I don't feel like eating at home tonight. Let's go out for dinner.

B: O.K., but I don't want to go to a fast-food place.

A: | 23 |

B: Wonderful. Will you call up to reserve a table?

1 Yes, thank you. I'll have some seafood.

2 Let's ask someone about the restaurant first.

3 Why not go to a Chinese restaurant?

4 I'm tired of hamburgers and fried chicken.

問17　A: What's the best way to the airport?

B: By subway, if you want to save time.

A: | 24 |

B: That depends on the traffic.

1 How many stops are there on the way?

2 How long will it take to go by taxi?

3 How often do I have to change on the way?

　　4 How much does it cost from here?

問18　A: Will you be free to come to dinner next Saturday night at my house?

　　B: ┃　25　┃

　　A: Good. I'll pick you up at six if you like.

　　B: Oh, that's very nice of you, but please don't go to the trouble.

　　1 I hope I'll be able to come another time.

　　2 Yes, I'd be glad to. It's very kind of you.

　　3 Thank you for the invitation, but I'm afraid I'm going to be out of town.

　　4 I'd like to come, but I'm afraid I already have another appointment.

問19　A: Could you tell me the way to the Central Post Office?

　　B: ┃　26　┃

　　A: How can I go there?

　　B: I think you'd better take a bus at that corner.

　　1 Well, it's just around the corner and easy enough to find.

　　2 Walk about a block and you'll see it on your right.

3 Yes, of course. Actually, it's rather far from here.

4 No, I'm afraid I can't. I've only been here for a few days myself.

　　試題評析：這裏總共有十九題「綜合測驗」的選擇題。其中，前面八題(問1—問8)只含有一個句子，中間五題(問9—問13)含有兩句對話，而後面六題(問14—問19)則含有四句聯貫的對話。問1到問4四題分別以 'in advance, at home, resulted from, (can't) afford' 等熟語的意義與用法爲測驗的對象，並配合形態相似或意義相近的熟語或詞語做爲「誘導答案」(distractor)。問5到問8四題則分別以 'one and a half dollars, (nothing more) could be done, (see her guest) eating, have this cassette recorder fixed' 等與句法有關的問題(名詞的單複數與無定冠詞'a(n)'的有無，主動、被動與單純貌(V)、完成貌(have V-en)的選擇，「知覺動詞」(perception verb) 'see' 的賓語後面動詞形式的選擇，以及「使役動詞」(causative verb) 'have'的賓語後面動詞形式的選擇)爲測驗的對象。問9到問13五題分別要求考生根據兩句對話的「語意」(semantic) 與「句法」(syntactic) 關係選出最適當的動詞 ('care (about)')、名詞('(have no) idea')、形容詞('modest')、動詞的時制與動貌('had sent')與「片語連詞」('as far as')來塡入空白。而問14到問19六題則含有在兩人間進行的四句對話，並把其中一句話留爲空白，然後要求考生根據「語意」與「語

用」（pragmatic）關係選出最適當的句子（'Yes, that's O.K.' 'Where are the rest?', 'Why not go to a Chinese restaurant?', 'How long will it take to go by taxi?', 'Yes, I'd be glad to. It's very kind of you.', 'Yes, of course. Actually, it's rather far from here.'）。第二問的試題中並未出現冷僻罕用的詞彙或複雜難解的句法結構，所採用的文體也都是淺近易懂的口語英語。試題大致按照從易到難、從簡到繁的順序排列，誘導答案的設計也尚稱妥貼。不過問3的誘導答案3 'took place'與4 'were caused'以及問4的誘導答案2 'find'與3 'spend' 似乎弱了些。類似第二問「綜合測驗」的試題，在我國大學聯考的英文試題中也經常出現。但是我們的試題不採用一個句子留一個空白的方式（如問1到問7），而只採用一段文章留好幾個空白的方式（如下面第二問的B題）。我們的英文試題也採用聯貫對話方式（如問9到問19）的題目，但是考生在語用上所要做的考慮似乎比日本的試題還要複雜一點。因此，一般而言，我國這一類型的試題難度似乎比日本同類試題的難度高，而誘導答案的誘導力似乎也比日本試題強。

B. 從下面一段文章的備選答案1到10中選出最適當的答案填入空白（ 27 — 34 ）。但是同一個答案不能重複使用。

One of the biggest decisions you have to make in your life is the decision about your job.

Between now and when you die, you will spend more hours at work than you will on any other single ⬚27⬚ . You can find out a lot about the job by reading and asking about it, but sometimes that doesn't ⬚28⬚ much. If you shop for a coat, you can ⬚29⬚ the color, the design, the material, and so on, but it is only after you have tried it on that you can ⬚30⬚ convinced that a particular coat is the right one for you.

How can you "try on" a job for a while before deciding that it is the right one for you? One ⬚31⬚ is through work experience. But how can you ⬚32⬚ such experience? Well, for example, while you are still at school, you could spend a few days working at a job that ⬚33⬚ you, one that you might like to do when you ⬚34⬚ school. That would give you work experience. It's a good way to "try on" a job.

1 activity   2 check   3 employment

4 feel	5 get	6 help
7 interests	8 learn	9 leave
10 possibility		

試題評析：這一個試題也是利用選擇填空的綜合測驗題。不過上面Ａ題都是四個被選答案，並在單一的句子或兩句對話裏留下一個空白來填入單詞、片語，或在四句對話裏留下一個空白來填入句子；而這一個試題則是兩段文章裏留下八個空白，並從十個備選答案中選一個單詞來填入。這一段文章總共一百八十四個單詞，平均每二十三個單詞要填入一個單詞。文章的文字與內容都很簡單，不但幾乎沒有生詞，而且只要求填入動詞(除了7 'interests' 的第三人稱現在式以外，都是動詞原形與第二人稱現在式)與名詞(都是單數形)。同時，填入動詞與名詞的語境都相當明確；例如，動詞與名詞的語境分別是 'doesn't (help), can (check), can (feel) convinced, can you (learn) such experience, a job that (interests) you, you (leave)school' 與 'any other single (activity), one (possibility)'。這一類型的題目經常出現於我國歷屆大學聯考的英文試題中，但是我國的試題在難度上似乎高於日本的試題。

第三問：在下列問題(問1—問6)裏，把1到7的詞句填入空白來完成句子。答案卡上只要填入附有題號 35-46 部分的答案就可以。(配分30分)

問1　You are waiting for the 10: 05 bus. It is 10: 40

now. You are very angry and say: "Oh, <u>35</u> __

<u>36</u> __ __ __ ?"

  1 time   2 why   3 never   4 this

  5 on   6 is   7 bus

問2 Your doctor asks you how you feel and you answer: "I feel quite well now, thank you. I certainly __ __ <u>37</u> __ <u>38</u> __ __ ."

   1 ago   2 much better   3 did   4 feel

   5 a week 6 I   7 than

問3 You went out and got terribly wet. Ten minutes later the rain stopped. You said to yourself: "I __ <u>39</u> __ __ <u>40</u> __ __ ."

 1 had left 2 have got   3 I   4 if

  5 so wet 6 ten minutes later   7 wouldn't

問4 You want to make sure that Nora will give your greetings to Jane. You say: "You <u>41</u> __ __ <u>42</u> __ __ , ___you?"

  1 say   2 for me   3 are   4 hello

  5 aren't   6 going to   7 to Jane

問5 You've received a phone call for Bill, but he is not in. You say: "I'm sorry, but Bill is out now. I suppose he'll be back by about five. May I take your message or __ __ <u>43</u> __ __ <u>44</u> __ when he returns?"

1 call　　2 have　　3 shall　　4 him

5 back　　6 you　　7 I

問6　The first great invention in the world was one that is still important today—the wheel. This ＿45＿＿＿＿46＿ and to travel long distances.

1 easier　　2 to　　3 heavy　　4 made

5 things　　6 it　　7 carry

試題評析：這一個類型的題目先提出有關「語言情境」(speech situation) 的說明，然後把最後一個句子的一部分留為空白，要求考生把附在後面的詞句「重新組合」(rearrange) 以後填入空白。六個題目裏所牽涉到的句型依次是「wh問句」("why is this bus never on time?")、「比較句」("(I certainly) feel much better than I did a week ago")、「與過去的事實相反的假設」("(I) wouldn't have got so wet if I had left ten minutes later")、「用 be going to 表示未來時間並帶上附加問句」("(You) are going to say hello to Jane for me, aren't (you)?")、「使役動詞」("shall I have him call you back?") 與「移尾結構」("(This) made it easier to carry heavy things")。又為了便於電腦閱卷，這個題目並不要求考生抄下整個詞句，而在七個空格中只指定兩個空格，要把填入這兩個空格的答號碼寫在答案卡上。要填入答案卡上的詞句，幾乎是清一色的「虛詞」(function word)，例

如 "this, never, than, did, are, have, you, it"，而且所牽
涉到的句型都屬於坊間的升學參考書上所強調的文法重點；因此
很容易成為補習班考前猜題的對象。我國歷屆大學聯考英文試題
似乎從來沒有考過這個類型的題目，不過這類題目可以利用客觀
測驗的方式來測驗考生重組句子的能力，這一點倒值得參考。

第四問： 下面1到4是一篇前後聯貫的文章。請仔細閱讀各段文
章，並從1到4的備選答案中選出最能吻合文意的答
案。（配分20分）

（1）Although he was an extremely shy young man,
he hoped for a chance to meet a pretty girl
when he went to live in Paris. He soon noticed
one, who lived nearby.

問1   ┌─────────┐
              │   47   │
              └─────────┘

  1 While he was in Paris he wanted to get to
know a pretty girl.

  2 While on a visit to Paris, he had a chance to
date a pretty girl.

  3 One of the neighbors he was introduced to
was a pretty girl.

  4 He didn't feel so shy in Paris because the
girls there were very bold.

（2）He wondered how to meet her. A French friend

told him it was easy: just wait till she dropped something—her handkerchief, perhaps—pick it up, hand it to her, and start a conversation.

問2 | 48 |

1 A French friend explained the way he himself had met the girl some time ago.

2 Until a French friend suggested a method, he wasn't sure how he could get to know her.

3 One of the girl's friends explained to him how he had got to know the girl.

4 She was a careless girl, so he hoped to make friends with her by offering to help her.

（3） Though he followed her each day, she never dropped anything. Finally, he got an idea: he would take something with him and pretend that she had dropped it.

問3 | 49 |

1 He thought his French friend's plan would take too long, so he didn't follow his advice.

2 The girl thought he was a thief following her and so she took great care not to drop anything.

3 After a while, he decided to deliver something

to her home as if it had been ordered.

4 He became impatient and so decided to use a quicker method.

（4）Nervously, he followed her when she went shopping one day. Outside the shop he hesitated, then approached her. "Excuse me," he said, "you've dropped this." And he handed her an egg.

問4　　　　50

1 He was as polite as possible because he was giving her only one egg.

2 He was feeling so nervous that he didn't realize that she would not believe him.

3 He thought he might succeed in his plan because he knew she liked eggs.

4 He was very nervous because he was afraid of breaking the egg.

　　試題評析：這一個試題把一篇文章分成四段，並在每一段文章後面附有四個備選答案來敍述這一段文章的大意或要旨，要求考生選出最適當的一個答案來。因此，在試題分類上屬於「閱讀測驗」。第二問B題的文章是比較正式而正經的「論說文」（ex-position），而這篇文章則屬於輕鬆有趣的「敍述文」（narration）

，而且難度都不高，幾乎沒有什麼生詞。如果把正確的答案串聯起來，幾乎可以形成一篇「摘要」（précis）："While he was in Paris he wanted to get to know a pretty girl. Until a French friend suggested a method, he wasn't sure how he could get to know her. He became impatient and so decided to use a quicker method. He was feeling so nervous that he didn't realize that she would not believe him."。我國歷屆大學聯考的英文試題也常出現類似的分段閱讀測驗題，但是日本的試題每段的字數較少（前後四段文章依次是32個單詞、34個單詞、28個單詞、32個單詞），每段文章的平均字數是31，難度也較低。同時，我國的試題還沒有出現過四段都考同一篇文章大意的題目。

第五問：下面(1)到(4)是一篇前後聯貫的文章。請仔細閱讀各段文章，並從1到4的備選的答案中選出最能吻合各段文意的答案。（配分20分）

（1）In modern life we depend on pictures for a good deal of the information we receive. The need for words has been reduced.

問1　　　　　51

　　1 We can find out more about modern life from pictures than from words.

　　2 Pictures are more interesting than words.

　　3 We often make use of pictures to get infor-

mation.

4 Good pictures do not need words to explain their meanings.

（2）As modern society has developed, the amount of information we have to use in our daily lives has grown rapidly. Much of it is communicated through pictures of various kinds—traffic signs, photographs and, above all, television.

問 2　　　52

1 Communication has changed to suit modern needs.

2 People are more educated now than they used to be.

3 Improvements in communications have given people new interests.

4 Nowadays, people spend most of their time watching television.

（3）Information can be presented clearly and effectively by means of pictures: a quick glance is all that is necessary for us to understand a fact or situation.

問 3　　　53

1 The speed of communication is more impor-

tant than its correctness.

2 To be effective, pictures should be very clear.

3 These days, people are too busy to read.

4 The information in pictures can be understood immediately.

（4）While pictures are useful for the fast communication of facts, they make things clear by making them simple. We must take care not to forget that ideas and thoughts, especially important ones, are seldom simple.

問4　　　 54

1 If something is communicated quickly, we remember it easily.

2 The most important things in life are usually simple.

3 Pictures are not always the best means of communication.

4 When facts are communicated quickly, they are not always clear.

　試題評析：第五問與第四問屬於同一類型的試題，只是敍述文改為論說文。文章的難度稍為提高了些。但是文中仍然沒有出現冷僻的詞彙或複雜的句型。前後兩篇文章的字數以及各段文章

的字數都相當接近(前後四段文章依次是 23 個單詞、37個單詞、27個單詞、35個單詞，每段文章的平均字數是 30.5 個單詞)。試題裏的正確答案也可以串聯成一篇摘要：'We often make use of pictures to get information,' (and) 'communication has changed to suit modern needs.' (While) 'pictures are not always the best means of communication.'。

第六問：仔細閱讀下面的文章，並從問1到問3的備選答案1到4選出最適當的答案填入空白(55 — 57)裏面。(配分18分)

Dear Tom,

　　With the summer holidays nearly here, I've been thinking about our visit to my grandparents. They're looking forward to meeting you. They're both pretty old now—my grandfather is almost 80. Don't expect too much, will you? They live a simple life, and their house isn't very big. It used to be a farmhoure, and it's right out in the country, a really great place.

　　There are plenty of things to do there. The sea is only about a ten-minute walk away. There's an old fishing village but it's not very busy now. A lot of people have moved away to the city. Don't forget your swimsuit!

　　There's another thing, too. It's not my idea really,

but my history teacher's at school. He was saying that the history we study is usually about big events— politics, revolutions, wars and so on, but that there's another kind: ordinary people's daily lives and daily work, and changes they've seen. He suggested asking old people about their experiences and writing them down. Well, my grandparents must have a lot of memories of life in the past, so I'm thinking of taking my tape-recorder and getting them on tapes. I'll take a notebook too, for comments and pictures. "Living History," my teacher called it.

I wonder if you'd be interested? We'd have to think of some questions to ask. Let me know what you think of the idea when we meet. We can arrange dates and trains then, too.

Till then,
Ted

問1　"Don't expect too much, will you?" (first paragraph) suggests that | 55 |

1 Tom was not expecting to meet Ted's grandparents.

2 young people usually expect too much of their grandparents.

3 Ted and Tom will have to share the old

people's way of living.

4 Tom had thought that he would meet more members of Ted's family there.

問2 The fishing village is not very busy now (second paragraph) because [56]

1 fishing is out of season.

2 during the summer people do not live there.

3 people do not eat as much fish as they used to.

4 the population of the village has been decreasing.

問3 The idea of "Living History" (third paragraph) was proposed because [57]

1 some world events are not mentioned in history books.

2 ordinary daily life is an important part of history.

3 old people easily forget the small events in their lives.

4 old people enjoy talking about the big events of the past.

試題評析：第六問也是屬於閱讀測驗的試題，但是不採取

「分段閱讀」的方式，而採取「整篇閱讀」的方式。同時，文章的
體裁也改為應用文 —— 書信。分段閱讀測驗以段為單元，每一段
文章後面的問題是針對這一段文章而提出來的；因此，在試題分
類上雖然屬於「成段題目」（passage item），而實質上卻接近以
語詞或句子為單元的「分項題目」（discrete item）。另一方面，
整篇閱讀測驗則可以針對整篇文章提出問題，要求考生除了個別
句子的結構與意義以外還要注意到前後出現於不同段落的幾個句
子間的語意或邏輯關係；因而在試題分類上可以真正發揮「成段
題目」或「整篇題目」（global item）的功用。可是第六問的三
個試題卻在題目中分別指明正確的答案出現於第一段（"3 Ted
and Tom will have to share the old people's way of
living"）、第二段（"4 the population of the village has
been decreasing"）與第三段（"2 ordinary life is an important part of history"）裏面，因此在實質上也與分段閱讀
測驗無異。不過，這一篇書信總共二百五十個字，扣掉第四段三
十五個字以後剩下二百十五個字，平均每閱讀七十一個字要回答
一個問題；也就是說，第六問的文章在長度上是第四問與第五問
的文章的兩倍半，因而難度似乎也較高。

第七問：仔細閱讀下面的文章，並從問1到問3的備選答案1到4
　　　　中選出最適當的答案填入空白（ 58 － 60 ）裏
　　　　面。（配分18分）

　　We have known for a long time that flowers of
different plants open and close at different times of

day. This is so familiar that there seems to be no need to ask the reason for it. Yet no one really understands why flowers open and close like this at particular times. The process is not as simple as we might think, as recent experiments have shown. In one, flowers were kept in constant darkness. We might expect that the flowers, without any information about the time of day, did not open as they normally do. In fact, they continued to open at their usual time. Their sense of time does not depend on information from the outside world; it is, so to speak, inside them, a kind of "inner clock."

問1 According to the first paragraph, a recent experiment showed that $\boxed{\quad 58 \quad}$

1 different flowers open and close at different times of day.

2 for their opening and closing, flowers do not need information from the outside world.

3 flowers are influenced by weak light even when they are in a dark room.

4 flowers can be used for telling the time.

This discovery may not seem to be very important. However, it was later found that not just plants but animals including man have this "inner clock"

which controls the working of their bodies and influenced by this mysterious power. Whether we wish
it or not, it affects such things in our life as our
need for sleep, our need for food, and our ability to
concentrate.

In the past, this did not matter very much because
people lived in natural conditions. In the modern
world, things are different: now there are spacemen,
airplane pilots and, in ordinary life, a lot of people
who have to work at night. It would be very useful,
then, to know more about the "inner clock." Such
ordinary things as flowers might help us to understand more about ourselves.

問2　According to the second paragraph, the "inner
　　　clock"　[59]

　　　1 was an unimportant discovery.

　　　2 is only found in animals.

　　　3 is now clearly understood.

　　　4 has an effect on human life.

問3　According to the third paragraph, further study
　　　of the "inner clock" will be useful because

　　　[60]

　　　1 for many people today, living conditions are

unnatural.

2 we do not yet understand plants and animals
   well enough.

3 the number of spacemen and airplane pilots
   is rapidly increasing.

4 we should try to live more naturally than we
   do now.

試題評析：第七篇也是整篇閱讀測驗，但是字數最多（總共
二百八十五個字，平均每閱讀九十五個字要回答一個問題），在
長度上是第四問與第五問的三倍多，比第六問的文章也多出三十
五個字來。第七問與第六問一樣，在每一個問題中指明正確的答
案出現於文章中的那一段；例如，問 1 的正確答案 "2 for their
opening and closing, flowers do not need information
from the outside world" 出現於第一段，問 2 的正確答案 "4
has an effect on human life" 出現於第二段，而問 3 的正確
答案 "1 for many people today living conditions are
unnatural" 則出現於第三段。日本共同考試採取這種方式，顯
然是為了減低英文試題的難度；因此，無論是文章的內容或是用
詞較難的詞彙也只不過是 'particular, constant, normally,
mysterious, sense of time, so to speak, inner clock,
influence, affect, concentrate, spacemen, pilot' 等。

三、昭和六十二(一九八七)年度共同英文科試題評析

這一份試卷七大題的總分為兩百分，其中「辨別單詞重音節母音讀法」的題目共五題，每題三分；「舉出句重音」的題目共兩題，每題三分；以單詞、兩句對話、四句對話為單元的「綜合測驗」共十九題，每題三分；附有備選答案的「克漏字測驗」（cloze test）含有八個空格，每個空格兩分；「詞句重組」的題目共六題十二個空格，每個空格二‧五分；「分段閱讀測驗」兩大題共八個小題，每個小題五分；「整篇閱讀測驗」兩大題共八個小題，每個小題六分。配分的高低大致上與題目的難度對應，而且題目出現的次序大致是由易到難。試題的類型清一色地屬於客觀測驗的選擇題，不含有翻譯與作文等非選擇題；因此不發生我國歷屆大學聯考英文科試題非選擇題有關閱卷評分的「品質管理」問題。試題的難度也顯然比我國試題的難度為低，無論就詞彙、句法結構或文意內容而言，都完全符合高中授課的範圍。同時，考生要在一百分鐘的時間裏回答五十二道題目，平均每兩分鐘就要做完一道題目；因此，要求考生做敏捷的思考與迅速的判斷，帶有「速度測驗」（speed test）的性質。以上的評析顯示：日本一九八七年度的共同考試英文科試題的出題範圍、方式、難度與配分都相當中肯。

　　＊ 本文原刊載於《人文及社會學科教學通訊》（1991） 2 卷 1 期122-127頁。

八十年度大學聯考英文試題的評析

　　一年一度的大學聯考，不僅直接關係著十幾萬考生的前途，而且在「考試領導教學」的現實環境下還間接影響全省高級中學與職業學校的教學內容與成效。因此，大學聯考命題的內容與方式，非但必須符合測驗理論的要求，俾能公平而有效地甄別考生成績的優劣，而且還應該遵照高中課程標準的規定，以求高中教學的正常化。本文有鑑於此，擬就八十年度大學聯考英文試題與標準答案，做一次客觀而詳盡的評析，以供聯招會與命題委員參考，並祈國內先進不吝指教。

　　八十年度大學聯考的英文試題，大致沿襲過去幾年的出題方式分為兩部分（卽單一選擇題與非選擇題）。在單一選擇題（共四十五題）下包括「對話」（十題，每題一分）、「綜合測驗」（二十

題，每題一分）、「閱讀測驗」（十五題，每題二分）；而在非選擇題下則包括「中譯英」（五題，每題四分）與「英文作文」（一題，二十分）。以下就這些試題的內容一一加以評介。

第一部分：單一選擇題

I．**對話**(10%)：附有答案(四選一)的填充題，總共十個空格。

May: Sue, you've been to Hawaii, haven't you?

Sue: Yeah, I spent my winter vacation there with my parents last year.

May: I heard 1 .

Sue: Yes. It's just like a paradise.

May: My family are planning 2 . I'm really looking forward to it.

Sue: Oh great! 3 .

May: When's a good time to go?

Sue: Well, I wouldn't go in summer. It's kind of hot. It's mild in winter, but sometimes it can be wet. If you're lucky, 4 . when we're there, it rained for only one afternoon.

May: I think 5 . I don't like hot weather. And what would you recommend me 6 ?

Sue: First, you can go to the beach. Then, I think you can visit some of the other islands.

May: 7 . And besides going to the beach, what can we

do on Oahu?

Sue: I think you can see a Hawaiian show. And 8 , there's an aquarium, which is very interesting.

May: What do you think of the sunset cruise off Waikiki?

Sue: Well, some people say it's fun, but 9 .

May: By the way, is it easy to get around on the island? Do you think we should rent a car?

Sue: 10. Public transportation is pretty good, though. There're plenty of buses, and you can take a bus trip around the whole island for only 60 cents.

C 1. (A) it's quite dusty

　　(B) it's pretty deserted

　　(C) it's very beautiful

　　(D) it's much polluted

D 2. (A) to leave Hawaii

　　(B) to invite some friends over

　　(C) to get together sometime

　　(D) to go there next year

C 3. (A) You'll be there

　　(B) You'll see me

　　(C) You'll love it

　　(D) You'll do your best

B 4. (A) You'll arrive on time

(B) you'll have nice weather

(C) you'll see many things

(D) you'll meet a lot of people

A 5. (A) I'd like to go in winter

(B) I'd go there in summer

(C) I'd be there anytime

(D) I'd go with my parents

A 6. (A) to do there

(B) to be there

(C) to eat there

(D) to stay there

C 7. (A) I don't mind

(B) It sounds annoying

(C) That's a good idea

(D) I don't understand it

D 8. (A) if you like old things

(B) if you want to buy fashionable shoes

(C) if you are fond of fresh flowers

(D) if you wish to see colorful fish

B 9. (A) we enjoyed it a great deal

(B) we didn't like it very much

(C) we took it several times

(D) we found it very pleasant

B 10. (A) You had better agree with me

(B) It's up to you

(C) Leave it to me

(D) You should take a bus

單一選擇題的第一題，沿襲過去幾年的題例，採取「對話」題，配分也是每題一分，共十分。但過去是總共十題的對話，每題都是獨立的，上下語義並不聯貫。而今年卻是上下一貫的對話題，在語義與語用上密切聯繫。對話的人是 May 與 Sue 兩人，話題是夏威夷之行。雖然也談及夏威夷風光，但是出題出得很謹慎；因此去過夏威夷的人不一定會佔便宜，沒有去過夏威夷的人也不見得會吃虧。又對話中所出現的詞彙與句型也控制得宜，除了在對話中出現的 'paradise, aquarium, cruise' 與在答案中出現的 'dusty, deserted, polluted, It's up to you…' 較難以外，幾乎沒有艱難的生詞或句型。

II. **綜合測驗**(20%)：附有答案(四選一)的填充題，總共三段文章，二十個空格。

第一大題：(11)～(20)

Jack was walking 11 the street when he saw a big dog. The dog looked very, very 12. It kept on barking 13 Jack, so Jack stopped walking. Jack saw a woman 14 near the dog, so he walked up to her and said, "15, does your dog bite?" "No," the woman 16, "my dog doesn't bite." 17 hearing this, Jack continued walking.

Suddenly the dog jumped up <u>18</u> bit.

Jack. "Hey!" Jack <u>19</u> to the woman, "you said yourdog doesn't bite!" "It <u>20</u>," the woman said, "but that's not my dog!"

D 11. (A) above   (B) over

    (C) at   (D) down

B 12. (A) sad   (B) mean

    (C) just   (D) fit

A 13. (A) at   (B) to

    (C) on   (D) up

D 14. (A) stood   (B) stands

    (C) to stand   (D) standing

B 15. (A) I'm sorry   (B) Excuse me

    (C) I beg your pardon (D) Please forgive me

C 16. (A) remembered   (B) requested

    (C) replied   (D) refused

A 17. (A) On   (B) From

    (D) In   (D) With

D 18. (A) then   (B) but

    (C) thus   (D) and

B 19. (A) confirmed   (B) complained

    (C) commanded   (D) conveyed

D 20. (A) does   (B) did

    (C) didn't   (D) doesn't

第一段文章是幽默有趣的短篇故事。文體是含有對話的口語英語，而且除了 'bark'（'（狗)吠'）以外，幾乎所有的詞彙都出現於國中英語的課本。這一大題的答案中，(11)題是根據上下文意選擇適當的介詞；(12)題是根據文意選擇適當的形容詞（其中 'just' 的誘答力似乎較弱；而 'fit' 也被解爲 '適宜'，非被解爲 '強健'，結果可能減低其誘答力。）；(13) 題是根據文意來選擇適當的介詞；(14)題是根據句法來選擇動詞 'stand' 的適當形式；(15)題是根據文意來從 'Excuse me' 等慣用說法中選擇適當的一種；(16)題是根據文意選擇適當的動詞；(17)題是根據文意選擇適當的介詞；(18)題是根據文意選擇適當的對等連詞或連接副詞；(19)題是根據文意選擇適當的動詞；而(20)題是根據文意選擇動詞 'do' 的適當形式。

第二大題：(21)～(25)

For years Italians have suffered with one of the 21 postal and telegraph services in Europe. To show 22 incompetent service is, Giorgio Benvenuto, secretary-general of the Italian Labor Union, 23 a test a few weeks ago. Benvenuto sent a telegram 24 the fourth floor in his office building to an office on the third floor. The telegram was 25 four days later.

D 21. (A) easiest   (B) fastest

      (C) greatest   (D) slowest

B 22. (A) such   (B) how

      (C) as   (D) what

C 23. (A) contested   (B) constructed

    (C) conducted   (D) contained

B 24. (A) to   (B) from

    (C) in   (D) at

A 25. (A) delivered   (B) canceled

    (C) delayed   (D) advanced

　　第二段是有關義大利郵政的短文，在文體上屬於書面語的敍述文。文中較難的詞彙有 'postal, incompetent, secretary-general, labor union' 等，但這些生詞的出現似乎對於文章的了解或題目的解答並不構成太大的妨碍。這一題的答案中，⑵題是根據上下文意選擇適當的形容詞；⑵題是根據句法從 'such, how, as, what' 等不同詞類的答案中選擇'how'（其他答案的誘答力似乎較低）；⒀題是根據文意選擇適當的動詞；⒁題是根據文意選擇適當的介詞；而⒂題又是根據文意選擇適當的動詞。

第三大題：⒃～⒀

The modern English name didn't come into common use 26 the late Middle Ages. Before that, only one name was 27 to a person. We now call 28 the first name. Because many people received 29 first name, they were additionally differentiated by another name, now called the last name. Many of the last names were passed down in 30 families.

A 26. (A) until　　　　(B) with
　　　　(C) for　　　　(D) while

D 27. (A) sent　　　　(B) made
　　　　(C) used　　　　(D) given

A 28. (A) this　　　　(B) which
　　　　(C) person　　　(D) family

C 29. (A) many a　　　(B) the only
　　　　(C) the same　　(D) more than

B 30. (A) typical　　　(B) individual
　　　　(C) entire　　　(D) particular

　　第三段文章是有關英文姓名的短文，在文體上屬於書面語的
說明文。文中出現'differentiate, passed down'等較難的詞彙
，但是題目本身並不艱難。這一題的答案中，㉖題是根據文意選
擇適當的介詞；㉗題是根據文意選擇適當的動詞；㉘題是根據文
意選擇適當的(代)名詞；㉙題是根據文意選擇適當的名前修飾語
（包括限定詞與數量詞）；而㉚題是根據文意選擇適當的形容詞。

　　以上綜合測驗，共有三篇文章，包括接近口語英語的短篇故
事以及屬於書面語英語的敍述文與說明文。所有的文章都相當簡
短，而且沒有太多太難的生詞。題目的安排，大體上是由簡而難
，因而可以幫助中下程度的學生由簡而難依序作答。不過總共二
十個題目中，動詞佔七題(35％)、介詞佔五題(25％)、形容詞三
題(15％)，單是這三種詞類就佔了十五題(75％)。相形之下，連
詞、慣用說法、名前修飾語、(代)名詞等都只出一題（每題佔５％）

。爲了周延題目的涵蓋面，似乎應酌量減少有關動詞與介詞的題目，而把這些題目分配到情態助動詞、包括冠詞的限定詞、介副詞等上面來。這些詞類都是屬於英語的虛詞或「功能詞」(function word)，不但是英語教學的重點，而且是我國學生最容易犯錯的詞類。另外，既然名爲綜合測驗，就似乎應該綜合考量詞彙、句法 、語意 、語用四項因素出題。在以上二十題中，只有⑭題有關動詞形式的選擇牽涉到句法，而其他的題目都僅與語意(包括詞彙意義與上下文意)有關。因此有關動詞的測驗題中不妨摻入含有情態動詞、完成貌 (have V-en)、進行貌(be V-ing)、被動態 (be V-en) 等的題目；有關形容詞的測驗題中也不妨加入有關形容詞原級、比較級、最高級或區別名前形容詞與名後形容詞等題目。

Ⅲ. 閱讀測驗(30%)：共有四段短文，十五個題目(每題兩分)，都是四選一的選擇題。

第一大題：(31)～(32)

One young woman, an only child, chose to live in a college dormitory in order to better learn to live with others. She considered dormitory living to be an invaluable experience. She said that someone "living in the dormitory becomes more involved in college activities. People depend on you to do more, and so do you. You learn to become involved." She went on to say, "You don't have a whole lot of privacy with all those people in one dormitory, but you learn how to get along. After a while, it's like having one big family."

A 31. The only child chose to live in a college dormitory because

(A) she would like to be more closely connected with people.

(B) she found it more convenient to go to classes and the library.

(C) she would like to enjoy more freedom and independence.

(D) her family was too big and complicated and she didn't like it.

C 32. According to the only child, the students living in the dermitory

(A) learned to cherish their privacy.

(B) considered dormitory life unbearable.

(C) shared many common experiences.

(D) thought little of their experiences.

　　第一段文章是有關大學寄宿生活的敍述文。文章簡短而容易，除了'dormitory, invaluable, involved'幾個單詞較難以外，沒有什麼艱難的詞彙或句型。又這一段文章簡短而容易，所以只附了兩個題目。而這兩個題目與答案都是屬於「解義」（paraphrase）的型式。例如，(31)題的原文'in order to better learn to live with others' 以 'because she would like to be more closely connected with people' 來解義；而(32)題的原文'learn to become involved' 與'learn to get along' 則以 'shared many common experiences' 來解義。雖然這些解義與原文的含義並不盡然相同也不完全吻合，但是在「選最適當的答案」這個條件下只能選這些答案。又(31)與(32)兩題題目都以 'the only child' 來指涉文章裏的主角，但是原文的 'an only child' (表示家裏的身份或地位)是 'one young woman' (表示人)的「同位語」，與其(31)與(32)兩題兩次重複使用'the only child' 而顯得上下的連貫有些不自然，不如改為 'The young woman……' 與'According to her,……'以求前後呼應來得妥貼。

第二大題：(33)～(35)

Drunken driving has become a serious form of murder. Every day about twenty-six Americans on the average are killed by drunk drivers. Heavy drinking used to be an acceptable part of the American masculine image, but the drunken killer has recently caused so many tragedies that public opinion is no longer tolerant.

Twenty states in the United States have raised the legal drinking age to 21, reversing a trend of 1960s to reduce it to 18. After New Jersey lowered it to 18, the number of people killed by 18-to-20-year-old drivers doubled, so the state recently upped it back to 21. Some states are also punishing bars for serving customers too many drinks. As the casualties continue to occur daily, some Americans are even beginning to suggest a national prohibition of alcohol. Reformers, however, think that legal prohibition and raising the drinking age will have little effect unless accompanied by educational programs to help young people develop responsible attitudes about drinking.

D 33. Drunken driving has become a major problem in America because

(A) most murderers are heavy drinkers.

(B) many Americans drink too much.

(C) most drivers are too young.

(D) many traffic accidents are caused by heavy drinking.

C 34. What is the public opinion regarding heavy drinking?

(A) It's a manly image.

(B) It can create a relaxing and happy atmosphere.

(C) Fewer and fewer people can stand it.

(D) People should be careful in choosing the right drink.

B 35. According to reformers, the best way to solve
the problem of drunken driving is to

(A) specify the amount drivers can drink.

(B) couple education with legal measures.

(C) forbid liquor drinking.

(D) raise the drinking age.

第二段是有關酗酒駕車的說明文。這段文章的文體是書面語，不但字數比第一段文章長，而且用詞也比第一段文章更為簡鍊而偏難。例如，'drunken (driving), murder, drunk (drivers), heavy (drinking), masculine (image), tragedies, tolerant, legal (drinking age), reverse, trend, up (something) back, bars, casualties, prohibition, alcohol, reformers, accompanied by' 等都可能不屬於一般高中學生的常用詞彙，就是在日常生活中也少有這類接觸或經驗。另外，在答案裏出現的 'manly (image), couple (something) with (another), (legal) measures' 等詞彙的難度也稍高。而且這些詞彙含義的了解，對文義的了解與選擇正確的答案具有相當密切的關係。由於這一段文章較長較難，所以附了三個題目。這三個題目在基本上也是屬於「解義」的性質，但是與第一大題不同，有些答案比較不容易在原文裏找出解義的對象。如上所述，第一大題的答案是針對原文裏某一個簡短的詞句加以解義的，但第二大題答案中㉝題的解義或了解對象至少涉及開頭兩個句子，而㉞與㉟題的解義或了解對象則分別涉及第三個長達三行的句子與最

後一個長達四行的句子。結果，除了文章以外，題目本身的難度
也無形中提高了。

第三大題：㊱～㊵

Ten years ago, there were more than 1.3 million
elephants in Africa. Over the past ten years, that
number has been cut down to around 600,000. African
elephants are hunted for their valuable ivory tusks.
Most have been killed by poachers. Poachers are hunt-
ers who kill animals illegally. An adult elephant eats
as much as 300 pounds a day. In their search for food,
elephants often move great distances. When they
cannot find the grasses they prefer, they may strip the
land of trees.

Today, the area in which elephant herds live is
much smaller than it used to be. Many areas in their
path have been turned into farms. And some elephants
have been killed by farmers for trampling their crops.

What can we do here in our country about a threatened animal that lives so far away? Our government
has passed a law to protect it. People cannot import
or bring in items made from ivory or any part of the
elephant's body.

Most countries throughout the world have also

stopped ivory imports. It is hoped that the ban on the sale of ivory will help save the African elephant. But the world's largest land animal needs other help. The countries where these animals live are often poor and unable to manage the herds. If the elephant is to survive, this animal is going to need our support for many years to come.

C 36. The number of elephants in Africa today is

    (A) the same as that ten years ago.

    (B) more than that ten years ago.

    (C) a little less than half of that in 1981.

    (D) a little more than half of that in 1981.

B 37. African elephants have been killed mainly because

    (A) they eat a lot.

    (B) they have beautiful tusks.

    (C) poachers kill them for fun.

    (D) there are too many of them.

C 38. The areas where African elephants live are much smaller today because

    (A) they tend to live in herds.

    (B) there are not so many of them today.

    (C) many of these areas have been turned into farms.

    (D) farmers have been killing them to save their

crops.

A 39. It is mentioned in the article that our country has

　(A) officially stopped ivory imports.

　(B) banned the killing of elephants in Africa.

　(C) threatened the elephants that live far away.

　(D) helped the African countries where elephants live.

D 40. Which of the following statements is true?

　(A) Poachers have a license to hunt for animals.

　(B) Elephants do a lot of good for the farmers in Africa.

　(C) We live too far away to help save the African elephant.

　(D) The African elephant needs the world's support for its survival.

　　第三段文章是有關保護非洲大象的說明文。這一篇文章含有四段文字，字數也在閱讀測驗所有四段文章中最長。但是用詞卻相當簡易，除了'ivory tusk, poacher, illegally, strip, herd, path, trample, ban, survive' 等單詞稍難以外，沒有什麼較難的成語或句型。而且，出題的人非常謹慎的把這些較難的單詞從題目的考慮中抽出；因此，不懂這些單詞並不會直接影響找出正確的答案。由於這一段文章的字數較長，所以總共附有五個題

目。第三大題的閱讀測驗題目顯然比前兩大題的閱讀測驗題目進步。因爲這一大題文章的難度比第二大題文章的難度適當，而這一大題的出題方式也比第一大題的出題方式高明。第一大題的題目不但以「解義」部分詞句爲主，而且解義的對象相當狹窄，因而是比較偏向「分項題目」（discrete item）的出題方式。這一類題目，只要了解文章的某一部分詞句就可以回答。相反的，第三大題的題目是以「了解」全文爲目的，問題的範圍比較廣泛，因而是屬於「成段題目」（global item）的出題方式。這一類題目，必須了解整段文章，還得做些推理推論。雖然難度較高，卻能眞正測驗考生的閱讀能力。

第四大題：(41)～(45)

Lincoln College Preparatory Academy, a secondary school for sixth to twelfth graders in Kansas City, Missouri, U.S.A., is proving a little money can grow a long way. About 45 of the 60 staff members at this school are giving $10 of their salaries each month to a college fund for Lincoln graduates who want to become teachers.

"Our area is short of teachers," explains Shirley Johnson, a math teacher who started the fund. "I know it wasn't going to get better unless we did something about it ourselves." Lincoln graduates can be considered for awards if they "maintain a B-or-above average in high school and a C-plus or above in college," says Johnson. "And they have to major in education and want to teach in Kansas City for two years."

Students who change their major from education in college can pay back the award later. If the fund—expected to reach $7,000 or more by May—proves successful, Johnson will introduce her program to other schools later on.

A 41. The secondary school in Kansas City is proving that

    (A) education funds can be started with small sums.

    (B) money can make anything happen.

    (C) money is more important than education.

    (D) good teachers always have chances to get awards.

C 42. The total amount of the fund raised each month is about

    (A) seven hundred dollars.

    (B) six hundred dollars.

    (C) five hundred dollars.

    (D) ten dollars.

A 43. The staff members have contributed to the college fund because

(A) they want to encourage their graduates to come back to teach.

(B) they think teaching is a rewarding profession.

(C) they expect their graduates to become famous scholars.

(D) their salaries are high and their living expenses are low.

B 44. One of the conditions for a student to receive the education award is:

(A) he must be a graduate of a college.

(B) he must be a graduate of Lincoln College Preparatory Academy.

(C) he must have outstanding grades in high school and college.

(D) he must want to teach in Kansas City for at least one year.

D 45. Who has to pay back the award?

(A) Those who maintain a B average in high school.

(B) Those who maintain a C-plus average in college.

(C) Those who have earned enough money for their education.

(D) Those who no longer major in education.

　　第四段文章是有關美國一所中學升學獎學金計畫的敍述文。整篇文章由三個小段而成，字數略比第二段文章短，但仍然附有五個問題。在文章裏出現的詞彙中以 'preparatory academy, grader, grow a long way, staff (members), salaries, (college) fund, area, awards, B-or-above average, C-plus or above, major in, (their) major' 等屬較難，但是這些詞彙的出現似乎並不妨礙基本文義的了解，考生仍然可以找出正確的答案。五個題目都以「了解」為主，除了(42)題(只與第二個句子有關，但是要了解句義後做 "$10 \times 45 = $450" 的計算)與(45)題(只與第三段第一個句子有關)比較接近「分項題目」以外，其他三題都含有「成段題目」的性質。

　　今年的綜合測驗共有四段文章，其中敍述文兩篇，說明文兩篇。以文章與題目的難度而言，第一大題最容易，而第二大題則似乎最難；因此，宜把第二大題排在第三大題或第四大題後面。由於綜合測驗在性質上多屬於「分項題目」，所以閱讀測驗宜注重「成段題目」。又綜合測驗的目的在於測驗學生主動運用的能力，所以試題中所出現的詞彙(尤其是四選一的備選答案中所提供的詞彙)應該屬於考生的「(主動)運用詞彙」((active) manipulation vocabulary；卽學生會聽、會說、會讀、會寫、會懂、會用的詞彙)。而閱讀測驗的目的則在於測驗考生被動認識的能力，所以文章裏所出現的詞彙(尤其是非關鍵詞)不妨包含一些考生的「(被動)認識詞彙」((passive) recognition vocabulary，卽學生會聽、會讀、會懂，但不一定會說、會寫、會用的詞彙)，甚至可以出現一些學生可能不認識的詞彙，藉以測驗考生

利用上下文意來推測或判斷這些生詞的能力。但是閱讀測驗的答案裏所使用的詞彙卻應力求避免生詞；甚至不妨在文章裏用較難的詞彙，而在答案中則用較易的詞彙來解義（例如：第四大題第三行的 'giving ($10)' 不妨用 'donating' 或 'contributing'，而⑭題第一行的 'contributed' 則改爲 'given money'；又如，第四大題倒數第四行的 'pay back' 不妨改爲 'repay'，而以⑮題第一行的 'pay back' 來解義。

第二部分：非選擇題

Ⅰ. 中譯英（20%）

(1)我生長在鄉下的一個小村落。

(2)那時，我家附近有一條清澈的小溪。

(3)我們常在夏天到那裏游泳、釣魚。

(4)現在溪水髒得魚都不能活了。

(5)不知道甚麼時候才能再見到童年的美景。

非選擇題共有兩大題。第一大題是中翻英。中文由語意連貫的五個句子合成，要考生翻成「正確」、「通順」而「達意」的英文（每題4分）。第一題的翻譯重點似乎在於 '生長'（'grew up; was brought up; was born and raised' 等）與 '鄉下的一個小村落'（'a small village in {the country/a rural district}' 等）。第二題的翻譯重點似乎在於 '那時'（'at that time, then, when we were children'）與 '我家附近有一條清澈的小溪' 的「存在句」（existential sentence；如 'there was in our neighborhood a stream clean and clear; there was a clean and clear stream in our neighborhood')。第三題的翻譯重點似乎在於'常'（'used to; would' 等）與'夏天到那裏游泳、釣魚'（'go swimming and fishing there during the summertime'）。第四題的翻譯重點似乎在於'髒得'（'{became/got} so dirty that…'）與'魚都不能活'（'(even) fish cannot live in the water'）。而第五題的翻譯重點似乎在於'不知道什麼時候才能再見到'（'I wonder when I can see…again'）與'童年的美景'（'the beautiful scenery in my childhood'）。在以上這些翻譯重點中'生長'、'我家附近有一條清澈的小溪'與'常'較難，但是仍然在高中英語敎學的範圍內。只有'童年的美景'，由於含義比較抽象，可能不容易翻譯出來。

II. 英文作文（20％）

寫一篇有關鐘或錶的短文，分成兩段：第一段談鐘或錶對我們生活的重要性；第二段談你最喜歡的一個鐘或錶。

非選擇題的第二大題是英文作文。與往年一樣，不硬性指定作文題目，而只交代文章的字數（以不超過 100 個單字爲原則）、段數（兩段）以及段意的主要內涵。但是今年的作文主題卻選擇了冷門的「鐘」或「錶」，而且有關段意的說明似乎也比往年簡略而抽象，因而難望觸動考生的「文思」。命題者或許擔心作文題目被坊間的補習班猜中，而有意出一個冷門的題目，不讓考生猜中

於事前。但凡事過猶不及，過分防備試題被猜中而出非常冷門的題目，結果反而極端限制了學生自由聯想與發揮的能力。其實，這類作文題事先限制段數與主要內容，即使考生或補習班猜到主題，也不容易猜到這些具體的內容。今年的作文主題不但冷僻，而且有關段意的指示幾乎沒有任何具體的內容；因此，許多考生與英文老師都反應今年的英文作文題不如往年題目的容易發揮。例如，以目前高中學生的英文能力，並且在考試時間的限制與壓迫下，如何描述他所喜歡的鐘或錶？是描寫它的形狀、大小、顏色、結構嗎？又如，第一段的"談鐘或錶對我們生活的重要性"與第二段"談你最喜歡的一個鐘或錶"，其實可以充當兩個獨立的作文題目；兩段文章的內容並不相干，因此也可能不容易上下連貫。為了幫助學生能夠比較容易就題發揮，不妨把作文的主題改為「我的錶」：第一段談一下你的手錶，例如，是什麼樣的錶？是那一個國家製造的？是你自己買的還是別人送的？那是什麼時候的事情了？第二段談你的手錶跟你的關係或對你的重要性；例如，帶手錶有什麼方便或不方便？你的手錶幫過你什麼忙或耽誤過你什麼事？你能想像沒有錶的生活嗎？

從民國六十七年到六十九年筆者曾在中央日報〈中學生副刊〉與《英語教學》等刊物為文批評該年度大學聯考英文試題的缺失。以六十七年度大學聯考英文試題為例，筆者所指出的缺失，計有：(一)試題種類過多、(二)複選題不合宜、(三)試題難度偏高、(四)文法分析題應該廢除、(五)中譯英題應加改進等五點。這幾年來，這些缺失都已見改進：

　　(一)試題種類由當年的十一大類、六十個題目(平均每做五

題就必須改換做另一類題目；如此考生不僅要耗費相當長的時間去了解每一類題目的題意與答題方式，而且每一類題目之間試題內容或答題方式的變化相當大， 很容易引起學生的慌張與混亂)減為今年的五大類、五十個題目。

(二)當年的複選題已改為單選題，因而不致於使題目的內容過於艱深，增加學生不必要的負擔。

(三)當年的試題難度偏高，因而考生成績的高標準與低標準都偏低。如今，除了少數題目以外試題難度都適中，很少出現使用頻率極低的詞彙、成語或文意與哲理太深的文章。

(四)當年容易引起爭論的文法分析題已從大學聯考的英文試題中消失。現在的英文試題都趨向「綜合性」(integrative) 的試題，不致於在某些試題中偏重拼字、發音、詞彙或文法而忽略了其他語言因素。

(五)過去兼考中譯英與英譯中，題目的內容常超出考生的實際生活經驗，所用或所要求的詞彙或成語也常超出考生的實際能力。如今，把英譯中納入英文作文而只考中譯英。無論是題目的內容或所要求的詞彙成語，都力求符合考生的實際生活經驗與實際英語能力。

這幾年來，大學聯考的英文試題一直都在穩定中求進步。今後或許可以在進步中求一點變化。例如，中翻英的題目不妨嵌在整段英文的文章中。也就是說，在一段英文的文章中空出五個部分要求考生依照中文填入英文。這一種出題方式的好處是考生必須參考整篇文章的文體、風格、用詞與節奏來做翻譯；因此，考生會對於整篇文章的「統一性」(unity)、「連貫性」(coherence)

、「強調性」（emphasis）與「變化性」（variation）更加注意。又如，英文作文題也不妨提供文章開頭的幾句英文，讓考生能參酌這段英文的文體、風格、用詞與節奏來寫底下的英文。這一種出題方式還具有防止猜題或背題的功效，因為預先背好的文章並不容易接上試題上預先提供的英文文章。

最後，我們必須鄭重指出：英文試題的改進必須配合英文閱卷的改進。筆者曾聽見許多考生與家長（其中不乏大專院校的英文教授）埋怨非選擇題（特別是英文作文）的評分並不公正，不能令人信服。關於這一點，筆者早於民國六十九年在中央日報〈中學生副刊〉與《英語教學》發表文章討論有關的問題。筆者曾指出：

（一）非選擇題題目、題意往往含混不清，很容易引起考生的誤解而答錯題目。

（二）非選擇題的答案如果要認真評分，必定要花費閱卷人很多時間與心血。考生可能犯的錯誤可以說是千差萬別，很難擬定公平而合理的扣分標準。即使是同樣的錯誤在前後兩張不同的考卷上出現，閱卷人也不可能一一加以記住而扣去同樣的分數。

（三）非選擇題的評分，可靠度很低。因為由同一個閱卷人評閱多份試卷的結果，可能由於情緒變化、身體疲倦或時間緊迫等因素，無法始終保持一定的評分標準。如果試卷數目過多而必須由許多人分開閱卷，那麼閱卷人彼此間評分的差距必然更大。對於英語測驗素有研究的美國語言學家 Robert Lado 在 Language Teaching: a scientific approach 一書中曾引用了 Henry Chauncey 所做的實驗報告。在一次實驗裏總共請了二

十八位英文老師，在前後兩次不同的機會為同一篇作文評分。結果，二十八位老師中有十八位老師對於同一篇作文在第一次評分中給予及格的分數，而在第二次評分中卻給予不及格的分數。另外有十一位老師則在第一次評分中打了不及格的分數，而在第二次評分中卻打了及格的分數。在另一次實驗裏曾經請了一百四十二位老師為同一篇論文評分。結果發現，其間評分的差距竟然達到最低五十分與最高九十八分之鉅。因此，Chauncey 所下的結論是：要求一百五十位閱卷人根據共同一致的標準，做客觀而公平的評分，簡直是不可能的事情。他還說：即使是經過精選的老師或教授，在經過一天的事前協調訓練與實習之後，於同一時間、同一地點在幾位老練的「主試人」(table leaders) 負責檢查與協調下閱卷，也難保評分之客觀與公平。

非選擇題測驗無法用評量或統計的方法來檢查題目的「信度」(reliability)、「效度」(validity)、「難度」(difficulty) 或「鑑別能力」(discriminatory power) 等。這也就是說，我們無法檢查非選擇題測驗是否有效地達成它的目標，或公正地完成了它的使命。

針對這些問題，筆者曾經建議：

㈠非選擇題在總分中所佔的比例不宜過高（現在佔總分一百分中的四十分）。

㈡作文的字數與段數最好能設一個限制（現在已限制為一百字兩段的文章）。

㈢作文的命題需要高度的技巧(現用提供「內容組織」(context) 的方式，而把作文的重點放在「文字表達」(expression))

，一方面讓考生有話可說，一方面讓考生不容易事前猜題而預先背好文章。

(四)作文的評分應該有相當客觀的標準(現在規定為"內容4分，組織4分，文法4分，用字遣詞4分，拼字、大小寫與標點符號4分"，但是閱卷人是否確實依照這些標準評分，不無疑問)。

(五)作文成績的高低應該從考生實際表現的比較中得來。因此，表現最好的學生應該得到滿分二十分，一如表現最差的學生應該得到零分。閱卷人千萬不能依個人的主觀預設滿分的英文作文；凡是未能達到這個預設標準的作文都一律扣分。同時，閱卷人不能只注意考生寫錯的詞句而扣分，也要注意考生寫對的詞句而給分。

關於中譯英與英文作文評分可能隱藏的缺失，筆者已籲請大學入學考試改進中心在一項研究計畫中針對已往考生的選擇題(即選擇題等客觀測驗題)與非選擇題(即中譯英與英文作文)兩項成績之間做統計調查與評量的工作。希望這項調查結果出現之後，能對非選擇題的評分提出更具體的改進意見。

＊本文原刊載於《人文及社會學科教學通訊》（1991） 2卷4期110-127頁。

英語疑難彙編

第一問：《國中選修英語》下册第十課，頁五二出現：'This wall lists American presidents who were born in Virginia.' 與 'Eight of America's forty presidents were born in our state.' 兩個句子。請問其中 American 與 America's 有何不同？

（臺北市石牌國中）

解答：

'American' 是 'America' 這個專有名詞的形容詞，做 'belonging to North, Central, or South America, esp.

the United States of America'或'（北、中、南）美洲，尤指美國的'解。'America'是由名詞加領屬標誌'-'s'而成的所有格名詞，做'美國的'解。在課文的用法裏，'American presidents'與'America's presidents'兩種說法都可以通用，而且在意義與用法上並沒有多大的差別。

但是一般說來，所有格名詞'America's'裏表示地域或國家的含義比較明顯，而形容詞'American'則從'美洲(人)的；美國(人)的'原義常引伸到'美國(人)典型的，代表美國人氣質的，美國特產的'等多種含義，因而意義與用法都較廣。例如，下面例詞裏的'American'都不一定能用'America's'來代替；或者雖然可以代替，但是所表達的意思卻不盡相同：'American {badger/buffalo/cotton/cranberry/crawl/crocodile/dream/eagle/English/footfall/Indian/organ/plan/poplar/robin/studies/tiger}'。同樣的區別也發現於'China's'與'Chinese'，例如'Chinese {boxes/cabbage/copy/Empire/evergreen/fire drill/forget-me-not/goose/hibiscuss/ink/lacquer/lantern/orange/pear/puzzle/restaurant/restaurant syndrome/Wall/wax/white/wood oil/yellow}'等說法的'Chinese'也不能用'China's'來代替。

第二問：北區公立高中七十九年度第一次模擬考試有一題四選一的選擇填空題：

1. A: Julia, you're looking most attractrive tonight.

B: Really? _____

A: Today is yours. The best of luck to you.

B: Much obliged.

(1) I am afraid you are making fun of me.

(2) Everybody looks nice.

(3) Yes, you can say that again.

(4) Anyway, thank you very much.

本題標準答案爲(2)。請問可否選(4)？

（臺北市光仁中學）

解答：

在第一句對話裏A說：'Julia, 你今天晚上看來漂亮極了'。而B回答說：'眞的嗎？大家看來都不錯啊'。參照上面A的對話與B的答話，還是答案 (2) 最爲合適。答案 (4) 如果刪掉 'anyway' 而改爲 'Thank you very much'，那麼還可以通。但是原答案有 'anyway' 這一句 'hedging word'，從上下文看來並不妥當。

第三問：《高中英文》第五册第一課，頁四：'It's unreasonable to regard any language as the possession of particular nations, and with no language is it more unreasonable than with English.' 中 'with no language is it more unreasonable than with English' 應如何解釋？其用法爲何？

（臺北市光仁中學）

解答：

此部份可以解釋為 'and it is most unreasonable with English' 或 'and it is especially unreasonable with English'，即 '就英語而言，尤其不合理'。在這一個句子裏含有否定詞 'no' 的介詞片語出現於句首，因而引起主語名詞與(助)動詞的倒序。這一種「否定倒序」(Negative Inversion) 的方式在原則上與一般英語疑問句的倒序方式相同。

第四問：《高中英文》第五冊第二課，頁四的：'No account of the solar system would be completely without mention of comet, for these are just as much members of the sun's family as are the major and minor planets.' 中的 'just as much' 應如何解釋？（臺北市光仁中學）

解答：

首先我要指出題目裏第一行第九個字的 'completely' 應該改為 'complete'。前半句 'No account of the solar system would be complete without mention of comets' 做 'we cannot talk about the solar system(= the sun's family) without mentioning comets' 或 'if we want to talk about the solar system, we must mention comets' 解；也就是做 '我們不能談太陽系而不談彗星；要談論太陽系，必須要談到彗星' 解。後半句 'for these are just as much members of the sun's family as are the major and minor planets'

做 'because comets are members of the sun's family just like the major and minor planets' 或 'because just as the major and minor planets are members of the sun's family, so are comets' 解；也就是做 '彗星與太陽系的大行星與小行星一樣，都是太陽系的一分子' 解。這裏的 'just as much' 要與後面的 'much' 搭配成為 '…just as much…as…'，並做 '…的…正如…的…' 或 '…是…一如…是…' 解；在這裏用來強調 '彗星與太陽系的大行星與小行星一樣，都是屬於太陽系'。因此，課文的句子本來可以說成 'for these (= comets) are just as much members of the sun's family as the major and minor planets are members of the sun's family'。但是為了避免 'members of the sun's family' 在前後兩個句子裏重複出現，把後半句的 'members of the snn's family' 刪略；並把 Be 動詞 'are' 調到句首，以便 'the major and minor planets' 能夠出現於句尾而充當句子的「信息焦點」(information focus)。

第五問：《高中英文》第六册第四課，頁五〇出現：'Like so many activities in life the more you are involved with music the more you get out of it.' 的句子。請問 'be involved with' 是否可用 'be involved in' 來代替？又此二片語又有何不同？

（臺北市光仁中學）

解答：

這裏的 'be involved with (something or someone)' 做 'have a close relationship with (something or some-one)' 解；也就是 '與…有關，與…有往來' 的意思，例如：

(1) You *are* much too *involved with* the problem to see it clearly.

(2) I have no special ambition to *get involved with* problems at ministerial level.

(3) The problem *is* closely *involved with* the man-agment of pastures.

(4) I don't want my son to *be involved with* criminals.

(5) How long has Grace *been involved with* that red-haired boy?

(6) He *is involved with* the police.

(7) I simply do not understand how you could *become involved with* a woman like that!

另一方面，'be involved in (something or someone)' 則通常做 'be part of, included in, mixed with, or deeply concerned in (something or doing something)' 解；也就是 '參與…，受到…的牽連' 的意思，例如：

(8) I *got involved in* the quarrel between Tom and Dick.

(9) *Were* you *involved in* an accident a few min-utes ago?

(10) He learned that his wife had *been involved in* an affair.

(11) I don't want to *get involved in* the matter.

不過，'be involved in' 有時候也可做'與…有關'解，例如：

(12) *Was* there gambling *involved in* the murder?

或做'(衣服等)被(機器等)捲進去'解，例如：

(13) A garment *became involved in* a piece of machinery.

從上面的解釋與例句可以發現：'be involved in'的含義與 'be involved with'的含義不盡相同，而且都可能含有「貶義」 (pejorative meaning)。又 'be involved with（人）'（如 例句(4)到(7)）固然常含有貶義，但'be involved with（事）' （如例句(1)到(3)）則並不含有貶義。因此，把課文裏的'be involved with'改為'be involved in'並不妥當。順便一提： 'be involved in' 也並不一定要表示貶義，例如下面(13)的主 動句與(14)的'be involved in V-ing…'就不含有貶義。

(13) Try to *involve* your mother *in* the general activity of the house.

(14) How many ofthe children *are involved in* preparing for the concert?

但是如果你多方蒐集例句，還是以表示貶義的為多，例如：

(15) His remark *involved* him *in* the argument.

(16) One foolish mistake can *involve* you *in* a good

deal of trouble.

(17) Don't *involve* me *in* your quarrel!

(18) The trouble with the relationship was that Ruby sometimes *involved* me *in* his capers.

(19) A city bus and a train *were involved in* a terrible crash at the railway crossing, in whick nine people were killed.

(20) Don't *involve* me *in* your crime — I had nothing to do with it!

　　我們花了相當多的篇幅來回答這個問題，因為我們想提醒老師們：上課講解或考試出題時，千萬不要隨便換個介詞或換成另外一個說法；務必要多方蒐集例句並深入研究意義與用法以後才可以介紹或補充其他說法。

第六問：《高中英文》，第六冊第四課出現：'They get a commitment to something other than the usual values they have in their lives' 的句子。請問此處'other than'為何意？（臺北私立光仁中學）

解答：

　　這一句英文做 'They commit (＝pledge) themselves to (seek) something that is not the usual values they have in their lives' 解；也就是'他們承諾（立誓）去尋求物質生活上一般利益之外的東西'。'other than' 在這裏是「片語介詞」（phrasal preposition），做 'aside from, apart from'

或‘除了……以外(的)，在……之外(的)’解。又‘other than’
通常都出現於否定句，但在課文裏卻出現於肯定句。試比較：

(1) There is nobody here *other than* (=except) me.

(2) She can hardly be *other than* (={anything but/ not}) grateful.

(3) You can't get there *other than* (={in any other way than/otherwise than}) by swimming.

(4) I have no *other* coat *than* this one.

(5) He could not be *other than* pleased.

第七問：本校高中英文補充教材中出現：‘The first full-scale giant recycling plants are, perhaps, years away’ 的句子。請問此處的‘years away’為何意？

（臺北私立光仁中學）

解答：

這一句話的大意是：‘要建造第一所大規模地回收廢棄物並加以利用的大工廠恐怕還要等好幾年(或是好幾年以後的事情)’。‘years away’在這裏做‘離現在好幾年’(‘many years away from now’) 解。相似的用例有：

(1) Christmas is still *three months away*.

(2) The debate on the Afghan crisis is only *a fortnight away*.

如果用‘away back’就做‘老早以前；早在……’(‘far back; as long ago as…’) 解，例如：

(3) I first met her *away back* in 1950.

(4) We sold our old house *away back* in February.

在臺灣出版的英漢辭典一般都沒有提起這裏 'away' 的用法（'away back' 的說法倒有辭典提起），但是由 Collins Birmingham Uuiversity International Language Database 出版的 Callins Cobuild English Language Dictionary 的 'away' 項倒有 'if an event is a particular time away, it will happen that amount of time in the future' 的英文解釋，並附有上面(1)的例句。

第八問：本校高三第一次月考出現下面的題目：

A: Do I look all right?

B: _____, you always do to me.

(1) You are like a fashion model.

(2) You are beautiful.

(3) Your beauty is beyond desciption.

(4) More than all right.

而標準答案為(4)。請問整篇對話為何意？可否選(2)？

（臺北私立光仁中學）

解答：

在第一句對話裏A說：'我看來還好嗎？'，而B則回答說 '（不只是好而已，）好得很呢，你什麼時候看來都不錯。'A句裏的 'all right' 不一定指容貌或外表，也可能指氣色或健康。因此以答案(4)的 'more than all right' 最為適當。答案(2)說得

未免太重了，太露骨了。

第九問：《高中英文》第三冊第十一課，頁一一九出現"Do not think that because Americans are in such a hurry that they are unfriendly." 的句子。請問此句中的從屬連詞去掉是否較好？

（臺北市立第一女子中學・英語科教學小組）

解答：

　　根據國立編譯館高級中學英文教科書編輯小組所言，這一課課文是採自 A. R. Lanier 編的 Visiting the U.S.A.。但是如讀者來信所指出，這一個句子似乎含有贅詞，似乎可以改為下面 (1)或(2)的句子。

(1) Do not think because Americans are in such a hurry that they are unfriendly.

(2) Do not think that Americans are in such a hurry that they are unfriendly.

　　(1) 句是從原句刪去出現於 'because' 前面的從屬連詞(新的語法稱為「補語連詞」(comqlementizer)) 'that' 而得來的。把這個 'that' 刪去以後，'because Americans are in such a hurry' 這個表示原因或理由的副詞子句就只修飾主要子句的 'Do not think'，而 'that they are unfriendly' 這個名詞子句就單獨成為 '(Do not) think' 的賓語。因此；(1)的句子表示：'不要因為美國人如此匆忙就以為他們(一定)不友善'。

　　(2) 句是從原句刪去出現於第一個 'that' 後面的從屬連詞

'because'而得來的。把這個 'because' 刪去以後，整個名詞子句'that Americans are in such a hurry that they are unfriendly'就成爲'(Do not)think'的賓語；而出現於這個賓語裏面的 'that they are unfriendly'就與前面的'(in) such (a hurry)'搭配而成爲表示結果或程度的副詞子句。因此， (2)的句子表示：'不要以爲美國人如此匆忙(所以)總不友善'。從課文的上下文來看，似乎(1)句的文字與解釋比(2)句的文字與解釋較爲妥當。

如果不改爲(1)句或(2)句，那麼在原句裏 'that because Americans are in such a hurry that they are unfriendly' 這整個名詞子句就成爲'(Do not)think'的賓語。而在這個賓語裏，'because Americans are in such a hurry' 與 'that they are unfriendly' 都因爲各自含有從屬連詞 'because' 與 'that'而成爲從屬子句；結果是賓語(子句)裏含有兩個從屬子句，而不含有主要子句，顯然是有語病的句子。我們會把這個問題送請國立編譯館高級中學英文教科書編輯小組注意；如果他們有什麼回答，我們也會利用《人文及社會學科教學通訊》的〈疑難彙解〉補答。

第十問：《高中英文》第三册第十二課，頁一三二出現："Of all the fibers now used by man, a very large percentage is man-made."的句子。請問此句中是否用複數動詞 'are'爲宜？

（臺北市立第一女子中學・英語科教學小組）

解答：

來信的讀者大概是以為課文的原句在結構與含義上等於下面 (1) 的句子，因此 Be 動詞應該與 'all the fibers (used by man)' 呼應，而用複數形 'are' 才對。

(1) A very large percentage of all the fibers now used by man are man-made.

一般說來，在含有 'all, most, half, quarter, more, none' 等數量詞的「表份結構」(partitive construction) 為主語的句子裏，動詞常與出現於數量詞後面的名詞的單複數呼應，例如：

(2) All of *the jam has* been eaten.

(3) All of *the boys have* been eaten.

(4) Part of *the blame is* mine.

(5) Part of *the prunes have* been picked.

(6) None of *it was* edible.

(7) None of *them were* going.

(8) The jar of *jam was* full. *Half has* now been eaten.

(9) There were *ten men* in the club. *Half are* now dead.

(10) I looked for *some jam,* but there *was none* left.

(11) I looked for *the boys,* but there *were none* left.

(以上(2)到(11)的例句採自 Paul Roberts (1954) Understanding Grammar, 281頁)

'percentage' 的有關用法，基本上也與一般數量詞相同，

例如：

(12) What *is* the percentage of *nitrogen* in air?

(13) It'*s* a tiny percentage of *the total income*.

（以上的例句探自 Collins Cobuild English Language Dictionary, 'percentage'項）

(14) What percentage of *babies die* of this disease every year?

（上面的例句探自 Longman Dictionary of Contemporary English, 'percentage'項）

(15) War is not an occupation in which death is certain, but only one in whch the percentage of *risk is* greatly raised.

(16) A good percentage of *the immigrants* coming to America *have* never left the neighborhood of the City of New York.

(17) A great percentage of *the automobiles* produced in Japan *are* intended for export.

(18) A large percentage of *the people are* illiterate.

(19) What percentage of *children* of school age *attend* school in Japan?

（以上 (15) 到 (19) 的例句探自 A New Dictionary of English Collocations, 'percentage'項）

但是有關英語主語名詞組與述語動詞在「數」(number) 的「呼應」(agreement; concord) 上所應遵守的規定並不是絕對

不變的。也有些人以'percentage'為名詞組的「主要語」(head)或「中心語」(center)；因而以'percentage'的單複數來決定動詞的單複數，特別是'percentage'後面沒有出現表示「總數」(total) 的名詞組的時候，例如：

(20) Unemployment *percentage rises.*

(21) Those *are* remarkable *percentages.*

(以上兩個例句採自 A New Dictionary of English Collocations, 'percentage'項)

課文裏面出現的句子也是屬於這種用例；動詞'is'因為與單數主語'a very large percentage'呼應而用單數，我們似乎不能說是錯誤的用例而非修改不可。但是在教學的時候則可以告訴學生依照上面一般的用例來造句或寫作。

問：國立編譯館編《高中英文》第四冊第八課87頁14行出現："I like you *the way you are.*"，的句子。請分析畫線部分在句中的結構。

（臺北市立北一女中・高二英文科教師）

解答：

句子中畫線的部份可以在前面補上介詞'in'，並在名詞片語'the way'與主語'you'中間插入關係代詞（嚴格說來是「補語連詞」(complementizer)) 'that'變成下面①的句子。

① I like you (*in*) the way (*that*) you are.

在這個句子裡'the way (that) you are'是名詞片語，而'in the way (that) you are'是介詞片語，但都充當修飾

'like you' 的「狀語」（adverbial）。傳統的文法把充當狀語的名詞片語叫做「狀語性的賓語」（adverbial object），例如：

② He came to see me {*the other day/last week*}.

③ I first met him{*one wintry night/three years ago*}.

④ Your dream will come true *some day*.

⑤ Mr. Smith weighs *two hundred pounds*.

⑥ She stands *six feet* tall.

⑦ The boy is *twelve years* old.

又①句中的 '(that) you are' 在句法功能上相當於關係子句，而修飾「前行語」（antecedent）名詞片語 'the way'。因此，在書面語裡 'that' 可以用 'in which' 來代替（這個時候，'the way' 前面的介詞 'in' 常加以省略），而且關係子句 'you are' 後面因為關係代詞的移位而出現「痕跡」（trace）或「空缺」（gap；用符號 'e' 來表示）。試比較：

⑧ I like you (in) the way [that you are *e*].

⑨ I like you the way [in which you are *e*].

從以上的討論，我們可以知道：'I like you the way you are' 裡的 'the way you are' 是含有關係子句 'you are' 的名詞片語，充當修飾謂語 'like you' 的狀語用；而且整句話做 '我（就）喜歡你這個樣子' 解。

　　問：國立編譯館編《高中英文》第四冊第八課87頁33行至88頁35行出現："Making something by hand has become the exception in many countries today

—*so much so that* giving a handmade gift is sometimes considered extraordinary." 的句子。畫線的部分應該做 'making something by hand is so erceptional that giving a handmade gift is sometimes considered extraordinary" 解。請問爲什麼不用 "so...that S" 的句型，而用 "so...so that S" 的句型？

（臺北市立北一女中・高二英文科教師）

解答：

我們先來討論 'so much *so* that' 裡第二個 'so' 的句法功能。這個 'so' 是「替代詞」（pro-form），可以替代動詞片語（如①句）、形容詞片語（如②句）、句子或子句（如③與④句）等。

① John *went to Japan last year*, and Bill did *so*, too.

② Mary is *good at mathematics*, and *so* is Jane.

③ *Did John go to Japan last year?* I think *so* (＝he did＝John went to Japan last year).

④ *Is Mary good at mathematics?* I guess *so* (＝she is＝Mary is good at mathematics).

由於替代詞 'so' 代表舊的信息，所以常出現於句首（如②句、⑤句與⑥句）。

⑤ *So* I {think/believe/heard/was told}.

⑥ *So* it seems.

替代詞 'so' 還可以用「加強詞」（intensifier; 也就是「程度副詞」）'very much' 等來修飾，例如：

⑦ A: Are you satisfied with our service?

B: Yes, *very much so.*

從以上的分析，我們可以知道：'so much so that' 的第二個 'so' 是替代前面的句子 'Making something by hand has become the exception in many countries today' 的替代詞，而 'so much' 是修飾這個替代詞的加強詞；因此，在句型上仍然屬於 "so (much so) that S" 的句型，做 '今天用手工製作東西在許多國家裡已不多見，以致於送人自己製作的禮物有時候成為很稀罕的事情' 解。相似的例句，如：

⑧ He is poor — *so much so that* he can hardly get enough to eat.

如果把原文裡面的 'so much so that' 改寫為 'making something by hand is so exceptional that'，那麼至少有下列兩個缺點：

（一）在 'making something by hand has become the exception' 的前文後面又加上 'making something by hand is so exceptional' 這一句話，顯得用詞上重複太多。

（二）'so *exceptional*' 只強調 'exceptional' 這個形容詞，而 'so much *so*' 則強調 'Making something by hand has become the exception in many countries today' 整個句子。

又 'so much so that' 應該分析為 'so...that' (即 '[so much so] that') 的句型，而不應該分析為 'so...so that' (即 '[so much] so that') 的句型。因為 'so...that' 表示「（程度

的)結果」，而 '...so that' 則常表示「目的」表示「目的」的時候，'that'前面的形容詞或副詞不用加強詞 'so' 來修飾，而'that'後面的子句裡常出現 'may, can, will' 等「情態助動詞」(modal auxiliary)。或「結果」。而表示「結果」的時候，'that' 後面的子句裡不出現 'may, can, will' 等情態助動詞，但'that' 前面的形容詞或副詞仍不能用加強詞 'so' 來修飾。試比較：

⑨ John worked *so hard that* he finally succeeded.

⑩ John worked *hard so that* he *might* succeed one day.

⑪ John worked hard *so that* he finally succeeded.

⑫ *John worked *so hard so that* he finally succeeded.

問：國立編譯館編《高中英文》第四册第十四課 152 頁26 至28行出現：As author and poet Samuel Ullman once wrote, "Years wrinkle the skin, but to give up enthusiasm wrinkles the soul."。

請問這裡的引用句是否充當動詞 'wrote' 的賓語？如果是的話，那麼整段文章就變成不完整的"sentence fragment"。另一方面，如果把引用句分析爲主要子句，那麼整段文章的文意似乎有些怪怪的。又這裡的 'as' 是否做 'just as' 解？

（臺北市立北一女中・高二英文科教師）

解答：

'as' 在這裡的用法應該是關係代詞用法，做 "according to what, in accordance with that which (在關係子句裡充當

主語或及物動詞賓語），the way in which（在關係子句裡充當狀語）"（參 *Third Webster Dictionary*, 'as' 項）或"in accordance with what, in accordance with the way in which" 參 *Longman Dictionay of Contemporary English*, 'as' 項）解，例如：

① *As* he said, the stream was full of trout. （賓語）

② His criticism, *as* I remember, were coldly received.

③ *As* you know, David writes dictionaries. （賓語）

④ He is a teacher, *as* {became/is} clear from his manner. （主語）

⑤ He is quite good *as* boys go. （狀語）

⑥ It was very cheap *as* the prices of cars go these days. （狀語）

⑦ *As* the song goes: I fell in love with eyes of blue... （狀語）

　　Collins Cobund English Language Dictionary （'as' 項，9.2）更以"when you want to mention where it has been said before, to indicate that you are quoting, or to point out that it is already known by the person you are speaking to"）（表示這句話曾經出現於什麼地方、表示說話者是在引用、或者表示這句話的內容聽話者已經知道）來詳細說明'as'的用法，並列舉下面的例句。

⑧ *As* I said a moment ago, we each want to write

a best seller.

⑨ *As* Peter Jenkins put it: "The Party was rotting at the grass roots.'"

⑩ *As* you know, I have spent a lifetime commuting.

⑪ *As* you can see we've got a problem with the engine.

因此，引用句 "Years wrinkle the skin, but to give up enthusiasm wrinkles the soul" 並不是及物動詞 'wrote' 的賓語（如果是賓語不可能在及物動詞與引用句之間標逗號），'wrote' 的賓語已經包含在關係代詞 'as' 裡面。這個賓語可以用符號 'e' 來表示，例如：

⑫ *As* author and poet Samuel Ullman once wrote *e*, "Years wrinkle the skin..."

在⑫的句子裡，引用句是主要子句，全句做'依照作家兼詩人 Samuel Ullman 曾經寫過的話："歲月使人的皮膚起皺紋（即變老），但放棄熱忱卻使人的心靈起皺紋"'解。

第十一問：《高中英文》第一冊第八課 Good Manners 中，用 'well-mannered' 與 'ill-mannered' 來分別表示'有禮貌的'與'沒有禮貌的'。請問：這裡可否用 'good-mannered' 與 'bad-mannered'？因為從字的結構而言，'well-mannered' 與 'ill-mannered' 是屬於 "Adv-V-en" 的結構，如 'well-behaved' 與 'ill-gotten'；而 'good-mannered' 與 'bad-mannered'

是屬於 'Adj-N-ed' 的結構，如 'good-natured' 與 'bad-tempered'。英語的 'manner' 是名詞，似乎應該用 'Adj-N-ed' 的結構纔對。請分析釋疑，謝謝。（左營高中英文教師）

解答：

這是一個很有趣的問題。如果只是要知道可否用 'good-mannered' 與 'bad-mannered'，那麼可以向英美人士或查英語辭典。但是如果要探求個中的道理，就非更進一步做語言分析不可。

首先，我們要知道：'mannered' 在古語裡可以單獨做形容詞用。因此，美國出版的 *Webster's Third New International Dictionary* 與日本研究社出版的 *Kenkyusha's New English-Japanese Dictionary* (5th edition) 都把 'mannered' 列為形容詞，並附上 '*mannered* pictures'（描寫風俗習慣的繪畫）、'delightfully *mannered*'、'beautifully *mannered* without verging on the precious'、'*mannered*, but imaginative'、'brief, *mannered* and unlifelike idiom' 等例句。但是在現代英語裡，'mannered' 卻在 'well-*mannered*'、'ill-*mannered*'、'rough-*mannered*' 等複合形容詞裡纔充當形容詞。

其次，我們也應該注意到：'well' 與 'ill' 都有副詞與形容詞兩種用法。下面以①、②、③、④的例句，分別舉一些 'well' 與 'ill' 的副詞與形容詞用法的用例。

① 'well' 的副詞用法

a. The work is *well* done.

b. The invalid is eating *well* now.

c. She dressed *well*.

d. The plan worked *well*.

e. He has a cold, but will do *well*.

f. That is *well* said.

g. All went *well*.

h. I was *well* rid of them.

② 'well'的形容詞用法

a. He began to eat like a *well* man.

b. The *well* are impatient of the sick.

c. I am perfectly *well*.

d. You don't look *well*.

e. All was *well* with him.

f. It is not *well* to anger him.

g. This is *well* enough, but I cannot afford the time.

h. It was *well* that he was our mutual friend.

③ 'ill' 的副詞用法

a. Don't {speak/think} *ill* of him.

b. Don't take it *ill* of him.

c. Never behave *ill* in public.

d. *Ill* got, *ill* spent.

e. I could *ill* afford the time and money.

f. It *ill* becomes him to speak so.

g. The affair turned out *ill*.

h. It would have gone *ill* with him.

④ 'ill' 的形容詞用法

a. He became *ill* through overwork.

b. You look *ill*.

c. The sight made me *ill*.

d. It has an *ill* taste.

e. He has an *ill* opinion of me.

f. It is an *ill* wind that blows nobody (any) good.

g. *Ill* news comes apace.

h. *Ill* weeds grow {apace/fast}.

最後，我們發現：用 'good' 與 'bad' 形成複合形容詞的例詞不多，而用 'well' 與 'ill' 形成複合形容詞的例詞則很多。試比較：

⑤ 'good-N-ed': good-conditioned, good-humored, good-natured, good-sized, good-tempered; good-looking

⑥ 'bad-N-ed': bad-tempered

⑦ a. 'well-V-en': well-acquainted, well-acted, well-advised, well-affected, well-appointed, well-armed, well-attested, well-balanced, well-be-haved, well-beloved, well-born, well-breathed, well-bred, well-built, well-chosen, well-conditioned, well-conducted, well-cooked, well-defined, well-deserved, well-developed, well-directed, well-disposed, well-done, well-dressed, well-earned, well-educated, well-established, well-favored, well-fed, well-fixed, well-formed, well-fought, well-found, well-founded, well-furnished, well-groomed, well-grounded, well-handled, well-heeled, well-hung, well-informed, well-intentioned, well-judged, well-kept, well-knit, well-known, well-laid, well-lined, well-made, well-marked, well-meant, welloiled, well-ordered, well-padded, well-paid, well-pleased, well-preserved, well-proportioned, well-read, well-regulated, well-remembered, well-rounded, well-seen (古語), well-set, well-set-up, well-shaped, well-sifted, well-spent, well-spoken, well-suited, well-tempered, well-thought-of, well-thought-out, well-thumbed, well-timbered, well-timed, well-trained, well-traveled, well-tried, well-trod (den), well-turned, well-worn

b. 'well-V-ing (現在分詞)': well-becoming, well-fitting, well-looking, well-meaning, well-pleasing, well-seeming, well-wishing

    c. 'well-V-ing'（動名詞）': well-being, well-doing

    d. 'well-to-V': well-to-do, well-to-live（蘇格蘭語），
    well-to-pass

⑧ a. 'ill-V-en': ill-advised, ill-affected, ill-balanced, ill-behaved, ill-bred, ill-clad, ill-come, ill-conceived, ill-conditioned, ill-considered, ill-cut, ill-defined, ill-disposed, ill-established, ill-fared, ill-fated, ill-favored, ill-fed, ill-formed, ill-founded, ill-given, ill-gotten, ill-housed, ill-humored, ill-informed, ill-judged, ill-kempt, ill-looked（古語）, ill-matched, ill-natured, ill-omened, ill-seen（古語）, ill-sorted, ill-spent, ill-starred, ill-suited, ill-tempered, ill-timed, ill-used, ill-willed

    b. 'ill-V-ing（現在分詞）': ill-becoming, ill-boding, ill-fitting, ill-judging, ill-looking

    c. 'ill-V-ing（動名詞）': ill-being, ill-breeding, ill-doing

    d. 'ill-V': ill-treat, ill-use

在以上的例詞中，'good-conditioned' 與 'well-conditioned' 都可以表示'情況良好的'；'bad-tempered' 與 'ill-tempered' 都可以表示'脾氣不好的'；'good-looking' 與 'well-looking' 也都可以表示'美貌的'，但是 'well-looking' 很少使用。又在上面含有 'ill' 的例詞中，'ill-fated'，'ill-humored'，'ill-natured'， 'ill-starred'，'ill-tempered' 都可以分析爲來自由形容詞與名詞合成的 'ill fate'，'ill humor'，'ill nature'，'ill star'，'ill temper'；但是一般較大的英文辭典都列有 'fated'，'humored'，'natured'，'starred'，'tempered' 的形容詞用法，所以仍然可以分析爲由副詞與形容詞合成。

從以上的觀察，我們可以獲得下列兩點結論。

（一）情狀副詞 'well' 與 'ill' 原則上與「由過去分詞（V-en）或現在分詞（V-ing）衍生的形容詞」（deverbal adjective）合成複合形容詞（如⑦與⑧的例詞）。'mannered' 在中古英語（大約在一千三百七十八年左右）具有 'endowed with good morals' 的意義而做形容詞 'having manner of specific kind' 解，因而也與 'well' 與 'ill' 合成 'well-mannered' 與 'ill-mannered' 這兩個複合形容詞。

（二）'good-natured, good-tempered, bad-tempered' 確實是由形容詞與名詞再加上詞尾 '-ed' 合成的複合形容詞，但是在 "Adj＋N-ed" 的複合形式中，形容詞 'good' 與 'bad' 的孳生力並不強；也就是說，'good' 與 'bad' 形成 "Adj＋N-ed" 這個複合形容詞的例詞並不多。這大概是由於已經有"{well/ill}-{Adj/V-en}" 的複合形容詞的存在，就不需要再借用較爲新型的 "{good/bad}-N-ed"的複合形容詞；這種詞彙現象叫做「阻擋」（blocking）。但是我們並不完全否認有些「方言」（dialect）或「個別語言」（idiolect）在「比照類推」（analogy）之下可能造出 'good-mannered' 或 'bad-mannered' 這樣的詞來。但是這樣的詞至少在目前並沒有獲得「標準英語」（Standard English）

的認可而收錄於一般英語辭典裡面。附帶一提：'soft-spoken' 與 'gentle-spoken' 都做'說話溫柔的'(speaking softly, having a mild or gentle voice' 解。這裡的 'spoken' 也做形容詞'用話說出來的，口頭的' (expressed, told, or delivered by word of mouth) 解，並且以 "Adj-spoken"的形式衍生 'fair-spoken'（很會說話的）、'pleasont-spoken'（談話令人愉快的）、'short-spoken'（談話很唐突的）等複合形容詞。可見，英語的複合詞有其獨特的「造詞規律」(morphological rule; word-formation rule)，不能完全從「句法規律」(syntactic rule) 的觀點來推論。

　　* 本文曾先後刊載於《人文及社會學科教學通訊》1 卷 1 期 140-144頁；1 卷 2 期128-130頁；1 卷 3 期 159-161 頁；1 卷 5 期120-123頁；2 卷 6 期132-136頁。

On Professor Fujii's 'Categories of Objects and the Verb BREAK: Conceptual Systems in Languages With and Without Classifiers'

I have studied with great interest Prof. Fujii's clearly written paper 'Categories of Object and the Verb BREAK: Conceptual Systems in Languages With and Without Classifiers'. In this paper Professor Fujii suggests a new linguistic typology which divides natural languages into two types: those with lexical classifiers and those without lexical classifiers. By carefully conducting a contrastive analysis between several uses of the English verb 'break' and the corresponding Japanese verbs; namely, *waru* (割る) for BREAK 1, *oru* (折る) for BREAK 2, *yaburu* (破る) for BREAK 3, *kowasu* (壞す) for BREAK 4, and *kuzusu* (崩す) for BREAK 5, Prof. Fujii tries to establish a correlation between verb categories and the categories of objects classified by classifiers, not only for Japanese but also for other languages which have classfiers, such as Chinese, Korean and Indonesian. In this comment, I would not recapitulate Prof. Fujii's analyses or conclusions. Rather, I would like to make a few remarks which, I hope, will supplement or reinforce Prof. Fujii's analyses and conclusions.

The correlation between verb types and classifier types, or objects classified by classifier types, I think, is semantic or pragmatic, rather than morphological or syntactic, in nature. The conceptual structure of the semantic verb BREAK (what Prof. Fujii calls in Note 1 the capital BREAK) in its broadest sense and transitive use might be paraphrased as something like 'CAUSE something to CHANGE INTO A CERTAIN STATE BY SEPARATING it INTO PARTS (suddenly or violently)'. Furthermore, despite the subtle semantic difference involved in different uses of the English verb 'break' and the corresponding Japanese verbs, they share certain common characteristics: (1) all the verbs involved are actional rather than stative, and can be used as accomplishment verbs as well as activity verbs; (2) the objects acted upon by the verb must be something 'breakable', which characterestic is described in Prof. Fujii's paper as 'thin' and/or 'fragile'. The variables involved in the different use of the English verb 'break' or the various corresponding verbs in Japanese, on the other hand, are (1) the shape of the objects, (2) the materials that the objects are made of, (3) the functional value of the objects, and (4) the 'broken image' or the resultant state of the object. after the action of breaking. These four variables, all of which are more or less correlated with choice of classifiers, however, do not seem to explain away all the differences involved in the different Japanese verbs which correspond to the different uses of the English verb 'break', since, as Prof. Fujii herself has pointed out, the parallelism between the classification of objects by the different verbs and the classification of objects by classifiers is by no means complete. Thus, despite Prof. Fujii's repeated claims that her analysis applies only to the core meaning of the verb or central members of the object, there seem to be numerous counterexamples to her generalization. For example, the use of the Japanese verb *waru* is by no means limited to 'thin, flat, fragile and inflexible objects', since the same verb may also apply to such hetrogeneous objects as 'watermelons, pumpkins, apples, walnuts, faggots, bamboo and cake.' Prof. Fujii also points out that the Japanese verb *kowasu* can be used not only with artificially made objects which have functional value but also with other objects that can be used ·in unmarked cases with the Japanese verbs *waru, yaburu* or *oru*. Prof. Fujii is of course correct in suggesting that the use of the verb *kowasu* emphasizes the functional value of the object, while the use of the verbs *waru, yaburu* and *oru* stresses the materials that the object is made of. This explanation, however, does not nullify the claim that the correlation between the various verbs of BREAK and classifiers is not complete. And the fact that the Japanese verb *kuzusu* can be used with objects which take a highly idiosyncratic classifier '*yama*', which is not included in the eight most frequently occurring Japanese classifiers, as well as the most frequently used Japanese general classifier '*tu*' further suggests that the relationship between verb types and classifier types is not as close as Prof. Fujii wants it to be. Thus she has to admit that while Japanese classifiers group objects by virtue of spatial configurations (namely, one-dimensional or two-dimensional), the verb BREAK groups objects not only by spatial configurations, which is reflected in the Japanese classifier system, but also based on the strength of the materials that the objects are made of (namely, flexible or inflexible), which'is not necessarily reflected in Japanese classifiers. Hence, the breakdown in the parallelism between verb types and classifier types.

The variable factor which seems to be somehow neglected in Prof. Fujii's analysis is the factor of manner, and perhaps the factor of instrument as well. Thus, the Japanese verb *waru* meens essentially 'damage something brittle by dropping or smashing it (into pieces)' in its non-instrumental sense, and 'separate something into two or more parts with an instrument (such as a knife)' in its instrumental sense. Here I use the adjective 'brittle', rather than the adjectives 'thin, flat and fragile' used by Prof. Fujii, because I think the adjective 'brittle', which means 'hard to the touch but easily broken', will better apply to include Prof. Fujii's exemplifying objects 'glasses, cups, windowpanes, plates, vases, tiles, Japanese roofing tiles'. I also add the instrumental use of the verb *waru* to include such examples as '*suika-o (naifu-de) waru* (cut a watermelon (with a knife))', '*take-o (nata-de) waru* (split a bamboo (with a hatchet))' and even '*roku-o ni-de waru* (divide 6 by 2)'.

The Japanese verb *oru*, on the other hand, means essentially 'separating something into two or more parts (usually with the hand)' which will apply not only to all of Prof. Fujii's list of objects, but also to such examples as '*kami-o futatu-ni oru* (fold a piece of paper in two)', '*hiza-o oru* (go down on one's knees)', '*eri-o oru* (turn down the collar)' and even accounts for the existence of the compound verb '*taoru*', which means '*te-de oru* (break off with the hand)'. This difference in the interpretation with regard to the manner of breaking (or what Prof. Fujii calls 'the broken image') also accounts for the acceptability of '*koppamijin-ni waru* (smash to bits)' and the unacceptability of '**koppamijin-ni oru* (snap into bits)'.

Next, the Japanese verb *yaburu* seems to essentially mean '*tateyoko-ni (hiki)saku* (tear or pull apart)' when the object is flexible or not solid, and '*ana-ya-hibi-o akeru* (make a crack, hole or opening in)' when the object is inflexible or solid. This interpretation with regard to the manner of breaking will account for the semantic difference invloved in such sentences as '*tegami-o yaburu* (tear the letter across)', '*kami-o komaka-ni yaburu* (tear up a sheet of paper)', '*ganjyoona kinko-no-kabe-o yabutte kane-o toru* (steal money by making a hole in the solid wall of a safe)', and '*to-o yaburn* (break a door open)'.

Fourthly, the Japanese verb *kowasu* seems to essentially mean 'damage in such a way that the object becomes useless or no longer stands use' and has a wide application in such examples as '*chyawan-o kowasu* (break a teacup)', *mon-o kowasite akeru* (force open a gate)', '*tokei-o kowasu* (put a watch out of order)', '*karada-o kowasu* (injure one's health)', and '*i-o kowasite iru* (have a disordered stomach)'.

Lastly, the Japanese verb *kuzusu* seems to essentially mean 'partially break something to make it smaller in size or amount, or less straight or rigid in posture', which is exemplified in sentences such as '*oka-o kuzusu* (level a hill)', '*ishigaki-o kuzusu* (demolish a stone-wall)', '*senyensatu-o kuzusu* (break a 1,000-yen note (intosmall money)', '*shisei-o kuzusu* (assume an easy posture)' and '*hiza-o kuzusu* (sit at ease)'.

Finally, I would like to add that the Chinese data provided by Prof. Fujii's informants are, in my opinion, far less than satisfactory. For example, it is *not impossible* in Chinese to say 'I broke a car', because we can say '我｛損壞/損毀｝了汽車', and it *is possible* in Chinese to say both 'My leg is broken' and 'I broke my **leg**', because we can say not only '我的腿(不小心)｛折斷/摔斷/跌斷｝了' but also，我(不小心)｛折斷/摔斷/跌斷｝了腿'. And the Chinese verbs which correspond to the five Japanese verbs discussed in the paper are, I think, in unmarked cases '打破'，'折斷'，'撕破'，'破壞/損壞' and '拆除/拆開'，respectively. Note also that unlike the corresponding verbs of BREAK in English and Japanese, the Chinese verbs are given in the form of verb-verb compounds or verb-complement compounds.

To summarize, though many of Prof. Fujii's generalizations seem valid and quite interesting, I do not think that the correlation between verb types and object types may be captured merely by virtue of classifier types without also taking manner types into consideration.

* 本文於1991年4月1日至6日在臺南市國立成功大學舉行的 Third International Conference on Cross-Cultural Communiction: East and West 上以講評人的身分發表。

高中英語教學：回顧與展望

一、我國英語教學的歷史背景

　　根據史載❶，英語或英文大概於一七一五年左右以「洋徑濱英語」(Pidgin English) ❷的形式傳入我國。在此以前，我國與外國的主要「通商語言」(lingua franca) 是葡萄牙語。❸ 從一七一五年到一八一八年的一百多年間，我國與歐美之間的主要通

---

❶ 有關英語傳入我國的歷史背景，主要參照 Stowe (1990)。我們在這裡向提供下面有關資料的 Dr. John E. Stowe (中文名'司徒約翰')致最高的謝意。

❷ 一般認爲 'Pidgin English'是由'business English' 訛化而來。

❸ 參 Hunter (1885)、Downing (1838)、Jespersen (1925)。

商語言是洋徑濱英語❹。美國與我國的通商自一七八四年開始增加❺，更是有助於提高洋徑濱英語在我國的重要性與普及性。但是洋徑濱英語到底不是真正的英語；因為當時我國通行的洋徑濱英語不但詞彙總數非常有限，而且大多數都是單音節或雙音節詞彙，有些習慣用法甚至混合使用葡萄牙語或由廣州方言直譯而來。例如，'No can do'是'不是'或'行不通'的意思，'No savvy'（'savvy'來自葡萄牙語的'sabe'（'知道'））是'不知道'的意思，'long time no see'表示'好久不見'，而'catchee wifo'（來自'(Did you) catch (your) wife?'）則表示'你結婚了沒有？'❻。在大中華思想的薰陶、重士輕商的傳統以及對於蠻夷之風的鄙視❼之下，當時的中國人都不屑學習洋徑濱英語，甚至羞於與使用洋徑濱英語的人為伍。

到了十九世紀之後，歐美有識之士纔開始對中國人教授較為「正式」（formal）的英語。這些有識之士主要是歐美的傳教士，而他們教授英語的主要動機是在中國推廣基督教。在中國從事英語教學的第一位新教（Protestant）傳教士是由倫敦傳教協會（London Missionary Society）派遣的 Robert Morrison❽。他於一八〇七年九月七日到達廣州。在未到中國之前，他已經

---

❹　參 Eames (1909)、Morse (1926)、Morrison (1834)。

❺　參 Morse a MacNair (1931:45-48)。

❻　參 Stowe (1990: 69)。

❼　當年外國水手的酗酒滋事、動輒開砲耀威、抓辮子取笑華人等作風更助長國人對"洋鬼子"的鄙視。參 Hunter (1885:33)。

❽　參 Morrison (1834)。

在倫敦跟一位受過教育的華人 Yong Sam-Tak 學過華語，而倫敦傳教協會派他到中國來的目的是"學會漢語並把聖經翻成漢文"('to acquire the Chinese language, and translate the Sacred Scriptures')。Robert Morrison 與 William Milne 兩人於一八一八年在廊六甲（Malacca）建立一所英華專科學校 (Anglo-Chinese College) 向中國人教授英語，並由 Milne 擔任校長。Milne 所採用的教學方法與中國傳統的漢文教學法頗為相似：嚴格而死板的紀律與浮淺而重死記的教學。在鴉片戰爭 (1839-1842年) 之後，這一所學校乃由廊六甲搬到香港來，曾於一八三五年成立摩里遜教育協會 (Morrison Education Society)。美國人 Samuel Robin Brown 也於一八三九年的二月二十三日帶著六個男學生到中國來，並在澳門開辦學校。Brown 受過良好的高等教育，並且有豐富的教學經驗。他反對當時的中國教育，認為中國的教育"極端忽略判斷、理性、想像、情操與良知等能力與德性的培養"('badly neglected judgment, reason, imagination, affections, and conscience')❾。他對於英語教學的貢獻是不注重「死背」(memorization) 而主張「解釋」(explanation)。他自己學漢語，也要求中國老師用同樣的方法來教他。他的另一個貢獻是於一八四七年第一次薦送三個中國學生到美國留學。

從這時候起，洋徑濱英語逐漸為眞正的英語所代替。在南京條約 (1842年) 之後，香港成為訓練英文通譯與買辦人才的大本

---

❾ 參 *Chinese Repository* (1851)。

營，大中華思想從此大受衝擊而瀕臨崩潰。一八五八年訂定的天津條約甚至把英國代表與中國政府交涉時所使用的官方語言規定為英語。開放五口通商之後，傳教自由就延伸到中國的腹地來，外國使節也開始駐紮於北京。而一八六一年從大中華思想的迷夢初醒之後，中國人第一次覺悟到了解歐美列強、學習他們的語言與科技的需要，同文館在北京的成立乃反映這種時代背景。從此，教授英語的學校乃雨後春筍般在中國各地相繼成立。❿

　　設立同文館的目的在於為政府訓練通譯人才，因而可以說是中國官方教授英語的開始。在此以前，所有的英語教學都由外國人在外國學校負責。這些學校訓練出來的英語人才雖然常由海關、軍隊甚或外交部來僱用，但是政府與國人對於這些人的能力與操守的評價並不高，常以鄙視與排斥的心態來對待。如今，在中學為體、西學為用的考量下獎勵英語的學習，必須造就更為優秀的英語人才。由於找不到通曉英語的國人來擔任教師，同文館所僱用的第一位英語老師仍然是來自英國的教士 John Shaw Burton, 並且在提供獎學金的條件下招募十四歲以下的學童十人開課。旋於一八六三年上海與廣州兩地也設立類似的學堂，而北京的同文館則除了英語之外也兼教法語與俄語，並於一八六七年升格為學院。這幾所學堂的成立，不但為國人敞開了學習外語之門，而且也打破了傳統舊式教育的壟斷而開放了接受現代教育之門。一八七二年滿清政府第一次派遣調查團赴美考察教育制度，

---

❿　根據 Mok (1951:99-100) 從一八六二年至一八九五年之間在北京、上海、廣東、福建、天津、武昌、湖北、湖南各地設立教授英語的學校多達十三所。

而同年八月則第一次保送三十位中國學生到美國留學。

二、日治時期在臺灣的英語教學

　　滿清政府於甲午戰爭失利之後便與日本締結馬關條約把臺灣割讓給日本，此後五十年（從一八九五年至一九四五年）臺灣卽被置於異族統治之下。在日本尚未統治臺灣之前，臺灣並沒有學校之設施，而只有書院或私塾的存在。在書院裏所講授的只是包含《三字經》、《千字文》與四書五經在內的漢文，而主要的教學方法是認字、背誦、書法與作文，當然並不包括外語在內。公學校的設立引進了日語教學，而師範學校的創辦則培養在公學校裏擔任日語、算術、家事、裁縫等課程的基本師資。至於英語的教學雖然列爲中學的必修課，但是全省只有十幾所公立中學（另有幾所私立中學），而且能進入中學的本省籍學生寥寥無幾。當時的中學是五年制（第二次世界後曾改爲四年制），不分初中與高中。英語教學一律採用傳統的「文法・翻譯法」（grammar-translation method），教師偏重課文內容與文法要點的講解，而教學活動則注重閱讀與翻譯。只有少數私立的教會中學（如淡水中學）在外籍教師的協助之下講授英語會話的課程。一般說來，日治時期的英語師資嚴重缺乏，而且英語教師的英語水準相當低落。因爲中學師資幾乎淸一色的由日籍教師包辦，而日籍教師一般都怯於開口說英語，上課時甚至用只能代表"(C)(y)V"音節類型的日語「片假名」（katakana）來注可以有"$C_0^3 V C_3^4$"這樣複雜音節類型❶的英語發音。再者，日治時期的臺灣只有一所大學

---

❶　例如英語的 'strengths' 可以讀成〔ˈstrɛŋkθs〕。

（臺北帝國大學）與三所專科學校（臺北醫學專科學校、臺中農業專科學校與臺南工業專科學校），而沒有專門培養中學師資的師範大學或師範學院（日人稱為高等師範學校）。因此，中學英語師資的主要來源是公私立大學英國文學系的畢業生（絕大多數為日人）或通過中學教員檢定考試的代用教師。這些教師都沒有受過嚴格的專業訓練，對於教材教法也沒有什麼特別的研究。上課時完全由老師講解，學生只管記筆記，很少有發問或討論的機會。一九四一年第二次大戰爆發以後，英國與美國都成為日本的敵人，反英、反美的風氣油然而生。影響所及，對於英語的學習興趣大為降低，當時的英語人口可以說少之又少。總而言之，日治時期臺灣的英語教學乏善可陳。

三、清末到民初時期大陸的英語教學

自從京師同文館於一八六二年（同治元年）在北京開設以來，大陸沿岸學習英語或其他外語之風氣漸盛。一九〇二年（光緒二十八年）清廷頒佈「欽定學堂章程」（俗稱「壬寅學制」），明定中等教育只有中學一級，修業年限為四年。其中外國語文（英文）列為必修課目，上課時數佔總時數的四分之一（九小時），可見當時對於外國語文教學重視之程度。但是此一章程頒佈以後，未及實行即又廢止。清廷復於次年頒佈「奏定學堂章程」，規定中學的修業年限為五年，所授課目凡十二種。英語仍是必修課目，而上課時數為每週八小時。這個時期的英語教材多由在華的英美傳教士提供，或由傳教士自行編著，或直接採用英美原版教材。一八九七年商務印書館在滬創辦，並於次年出版《華英初階讀本》

(English Primer) 做為初學英語之用。但是事實上這個讀本係來自印度的英文讀本，只是用中文譯注而已。

一九一一年（民國元年）國民政府推翻清廷，當年四月成立教育部，而教育部於九月即頒佈學制系統。一九一二年教育部更頒佈各種學校令與課程標準，規定中學的修業年限為四年，而英語仍然是必修。每週的上課時數為第一年男生七小時、女生六小時，第二年至第四年男生八小時、女生六小時。英語的每週上課時數略高於國文的每週上課時數（第一年男女生均七小時，第二年男生七小時、女生六小時，第三年與第四年男女生均五小時），尤以男生為然。至於教學內容，則第一年注重發音、拼字、讀法、譯解、默寫、會話、文法、習字等項目，第二年注重讀法、譯解、默寫、造句、會話、文法等項目，而第三年與第四年則注重讀法、譯解、會話、作文、文法等項目(第四年另加文學要略)。從這些教學內容可以發現，當年的英語教學仍以閱讀、翻譯、文法與講解為主，但是已經開始會話與作文的訓練，而且也注意到文學的欣賞。這時期各校常用的英語教科書，除了商務印書館出版的《英語初階》、《初學英文規範》、《新法英文教程》、《英文益智讀本》以外，尚有 Nesfield 所著的《納氏英文文法》、Charles Lamb 所著的《莎氏樂府本事》與 Williams Irving 所著的《歐文隨筆集》等。

四、民初到抗戰結束時期大陸的英語教學

一九二二年（民國十一年）國民政府提出學校系統改革案，並於次年六月正式頒佈「中小學課程標準綱要」。這個課程標準綱

要，除了取消男女生間的課程差別以外，首次採用小學六年、初中三年、高中三年（俗稱「六、三、三制」）的美國學制系統。此後教育部曾於一九二九年（民國十八年）八月、一九三三年（民國二十二年）三月、一九三六年（民國二十五年）與一九四〇年（民國二十九年）先後頒佈「中學暫行課程標準」、「中學規程」、「修正中學課程標準」與「修訂初高中課程標準」，對於高中與初中英文的課程目標、每週授課時數、教學內容以及選修或必修（學分制自一九三三年（民國二十二年）起取消）等做了幾次內容不同的修訂。令人遺憾的是，我們屢經尋找卻無法獲得這些課程標準的原始資料❷，因而也就無法針對修訂內容做詳細的評述。

　　同時，對於民初到抗戰結束時期有關大陸英語教學的實際情形，我們也只能從沈宗翰先生的《克難苦學記》窺見一斑而已。例如，該書四十二頁提到：沈先生於一九一五年（民國四年）進入國立北京農業專門學校本科一年級，校中所採用的英文文法課本為《納氏文法》第三本，而英文讀本則似為 *National Reader* 第三與第四冊。此時，商務印書館的《英語週刊》已經出版，而沈先生的讀書方法是利用黎明後的散步讀英文生字、傍晚朗誦英文讀本、夜間則做文法練習與造短句。該書五十四頁更提到：沈先生於一九一八年（民國七年）入夜校補習英文，經口試後進入高級英文班，由美籍教師教授讀本、演講與作文（規定每週一篇），而所採用的讀本為 George Eliot 的 *Silas Marner*。次年，沈先生的英文已有進步，讀 *Millard's Review* 並寫英文日記；

---

❷　我們曾向師大英語系的資深教授黃自來先生討教，也向國立編譯館館長曾濟群先生求援，但是均以年久失散為由未能獲得這些資料。

英文寫作不但能清通達意，更能文法無誤。該書七十三頁也提及：沈先生於一九二〇年（民國九年）到南京第一農校任教英文時，曾被該校另一英文教員評論他的英文文法與作文頗好，而英文發音則不甚正確。沈先生認為他的學習英文幾乎完全出於自修，而他的啓蒙老師又是發音不正確的留日教員，因而不容易克服英文發音上的困難。

五、光復以後臺灣的英語教學

一九四五年八月日本投降，臺灣終於脫離了異族的殖民統治。同年十月，國民政府派員接收臺灣。由於日治時期中學以上的師資大都由日籍人士壟斷，所以光復以後臺灣的中等與高等教育都在行政與教學兩方面產生了嚴重的人才斷層的現象。同時，教學語言也遽然由日語改為國語，因此也產生了嚴重的教材缺乏的問題。另外，學制系統的改變也引起了不少困擾。日治時期的中、小學教育是小學六年、中學四年的「六、四」制，而光復後則忽然要改為「六、三、三制」；而且，原來三月開學、二月結束的學年制度也一下子改為九月開學、七月結束的新學年制度（結果全省所有的學生都要延長半年纔能升級或畢業）。這些激烈的變化都為過渡時期的臺灣教育帶來了相當大的衝擊與震撼。

為了解決英語師資缺乏的問題，凡是本省籍或外省籍的大學或專科學校畢業生都獲聘擔任中學教員。結果，非本科系畢業的教員擔任英語或本科系畢業的教員兼教英語以外科目的現象比比皆是，教員的專業水準也良莠不齊。本省籍出身的教員多半都擔任數理科，因為英語的課程在剛光復時還有人用日語講解，但後

來則規定教室用語必須一律使用國語，而大多數本省籍教員都無法勝任用國語來講解英語。因此，光復初期的英語教師都幾乎清一色的由外省籍教員來擔任。這些英語教師中有不少是非本科系畢業的，就是本科系畢業的也都沒有受過嚴格的專業訓練，結果是幾乎千遍一律的採用「文法·翻譯法」來教英語。臺灣中等教育的師資問題，無論是在量或質的方面，都到了嚴重的地步。政府有鑑於此，終於在一九四六年（民國三十五年）利用日本臺北高等學校的舊校址創辦了省立臺灣師範學院(即國立臺灣師範大學的前身)，負責中學師資的培養。推行九年國民教育之後，中學師資養成的需要更為迫切，因而先後有省立高雄師範學院（現為國立高雄師範大學）與省立彰化教育學院（現為國立彰化教育大學）之設立。教材方面，在光復初期也直接採用大陸開明書局、世界書局等出版社所印行的教科書，而不問這些教科書在難度上是否與本省初中畢業學生的英語程度相銜接。後來大陸淪陷，許多大陸的出版社都遷移到臺灣來繼續出版教科書，而在臺灣創辦的出版社如復興書局與遠東書局等也開始委託臺大與師大等學校的教授來編寫高中英語教科書。

為了配合行憲需要，教育部於一九四八年（民國三十七年）修正公佈「高級中學英語課程標準」，並把高中英語的教學目標訂為：(一)練習運用切於實用之普通英語；(二)就英文詩歌散文中增進其語文訓練；(三)從英語方面加增其對於西方文化之興趣；(四)從語文中認識英語國家風俗之大概；(五)從英美民族史蹟記載中，激發愛國思想及國際了解。從這些教學目標不難看出：(一)雖然注意到"運用"與"實用"，並要求寫的是淺近易懂的"普

通英語"，但是課文內容卻選"詩歌散文"等「高度格式化」（highly stylized）的文章；（二）已經注意到語言與文化之間的密切關係，因而強調認識西方文化與風俗的重要；（三）仍然脫離不了"文以載道"的傳統思想，因而列入"激發愛國思想"的要求。關於時間支配則規定：每週上課五小時；以他種外國語為外國語者每週六小時，但仍需學習英語三小時。❸ 這個課程標準，除了目標與時間支配以外，還列有教材大綱與實施方法。教材大綱對高中第一、第二、第三學年分別規定該學年的教材內容（如短篇選文、普通應用文件、普通應用套語、系統化詞彙、普通定期刊物、特種參考書、外國文化、其他臨時教材等），而實施方法則針對聽音、發音、語法、作文、修辭等提出二十六項相當扼要而明確的指導要領。教材大綱並規定：高中英語的新詞數量約四千字（連初中共約六千字），其中三分之一可不必盡行根據 Thorndike 的 *Teachers' Word Book*。而實施方法則提出「耳聽」、「口說」、「眼看」、「手寫」四種基本練習方法；這四種練習方法可以互相搭配使用，並需要多次反復直到純熟為止。

　　為了配合九年國民教育之推行與高中自然科與社會科分組之需要，「高級中學英文課程標準」於一九六二年（民國五十一年）

---

❸　課程標準實施方法第二十六項規定：‘其他外國語係指東方語言之印度語、日語、韓語，或其他東方語；西方語言之法語、德語、俄語、西班牙語，或其他西方語而言。其課程標準與實施方法均準英語一切規定。’但是事實上臺灣的高中教育從未講授英語以外的第二外語。同時，一九五五年（民國四十四年）五月修正公佈的課程標準把每週教學時數改為第一、第二學年四小時，第三學年五小時。

七月公佈，並把高中英文的教學目標訂爲：(一)練習運用切於實際生活之英語；(二)加強閱讀英文書籍之準備；(三)培養英文寫作及翻譯之能力；(四)啓發研習英語民族文化之興趣。這些目標可以說是「功能取向」（functon-oriented）的目標：強調學習的對象是"切於實際生活之英語"，而不是文學意味濃厚的詩歌散文；並且著重學習的技能是"閱讀"、"寫作"、"翻譯"與"文法"，但是似乎忽略了"聽說"的重要。關於時間支配則規定：自然學科組學生第一學年每週五至六小時，第二與第三學年每週五小時；社會學科組學生第一學年每週五至六小時，第二與第三學年每週六小時。❹ 至於教材大綱與實施方法，則比舊課程標準大爲簡化：前者只列短篇選文、普通應用文、普通應用套語、詞彙、句型、系統化語法、參考書、其他臨時教材等；而後者也把注意事項從二十六條減爲十八條。高中英語的新詞數量也從四千字減爲三千二百字，並且規定其中一千二百字爲必須「主動運用」（active manipulation）的「主動詞彙」，其他兩千字爲只要「被動認識」（passive manipulation）即足的「被動詞彙」。練習方法仍然以「耳聽、口說、眼看、手寫」爲主，仍然強調這些練習方法必須"分別及聯合加以運用"，但是實施方法第十八條第一次指出："說話教學須特別注意英語與國語不同之處，便易學得比較純粹之英語，並覺察兩種語言構造上之特點"。又這個課程的另一特色是附有句型表(包含五十九個英語基本句型)，以供高中英語教

---

❹ 課程標準並規定："每週上課以不分幾小時專屬讀本，某幾小時專屬語法（舊稱文法）爲原則"以及"一日之內，均以上課一小時爲原則"。

科書編者參考之用。

　　從一九四五年(民國三十四年)到一九六二年(民國五十一年)之間，在臺灣一般高級中學裏所盛行的教學方法仍然是「文法・翻譯法」。雖然臺灣師範大學的英語中心在五〇年代末期卽導入「口說教學法」(Oral Approach)，但是該中心的畢業生數目有限，未能對全省的英語教學發生深遠的影響。結果，高中英語教學都偏重閱讀與翻譯的學習，而忽略了聽說與寫作的訓練。針對這一缺失，臺灣師範大學英語系與美國德州大學（The University of Texas, 後來改稱爲 University of Texas at Austin) 在我國教育部與美國國際開發總署 (Agency for International Development, 簡稱 AID) 的贊助下於一九六二年七月起合作主持爲期兩年七個月(到一九六四年二月止)的「在職英語教師訓練計畫」(In-service Teachers Retraining Program)。❶❺前後舉辦了十一屆訓練班，訓練了一千一百八十九位英語教師。每一屆訓練班爲期八週，課程的主要內容是英語的密集訓練與口說教學法的灌輸。每一位學員每週都要上平均三十二小時到四十小時的課(包括發音訓練、句型練習、會話練習與上課實習等)，並且還要做平均五小時到十小時的作業。根據統計❶❻，當時臺灣的英語老師中幾乎有百分之四十五的人是非本科系畢業的，就是本科系畢業的人也大都沒有經過嚴格的專業師資訓練。因此，「在職英語教師訓練計畫」對於提昇一般英語老師的「英語能力」(English proficiency) 與「教學技巧」(teaching technique)

❶❺　關於此一訓練計畫的內容，參 DeCamp (1965)。
❶❻　參 DeCamp (1965:120)。

頗有貢獻。同時，由於「口說教學法」的推廣，英語的聽說教學首次獲得重視，各種「口說練習」(oral drill)，如「反復仿說練習」(Imitation-Repetition Drill)、「單項代換練習」(Simple Substitution Drill)、「代換呼應練習」(Substitution-Concord Drill)、「依次代換練習」(Progressive Substitution Drill)、「完成練習」(Completion Drill)、「重組練習」(Restoration Drill)、「改說練習」(Restatement Drill)、「變換練習」(Transformation Drill)、「聯句練習」(Integration Drill)、「擴充練習」(Expansion Drill)、「聯想練習」(Association Drill)、「變換‧擴充混合練習」(Transformation/Expansion Drill)、「擴充‧代換練習」(Expansion/Substitution Drill)、「推斷練習」(Deduction Drill)、「引導回答練習」(Guided Question Drill)、「引導反應練習」(Guided Response Drill)、「引導評論練習」(Guided Comment Drill)、「引導問答練習」(Guided Question Drill)、「應答練習」(Rejoinder Drill)、「翻譯練習」(Translation Drill)、「問答練習」(Question-Answer Drill)、「自由回答練習」(Free Reply Drill)、「自由反應練習」(Free Response Drill)、「自由評論練習」(Free Comment Drill)、「推託回答練習」(Evasive Reply Drill)、「引導造句或作文練習」(Guided Sentence-Making or Composition Drill)、「溝通練習」(Communication Drill) 等❶，都在全省各地的英語課堂大行其道。

---

❶ 關於這些口頭練習的內容與方法，參湯廷池(1989: 161-203)＜口說教學：理論與實際＞的討論。

這個在職英語教師訓練計畫先後由美國德州大學的Prof. Archibald Hill 與 Prof. David De Camp 及臺灣師範大學的林瑜鏗教授與揚景邁教授共同主持，而由一九六三年八月起到一九六四年二月止則由藍德而 (Earl Rand) 與湯廷池兩位先生負責巡廻全省訪問結業學員，以教學觀摩、專題演講與疑難解答的方式做「追踪」(follow-up) 與「回饋」(feed-back) 的工作。

　　一九七一年(民國六十年)二月教育部重新修訂公佈「高級中學外國文(英文)課程標準」，更進一步把高中英文的教學目標簡化為：(一)學習運用切於實際生活之英語；(二)加強閱讀及寫作英文之能力，以建立學術研究之基礎；(三)啓發研習英語民族文化之興趣。在時間支配上規定：自然學科組與社會學科組學生的第一學年的授課時數都每週六小時(以前係每週五至六小時)，而第二與第三學年則自然學科組每週五小時，社會學科組每週七小時(比以前增加兩小時)；並特別強調社會學科組的口頭與手寫練習時間在分配比重上應大於自然學科組，同時也提及個別練習的重要性。新詞數量則仍維持總數三千二百(包括運用字彙一千二百與認識字彙二千)的舊規定。但是實施方法則由原來的十八條經過細分與擴充而成為(一)教學原則(共五條)、(二)教學過程(共七條)、(三)教學要點(共八條)、(四)成績考查(共四條)、(五)教材編輯原則及各科連繫(共十一條)，在內容方面顯得更加詳細而充實。其中較為新穎或特殊的規定為："新舊教材間，即次一課與上一課間，應力使其能有相當之關聯，俾使學生將已習之經驗能運用於將習之情況中"(教學過程第二條)、"成績考查以聽、說、讀、寫四項並重為原則"(成績考查第一條)、"隨時注意

學生之成績、以便按照預定計畫調整其進行程序，尤須使學生覺察自己之進步，使能增加興趣、勇於學習"（成績考察第四條）、"各課取材如能與高級中學與其他學科相關者，應盡量使之配合"（教材編輯原則及各科連繫第七條）、"字彙注音以採用 D. Jones 萬國音標爲準，俾能與國中英語之音標相配合"（教材編輯原則及各科連繫第九條）。課中標準所附列的句型表也由五十九個擴充爲六十五個，並以教材編輯原則及各科連繫中第三條特別規定這些句型應分別編入高中英文課本前四册中。

最近一次的高中英文課程標準修訂爲一九八三年（民國七十二年）七月公佈的「高級中學外國文（英文）課程標準」。這一次高級中學課程標準的修訂與國民中學課程標準同時修訂，而且高中英文與國中英語的課程標準修訂委員會都由張芳杰教授擔任主任委員，並由湯廷池教授負責起草。因爲由同一個人負責起草並經過審慎的討論與推敲，所以國中英語課程標準與高中英文課程標準，無論就教學目標、教學觀、教學法以及課程設計、內容與文字而言，都在一貫的理念與精神之下串聯起來，兩級學校的英語文教學首次取得密切的銜接與配合。可惜，高中英文課程標準與國民中學英語課程標準都在總綱小組預設底線的限制下人爲而瑣碎的被分割爲「高級中學外國文（英文）課程標準」、「高級中學選修科目文法與修辭課程標準」、「高級中學選修科目英語會話課程標準」、「高級中學選修科目英文作文課程標準」、「高級中學選修科目英文文法課程標準」、「高級中學選修科目英語聽講課程標準」以及「國民中學英語課程標準」與「國民中學選修科目英語（甲）課程標準」等應該密切相關但是並不完全整合的課程標準。撇開這

一點不談，這一次高中英文課程標準的修訂，無論就質或量而言，都有顯著的改進。例如，教學目標第一條規定："從聽、說、讀、寫各方面，培養學生運用切於實際生活的正確英語的能力：(一)能聽懂教師講的英語；(二)能用英語回答教師的問題；(三)能流暢地朗誦課文並正確地了解意義；(四)能利用學到的詞彙、慣用語、句型、生活習慣、文化背景等簡明地用口頭與文字表達自己的意思"，不但明白地揭示聽、說、讀、寫四種語言技能兼顧並重的主張，而且也從「目標行為」(terminal behavior) 的觀點為這四種語言技能的訓練，提出具體明確的學習目標。這一次課程標準也取消了以往在教學分配與教材編輯上徒增困擾的自然學科組與社會學科組學生的區別，而在時間支配上一律規定：第一與第二學年每週授課五小時，第三學年每週授課六小時。高中三學年英文教材的新詞數量由原來的三千二百字提高為三千六百字(國中英語教材的新詞數量也由一千三百字提高為一千四百字)，不但規定這些新詞在不同學年的出現分佈(第一學年約為九百字、第二學年約為一千二百字、第三學年約為一千五百字)，而且還規定不同學年裏英文教材的選文字數、新詞字數與這些新詞的常用率(第一、第二、第三各學年的選文字數每課分別不超過六百字、八百字與一千字，所出現的生字分別以不超過三十字、四十字與五十字為原則，生字的選擇分別在常用率最高的五千字、六千字與七千字以內；另外在教材編輯原則及各科之聯繫第五條規定"超出常用字彙限制之生字宜在字彙解釋 (glossary) 中以星號「＊」標示"。教材大綱中，每一學年的教學綱要也比以往的課程標準更為具體(但是以往所附列的英文句型表則以不切實

際、形同具文的理由加以刪除），而實際方法則極其詳細地分為：(一)教學原則(共八條)、(二)教學過程(共八條)、(三)教學要點(共十四條)、(四)成績考查與學生輔導(共七條)、(五)教材編輯原則與各科之聯繫(共十六條)與(六)教學評鑑及輔導(共五條)。其中，比以往較爲新穎而進步的規定包括："聽、說、讀、寫四項訓練，必須兼顧並加以綜合運用"(教學原則第一條)、"教學活動宜以學生的練習爲主，以教師的講解爲副"(同前第二條)、"教學與測驗的實施宜注重整個句子的活用，而避免零碎字詞的死記"(同前第五條)、"教學的重點宜在常用的字彙、成語及句法，而不在冷僻或例外的用法。測驗的範圍，宜以實際教學的內容爲依據"(同前第六條)、"教師評閱後之作業或測驗中之錯誤，宜指導學生自行改正，以培養審慎之學習態度"(同前第七條)、"隨時抽查作業或觀察學習情形，一經發現錯誤，除適時糾正外，並宜使學生反復練習正確的用法"(同前第八條)、"一切作業與測驗，宜事先明確說明其範圍與方法，並作簡要之範例演示，務使學生確切了解其需要與內容，以培養學習興趣"(教學過程第八條)、"聽、說、讀、寫四種語言能力宜平均發展"(教學要點第一條)、"練習比講解重要，在講解課文之後，宜充分訓練學生主動運用的能力。學生的練習時間應占整個教學時間的一半以上"(同前第二條)、"練習的內容要有意義，方法要有變化，如此始能引起學生興趣而切合實用"(同前第三條)、"口頭練習與書寫練習，團體練習與個別練習宜相輔而行，如此方能普及全面而又能顧及個別需要"(同前第四條)、"會話訓練應以使用簡單易懂的英語表達自己的意思爲目的，在練習的過程中應將重點置於表達與流利，不必

一開始即苛求正確無誤，以袪除學生畏懼用英語交談之心理"(同前第八條)、"語法之講解宜有系統而重簡明實用，語法規則須根據實際語言資料加以歸納整理所得者，不宜沿用以分類與分析為主的傳統抽象文法。語法練習以運用整句，發揮表情達意之功用為原則"(同前第十一條)、'教師應隨時監聽學生使用英語，如果發現發音、用詞或語法上的錯誤，應即改正並輔以練習。教師也應鼓勵學生自行監聽與自行改正自己的錯誤"(同前第十二條)、"鼓勵學生利用問答、對話、說故事、演角色等各種方式將已學得之英語加以應用，以期與實際的語言情況發生聯繫。學校宜設法舉辦英語會話、英語歌唱、英語短劇等課外活動，並定期舉行演講比賽、背誦比賽、聽寫比賽、聽力比賽、閱讀測驗比賽等各種競賽，以提高學生學習英語的興趣"(同前第十三條)、"成績考查以聽、說、讀、寫四項語言能力並重為原則"(成績考查與學生輔導第一條)、"測驗與考試之內容必須符合教學目標與實際內容，決不可鑽入艱深冷僻的牛角尖。測驗與考試的方式應力求變化，並盡量設計避免死記而重活用的題目"(同前第四條)、"作業與試卷應盡速評閱並發還學生。學生在作業與試卷上所犯之錯誤，應令其自行改正並回家復習"(同前第六條)、"程度較低的學生應設法施予個別輔導，並鼓勵成績較優學生協助其他學生學習"(同前第七條)、"高中一年級教材與國中教材銜接，並按年級逐步加深，前後統一"(教材編輯原則及各科之聯繫第三條)、"生字中的虛詞 (function words)，如代名詞、助動詞、連詞、介詞、冠詞等宜做為主動運用字彙(active production vocabulary)學習。生字中的實詞 (content words)，如名詞、動詞、形容詞

、副詞，在各學年度常用字彙限制之內者宜做主動運用字彙練習
；在常用字彙限制之外者宜做被動認識字彙（passive recognition vocabulary)學習"(同前第六條)、"主動運用字彙除了於
第一次出現時詳加解釋，並舉例句以外，宜設法在以後的課文或
練習內反復出現，以期學生能確實掌握這些字彙的意義與用法"
(同前第七條)、"字彙解釋（glossary)中除了生字的中英文注解
以外，宜附與該字有關之詞類變化、相似詞、相反詞等，藉以幫
助學生增加認識字彙。生字與成語之英文注解，切忌用生字注解
生字"(同前第八條)、"作業的方式力求有意義、有變化，不應完
全抄襲課文的句子為習題"(同前第十四條)、"英語教學之評鑑與
輔導，應由專業人才依據高級中學英語文課程標準之規定為之"
(教學評鑑及輔導第一條)、"各地區高級中學應定期舉辦地區英
語文教學觀摩會，每年至少舉辦一次，並邀請師範院校中等教育
輔導會及該地區大學有關科系派遣英語文教學專家參加輔導"(同
前第二條)、"大學及三專入學考試之英語文試題，其內容應根據
高級中學英語文課程標準，並參酌高級中學英語文之實際教學內
容"(同前第三條)、"除了全國性的高級中學英語文教師在職訓練
以外，應酌情舉辦地區性的高級中學英語文教學研習會，並編纂
「英語文教學輔導叢書」或「英語文教學輔導月刊」等刊物，以
利在職教師進修"(同前第五條)。

六、一九七六年的全國英語文教學研討會

　　教育部於一九七五年（民國六十四年）十二月卅一日召開英
語文教學研討籌備會，其目的在於成立英語教學研討會，以便研

討改進全國的英語文教學。次年二月十七日，教育部復召開英文教學研討會各組召集人聯席會，商討分組研討與大會進行事宜。開會結果由俞成樁教授任國中組召集人、張芳杰教授任高中組召集人、侯建教授任大學組召集人、楊景邁教授任師資訓練組召集人、湯廷池教授擔任職校與專科組召集人，並聘請專家學者八十餘位爲委員。各組經過三個月的實地參觀、考察與研討之後，於同年六月提出各組綜合報告，由湯廷池教授起草綜合意見與建議。綜合意見與建議分爲：(一)教學目標與課程標準、(二)教材與教法、(三)測驗與考試、(四)師資的栽培與進修四項內容，針對當時英語文教學的問題與缺失提出相當具體的分析與明確的建議。其中，較爲重要的意見與建議如下：

(一)英語教學的內容 —— 聽、說、讀、寫：聽、說、讀、寫四種技能在理論上應該立於平等的地位，具有同等的重要性，而在教學的實效上亦以「四管齊下」互相配合爲宜。但是事實上由於個人或社會現實需要的不同，在這四種技能的培養上可能有輕重或緩急之分。例如，在高中與大專的英語教學中應該特別注意培養學生的閱讀能力，而在高職與專科學校的英語教學中，應該特別強調實用性。

(二)英語聽力測驗的應用：今後各級學校的英語入學考試（包括高中、高職、五專與大專聯考）應該列入英語聽力測驗（listening comprehension），用以改進考試的方式，而確保教學目標的完整性，並領導國中與高中英語教學的內容。聽力測驗的內容與方式可以參照臺北語言中心所主辦的英語托福考試，也可以選定幾個地區（如某地區高中或高職聯考）試辦。這項建議

應向教育部、教育廳、大專聯招委員會正式以書面報告提出。孫委員志文更進一步強調，聽力測驗的採用對於整個英語教學狀況有莫大影響，無論如何應於下（一九七七）年度立卽實施。

(三)英語教學成績的考察：目前中學英語教學偏重字彙與文法的講解，而忽略聽說的運用與閱讀寫作的訓練。因此建議臺灣省教育廳及臺北市教育局，今後成績考查（不論日常測驗或月考、期考）均應兼顧筆試與口試，同時也應該酌情舉辦國中與高中的英語聽力測驗、閱讀測驗或寫作比賽等。現行高中英語能力評量測驗中閱讀的比重應仿聽力部份予以加重，評量對象也應擴及到省市的每一個學校，藉以糾正目前英語教學的偏頗。

(四)教材偏纂的原則 —— 漸進、累積、反覆：語言教學是一個有組織有系統的過程。每一個新的教學單元必須與以前學過的教學單元以及以後卽將學習的教學單元融會貫通。每一節課的進度也必須與前幾課的內容相互呼應，不能隨意分化教學的單元、混亂教學的進度。因此，教材的編纂應該是「漸進」(progressive)、「累積」(accumulative)、而「反覆」(repetitive) 的。所謂「漸進」是指教材與練習的設計要由易到難、由簡引繁，使學生在學習的課程中能按部就班、循序漸進；所謂「累積」是指學習的分量要有計畫地支配，使學生積少成多、腳踏實地進步；所謂「反覆」是指教材與練習的編排要有適度的重覆，使學生在練習一次以後，仍有複習或再學習的機會。

(五)提高學生學習興趣的方法：據一般學生的反應，對於學習英語的興趣並不高，因此建議採用下列各種方式以提高學生學習的興趣。

（1）教材的難度要適合學生的程度，課文的內容要符合學生的需要。

（2）考試的題目要難易適度，避免出零碎、冷僻的題目。大多數學生在某一次考試中做錯的題目要在下一次考試中再考。

（3）儘量使教室的氣氛在嚴肅中仍保持輕鬆，教學方法要有變化，並應該增加學生主動運用英語的機會。

（4）舉辦英語會話、歌唱、話劇等課外活動與「演講」、「背誦」、「聽寫」、「閱讀」、「造句」、「拼字」、「用英語說笑話」等各項比賽。這種比賽可以是全校性的，也可以在班際或班內舉行。有些比賽，除了每班推選代表或隨個人志願參加以外，也可以採用由全校學生中臨時抽籤的方式來決定參加比賽的人選。

（六）英語測驗的方法 —— 綜合測驗聽、說、讀、寫四種能力：測驗與考試應該避免孤立而死板的語言項目（如單考發音、單字或孤立的句子），因為這種考試方式把整個語言分割得支離破碎、互不關連，失去了溝通的意義與價值。測驗與考試應該綜合地顧慮到語音、構詞、語法、語意、語用等各種語言要素，而且應該設法要求學生同時運用各種語言能力，藉以測驗學生綜合運用聽、說、讀、寫的能力。符合這一種「綜合測驗」（integrative test）的原則的考試方法計有：

（1）利用「聽寫」（dictation）（由教師或錄音帶唸出一段文章，第一遍用一般說話的速度，第二遍以適度的詞組為單位做一停頓，大約每隔四至七字；第三遍再用一般說話的速度讓學生校正）或"cloze test"（即填入一般文章中所省略之空白，如每隔第五字或第六字或第七字予以省略，或將某段文章中某一特殊語法

形式，如冠詞、介詞或時式標記等予以省略）來測驗字音、拼字與文法。

（2）利用各種「聽力測驗」（listening comprehension）（如對話、故事、演講等）來測驗發音、字彙與文法。

（3）利用「口說測驗」（oral test）（由一位或兩位以上的老師聯合考試，方式是採用一問一答、或團體討論、或當場抽題即席說話三至五分鐘）來測驗幾乎所有的語言要素。

（4）利用「寫作測驗」（essay writing）（這是傳統的測驗方法，學生用筆寫來回答幾個問題，也可以選題作答）來測驗字彙、文法、語意與邏輯結構。

（5）利用「閱讀測驗」（reading comprehension）來測驗字彙、文法、語意、邏輯結構、思考推理能力與欣賞能力等。

（七）入學考試必須列入「聽力」及「寫作能力」：目前大專聯考的英文試題，有關聽、說與寫的能力的測驗完全闕如。至於讀的能力，在一些專為測驗文法與翻譯的題目中也無法真正地測驗出來。連標明為「閱讀測驗」的部份，也因為所選的文章過於艱深，以致大多數的學生都無法了解。因此，我們建議：

（1）「說話能力」：首先必須研究如何客觀地測驗說話的能力。就目前的情況而言，若在入學考試時採用，困難諸多。但是說話能力與聽力關係密切，而聽力測驗則已有相當客觀的測驗方法。

（2）「聽力」：利用預先錄好的句子、對話、故事、演說、討論等來測驗。

（3）「寫作技巧」：原則上此項技巧應納入考試中，至於如何訂定客觀的評分標準，則必須加以研究。如果作文暫時不能作為

單獨的測驗題目，那麼至少也要包括測驗學生判斷文章或句子的語法、語意或邏輯關係的能力的題目。

(4)「閱讀技巧」：閱讀不僅是辨認單字與文法要素，而是從牽涉到字彙、文法、觀念與邏輯的複雜結構中去了解語意與推論的思維過程。而所謂英文的閱讀，實際上包括許多不同的文體(如對話、故事、簡易散文、論文、新聞專題、演說、戲曲、科學的文章等)，大學的閱讀測驗應該考慮到這些因素。

(5) 大專聯考的英文試卷必須由一個稱職的委員會在完全保密與隔離的環境中擬定。全部試題必須是新的，也就是為這次考試而特別創造出來的。如此，補習班的「題庫」或死背考題答案，都將失去用處。準備這種考試的唯一方法乃在課堂上確實而不斷地運用聽、說、讀、寫的教材來練習。

七、高中英語教學的展望

為了響應改進高中英語教學的呼籲，教育部乃在人文及社會學科教育指導委員會之下設立高級中學英文學科小組，以便研討高中英語教學的改進事宜。這一小組，由余玉照教授擔任召集人，並公推湯廷池教授負責起草「高級中學英文學科教材大綱研究報告」。先是於一九八六年(民國七十五年)十二月研訂高中英文課程的兩大教育目標如下：

(一)培養學生聽、說、讀、寫一般英語文之能力。

(1) 能聽懂與一般事物有關的英語。

(2) 能應用淺近的英語與人交談並敘述或解釋一般事物。

(3) 能讀懂各種不同體裁與內容的淺近英文讀物並能流暢地

朗誦。

(4) 能寫作簡明的英文以表達情意及描寫一般事物。

(二)激發學生瞭解英語國家社會文化及社交禮儀之興趣，並培養
　　以淺近英文介紹我國社會文化之能力，以促進民族文化之交
　　流。

接著從一九八七年（民國七十六年）一月至次年六月間分兩期蒐
集資料、研擬草案與討論修正，提出了如下的「高級中學英文學
科教材大綱草案」：

「高級中學英文學科教材大綱草案」

一、第一學年

　　　甲、課文內容與字數

(一)選文內容以淺近明易之當代英美短篇作品為原則，須兼採有
　　生活意義、文學意味、科技色彩、或其他饒有興趣之各體文
　　字。以小品文為主，以對話、故事、短篇小說、詩歌、戲劇
　　等為副。在內容方面應顧及學生的生活背景與心智成長的階
　　段，並特別注意啟導人生意義、喚起民族倫理、培養民主風
　　度及科學求知精神。

(二)選文字數每課不超過六百字，所出現的生字以不超過三十字
　　為原則。生字的選擇宜盡可能在使用率最高的五千字內。

　　　乙、複習與矯正（第一學年第一學期開學後第一至四週）
高一新生英語程度參差不齊，有些學生在國中階段中聽、說
與口頭練習的機會較少，常犯許多發音或語法上基本的錯誤
而不自覺，似應撥出為期四週的時間作為複習、再學習與矯

正之用，並指導學生正確的學習英語的方法。

(一)聽音與發音

    (1) 利用「對偶詞」與「對偶句」的「最小對比」作辨音與發音的練習。

    (2) 能分辨並掌握「重音節」與「輕音節」的區別，「輕音節」與「輕元音」'ə'的關係。

    (3) 能分辨並掌握詞尾輔音（羣）的發音。

    (4) 能分辨並掌握「升調」、「降調」、「平調」、「停頓」以及這些節律音素與句型、標點符號之關係。

(二)拼字與詞彙

    (1) 能注意並利用「發音」與「拼字」間的對應關係。

    (2) 能拼讀國中英語的基本詞彙並利用這些詞彙造句。

    (3) 指導學生如何利用英英辭典或英漢辭典查閱發音、拼字、詞類、詞義與有關句型。

(三)句型與語法

    (1) 能熟悉英語基本句型並能運用這些句型造句。

    (2) 能熟悉「直述句」、「否定句」與「疑問句」的變化，並能運用這些句型造句。

    (3) 能熟悉英語動詞的基本時式包括「單純式」、「完成式」、「進行式」的運用，並造句。

    (4) 能熟悉「主動句」與「被動句」的句型，並利用這些句型造句。

(四)閱讀與寫作

    能自行了解前四課課文內容並能完成課文練習。

丙、教材內容（開學後第五週起）

(一)聽講與會話

  (1) 加強「基本元音」、「輕重音」與「語調」的訓練。

  (2) 練習在課堂上用英語作簡單的問答。

(二)詞彙

  (1) 熟練「人稱代名詞」、「限定詞」、「助動詞」、「介詞」、「連詞」等英語虛詞的意義與用法。

  (2) 增加「名詞」、「動詞」、「形容詞」、「副詞」等英語實詞的「主動運用詞彙」並熟練運用這些詞彙的意義與用法。

  (3) 利用課內與課外閱讀增加「名詞」、「動詞」、「形容詞」、「副詞」等「被動認識詞彙」。

(三)句型與語法

  (1) 加強訓練「單句」、「合句」、「複句」的辨認與運用。

  (2) 加強訓練動詞的基本時式的辨認與運用，特別是「現在完成式」、「過去單純式」、「過去完成式」與「過去進行式」。

  (3) 練習以各種修飾語修飾名詞與動詞。

  (4) 練習以「子句」、「不定詞」、「動名詞」做為動詞的補語。

(四)閱讀與寫作

  (1) 除了閱讀課文以外，利用課外閱讀與閱讀測驗的方式訓練學生閱讀與課文難度相當的文章。

  (2) 熟練在課文中出現的重要詞彙、成語、句型並且運用這些詞彙、成語、句型造句。

  (3) 練習用英文寫便條或日記。

(五)其他

　　鼓勵學生參加校內外舉辦的英語課外活動，並舉辦用英語說故事、說笑話等競賽活動。

二、第二學年

　　　甲、課文內容與字數

(一)與第一學年同。

(二)選文字數每課不超過八百字，所出現的生字以不超過四十字為原則，生字的選擇宜盡可能在使用率最高的六千字內。

　　　乙、聽講與會話

(一)訓練學生流暢地朗誦課文的能力，除了單字的發音以外，尤宜注意整句的重音、停頓、語調及節奏。

(二)盡量以簡易的英語解釋課文中的新詞成語，並以簡短的英語問答討論課文的內容。

(三)鼓勵學生在課外接觸英語廣播或電視敎學節目，並練習在日常生活中實際運用的英語。

(四)能聽懂老師的英語說明，能以英語回答老師與錄音帶上的問題，能積極參與課堂上的口頭練習。

(五)能運用基本的詞彙與句型操用簡易的日常會話，包括問候、介紹、問路、搭車、購物等。

　　　丙、詞彙

(一)利用拼字與發音間的對應關係推測生詞的發音並加強拼字的記憶。

(二)指導學生注意並分辨「詞類」的區別，練習動詞、名詞、形容詞與副詞的詞類變化。

(三)指導學生注意「詞首」、「詞根」、「詞尾」的結構，並從課文
　　的詞彙中舉例說明。

(四)鼓勵學生利用上下文猜測生詞的含義並自動翻查辭典來學習
　　這些生詞的詞音、詞類、詞義與有關句型。

(五)利用課堂上的造句練習來訓練學生運用「主動詞彙」的能力
　　；鼓勵課外閱讀來增加學生「被動詞彙」的數目。

(六)能利用動作、表情、舉例、「同義詞」、「反義詞」、「解義」、
　　「造句」等方式來說明課文中「主動詞彙」的意義與用法，並
　　能把這些「主動詞彙」應用在問答與對話中。

　　丁、句型與語法

(一)指導學生辨別英語動詞的分類，並了解動詞分類與基本句型
　　的關係。

(二)繼續訓練動詞時式的辨認與運用，包括「單純式」、「進行式」
　　、「完成式」、「完成進行式」以及各種表示未來時間的說法。

(三)配合各種時式的「主動句」，繼續訓練「被動句」的形態、意
　　義與用法。

(四)繼續訓練動詞、形容詞與「不定詞」、「動名詞」、「子句」的
　　連用。

(五)指導並訓練情態助動詞的「義務用法」與「認知用法」。

(六)指導並訓練各種「假設語氣」的說法，包括「可能的假說」、
　　「可疑的假設」與「不可能的假設」。

(七)指導學生了解與辨別「可數名詞」與「不可數名詞」的區別
　　以及這兩類名詞與「數量詞」的連用，包括「全稱用法」與
　　「偏稱用法」。

(八)指導學生了解與辨別名詞與冠詞的「定性」，包括「定指」、「殊指」、「任指」、「虛指」與「泛指」。

(九)指導學生辨別連詞中「對等連詞」、「句連詞(又稱「連接副詞」)」、「從屬連詞」的分類，並了解這些連詞的分類與「合句」、「複句」與「合複句」的關係。

(十)加強練習以「形容詞片語」、「介詞片語」、「不定詞片語」、「分詞片語」與「關係子句」修飾名詞。

(十一)加強練習以「副詞片語」、「介詞片語」與「從屬子句」修飾動詞與句子。

(十二)指導學生以各種「程度副詞」或「加強詞」修飾形容詞與副詞，包括形容詞與副詞的「比較結構」。

(十三)指導學生了解並運用英語的「雙字動詞」與「三字動詞」，包括「動詞與介詞」、「動詞與介副詞」、「動詞、介副詞與介詞」以及「動詞、名詞與介詞」的連用。

戊、閱讀與寫作

(一)配合(丙)與(丁)的詞彙、句型與語法教學，利用課文、口頭練習、書寫練習來進行閱讀與寫作教學。

(二)除了閱讀課文以外，利用課外閱讀(包括英文報刊雜誌或簡易小說)與閱讀測驗的方式訓練學生閱讀與課文難度相當的文章。

(三)指導學生辨別「描寫文」、「敘述文」、「論說文」等文章的種類與組織結構，並且訓練學生能熟悉運用各類文章常用的「連貫詞」與「嚮導詞」。

(四)指導學生辨別「口語」與「書面語」以及「正式體」與「非

正式體」等語體、文體上的差別，並利用課文與練習上的文章說明這些差別的實際運用。

(五)寫作練習，除了造句、翻譯與作文以外，還可以指導學生寫出課文的大意，或把課文改寫為對話或戲劇的方式來表演。

(六)鼓勵學生用英文寫日記、週記、便條，並鼓勵學生以英文辦壁報或與國外學生通信。

(七)鼓勵學生在班內組織「小型英文圖書館」，以交換英文書籍與發表讀書心得的方式提倡課外閱讀與寫作。

　　己、其他

鼓勵學生參加校內外舉辦的英語課外活動，並舉辦英語演講、辯論或寫作等競賽活動。

三、第三學年

　　甲、課文內容與字數

(一)與第一學年同。

(二)選文字選每課不超過一千字，所出現的生字以不超過五十字為原則。生字的選擇宜盡可能在使用率最高的七千字內。

　　乙、聽講與會話

(一)訓練學生以簡潔易懂的英語表達自己的情意，除了注意輕重音、停頓、語調與節奏以外，並以適當的語氣表情與手勢來配合所要表達的情意。

(二)訓練學生以解義的方式解釋課文，並以簡短的英語說明課文的大意或與同學討論課文的內容。

(三)鼓勵學生以英語介紹自己以及自己的家庭、朋友、嗜好、國家、文化、風俗、習慣等。

(四)鼓勵學生在課外接觸英美人士，並練習在日常生活中如何實際運用英語。

　　丙、詞彙

(一)指導學生繼續擴大「主動詞彙」，並且鼓勵學生盡量把這些詞彙運用在會話與寫作中。

(二)指導學生繼續擴大「被動詞彙」，並且訓練學生如何從上下文的文義中推測這些詞彙的含義。

(三)利用「同義」、「反義」、「解義」、「同形」、「同音」、「派生」等聯想與對比的方式，複習高中全三年所學過的全部英語詞彙，並配合(乙)、(一)(二)(三)的教學活動訓練主動詞彙的**運用**。

(四)利用聽寫、拼字競賽等方式複習並測驗學生的拼字與讀音能力。

　　丁、句型與語法

(一)指導學生辨別英語介詞的語意分類，並對照國語介詞的意義與用法訓練學生熟悉英語介詞的意義與用法。

(二)指導學生辨別英語連詞的語意分類，並對照國語連詞的意義與用法訓練學生熟悉英語連詞的意義與用法。

(三)指導學生辨別英語情態助動詞與副詞的意義與用法，並對照國語情態助動詞與副詞的意義與用法，訓練學生熟悉英語情態助動詞與副詞的意義與用法。

(四)指導學生辨別修飾全句的副詞與狀語，並對照國語修飾全句的副詞與狀語訓練學生熟悉英語修飾全句的副詞與狀語。

(五)指導學生複習英語的「時制」、「動貌」、「語態」與「語氣」。

(六)指導學生複習如何修飾動詞或動詞片語。

(七)指導學生複習如何修飾形容詞與副詞。

(八)指導學生如何修飾名詞。

(九)指導學生注意在課文與練習中出現的「倒裝句」、「省略句」、「分裂句」、「準分裂句」、「名物化」等，並了解這些句式與「從舊到新」、「從輕到重」、「從低到高」、「從親到疏」等語用與節奏原則的關係。

(十)指導學生如何「擴展」或「簡縮」句子，並且訓練學生用幾種不同的句式表達同樣的意思。

戊、閱讀與寫作

(一)配合(丙)與(丁)的詞彙、句型與語法教學，利用課文、口頭練習、書寫練習等方式來進行閱讀與寫作教學。

(二)指導學生如何尋求文章的「中心思想」、每一段落的「主題句」，並且就各種不同體例與內容的文章向學生說明如何展開「主題句」來表達「中心思想」。

(三)指導學生了解「統一性」、「連貫性」、「清晰性」、「強調性」、「變化性」等修辭原則，並且利用課文與練習舉例說明這些原則的實際運用。

(四)配合(丁)、(九)與(十)的教學活動，指導學生如何運用具體的句型與語法來達成「強調性」與「變化性」。

(五)配合(丙)的詞彙教學，指導學生辨別「口語詞彙」與「書面語詞彙」以及「抽象詞彙」與「具體詞彙」的區別，並了解這些區別在寫作上的實際運用。

(六)以指定課外閱讀與閱讀測驗的方式，訓練學生閱讀與課文難

度相當或與課文內容相近的文章(包括介紹我國歷史文物與風俗習慣的文章)，並且鼓勵學生以簡潔有力的英文寫下閱讀心得。

綜觀以上教材大綱草案，與一九八三年(民國七十二年)教育部所頒佈的現行高中英文課程標準的內容，主要有下列三點不同之處：

(一)對於教材的廣度有較周延而縝密的規定：現行教材大綱對於每一學年的教材內容僅提出八點內容相當籠統的規定，除了對於選文內容、字數與生字數目有較具體的規定以外，有關語言知識與能力的內容則過於簡單而含糊。而本研究所訂之教材大綱則把語言知識與能力細分為「聽講與會話」、「詞彙」、「句型與語法」、「閱讀與寫作」四項，並把各項教學活動的教材單元詳加列舉，在教材的廣度方面顯然較為周延而縝密。

(二)對於教材的深度有具體而有系統的規定：已往的教材大綱對於教材的深度幾無考慮，因而在現行教材大綱中屢次出現"同等○學年第○項"等文字。而本研究所訂之教材大綱則首次顧及教材的深度，具體而有系統的把「漸進、累積、反覆」的編纂原則應用於教材大綱之中。因此，各學年的教材進度均按由易到難的漸進原則與由簡而繁的累積原則設計，並且也提供適度的反覆以供複習與再學習之用。同時，同一學年同一項目的教材單元都依重要到次要的順序排列，並把教學重點與行為目標相當清晰的加以釐定。

(三)對於都市與僻遠地區學校之差距及學生個別程度的差異有較為妥切的考慮：高中英文教材大綱及依據大綱而編纂之高中

英文教科書將由全省高級中學學生一體奉行與使用。但是都市地區與僻遠地區學生程度的差距是無可否認的事實，而且即使是同一學校的學生亦因出身與學習背景的不同而難免產生個別程度上的差異。本研究所訂之教材大綱爲此特於第一學年第一學期撥出前四週爲複習與矯正之用，並詳細規定此一階段之教材內容，以使各地學校有調整學生程度的機會。另外，教材大綱中有關語言知識、語言能力、教材單元、行爲目標的規定，都以中等程度的學生爲考慮對象，以期將來所編纂之高中英文教科書不致失於偏難。至於國中英語與高中英文之間縱的銜接，以及高職英文與高中英文橫的配合，本研究所訂之教材大綱亦於可能範圍內妥善加以規畫，以免發生脫節的現象。

八、結　語

以上就我國的英語教學，特別是高中英語教學，做了一番回顧與展望。從十八世紀初葉的洋徑濱英語開始，經過十九世紀後歐美傳教士的教授與推廣，國人學習英語的風氣漸盛。一八六二年京師同文館的設立象徵我國英語教學的開始自立，而一九〇二年「壬寅學制」的頒佈則表示包括英文的外國語文正式列爲中等教育的必修課目。英語教學的師資來源在早期完全依賴歐美的傳教士或外籍人士，接著是倚重留學歐美日歸來或與教會外商有接觸往來的國人，而如今卻可以完全靠國內的師資培訓來自給自足。英語的教材也從英美讀物的翻版或國外教科書的抄襲，發展到完全由國人爲各級學校的英語教學自編教材的地步。而英語的教學方法則從早期模仿私塾教育的「塡鴨式教學」，經過「文法・翻

譯法」、「直接教學法」(Direct Method)與「口說教學法」(Oral Approach) 等進到「認知教學法」(Cognitive Approach)、「溝通教學法」(Communicative Approach) 與「自然教學法」(Natural Approach) 等反映當代歐美語言教學理論的水平。回顧過去三百年國人接受英語的經過與近百年我國英語教學的演進,歷史的軌跡雖然崎嶇嶙峋,進步的腳印卻也歷歷可見。英語教學的改進好比是漫長而永無終點的旅程,前人披荆斬棘的成果必須由我們以及後人繼往開來的努力來發揚光大。

本文為國立編譯館(1992)《八十年來我國中小學教科書之演進專輯》而寫。

參 考 文 獻

一、英文參考文獻

（1）Chinese Repository. (1851). Bridgman, E.C. and Williams, S.W. (eds.), 20 Vols., Canton.

（2）DeCamp, D. (1965). 'The training of English teachers in the Far East,' Language Learning, Vol. 15, 119-127.

（3）Downing, C.T. (1838). The Stranger in China. Philadelphia: Lea and Blanchard.

（4）Eames, J.B. (1909). The English in China, being an account of the intercourse and relations between England and China from the year 1600 to the year 1843 and a summary of later developments. London: Sir Isaac Putman and Sons.

（5）Hunter, W.C. (1885). Bits of Old China. London: Kegan Paul, Trench, and Co.

（6）Jespersen, O (1925) Language: its Nature, Development and Origin. London: Allen and Unwin.

（7）Mok, P.K. (1951). 'The history and development of the Teaching of English in China,' Dissertation Abstracts International, 11, 594 A. (University

Microfilms No. 0002, 546).

（8）Morrison, E.A. (1834). Memoirs of the Life and Labours of Robert Morrison. London: Longmans.

（9）Morse, A.B. (1926). The Chronicles of the East India Company Trading to China, 1634-1834. Oxford: Oxford University Press.

（10）Morse, A.B. and McMair, H.F. (1931). Far Eastern International Relations. Boston: Houghton.

（11）Stowe, J. E. (1990). English Language Instruction in the Schools in Transition: the case of Taiwan in the 1980s, Ph. D. Dissertation, Columbia University.

二、中文參考文獻

（1）中華民國三十七年十二月十四教育部公布《修訂中學課程標準》，出版時地不詳。

（2）中華民國五十一年七月教育部修正《中學課程標準》，正中書局，民國五十一年七月。

（3）中華民國六十年二月教育部公布《高級中學課程標準》正中書局，民國六十年二月。

（4）中華民國七十二年七月教育部公布《高級中學課程標準》正中書局，民國七十二年七月。

（5）教育部人文及社會學科教育指導委員會《教育目標文集》民國七十五年八月。

（6）教育部人文及社會學科教育指導委員會《學科研究工作參

考資料（二）》民國七十六年四月。

（7）教育部人文及社會學科教育指導委員會《教材大綱文集》
　　民國七十六年五月。

（8）國立臺灣師範大學《中等學校人文社會學科教育研討會報
　　告書》民國七十五年六月。

（9）沈宗瀚(1954)《克難苦學記》正中書局，民國四十三年九
　　月。

(10)湯廷池〈民國六十五年英語文教學研討會綜合意見與建
　　議〉，收錄於湯廷池(1977)《英語教學論集》二一三頁至
　　二三八頁。

(11)湯廷池(1977)《英語教學論集》臺灣學生書局，民國六十
　　六年十二月。

(12)湯廷池(1981)《語言學與語文教學》臺灣學生書局，民國
　　七十年四月。

(13)湯廷池(1989)《國中英語教學指引》臺灣學生書局，民國
　　七十八年九月。

國立中央圖書館出版品預行編目資料

英語認知語法：結構、意義與功用／湯廷池著.--初版.
--臺北市：臺灣學生,民81
　　冊；　　公分.--（語言教學叢書；9）
參考書目：面
ISBN 957-15-0439-4（中集：精裝）
ISBN 957-15-0440-8（中集：平裝）

1.英國語言

805.1　　　　　　　　　　　　　　　81004723

英語認知語法:結構、意義與功用
(中集)

著　作　者：湯　　　　廷　　　　池
出　版　者：臺　灣　學　生　書　局
本書局登
記證字號：行政院新聞局局版臺業字第一一〇〇號
發　行　人：丁　　　文　　　治
發　行　所：臺　灣　學　生　書　局
　　　　　　臺北市和平東路一段一九八號
　　　　　　郵政劃撥帳號〇〇〇二四六六八
　　　　　　電　話：3 6 3 4 1 5 6
　　　　　　FAX:(0 2) 3 6 3 6 3 3 4
印　刷　所：淵　明　印　刷　公　司
　　　　　　地　址：永和市成功路一段43巷五號
　　　　　　電　話：9 2 8 7 1 4 5
香港總經銷：藝　文　圖　書　公　司
　　　　　　地址：九龍偉業街九十九號連順大廈
　　　　　　五字樓及七字樓　電話：7959595

　　定價　精裝新台幣四九〇元
　　　　　平裝新台幣四三〇元

中　華　民　國　八　十　一　年　十　月　初　版

80507-2　版權所有・翻印必究
ISBN 957-15-0439-4（精裝）
ISBN 957-15-0440-8（平裝）

語文教學叢書編輯委員會

現代語言學論叢書目

⑧ 湯廷池等著：漢語句法、語意學論集（英文本）
　　十　　人

⑨ 顧百里著：國語在臺灣之演變（英文本）

⑩ 顧百里著：白話文歐化語法之研究（英文本）

⑪ 李梅都著：漢語的照應與刪簡（英文本）

⑫ 黃美金著：「態」之探究（英文本）

⑬ 坂本英子著：從華語看日本漢語的發音

⑭ 曹逢甫：國語的句子與子句結構（英文本）

⑮ 陳重瑜著：漢英語法，語意學論集（英文本）

語文敎學叢書書目

① 湯廷池著：語言學與語文敎學

② 董昭輝著：漢英音節比較研究（英文本）

③ 方師鐸著：詳析「匆匆」的語法與修辭

④ 湯廷池著：英語語言分析入門：英語語法敎學問答

⑤ 湯廷池著：英語語法修辭十二講

⑥ 董昭輝著：英語的「時間框框」

⑦ 湯廷池著：英語認知語法：結構、意義與功用（上集）

⑧ 湯廷池著：國中英語敎學指引

⑨ 湯廷池著：英語認知語法：結構、意義與功用（中集）